DEATH IS A
CERTAINTY

DEATH IS A
CERTAINTY

TED YORK

Matador
9 Priory Business Park
Kibworth Beauchamp
Leicestershire LE8 0RX, UK
Tel: (+44) 116 279 2299
Fax: (+44) 116 279 2277
Email: books@troubador.co.uk
Web: www.troubador.co.uk/matador

This book is a work of fiction and, except in the case of historical fact, any resemblance
to actual persons or events is purely coincidental.

ISBN 978 1783060 368

British Library Cataloguing in Publication Data.
A catalogue record for this book is available from the British Library.

Typeset in Palatino by Troubador Publishing Ltd
Printed and bound in the UK by TJ International, Padstow, Cornwall

Matador is an imprint of Troubador Publishing Ltd

MIX
Paper from
responsible sources
FSC® C013056

For all my family

PROLOGUE

Colonel Harriman sat down in his winged leather chair. Leaning forward he picked up another log and put it in the burner.

It had been a difficult day. He had attended the funeral of Major Marcus Bridge, a colleague from his service in the SAS. The ice clinked in the crystal glass as he sampled the twenty-one-year-old Glenlivet. A grateful client had given him a bottle of the malt whisky, but in truth he preferred Cardhu – a twelve-year-old single malt.

His friend's obituary was in *The Times* today, but the short paragraph didn't tell it all and he leaned back and rested his head on the wing back chair as he remembered his old friend and colleague.

On the 2nd August 1990, Iraq launched the invasion of Kuwait. The soldiers of Kuwait fought hard, but could not prevent the Iraqi commandos taking Kuwait City. Quickly the country was overrun by the Iraqi Republican Guard. A meeting of the UN Security Council passed a resolution condemning the invasion and demanding the withdrawal of Iraqi troops. The Arab League, the registered organisation of Arab states, passed their own resolution calling for the League to resolve the conflict and warned against outside intervention

Colonel Harriman put down his glass. At that time there was a high alert, including the SAS unit he commanded. The hope was that the Iraqis could be persuaded to withdraw, but behind the scenes diplomacy was taking place between the USA and Saudi Arabia. The fear of Saddam Hussein attacking Saudi Arabia to capture the oil installations prompted US President George H W Bush to launch what he described as a defensive mission – Operation Desert Shield. Colonel Harriman knew the background, but didn't involve himself in the politics and on the 17th January 1991 a major air campaign began.

His SAS regiment was flown to Saudi Arabia. Three days later on the night of the 24th January, the then Captain Harriman and Lieutenant Marcus Bridge led a patrol, transported by RAF Chinook helicopter deep into Iraq. The eight-man patrol walked ten kilometres to the proposed observation post and dug in.

After a day watching an empty road, supposedly a route for mobile Scud missile launchers he took the decision to move position. There was very little traffic on the road, but the night before, in the distance, they had seen many headlights heading south. There must be another road, he concluded, and they were watching the wrong one. They hiked a further two kilometres and dug in. The radio operator, Willy Norton, had problems with his kit, the radio frequencies he had been issued were not correct. They were spotting Scud transporters, but couldn't report the Intel as the bloody radio didn't work.

The colonel sighed and went upstairs to his bedroom clutching the bottle of Glenlivet. He had obeyed the rules. When you had a problem you reverted to where you landed. He led the patrol back towards the original infiltration point, where a helicopter would land in the next twenty-four hours. Later, the enquiry said that it was simply unlucky, but he pondered once again how they had walked into an Iraqi tank exercise. They went to ground, but not before they had been spotted. A fire fight followed, but they were not equipped to fight tanks. He sipped his scotch as he thought about his decision. He had instructed the patrol to split: Marcus was to lead three men toward the infiltration point, and he would lead the others north toward the Syrian border, hoping to draw off the Iraqis.

He was not an emotional man but tears squeezed into his eyes. Four of the patrol were lost. One of the men he led toward the Syrian border succumbed to hypothermia and one of Marcus's men was killed when they were surrounded by an elite Republican Guard unit before reaching the infiltration point. Later, Marcus told him that they fought well but were only equipped with M16 assault rifles; too light weaponry for a fire fight with several hundred Iraqis. After Marcus had lost Corporal McDonald and both he and another soldier were wounded, Marcus decided to surrender. Later Marcus had told him that they were not badly treated. Beaten but not tortured, and eventually taken to Abu Ghraib prison to the west of Baghdad.

At the end of the conflict Marcus was repatriated. His flesh wound had healed. Thommo, Private James Thomas, had not recovered from his wounds. Private Lawson had been beaten, but survived and was released with Marcus.

Colonel Harriman was not the sort of man to dwell on his past but he wondered if there had been an alternative. One man had died during the third night from hypothermia and after four days and one hundred miles Corporal Danvers, Billy Watson and he had reached the Syrian border. Crossing the border had been easier than he thought it would be. But they had to swim the Euphrates river and shortly after leaving the river bank they had lost sight of Billy Watson.

The Times obituary described Major Marcus Bridge without discussing his SAS career. A brief statement said that Marcus had died of lung cancer at the age of fifty-two, leaving a widow, Pat, and two sons. Colonel Harriman knew it had been a long and lingering death and more than once Marcus had asked him to finish him off. But he couldn't do it and he knew his friend's end had been a blessed relief to his wife Pat.

As he finished the malt whisky he turned his mind to today's events. He had started Harriman Security when he left the SAS in 2001. He predicted the need for the rich and famous to pay for bodyguards and recruited many of his old colleagues and others he knew from the SBS and Special Branch. Men and women who had retired early from the specialist divisions or were invalided out with relatively minor injuries. He recruited them and built his company based in Park Lane, London.

The telephone rang on the bedside cabinet and he rolled over and answered.

"Hello."

"Colonel," said a male voice.

"Yes, who is that?"

"It's Sergeant Boyes sir." Despite having retired six years ago, the men who worked for his security firm continued to call him colonel and it seemed reasonable that when they referred to themselves, they did so by their old rank.

"Yes sergeant," colonel Harriman replied.

"We have a problem with Dustin, sir."

"What sort of problem?" It was 3am and he needed his sleep these days.

Now sixty-two years of age, he had left the army six years ago, having served with distinction for over thirty-five years. Colonel John Harriman MC had retired, as far as he was concerned, at the top. He had been commander, and acting brigadier, of the SAS Regiment based at Hereford and as a young lieutenant had orchestrated some of the unit's activities, notably in the Middle East, Ireland and at the Balcombe Street siege in London.

Sergeant Boyes was talking about a pop star now – Dustin Starr. Whereas the colonel regarded all the young men and women who performed music, ranging from opera to reggae, as pop stars, in fact, Dustin had first worked as an actor in an Australian soap and then come to London, having hit record, after hit record. The teenagers loved him.

"I'm outside Alice's nightclub. He's inside totally stoned on the cocaine he's been sniffing. I have had to intervene in a fight he started and at the moment he's sitting in the manager's office being sick."

"Well what's new?"

The colonel was used to some of his immature, but rich clients taking drugs and/or drink and making a fool of themselves.

"The bloke he had the fight with, a young geezer."

"Yes, get to the point sergeant it's three o'clock in the morning," he said, beginning to get agitated.

"The other geezer's dead, sir."

"Dead," said a surprised Colonel Harriman.

"Yes, the doctor's just been and the fuzz are arriving now."

"Right, Alice's you say?"

"Yes, sir."

"Okay, phone Mr Toomey, he will meet you at the police station they take him to. Tell the police who you are and tell that idiot not to say one word until Toomey arrives."

Nathan Toomey was Colonel Harriman's tame barrister, who he used when his client was not likely to have a decent brief of their own.

"Phone me as soon as you know where they're taking him."

"Yes sir," said Sergeant Boyes, cutting the connection.

Most of the colonel's employees were ex-forces personnel. Many were ex-SAS or ex-SBS, but some were ex-Military Police and Captain Danders was one of those. The Colonel dialled out.

"Danders?"

"Yes sir," said Captain Danders, immediately recognising the colonel's distinctive voice.

"That punk, Dustin, is about to be arrested at Alice's Night Club."

The colonel explained the story as he knew it and dispatched Danders to take photographs and collect witness statements before everyone disappeared.

As he settled down to try to sleep, the colonel saw the light flashing on his bedside warning system. His instincts, honed over forty years, made him freeze…

CHAPTER ONE

25TH JULY 2006 – NEW YORK

Morgan Fryer, ex-CIA head of station, now a private contractor for the CIA, had arranged to meet an old colleague at the Guggenheim Museum off Central Park. The man had approached him with a proposition. It seemed an easy way to earn two million dollars, so Morgan had already put some wheels in motion to find Ludvig Korotski who would be perfect to run the operation in the UK.

Morgan Fryer read the report which he had obtained from his source in the CIA and sat back in his chair. He knew all about the Russian Ludvig, from his CIA days. Ten years he had spent trying to capture the bastard, but now his talents might just be what he was looking for. He picked up the papers again: they were headed 'Stanislav Alexandrov alias Ludvig Korotski and Karl Sobcha'. Now living as Ludvig Korotski, but possibly under another assumed name – 'whereabouts unknown'.

History (note-on CIA most wanted list 1975-). First came to notice in 1974 as a member of the Soviet Mission to the United Nations Committee on Foreign Trade Relations in New York. He was clearly on a clandestine mission, which was not discovered by the FBI. In 1975 he surfaced in Berlin as deputy head of the KGB. At least three CIA agents 'disappeared' during his stint in Berlin.

He skipped past the horrific stories of murder instigated by this man over 3 years in Berlin.

Transferred in 1978 to 'Directorate S' in Afghanistan, which engaged in murder, terrorism, sabotage, poisoning and arson. Carried out guerrilla campaigns 1980-1981 training mujahedeen groups to penetrate CIA-backed militia.

Seen in Moscow in 1981 was deputy head of ALFA group set up by KGB's Seventh Directorate. Seen again in Yasenevo, southwest of Kabul in June 1983, rumoured to be training the 'Khad', the deadly Afghan Communist Intelligence Service, feared for their use of torture and assassination.

1

Disappeared August 1983. Possible sighting Moscow December 1983. Seen in Berlin January 1984. Left KGB 'under a cloud'. Involved with Mujahedeen and Al Qaeda 1988-1994, seen at training camps in Pakistan, Iran and Libya. No sightings since 1994.

Inactive, retired or dead was penned in the margin. There was a separate handwritten note – *rumoured to have contracted to CIA in 2003.*

Morgan Fryer sat at his desk in his New York office reading the notes his senior operations manager had prepared. When he retired from the CIA in 2001, he had been a deputy director of the National Clandestine Service (NCS) described by many as the brains of the CIA. Morgan saw that the CIA would have to resolve many of its operational difficulties by outsourcing to private firms. He smiled to himself as he remembered the report he had prepared for the director. Once they had adopted the approach he recommended, he had retired and set up Infotek, his own private security agency. Since then industrial contracts, 'green badgers', the name for private contractors as the CIA called them, made up approximately fifty percent of the NCS, his old department, and he had enjoyed becoming very rich on the proceeds as Infotek received many of the contracts.

Morgan put down the file and pressed the intercom.

"Jack," he buzzed his number two, who dealt with most of the day-to-day matters. Jack Deveroux was also ex-CIA, having worked for Morgan over a twenty year period, mainly in the Middle East, Pakistan and Afghanistan.

"Yes boss."

In breezed the tall, dark-haired man who was regarded by all the men and most of the women in Morgan's firm as a ladies' man.

"This report on Ludvig Korotski, I want to set up a meet, can you find out his contact details?"

"Sure, I'll get to it straight away."

Morgan knew that Jack would contact their source in the FSB (the Federal Security Service), the Russian state security agency which had replaced the KGB in 1991, and hopefully have the information he needed in the next few days.

He picked up his mobile, dialled a number, and was answered on the second ring.

"OK I'll do it, meet me usual place 10.30 tomorrow morning," he said.

Morgan walked up the sloping ramp at the Guggenheim Museum. Frank Lloyd Wright's distinctive modern architecture was home to one of New York's finest collections of twentieth-century art. The grand ramp, which curved from the ground floor to the dome, had paintings, prints and drawings on the walls and important exhibitions, currently Picasso. But Morgan, not really an art lover, was not here to look at Picasso paintings and he went into the men's toilets on the second floor. Checking the cubicles were all empty, he waited. Two minutes later a well-built man in his fifties came in. The two did not exchange pleasantries; they had previously been rivals in the CIA for twenty-five years.

"You'll do it then?" asked the man.

"Yes. Send me one million dollars on account to this bank address." Morgan handed the man a single sheet of paper.

"I will text you with 'The Eagle has Landed' when you should start," said the man, who always had a sense of humour not shared by Morgan Fryer.

Morgan looked at him with disdain and said, "We will need the names and as much background as possible."

"You'll have it. I am preparing material now. Keep this on a need-to-know basis." At that, he left the toilet. Morgan followed a minute later.

He fancied a walk through Central Park and it enabled him to check for a tail, a habit he couldn't stop after a lifetime of fieldcraft. He thought about the Russian Ludvig. *Would he do it?* he wondered.

Ludvig picked up his passport and checked his identity. He was travelling, at the moment, as Ludvig Amst, a Swiss national. He clicked the hidden compartment on his leather holdall. Inside were three other passports, credit cards matching alternative identities and a wad of sterling and euro notes. He checked his apartment carefully, making sure he was not leaving any documents or links to his past. He thought that his identity as ex-station head of the KGB in Berlin in 1984 was unknown and he was living anonymously in Stockholm, but he had been shaken up when Morgan Fryer, an old CIA adversary, contacted him on his mobile two days ago. Ludvig was by nature a cautious man: he did not intend to return to his flat in Stockholm and was cleaning it meticulously.

The Old Town was built on fourteen islands around the well – preserved medieval city centre; Ludvig had enjoyed living here, but knew he had to move. He was watching out for a tail as he walked to the junction on Biglioteksgatan to catch a passing taxi. He had never stopped practising the KGB fieldcraft he had learned thirty years ago, but just of late he had relaxed more. That had been a mistake; otherwise how else had Morgan Fryer got his mobile number? Ludvig had lived in Stockholm's picturesque Old Town for six years, but when he left the apartment he knew he would not go back and looked for a taxi to go to Stockholm Arlanda Airport. Booked on the Air Berlin flight at 6.55am, landing at Berlin Tegel at 8.30am, he had arranged to meet Katya, one of his former officers in the KGB, at Starbucks and was booked on the 10.35am flight returning to Stockholm just after midday. What he wanted to talk to Katya about would only take five minutes. Ludvig rarely used mobile phones – he knew that all calls were monitored and any key words used in a conversation would immediately alert security forces across the world. Other than the occasional 'job' he had done for the CIA or the Russians, he had been inactive for three years but he had survived by being careful, hence the face-to-face meeting with Katya.

Taxis were common, even at 4am, and after walking for five minutes Ludvig hailed a passing cab. The driver, a rather chatty elderly man, was very proud of the fact he was an eco-taxi, an environmentally friendly scheme being operated in the Stockholm area – but Ludvig didn't return the conversation and the driver eventually got the message. Fifty minutes later, Ludvig was dropped off at terminal two, the international departure terminal, where he went to the men's toilet. Locking himself in a cubicle, Ludvig took off his wig and combed his now grey hair, whilst examining his eyebrows as he coloured them in part-grey. Satisfied, he opened the compartment in his holdall and selected a passport for Niklas Mueller, a retired schoolmaster from Berlin, and placed his Swiss passport and wig in the lead-lined compartment. Ludwig used the technology developed by the KGB. Cases and bags made with a thin, lightweight lead lining enabled the contents to remain undetected by screening equipment at airports. Taking a final look in the full-sized mirror in the toilet, he went to the information desk and enquired if the Air Berlin flight to Berlin was on time. Satisfied, he went upstairs to a coffee bar, ordered a cappuccino and a croissant and sat facing the bustling café, his back against the far wall. Shortly before the check-in was due to close, Ludvig presented his passport. He had bought an e-ticket three hours ago and felt confident nobody was tailing him – still better to be careful, if Morgan Fryer knew where he was, who else did? Collecting his boarding card he went through to the departure lounge. His bag went through the electronic surveillance with no trouble. Choosing to board the flight at the last moment, he looked at the passengers on the plane; he had selected a rear row and outside seat. The plane was not full and no one boarded after Ludvig.

The short-haul flight landed at Berlin's Tegel Airport an hour and a half later. Ludvig passed through immigration control as a German national, Niklas Mueller, and went to Starbucks on the first-floor concourse. Katya Gatchevske was already sitting at the back of the coffee bar, facing the open-plan entrance. Ludvig ordered a coffee and joined her. There were no pleasantries, Ludvig had no friends, just working colleagues, and in any case familiarity breached security. Katya already knew the reason for the meet. He wanted Katya and her partner, Ivan, to act as security for a meeting he had arranged in Stockholm with the ex-CIA field officer, Morgan Fryer.

He handed Katya five thousand euros for expenses and agreed to credit her Swiss bank account with fifty thousand euros after the job was done. Katya listened, nodded, picked up a plain napkin where she had made shorthand notes, omitting the destination, put the five thousand euros in her bag and left. Satisfied, Ludvig went to the men's room. Catching the return flight to Stockholm, Ludvig settled down to nap for half an hour – was it his imagination or did he feel much more tired these days? Perhaps he really ought to retire, but he hadn't got much of the money left that he had transferred out of Berlin before the wall came down – he needed a top-up and perhaps Morgan Fryer would provide that money.

*

Katya Gatchevske looked at the man sitting at the table opposite her, caught his steel-grey eyes staring at her and quickly looked away. Ludvig Korotski was the ex-station head of the KGB in Berlin, a cruel, ruthless man, who she had seen personally torture and kill women, children and numerous men, during the time she had worked for him. Now, twenty-five years after they had initially worked together he wanted her to provide security for him to meet an old adversary, an ex-CIA man, Morgan Fryer. Katya knew Ludvig had been hiding, she suspected in Sweden, for over ten years. She thought he probably lived on the money, mostly dollars, he had smuggled out of Berlin shortly before the wall came down.

Katya had been Ludvig's chief of staff in those turbulent days of Gorbachev, détente and worse the break-up of the old Soviet Union. Katya knew many people regarded the changes as positive, but the hardliners, especially those that had been in real power, were resentful. Katya had carried on working for the KGB 'during the changes'. Her past however, caught up with her when an old hardliner an ex-KGB officer began to take power: his name was Putin . She had fled Russia with her lover, Ivan, also ex-KGB, to Libya in 1995. After Libya, her freelance work had taken her to Afghanistan, Iraq and Saudi Arabia, training security forces .

Ludvig was proposing she cover him at a meeting; should she involve herself with him again? But, she needed the money, agreed to the job and left.

TWO MONTHS LATER… CYPRUS

Ludvig sat on the sunbed observing the rear of Gelda, the prostitute he had brought with him to Cyprus. Ludvig had purchased a four – bedroom villa on the prestigious Aphrodite Hills resort a year ago. It was nearer to his Stockholm home than his flat in Buenos Aires and when he wanted a quick 'sunshine fix' he preferred the shorter flight.

Ludvig had met an old CIA adversary two months ago, Morgan Fryer, who had offered him an interesting and lucrative contract.

Having deliberated on the American Fryer's proposition, Ludvig had quickly put out feelers and persuaded Katya, who he had worked with in the good old days, to join him. She was a first-class organiser and together with her partner Ivan Dinov, they were a ruthless and efficient team.

He had first met Katya as a twenty-year-old student from Moscow University in 1979. Quickly he realised her potential. Fluent in three languages, English, German and French, Katya had a photographic memory and as Ludvig discovered early on, no scruples. He recruited Katya into the Saboteur Training Centre of the KGB's First Chief Directorate. At the time Ivan Dinov was also at the Centre. The two comrades became inseparable and lovers. Katya became Ludvig's number two in the Berlin Station and set up a spy network in Britain, France and West Germany. Ludvig later ran a KGB department, principally to engage in what was known as 'wet jobs' i.e. murder, sabotage, arson, poisoning and terrorism. Katya and Ivan were important members of his team who liaised with the KGB Third Section, setting up clandestine premises and postal addresses. Ludvig reflected on those happy days, before the liberals Gorbachev and Yeltsin, training sabotage and intelligence groups. *Luckily*, he thought, *Katya had kept tabs on many of the old team which was going to be useful.*

Ludvig resumed his study of Gelda's rear end and wondered if he should kill her, she was becoming very demanding – perhaps not, might mean he couldn't come back to Cyprus. But he was tiring of her posing and demands; perhaps he would pass her on to one of the bodyguards that he had recruited since accepting the job from Morgan Fryer. He pondered on Katya and sent a coded email, 'Are you ready to commence export operations?'

Katya and Ivan had begun the process of setting up the team of operatives that Ludvig required immediately. They made a list of their previous colleagues and then, crossing out some names that were either unreliable, in prison or dead, they narrowed down their search

"We need three other Russian-born agents," said Ivan.

"Why only three?" Katya asked.

"These agents may need to be expendable, it is better to use Bulgarians and not recruit too many people known to us – and us to them."

"But the Bulgarians know me, I recruited and trained many of them," she replied.

"Yes, but they haven't met me and I may have to eliminate them."

"H'm, I take your point – so who have we got?"

Ivan reeled off a list and after each name Katya agreed or said no. The only name they didn't agree on was Leonid Kokorov, a Bulgarian.

"He is inclined to be careless," said Ivan.

"I know but he has a fantastic ability to change appearance and has killed many times."

They agreed to disagree, but nevertheless, Katya added his name. The list, now typed on Katya's laptop, showed eight of the most deadly killers the KGB had ever trained. All the people on the list would kill without remorse.

The next stage was to make contact with each person – but first they had to ascertain their whereabouts. The three Russians Katya found in an Afghanistan training camp. Since the Russians had left Afghanistan, ex-KGB members regularly hired out their skills for training and sabotage. Katya, with Ivan shadowing her, boarded the Lufthansa flight from Berlin to Karachi, where they had arranged to meet Anton Hineva. The other two Russians, a woman, Anastasiya Stoickkev, and Hristo Penev, were on the Pakistan and Afghanistan border, twenty-five miles inside Pakistan at a training camp, which, according to the Pakistan government, didn't exist.

The meeting with Anton, one of many agents trained by Katya in East Berlin, went well and they hired a car to drive to the border with Afghanistan.

Katya had met both of her ex-colleagues, Anastasiya and Hristo, at a Russian training camp in 1980. The commander of the Al Qaeda camp in Afghanistan knew her from her training Al Qaeda and Taliban operatives in the late 1990s and as recently as 2004. He also knew Ivan, Katya's partner, but Ivan kept out of sight, not wishing the two prospective recruits to know he was involved. Anastasiya Stoickkev was a very attractive woman and this was how, in the 1980s, her skills enabled her to entrap many men and women and kill if required. She had a ruthless streak, rare in a woman operative. Hristo Penev had joined the Red Army aged sixteen in 1978 before his talent for killing became apparent. He was then transferred to the KGB training unit in Moscow, where he met Katya, who was an instructor. He had made several moves on Katya before she told him she was with somebody else, but he proved reliable and had killed under Katya's instructions in London and Berlin. The two ex-KGB agents welcomed the change of scene and happily agreed to the contract proposed by Katya. Hristo was so keen that he left the Pakistan training base immediately. The commander of the base would have been less than happy about losing three of his trainers, but he welcomed the gift of twenty-five thousand dollars that Katya gave him.

The Bulgarians were not easy to track down. Viktorya Abamova and Dmitri Baich worked for the Russian Mafia in Sofia, grooming young girls as prostitutes, to be shipped all over Europe. Egor Dunayavskaya was employed as a bodyguard in London by a Russian oligarch. Ivan Gelperin was training recruits in Libya for Al Qaeda and Leonid Kokorov worked as a hit man in Moscow for a mafia group. It took Katya a further two weeks to meet and recruit the proposed members of the hit squad. All were more than happy to receive the ten thousand dollars upfront and a further fifty thousand sterling each month, guaranteed for twelve months.

Ivan and Katya then spent two weeks arranging false passports for all eight team members and themselves. The man who forged the documents in Berlin had been given three photographs of each team member, some with grey hair, and others blond or dark-haired. Katya had decided on initially using Dutch passports and held German and Swedish passports as a reserve. The Bulgarians were not proficient linguists when compared to the three Russians or Katya and Ivan. Only Viktorya spoke passable Dutch. So Katya decided they should initially travel as Bulgarians and obtained five false Bulgarian passports, each person having disguised their appearance by dyeing their hair.

Ivan had been shadowing Katya when she met Ludvig to receive the first set of targets in Britain. Ludvig gave her a tennis sports bag; inside was a box containing small bottles of the poison and adapted umbrellas which they were to use to inject a deadly liquid. Ludvig had warned Katya that the poison was lethal, but she must test it to determine the length of time taken before death after the injection. A quick prick, probably in the leg, should guarantee death within six seconds, Ludvig had said. Katya didn't enquire where the poison came from, but knew of several eliminations using the umbrella technique.

Later in Berlin the eight members of the team were each given a laptop computer and six disposable mobile phones by Katya and holdall bags with a hidden, lead-lined compartment. They were also shown that their laptop contained details of 'safe' bed and breakfast accommodation and journey details to the first list of intended victims. Each victim on the assassin's initial list of six persons had been researched by Ludvig, Katya or Ivan and details shown with their photograph, often a passport photograph, address and details of partners or spouse, if any.

The instructions to the group of assassins were simple: they were urged to mostly use the poison umbrella to kill the victims as it simulated a heart attack. However, if need be, always make it look as though there had been an accidental death. Outright physical murder, using guns or knives, was a last resort – but the victims must all be killed. None of the agents, except the three Russians recruited in Pakistan, knew any of the other members of the hit squad. They all knew Katya was the leader, except one of the Bulgarians, Leonid Kokorov, who had been recruited by Ivan as he had disagreed with Katya on an operation in 1987 and been demoted.

With the team assembled, they all journeyed separately to Britain. Most of them chose the easier border crossings, on the Eurostar from Paris or flying to Belfast or Dublin then taking a sea crossing. Katya and Ivan had developed, as their cover, that they were the advance party for a Swedish junior football team to tour the UK and that way the kit bags, corner flags and the VW Golf with a false floor, passed through Dover undetected. A week earlier they had travelled to the UK on the Eurostar from Bruges to Ashford and hired a garage on a housing estate just outside the town.

They drove the car to Ashford from Dover, stole a second car and then took out a quantity of the poison, wearing rubber gloves and taking great care not to touch the substance or the umbrellas. One by one they met the assassins and showed them how to load the poison and use the umbrella to deadly effect. The team were assembled and ready to strike, each had sent a coded text to Katya, except Leonid who thought he was sending a message to Ivan.

MURDERS

2ND JANUARY 2007 – CORNWALL, ENGLAND

Muriel Steadman is cordially invited to address the Cornwall Business Enterprise members on Monday 2ⁿᵈ January 2007

Muriel read the invitation again, wondering what she should include in her talk to the members of the local business community. Contemplating her long career as a successful producer of plays in London and provincial theatres, this was perhaps the subject with which to engage her audience. But was it? The audience were likely to be men and whilst she had many interesting anecdotes following a lifetime in the theatre would the audience be sufficiently engaged?

Muriel had noticed from the Cornwall Business Enterprise website that the speaker before her was talking on 'motivating your employees' and the speaker after her on 'cross-selling opportunities.' Perhaps she should broaden her talk to include her directorships of *Steadman Fashions* and *Women and Fashion* which were popular magazines run by Fleet Street Magazines Ltd.

She smiled to herself as she thought of her other occupation, which had been running a fetish dungeon in London's fashionable Soho. During the last twenty years, when her success brought with it some financial security, Muriel had become bored. The world of theatre and showbusiness necessitated that she socialise with many people and it was one such contact, Lord Manley-Willis, who prompted her to use some of her 'pretty young things' to greater advantage, as he put it.

One night, having had more champagne than wisely she should have and in the company of George Manley-Willis and two other titled friends, the conversation once again had turned to abstract sexual practices – George's favourite subject. Cassandra and Melanie, two of her young actress friends, giggled as George elaborated, and then, much to Muriel's surprise, said that they would be willing to whip any man who was prepared to pay.

George took up the suggestion with great gusto, but wanted a dungeon built – dark lighting and the full regalia handcuffs on the walls, chains and posts to be tied up to. At first Muriel thought they were all joking, but a prompt two days later by George and an enquiry by Cassandra, who it turned out needed cash urgently to feed her drug habit, prompted Muriel to consider the matter further. Why shouldn't she run a discreet, invitation-only, meeting place for like-minded people?

She already owned a shop in Soho that she rented to a Turkish man, selling risqué lingerie, peek-a-boo bras, that sort of thing, and the basement was empty. Finding a builder to convert the basement had not been difficult, as once she told George about her plan, he recommended a man who he had met at another similar 'club'.

By restricting her membership and only using girls who were usually desperate for money, or owed her for a part in a play or media exposure, Muriel built up an interesting sideline. It didn't make her rich, but was a nice, tidy earner.

When Lord George died in 2004 she decided to sell up – after all she was sixty herself and had successfully carried on a number of careers, without attracting undue attention. Now was the time to stop. A Romanian man was introduced to her by Natalie, one of her girls, and he made her a satisfactory offer for the freehold of the premises, now a sex shop, and the S&M business in the basement. Muriel wasn't surprised he was interested, her clients included a police commander, five MPs, seven titled members of the nobility and numerous rich patrons. Bondage was big business.

But Muriel giggled as she thought of the shock on the faces of the Cornwall businessmen if she talked about her diversified commercial affairs – best, after all, to stick to anecdotes from the theatre and some reference to her directorships.

The doorbell rang. Opening the door of her picturesque thatched cottage in the seaside town of Fowey in Cornwall, she saw a middle-aged woman standing there.

"I wonder if the charming cottage is for let," she asked in good, but accented, English.

Muriel was not surprised by the request – she had been asked before if her picture-book cottage was available for holiday let.

"No dear, I never let the cottage." Muriel smiled and went to close the door when the woman barged in, pushing Muriel backwards.

"What do you want?" said Muriel, now very frightened.

The woman looked at her, then raised her umbrella and poked it into Muriel's leg.

"Shit," said Muriel before slumping to the ground.

*

Katya timed the moment she injected the deadly cocktail into the woman's leg, until it took effect.

"Three, four, five." The woman fell to the ground, clearly dead. *That's very fast*, thought Katya.

Katya knew that the woman had a cleaner who came twice each week and tomorrow Muriel Steadman's body would be discovered, but that didn't matter. Checking the hall and her handiwork, satisfied, she left the house, pulling the door closed behind her.

Katya walked to the bus stop in the town and after a twenty-minute wait, caught a bus to Penzance railway station and boarded a train to London. Katya got off at Reading Station and connected to a train to Gatwick Airport. Leaving the station she went up the escalator and along the passage to the Gatwick Hilton and went to room 543.

Ivan was sitting in a rather comfortable-looking chair watching television as Katya entered the room.

"Successful trip?" he asked, putting the pistol back in his belt.

"Yes, very. Do you know it only takes four seconds and the target is dead?"

"Useful, very useful. Tomorrow I will go to Brighton and eliminate this man." He pointed to Katya's laptop. Katya looked over his shoulder. "Meredith Lineham, retired accountant, lives in Hove."

"Good choice and once we have tested again the effectiveness of the poison we will confirm the team can proceed with their list of targets."

Looking at himself in the mirror, Meredith Lineham saw a grey-haired, elderly man – *still quite sprightly though*, he thought. He had dressed meticulously for his lunch with Melanie Johnson, the daughter of Harold Johnson, a long-standing client. Meredith had retired from his accountancy practice five years ago, but still looked after a dozen clients, who were close acquaintances or in the Lodge. One of these, Harold Johnson, was an interesting character, who owned an antique shop in the Lanes in Brighton. Meredith suspected Harold did not disclose all his income from cash sales as he had some other, probably illegal, business running, as he seemed to live way beyond his means. Harold's daughter, Melanie, was a divorcee who handled much of the day-to-day business in the shop and Meredith was having a business lunch to go through the accounts for the last financial year. He lusted after Melanie even though she was twenty-five years younger, and was looking forward to the harmless flirting which normally took place when the two of them met.

Lunch was at 12.30pm at Claudine's, the upmarket Italian restaurant in Hove and Meredith arrived early to make sure he got the booth he wanted. Melanie breezed in five minutes late, but looking gorgeous, gave him a kiss on each cheek and enthusiastically explained that she had just sold a pair of George III silver candlesticks for four thousand pounds, hence her late arrival. They ordered a fillet steak each, washed down by a very pleasant red Burgundy. Meredith didn't eat pudding, but Melanie ordered a tiramisu. After a pleasant and enjoyable lunch, they decided to look at the accounts over coffee. This was the bit Meredith liked, as Melanie came and sat alongside him. He could see that her short skirt had ridden up, was that stocking tops he glimpsed? Melanie also wore an intoxicating perfume, Chanel No 5, she told him. It was difficult to concentrate on the accounts, but he made an effort.

Meredith hadn't noticed the dark-haired man that casually watched the couple from a table across the restaurant.

"Can you excuse me, Melanie?" he said. Meredith needed the toilet and took delight in watching her legs, as she slid across the bench seat.

As he walked to the toilet he contemplated – *should he make a move on her*? He knew she responded to his jokes. The slight touch of her hand on his arm. She seemed enthralled with his stories of the rich and famous clients he had done work for. Still, he had known Harold since Round Table in 1962 – could he shag his daughter?

A dark-haired man followed him into the tiled toilet area, the owners had made an effort with large mirrors and paper hand towels, almost unheard of these days – strange he was carrying an umbrella. As he leaned into the toilet stall, he felt a sharp prick on his calf, he jumped and turned, but as he did so, blackness.

Ivan had already paid for his lunch in cash, but decided to haul the man into a toilet compartment, lock the door, and climb over the top. *Christ, he was getting too old for all this*, he thought.

Melanie waited with some apprehension. She had more or less decided to let the old bugger screw her this year. She liked older men with no baggage. In any case it would be fun screwing one of daddy's friends. Smiling to herself she waited. Ten minutes passed by – where was he? She asked a waiter to go and have a look: he came rushing back a few minutes later.

"He's collapsed in the toilet," he said.

"My god, is he okay?" asked Melanie.

The manager went to the toilet area, having called an ambulance. One of the young waiters had climbed over the partition separating the toilets and unlocked the door. The manager, a normally cheerful Italian, felt the man's pulse. No signs. The paramedics arrived and after a few minutes declared the man was dead, probably a heart attack. Melanie couldn't help herself. She cried.

*

Ivan had left the restaurant and walked along the road he knew led to the town centre. He went into Burtons the tailors and purchased a new raincoat, telling the sales assistant he would wear it straight away as it looked like rain. Ten minutes later he was at Brighton Station and boarded a train to London's Victoria Station. He got off at East Croydon and then caught a train back the way he had come to Gatwick Airport, all the time checking for a tail. Satisfied at Gatwick, he nevertheless went upstairs and sat with a coffee in Starbuck's, watching. Finally he went to the hotel room he shared with Katya.

"How did that go?" asked Katya. Ivan had left six days ago to kill the man on the list.

"Fine – he took a woman to a restaurant. I followed him and killed him in the toilet."

"And the time?"

"Less than yours. Must have been only two or three seconds before death."

"Perhaps he had a weak heart, they said heart failure would be brought on quicker if the target had any prior condition."

"The important thing is we have trialled the equipment. Now we can get on with it," said Ivan, carefully putting down the umbrella.

15TH JANUARY 2007 – MAIDENHEAD, ENGLAND

John Mooney was very content. He had enjoyed a pleasant lunch with his fellow Rotarians at the Bull's Head pub in Maidenhead and had been presented by the club president, Jack Toomey, a Paul Harris Fellowship, the prestigious award given by Rotary Clubs. In this instance the award had been presented to John on his seventy-eighth birthday for his long service – he had been a member of Maidenhead and District Rotary Club for thirty-seven years. As he sat listening to the after dinner speech – a very pleasant young lady talking about riding for the disabled – he pondered on his Rotary career. In 1970, he had been recruited by the then president Maurice Small, straight from Round Table. He had passed the age when you had to reluctantly leave Round Table, but on attaining age forty-one he had been approached by Maurice asking him to consider becoming a Rotarian. John loved the service clubs – service above self, which Rotary stood for, was right up John's street. In 1970 when John had joined Rotary it was an honour to be approached to join the thriving service clubs Rotary, Round Table and The Lions.

Today, he thought, *youngsters don't seem to want to join service clubs. Sad really, they miss so much.*

He carried on day-dreaming until he heard his name and his pal Reg nudged him. Reg and John had sat side by side at lunch every Monday, bar holidays and enforced absence, for thirty-six years. Reg had joined Rotary the year after John and they had been firm friends ever since. The President of the Rotary Club was once again congratulating John on his award, and the slightly inebriated and enthusiastic membership clapped.

John left the club slightly tipsy – he had enjoyed a few glasses of rather pleasant claret. As he weaved his way along the High Street, clutching his Paul Harris Fellowship badge, he felt really proud. His wife, May, whom he was due to meet at the car park behind Safeway's supermarket, would be delighted. May had always supported John's charity work through Rotary and before that Round Table. John had always had the bold ideas, leading from the front they used to call it. Suddenly he felt a sharp prick in his leg and looked up as a swarthy, dark-haired man walked by.

Bugger, he thought, *that hurt. Must have been the umbrella.*

That was the last thing John thought in this world. He collapsed on the pavement. An ambulance was called and he was pronounced dead at the scene by the paramedics.

May waited half an hour before trudging to the Bull's Head. Finding this year's President, Jack Toomey, she had a joke and spoke about how happy John would have been to receive the Paul Harris Fellowship. May had a sense of humour and asked, "What have you done with dear old John?"

"He left over half an hour ago," said Jack.

May wasn't really concerned; he had probably had a glass or two of wine and gone home for a sleep.

When she got back home, May found a young lady constable on her doorstep.

"Mrs Mooney?"

"Yes," replied May, looking at the young policewomen with the respectful look of a senior citizen who was slightly apprehensive.

"Can we go inside?" the policewoman asked.

May opened the door and invited the young lady indoors.

"Tea, dear, or would you prefer coffee?" May knew the young did not drink as much tea these days.

"No thank you mam, but let's put the kettle on."

May busied herself and came back in with a mug of tea in her hand.

"Now, dear, you wanted to talk to me."

"I have some bad news, I am afraid."

May stopped drinking and looked at the young woman.

"I am sorry, Mrs Mooney" She paused. "Your husband collapsed on the High Street at 2.10pm this afternoon and died."

May dropped her mug of tea and cried out.

"No, it can't be, he was as fit as a fiddle – you must be mistaken. He can't be dead."

The woman police constable moved toward May and wrapped her arms around the elderly lady. You were not supposed to have contact these days – but what the hell, she needed a hug.

"I'm here to accompany you to the hospital to identify your husband, but we are pretty sure, from ID in his pocket, it is John Mooney."

*

The funeral was a week later. The President of Maidenhead Rotary Club had tears streaming down his face as he gave a most moving eulogy about dear John. John's son, Frank, an Inspector in the Metropolitan Police, followed with his own tribute to his beloved father. May silently cried and hugged her daughter, Matilda, and her four grandchildren – all of whom cried throughout the service. Reg, his old friend, came up to May afterwards.

"You know it seems daft to me. John was as fit as a fiddle. I just don't understand it."

John's son didn't understand it either. A post mortem had shown the cause of death as heart failure, but Frank knew his dad had never had a problem with his heart. Furthermore his granddad and grandma had both lived into their late eighties – so no hereditary heart problem was obvious.

Reluctantly the family said goodbye to dear John and life carried on in Maidenhead and at the Rotary club. May had dropped the Paul Harris Fellowship badge into the coffin before he was cremated.

Anton Hineva, a Russian, was now travelling as Bastiaan Meijer, a Dutch national. He was an exporter of bulbs, at least according to his passport. In fact, he exported death. It had been easy to kill that silly old man. He looked at his list, another man this time, in Reading, he studied his train timetable and then sent a text to Katya. The notes and photograph Katya sent him were extremely useful to pinpoint the target.

Wendle Baptiste was a character. He had come to the UK with his parents in 1951, who had responded when invited by the British government, as had thousands of West Indians, to fill the acute labour shortage after the war. Wendle's father had worked hard, firstly as a porter and then a train driver for British Rail. Ruby, his mother, also did cleaning and took in ironing and together they planned for Wendle to have a good education. Wendle went to Aristotle School in Brixton and was only the second black boy ever to go to the Central School, which was a cut above a secondary school, but not a grammar. His parents paid for him to have private lessons of English and maths and Wendle was in the top three in all subjects from the age of fourteen. Wendle was very bright and his teachers were not surprised when he gained the examinations needed to go to Kings College, London, a prestigious university which offered courses in engineering. Wendle wanted to build bridges and had excelled in all the sciences and mathematics. The year he took GCEs, he was top in the whole country in maths – "The whole country," his father said proudly showing the letters to Eustace, his West Indian drinking friend. Actually three pints of Whitbread's best bitter was their limit on a Friday night and a game of dominoes at The Lamb usually resulted in friendly banter and a shilling changing hands to the winner.

Wendle left Kings College with an honours degree in engineering and was recruited immediately by Huckerby and Bell, a prestigious London-based firm. He worked extensively all over the world, building bridges and boring tunnels. In 1988 he had collaborated with the French boring the Channel Tunnel. His French colleague had been astounded when he showed him his plan to leave the huge boring machines 'parked' under the ocean when they finished the tunnelling. "What's the point of trying to get them out?" he argued in French, and in the end he won the day.

Six years after he had finally retired he had been surprised to receive a letter advising him he had been awarded an OBE. On the day of the investiture Wendle was dressed up in the morning suit he had hired, and at seventy-six years old was accompanied by his daughter, Clarity, and two of his three sons, Melvin and Winston. His other son, Major Henry Baptiste, was in Afghanistan serving with the Grenadier Guards.

How proud he would be now, Wendle thought. *Here I am, on my way to Buckingham Palace to meet the Queen.*

"To Mr Wendle T Baptiste," the letter had been addressed. He had known it was official as no one knew his middle name was Tobias; he had taken enough stick at school and after that had kept it to himself. Opening the envelope, which had a crest on it, he was astonished to read that he was to be conferred with the Order of the British Empire or OBE as it was usually known, 'For Service to Engineering.'

How his dear departed wife and his parents would have loved this moment, he thought, as he approached Buckingham Palace with his daughter Clarity and his sons. He presented his pass and was admitted to the Palace and directed to the entrance. He was met and shown to the ballroom which was richly decorated in reds and pastel colours, with striking rich red curtains embroidered at the bottom with a coat of arms, he presumed the Royal Family crest. He was to be the fifty-sixth person on the list of investitures that day and Her Majesty the Queen was personally presenting the honours. The ceremony began as the Queen entered the room, attended by two Ghurkha orderly officers. The national anthem rang out and when the military band had finished, a distinguished-looking gentleman – who Melvin told him was the Lord Chamberlain – began calling names. It seemed to take ages and Wendle wondered if the Queen was getting tired standing there presenting honours – she had a few words for everyone. Then his name was called by an usher and he stepped forward and after a brief few words from Her Majesty he was presented his OBE.

Wendle and his children had a family photograph taken in the Quadrangle at Buckingham Palace. As it was a special occasion they had arranged for a limousine to pick them up and take them for lunch at Rules Restaurant just off the Strand in London. Wendle had arranged to meet his friend Eustace, his sister Susan and her husband Clyde, his son's wife, his grandchildren and the widow Margo, his next-door neighbour, who Susan suspected was her father's new bedwarmer, which was how she described her to husband Clyde. The meal Wendle had chosen was traditional, steak and kidney pudding followed by a fruit crumble. Rules had given them the upstairs private dining room and Wendle was amazed when in walked his son, Henry, who had been given special leave to fly into RAF Uxbridge and had rushed to the restaurant as he only had two hours before he had to reverse his journey.

That night Wendle slept soundly with the ribboned OBE on the pillow beside him. A shot of rum, or several, with his sons had well and truly knocked him out. He didn't hear the door to the bedroom open and was blissfully ignorant of the small dark-haired man who entered.

Taking out a hypodermic from the case in his pocket, he rolled up the bedclothes, careful not to disturb the snoring black man. He injected the substance in between Wendle's toes, he moaned in his sleep as he inserted the needle. Carefully he withdrew the hypodermic and left the room, exiting the way he had entered, through the front door, with the duplicate key he had copied a week earlier after Wendle had foolishly left his keys in his overcoat, which he had hung up in the passageway of the Working Men's Club in Brixton.

The following day Margo called as usual, and not getting any response from the bell let herself in. *I expect the old duffer is still asleep*, she thought. Knocking on his bedroom door, she was unable to wake him and went in. Margo had seen many dead bodies, she was a retired nurse, and knew immediately her dear friend was dead. *How could life be so cruel*, she thought, as tears streamed down her face.

The funeral was a joyous affair. Wendle's family made sure his wake was a happy reflection on a fine man. His son Henry could not understand how his father, who he had insisted went for a medical with his doctor last month, had died of a heart attack, but he only had compassionate leave for one day and returned to the Afghan capital, Kabul, where he commanded a tank division.

The Bulgarian Egor, now carrying a Dutch passport which showed his name as Filip Gerritson, a schoolteacher, examined the London A-Z. The fourth target on his list was a couple who lived in Beckenham. The notes on the victims were never brilliant, but once again he noted an elderly couple were to be eliminated. Fleetingly he wondered what these people had done. *Probably dissidents or Jews*, he thought as he planned his route. *Curious though a black man, still the money was good*. He sent a text to Katya.

"Exercise, that's the key," said Ellen to her friend Agnes. "I go dancing down the Co-op hall once a week and I walk as much as possible," she said winking at Sheila who knew Ellen regularly got the bus into town, "and I take the pooch out every day."

Ellen was entertaining her two friends to lunch, they were all seventy-five this year, but today was Ellen's birthday. She was a widow, had no children and had lived in her semi-detached house for over forty years. When her Bert had suggested buying the house, she had argued long and hard. Why did he want to leave the two-up-two-down in Lark Street? But he had been right, even though the mortgage stretched them in the early years. *Goodness,* she thought, *we bought our house for five thousand pounds and now they tell me it's worth over a quarter of a million. Not bad for a retired secretary.*

Ellen was very well off in comparison to many of her contemporaries. She had worked for an accountant in Solihull for nearly fifty years before she retired. He had paid 15% of her salary into a pension scheme and she had topped up to the maximum each year. She had been a continuous investor, but nevertheless had been surprised when the insurance company told her that her pension 'pot' was nine hundred and ten thousand pounds and that would entitle her to a lifetime annuity of over thirty thousand pounds each year. Goodness, with her old age pension and other savings she could manage nicely – very nicely, thank you.

Ellen loved to go to Blackpool each year and always stayed at The Beachcomber, a small guesthouse off the front. The owners, Mr and Mrs Jarvis, were nice people who reserved her a room for two weeks every August. *What would she do when they retired?* she thought to herself.

"Penny for them?" said Agnes.

"Oh, I was thinking about my holiday next week in Blackpool," replied Ellen.

Agnes looked resentful; she couldn't afford two weeks in Blackpool every year and secretly was jealous of Ellen, who seemed to be able to afford lots of nice things.

"Did you see that Nora has divorced her husband?" Sheila, the other woman at the birthday party, chirped in.

"No! That's her third divorce in ten years," replied Ellen. Sheila could always be relied on to keep them up to date on the local gossip.

"And what about her in Risley Street?" They all looked at Sheila expectantly.

"Arrested last week." Sheila looked triumphant.

"Arrested, what for?" asked Agnes. They leaned closer, not to miss what Sheila was about to tell them.

"Well" she paused looking at her audience. "I heard it was prostitution." Sheila sat back triumphantly.

"Nah, it can't be, she must be fifty, if she's a day," said Agnes leaning back into her chair.

"I can only tell it as I heard. The police came round and that Mrs Jones, next door at fifty-one, told me she was arrested for prostitution."

"You shouldn't listen to such gossip, Sheila," said Ellen.

"Cake ladies?" Agnes offered another slice of the delicious Marks & Spencer chocolate cake, a weekly indulgence.

The ladies chatted away until 3pm, when the birthday party broke up for her friends to go home for a snooze before bingo that night. All three ladies met at the Roxy Bingo Hall in the High Street three times a week. Occasionally Ellen was very lucky and only last month won the national accumulator, a total of five thousand pounds.

"My gaud," said Agnes resentfully to Sheila, "money goes to money." That was, of course, before she had received, from Ellen, the tickets. Ellen gave her friends the tickets on her birthday and she smiled as they looked taken aback.

Ellen had planned that all three of them travel to Austria in May by Churches Coaches, a local firm who arranged escorted tours. Through the Channel Tunnel of all things! Sheila and Agnes had been touched by their friend's generosity and when she left the room decided they really ought to buy her a birthday present.

Ellen had been out for a lengthy walk to the shops in Wrexham Street that morning, but after the ladies had gone, decided to put her coat on and take her Jack Russell terrier, Sally, up to the field for a walk. Sally was thirteen years old and didn't walk too fast! Reaching the field, which was really the only piece of green nearby and was a large municipal park, Ellen let Sally off the lead. Ellen noticed the woman walking toward her. Not recognising a fellow dog-walker, she briefly wondered who she was. When the dark-haired woman, who was very wrapped up for quite a warm afternoon, reached Ellen, she suddenly seemed to trip and the tip of the umbrella she was carrying struck Ellen's leg.

"Blast!" said Ellen, expecting an apology, but the woman simply kept walking.

Ellen started to feel unwell, and dropped to the ground before she had gone two steps further.

Another dog-walker found her ten minutes later with the faithful Sally, who had remained close to her mistress, crying as she had been unable to get any response – as her mistress was dead.

Not many attended Ellen's funeral at St Mary's Church. Sheila and Agnes were there, with several other ladies who went to the whist drive or played bingo. Sally, the dog, was taken in by Jack next door. The autopsy declared Ellen had died of a heart attack. Sheila and Agnes decided that they would use the two tickets and go on the coach trip to Austria – and very nice it was. Toasting their friend in Vienna, Sheila said, "I always thought she was as fit as a fiddle – still I suppose you never know what fate has in store."

*

Viktorya Abamova was a Bulgarian by birth, who in the early eighties had lived in Germany and Russia as a member of the KGB. She looked at her laptop, deleted the third name on the list, the woman she had killed walking her dog, and sent Katya a coded message using her disposable mobile phone.

That was the third this month, she thought. *Now who is next? Ah, yes, a man in Birmingham.*

Murdo McCleod spun the wheel of the *Miss Janet*, a sixty-five foot trawler, and set course for Fraserburgh. He had been fishing the North Sea for fifty years and this was to be his last trip. The decision to hand the boat over to his nephew, Magnus, had not been easy, but finally the arthritis affecting his hands made running his own boat impossible. Murdo had inherited his father's boat when he died in 1971 and had built up a fleet of six large trawlers over thirty-five years. His sons, Roddy and Ian, were skippers of their own boats now and he had sold the other three boats over the last five years as catches diminished. You could still make a living out of the business but successive British governments had not helped the industry and they had to scour the fishing grounds using the most sophisticated fish-finder to find shoals of fish.

"One day," said Murdo, talking to his old friend Robbie, they had worked together for thirty years, "there won't be any cod to be had anywhere in the North Sea."

"Aye, the buggars couldn't regulate a piss-up in a brewery," Robbie replied.

"Storm coming," said Murdo, as he looked at the sky and the barometer falling.

"Aye," said Robbie, using his favourite word.

"Can you see Roddy?"

Murdo had set out with his two sons in convoy searching for cod. Roddy skippered *Miss Julie* and his other son, Ian, skippered the ageing *Miss Betty*. *Miss Betty* had broken down, not for the first time, and Roddy was towing his brother's boat back to Fraserburgh.

"The old girl is struggling," said Robbie, talking about the ageing trawler.

"Yes, I think Ian may have to invest in a new engine." Robbie sighed; he was godfather to both boys.

"So expensive these days and for what – there's no fish!"

"Come on, Robbie, it's not quite that bad."

"Well it's getting that way and if we didn't have that gismo, we might as well give up." He pointed to the sonar machine.

"I wonder what the two lads will do?" said Robbie, indicating with his hand the two crew-men, who were busy cleaning the nets.

"We'll find them something," said Murdo lighting up his pipe.

"I don't think it will be that easy," said Robbie.

Suddenly there was a huge explosion toward the bow of the boat, but before Murdo and Robbie could react another explosion wrecked the wheelhouse.

Jonno and Ben Fowler were checking for tears as they rewound the nets when the first explosion ripped through the boat, knocking them both off their feet. As Jonno got up he looked around and realised the old girl was sinking fast. Ben lay crumpled on the deck and Jonno turned him over. Something had struck Ben and he was unconscious. Jonno looked for a moment toward the bow and reckoning that he had seconds to live, hauled Ben up and threw him overboard, jumping after him. Hitting the ice-cold North Sea, Jonno struggled to find Ben. Luckily it was a gentle swell and he spotted him just as *Miss Janet* slipped beneath the waves. *Christ*, he thought, *did the boss and Robbie get off?* He began to feel incredibly cold.

Half a nautical mile back, Roddy had heard the explosion, looked toward his father's trawler and shuddered. Immediately he got on the radio to his brother.

"Did you see that? *Miss Janet* has exploded. I'm detaching the bow line and going to look for survivors."

"Hurry brother, hurry," said Ian, knowing a man could not last long in the freezing water.

Five hours later two trawlers came into the harbour at Fraserburgh and the brothers saw that a crowd had gathered on the quay. As *Miss Julie* edged alongside the mooring, Sally, Robbie's wife and the wives of Jonno and Ben felt the cold dread many women had endured since men invented ships able to trawl these seas. An official and a policeman were the first Ian McCleod spoke to, and then he turned to the women. The look was all it needed – all hands were lost.

The fishing community of Fraserburgh had endured many a loss of good and brave men, but the turnout for Murdo and his crew to listen to Chaplin Peters was moving and tearful. The Admiralty had not been able to send divers down to the wreck to ascertain the cause as it was lying in sixty fathoms and would probably never be investigated. Ian and Roddy McCleod took out *Miss Julie* and the repaired *Miss Betty* looking for cod the following day – it was what their father would have wanted.

The Bulgarian, Leonid, had been an explosives expert plying his trade in Afghanistan before Katya found him. He didn't care for poison-tipped umbrellas and had set two simultaneous explosions to kill the occupants of the cabin and sink the boat rapidly. It was unfortunate all the men on board died because he only got paid for the old man, Murdo McCleod. Fleetingly, he was curious what the old man had done, but then sent a text to Katya informing her of the kill.

The following day Katya read the report of the sinking in *The Times*.

"I told you Leonid was unreliable," said Katya.

"He's killed three others in that explosion," replied Ivan.

"Well you better tell him no more explosions. This isn't fucking Afghanistan," said Katya.

"Who is his next target?"

Katya examined her laptop and showed Ivan.

"A man in Edinburgh," she said. "You will send him a text. No more explosions or he'll bring the whole operation down."

Leonid grunted as he saw the text, well he only had half the semtex left anyway and he needed the money, so he would do what Ivan told him – pity, he liked rigging explosives.

Elspeth and Rodney Jackson sang along to the Beatles song 'Yesterday', that was blaring out of the car radio. Rodney had turned up the volume as soon as the first beats of their favourite group transported them back to the mid-sixties.

"Do you remember the Locarno Streatham, Els?"

His wife smiled, of course she did, but she would tease him for a while. "No, what about it, dear?"

"Oh, come on. You must remember the first record we danced to at the Locarno was The Beatles ' Yesterday'?"

Els remembered the dance hall very well. Every saturday she travelled with Sue Harvey to Streatham Hill station from Norwood, where they lived, to go dancing at the Locarno. Not as though the boys danced much, most of the time they spent drinking beer in the bar and the girls danced with each other. But from time to time a boy did break ranks with the boozing crowd and ask for a dance. On the particular night Rod was talking about, her friend Sue had been asked to dance and she was standing watching her friend longingly when she felt a tap on her shoulder. Turning, she found herself gazing into the eyes of the most handsome boy she had ever seen.

"Would you like to dance?" he asked as the DJ put on a new record.

"Yes," she remembered murmuring. Why did she suddenly feel tongue-tied? But her dancing did the talking to the Beatles record and then to the Rolling Stones, then a slow dance to the Drifters – she remembered them all.

"Of course I remember, you silly idiot – it was the first time you trod on my foot," Els laughed.

"I did not," he said squeezing her knee.

"Watch the road now, Rodney," Els said using her officious voice.

"Oh come on, let's find a lay-by – it will be like old times."

She giggled. "Just drive, Rodney, Sandra is expecting us."

They had married in 1972 and bought a maisonette in Bromley near the Bromley Court, one of their favourite dance venues. In 1975, at the age of thirty, he was made a partner in Dearing and Adams Solicitors. He was the youngest partner in the firm's one hundred-year history. Then along came Sandra – their daughter and only child. Els had been devastated when the doctors told her she shouldn't have any more babies and thought she noticed a wistful look on her husband's face when he stared at Sandra who, at thirty-two, already had two children. Sandra had married five years ago and quickly had two children, a boy and a girl. They loved their grandchildren and often volunteered to babysit.

"Whilst we're young we can do it," she joked with her daughter.

Rodney had retired from the solicitors practice two years ago, thanks to the generous non-contributory pension scheme. He played more golf and they often went with his daughter and her husband and the grandchildren to an apartment they owned in Los Cristianos, Tenerife.

*

Egor didn't enjoy this part of the contract – shadowing people, always making sure to keep out of sight. They were obviously going to their daughter's house; he had followed them there before.

Egor had nearly got him at the golf club last weekend, but just at the moment he was about to deliver the deadly toxin, a car pulled into the car park. The man, his target, Rodney Jackson, knew the driver and they chatted and he went back inside the club-house. Egor waited for another thirty minutes, but when he came out it was with a crowd and he didn't get another chance. Egor sat somewhat impatiently in the stolen Vauxhall Nova, full of pent-up energy. The KGB trainer in the Moscow centre had said he was a time bomb waiting to go off. He had shown them he could control his temper but he found a long run every day essential to reduce his tension. The BMW with the man Rodney driving pulled into his daughter's driveway – Egor knew that because he had been to this house following them twice before and had casually asked a neighbour if Mr and Mrs Jackson's daughter lived nearby. The neighbour happily confirmed Sandra and Gary Tucson lived at number five.

He sat waiting impatiently, turned on the radio trying to find a medium wave station speaking something other than English, and then the front door of number five opened. His target led the way, followed by his wife and two young children running happily toward the BMW. The man got in the driver's side, as his wife strapped the children's seat belts in the back of the car. Reversing out of the drive, the BMW headed the way Egor was facing and he tailed the car at a suitable distance.

31

Egor was familiar with the roads around Beckenham and saw they were heading toward the town centre. His target parked down a leafy wide road and they all got out and began walking toward the centre of Beckenham. Egor parked and followed.

When they reached a restaurant called Ask they all went inside. Egor was just thinking this was not a good opportunity to kill the man when the target appeared at the front door hurrying past him. He followed, closing the distance between them . *He was going back to the BMW*, thought Egor. As Rodney reached his car, he used the remote to click the automatic boot catch and went to pick out his coat. Just at that moment, he felt a sharp stab to his calf. He turned, saw a dark-haired man right behind him, then collapsed in the road.

Egor looked around – nobody was within one hundred metres and the target had fallen between two cars, so the body was mostly out of sight. He walked away from the BMW, down the road, got into his car and drove off back to the main road, turning left toward Croydon. He would dump the Vauxhall in Croydon and catch a train to London – his next target lived in east London.

When her husband didn't come back to the restaurant, Els phoned Sandra and told her she was taking the children back to the car. That was when she saw the flashing light of an ambulance right alongside their BMW. Rushing down the road urging on the children, she reached a small crowd of onlookers.

"Excuse me," she said, "is my husband hurt?"

One of the paramedics, called a few minutes ago by a passing dog -walker who had spotted the man on the floor behind the open boot of the car, replied, "Come to the ambulance, madam."

She held both children's hands as she approached the rear doors. A small fair-haired paramedic got out of the rear of the ambulance, clearly the colleague of the man who had talked to her.

"I'll hold the children's hands, ma'm," she said, indicating she should go inside with the other paramedic.

"I am sorry to ask Madam," he said, "but is this man your husband?" Els had a terrible feeling and moved forward. There was Rodney lying quite still, eyes closed, looking peaceful.

"Rodney, oh Rodney," she cried.

The paramedic held this lady in his arms as she began to sob, large tears rolling down her face, not PC these days, but what the hell.

The police arrived and took charge of the scene, followed ten minutes later by Sandra and Gary. Sandra found her mum cuddling the two children in the back of the police car.

The family were devastated by the loss of Rodney.

"He was only in his sixties and seemed so fit," said Gary, her son-in-law, at the funeral.

The autopsy declared death due to a massive heart attack, but long before that Egor had sent a text to Katya confirming the kill and moved to his next target in east London.

1ST FEBRUARY 2007 – EAST LONDON, ENGLAND

Ludvig was due to visit the post office in Dalston Lane, East London. He went once a month to pick up the latest package. Sitting on the number 149 bus, he wiped the steamed-up window; it was a bitter, cold day. Ludvig usually travelled by public transport, less conspicuous than cars or taxis in London these days and unlike Moscow the buses were heated.

As he sat on the bus, passing through Shoreditch, he reflected on his good fortune. It was over six months ago that he had received a message from an old adversary.

In August 2006 he was living in Stockholm when an ex-CIA field officer, Morgan Fryer, with whom he used to cross swords with in Berlin, contacted him. At first he was cautious, they hadn't exactly been friends. But after a carefully planned meeting in the foyer of the Central Hotel, Stockholm, he agreed to go for a walk.

Morgan Fryer, the American, did not know that Ludvig had asked two of his colleagues from the old days to shadow them – he wasn't taking any chances. As they walked, Morgan explained that he wanted to hire his administration skills. It all started off quite innocently as Morgan ascertained whether he still had his contacts with ex-KGB officers. He nodded to Morgan, Ludvig was a cautious man and always said as little as possible as directional long distance microphones were a real nuisance. As they walked into a park, Morgan indicated they should sit. The seat was in the open so Ludvig didn't foresee any problem. In any case he saw Katya in the distance walking a dog (*where did she get that from*? he momentarily thought).

Morgan explained that he had a proposition and asked him if he would like to earn a million pounds sterling every other month, for the next three years. Ludvig was initially taken aback by the sums suggested, but tried not to show it – in any case what would he have to do to earn that sort of money? Morgan went on. "I'll wire your bank account in the Caymans, one million pounds each month. Half of that you will pay your field operatives, the rest you keep".

Ludvig remembered that he looked up to see Katya approaching and took his hat off to denote no action was required. Katya was ex-KGB and a deadly agent, having killed many times working for Ludvig in Russia, London and in Berlin. He couldn't see Ivan, his other shadow.

As he watched the east London shoppers from the bus, he continued to think about that first meeting with Morgan.

"Tell me more," he had asked.

"All you have to do is put together a team of assassins who will stay in Britain and kill targets on a list which I will send you each month." Ludvig reflected on his response, as he remembered Katya passing within five feet of their park bench leading a black and white terrier.

"Who are these targets?" he asked the ex-CIA man.

"That doesn't concern you. But you will pay each of your assassins fifty thousand pounds sterling for each month they are working for you."

Ludvig remembered sitting silently contemplating this offer. He knew Morgan now worked as a security consultant in New York. What on earth had this to do with killing people in England, or rather he had specifically said Britain? "I need to know more... What is it all about? What might I be up against?"

"You are on a need-to-know basis, Ludvig. You will be paid handsomely to co-ordinate the hits. There is no connection between any of the targets and they will be mostly old folk, often living alone."

"What are they? Defectors, agents?"

"I repeat, this is need-to-know. You will personally make five hundred thousand pounds sterling every month – you need to build a team of ten operatives, all used to killing without question or remorse."

Ludvig reflected on his response at the time as he had asked for twenty-four hours to 'think about it'. Morgan agreed and said he would call him in twenty-four hours, giving him a mobile phone. "Dispose of it after the call," he had said.

It didn't take him long to make up his mind. After leaving the KGB under a cloud in 1984, he had fled to Switzerland. Several of the international agencies were looking for him, so he used some hard-earned cash to have some facial work carried out and changed his appearance and nationality. He was a Swiss national now, Ludvig Amst from the German-speaking area of Zurich. Always on the move he went to live in Sweden. He thought he had shaken off his pursuers until he got a telephone call from Morgan. It must have been one of his ex-colleagues who told him where he was – so much for loyalty. For the last fifteen years he had been 'working' as a hit man for various criminal organisations, even the CIA had used his services, but the American dollars he had smuggled out of the old Soviet Union were nearly all gone and this sounded a lucrative scheme to rebuild his finances.

Sitting on the bus in east London, Ludvig smiled to himself. He remembered that after making up his mind to accept the assignment, he demanded a half-million dollars up front, as a retainer. The American readily agreed and he wondered if he could have got any more. Still, mustn't be greedy. Since then he had used Katya and Ivan, two of his most trusted ex-KGB officers who had worked under his command in Berlin, Russia, London and Poland, to recruit eight other assassins and given them two hundred thousand dollars for their trouble. They had given him a list a month later.

He was not surprised to see five Bulgarians, all ex-KGB, on the list. They were hard, those Bulgarians, and even the woman Viktorya, whose name was on the list, was a deadly killer. The others listed were Russian, all ex-KGB assassins.

Having assembled the team, Ludvig sent the pre-coded text message on his disposable mobile and six months ago, he had picked up the first list of names of people to be eliminated from the post office box, then located in Stockholm. He had fitted all the team out with false Dutch and Bulgarian papers.

It was easy to get into Britain if you were an EU national and cover stories were agreed for all the team. He never met any of the people on the list of ex-agents. Katya and Ivan passed on the passports, identity papers and cover stories to the other eight. Safety first, safety first, he had survived in West Berlin in the early eighties for five years by being careful, nothing had changed.

The American, Morgan Fryer, had been as good as his word and now, sitting downstairs on a number 149 bus, Ludvig reflected that he had three million pounds in his Cayman Islands bank account and all ten assassins were each three hundred thousand pounds better off. Sixty people were dead; much fewer than he had hoped as it was taking longer to plan the hits and he knew nothing about any of them. Curious – you bet, but why spoil an easy earning situation by unwanted questions.

He got off the bus at the stop two roads from the post office where he had a mailbox. Dalston High Street was very busy and as usual, he followed years of training by checking for 'tails' or anyone showing too much interest. He used Katya as his back-up and she rang his mobile.

"It seems all clear to me."

That was good enough and he went into the dingy shop which doubled as a mail-drop centre, currency exchange and a post office. Unlocking his safe deposit box and removing some cash, sterling and euros, he walked to the counter, paid for another three months rental in cash, collected an envelope which was postmarked Washington and left the shop. This time he went to the Dalston Broad Street tube station and got on a 277 bus to Highbury and Islington tube station. Katya followed him, operating counter-surveillance procedures. His mobile rang again it was Katya "No sign of anyone."

"Okay, when they have finished their tasks, change all their disposable mobiles, give them two weeks' break for research and then to report back at the end of the month. Meet me at the usual place tomorrow."

Ludvig went down the underground station to disappear in London; even Katya didn't know where he lived.

Carol muttered to herself as she closed the front door of her semi-detached house. *Raining again*, she thought and buttoned the top button of her raincoat and opened her umbrella. Once a week, she went into Bromley to the post office, to collect her pension. Such a nuisance since they had closed that nice Mr Ali's post office in the precinct, nobody had any choice. The number 336 bus was on time. She showed her senior citizen pass and sat next to a chubby young girl. She loved to chat and gossip, but there was no chance with this young girl, who appeared locked into a device attached to both ears. *My goodness – the young today*, she thought. That Mrs Doughty from Southlands Grove got on the bus. "Morning dear," said Carol as Mrs Doughty walked down the bus. The newcomer sat across the aisle and the two ladies began to chat.

"What a miserable morning," she said.

"They say it's going to brighten up after," replied Mrs Doughty.

"You going to the post office?"

"Yes, you?"

"Yes."

Mrs Doughty leaned slightly across the aisle.

"Did you hear about the shenanigans at number six, Hawthorne Road?" Carol looked at Mrs Doughty expectantly.

"Raided by the police." Her friend looked triumphant. Carol waited for her to continue.

"Yes," she nodded, "what for?"

"Well," the two ladies leaned even closer, "Mrs Spring has been living with a black man – Mrs Johnson at number eight said he comes and goes at all hours." Pausing to catch her breath Mrs Doughty continued. "Well the police arrived at seven o'clock in the morning. My Sid was just going to work when Mrs Johnson rang to tell me."

"What happened next?"

"Both of them, Mrs Spring and her 'lodger' were both shoved into a police car; Mrs Johnson thought he was handcuffed."

"My, my – what had they done?"

Her friend looked crestfallen, "I haven't been able to find out yet – but Mrs Johnson thinks it's drugs."

"Oh dear," replied Carol looking up. "Here we are dear," and both elderly ladies got up as the bus came to a halt outside Sainsbury's.

"Still raining," said Mrs Doughty.

Both ladies walked slowly to the main post office. It was a typical Friday at Bromley post office with queues alongside the roped area. "Why on earth they closed Mr Ali's post office, I shall never know," said Carol.

"Disgraceful – what do a load of big-wigs care about the likes of us," her friend replied. Slowly the ladies edged forward.

Dmitri, who had been following this elderly woman for three days now, was getting impatient. As he had strangled three of his previous victims and knifed the other, he wanted to try out the umbrella to confirm it was true – the victim died inside three seconds. *She can certainly talk*, he thought, *worse than my sister in Sofia.*

Dmitri had been recruited by Katya five months ago for a job in England. It all sounded easy enough: fifty thousand pounds a month to eliminate a few old people. *I wonder what she has done*, he thought. *Seems harmless enough to me – still a job's a job.*

Trailing the two elderly women, he watched them get on a bus and assumed they were returning to the terraced row of houses where they lived. He got on the same bus and walked past the women who were sitting together and positioned himself at the back.

As the bus reached the opposite side of the road where the journey had begun, both ladies got up, Dmitri followed. At Southlands Grove, Mrs Doughty gave a cheery wave and turned down the road, Carol continued.

Since her Albert had died, Carol had been comfortable in the red-brick terraced house – not too big and easy to keep. Albert had left her well off, arranging for a regular monthly amount to be paid into her building society account. As Carol glanced into the garden of number twenty-eight she felt a sharp prick in the back of her leg. She turned and then… blackness.

Dmitri turned around and walked quickly, but not too fast, back toward the main road. There were no CCTV cameras and he had a large brown trilby hat on to obscure his face. A number 336 bus pulled up and he got on, walking to the back, after paying for a single fare to the town centre. He got off and walked to Bromley South railway station, checking twice that he didn't have a tail. His next target was in London, and he was returning to his bedsit in Paddington. He had a small dingy basement flat near Paddington station, paying one month's rent in advance. Dmitri liked to be close to stations.

He sent a text to Katya, 'target five complete'. He didn't like mobile phones, they left a trace, but Katya had said to throw this one away after using it twice and she had given him two other Nokia phones, with his instructions written in Bulgarian on a small laptop computer. *She is very thorough*, he thought, as he boarded the train to London's Victoria station where he intended to catch the underground to Paddington.

Mrs Doughty heard about the sad death of her friend the following day. "Well I never," she said. "I was only with her ten minutes before – she seemed alright to me."

Carol's daughter Melanie listened to Reverend Proudfoot's eulogy; a tear ran down her cheek. *Why is life so unkind? Mum seemed as fit as a fiddle and they had just arranged a trip to Torquay in a few months time.* Melanie was an only child, divorced three years ago and only a few cousins, and her mother's friends shared the kind words of the Reverend. Melanie's son, Jake, reached out and held his mother's hand. *Why had his grandmother died now just before he was due to graduate from Kent University?* She would have been so proud – still both his mother's parents were gone now and mum was upset, so he held her hand.

Lady Woodfield cantered slowly across the lower field, heading out cross-country on her usual early morning ride. Anton, using the high-powered binoculars he had acquired from a second-hand shop in Guildford, observed from a distance.

Lady Woodfield was the widow of Sir Philip Woodfield, a prominent industrialist, who had built up Woodfield Technology plc, to take its place as a Footsie One Hundred company. A ruthless man, he had devoured many small businesses and his company steadily grew in the 1980s. But the key to his ultimate success was an invention by one of his group companies. The trioxym wheel enabled manufacturers to deliver less power to their processes and thereby reduce carbon emissions and more importantly, cut the cost of power significantly, by up to sixty per cent. Several large energy companies started a bidding war, trying to buy Woodfield Technology shares, and the share price quadrupled in one week from two hundred and eight pence per share, to over eight hundred and thirty pence. Sir Philip became a billionaire, largely due to his strategy of retaining over fifty-one per cent of the shareholding, which he drip fed to the stock market. Eventually the shares reached the ten pounds per share price and he dropped his holding to fourteen per cent. Sir Philip never knew entirely how the trioxym wheel worked, except it converted oxygen in the air to power, therefore reducing the electricity needed to drive a machine. In any case after Electrogen, the large French power company, got overall control of Woodfield Technology, the invention was mothballed – much to the relief of electricity companies worldwide.

Never one to do nothing, Sir Philip, who had been knighted in 1989, decided to take up politics. Surprisingly, he joined the Labour Party and through generous donations to the party funds, he was offered a safe seat in 1994 for Middlesbrough East, when the sitting MP died. During the nineties Sir Philip plotted his way towards the summit of the Labour Party. Most of the other rising stars had left-wing leanings, several having publicly extolled Marxism during their days at university. The jealousy and petty manoeuvring of these 'lefties', as he used to describe them, was the most enjoyable part of Sir Philip's rise up the ranks of the Labour Party. He was often called a hypocrite, but always rounded on his accusers with his history of donations to the party and charitable causes. He also employed a team of private detectives to collect dirt on all prospective rivals. He was often able to persuade a colleague to join his growing group of admirers, even though his following was more or less built on the sands of corruption and lies. When the Labour Party won the general election of 1997, as he had been an ardent supporter of Tony Blair and had donated over ten million pounds by nominees to the election campaign, he was given a ministry. Sir Philip didn't consider this was his finest political hour, merely a stepping-stone toward the top post – prime minister. However, Minister for Fuel and Power suited him as he had an in-depth knowledge of these resources. This set him aside from most other ministers who headed up departments when they had no clue as to the running or administration of that department. The fifty or so MPs who also became known as 'Woodfield's Wagon Train', also meant he could not be ignored and one year later, when the then home secretary wanted a change of ministry, he was promoted. He had now amassed a considerable following in the party amongst the sitting MPs and knew Tony was beginning to eye his meteoric rise with some suspicion – and then the bombshell…

A *Sunday Times* reporter uncovered details of ten dummy companies, most based in the Cayman Islands, who had each donated one million pounds to the Labour Party before the last election. Worse was to come. One of Sir Philip's most trusted accountants had been arrested by the City of London Police Fraud Squad on an unrelated matter, but was offering up proof and full details of Sir Philip's illegal donations as his way out of the charges he was facing. Sir Philip did consider arranging for the man to quietly disappear, but after pressure from the cabinet he fell on his sword.

It was said afterwards that it was the scandalous headlines and the shame that led to his fatal heart attack and he died without having achieved his second monumental rise – prime minister.

Lady Woodfield and their two sons were joined at the funeral by leaders of industry and cross-party politicians who secretly thought it ridiculous 'Woody' couldn't donate money to whom he liked. The trust funds set up to protect from inheritance tax and the massive pension fund accrued by Sir Philip provided Lady Woodfield with a millionaire lifestyle and she was often photographed with members of the Royal Family and notable celebrities. She was also a generous benefactor of the arts and purchased a number of up-and-coming British artists paintings and donated them to the National Gallery.

Lady Woodfield had inherited, through a complicated trust, the right to live at Amsleigh Manor, the huge estate in Dorset, and it was here that Anton studied her early morning movements. He knew all about Lady Woodfield; Katya's notes had been very extensive. She owned three other houses, including a mansion in Hampstead and a massive villa in the South of France overlooking Nice. As there was a bonus of fifty thousand pounds for eliminating this woman, Anton had spent the past week watching her movements. It would be difficult to kill her, but not impossible. In fact it had turned out to be easy.

Anton lay in wait, dressed in camouflage clothing, just before the hedge she jumped on the chestnut colt every morning. This morning she rode alone and just as she prepared to jump, Anton scared the horse by jumping up from the base of the hedge and shouting. Lady Woodfield was thrown and landed badly on the hard ground. It was just as well she was unconscious as Anton injected the poison between her toes. It had been difficult to remove one of her riding boots and he was tempted to inject her in the leg, *but endeavour to cover up the murder* had been the order and so he struggled with the leather boot. Lady Woodfield was dead before he managed to replace the boot and looking at his stopwatch he knew the horse would probably have returned to the stables about now. Checking the scene he walked across the field, reaching the Ford Fiesta he had stolen in Bridport yesterday, and drove toward the M3. Anton dumped the car in Fareham High Street car park and walked to the railway station. Safely on board the train to Portsmouth, he sent a text to Katya and thought about the extra £50,000 he had earned by killing the woman.

"Lady Woodfield, the well-known philanthropist and supporter of the arts, died of a heart attack whilst out riding," the reporter said on the midday Sky News.

Katya was delighted.

Miles Easeby turned on the radio and tuned in first to BBC Radio 1, then after ten minutes switched to Radio 2. He was monitoring the performance of two of the BBC's disc jockeys as the corporation was proposing cutting two jobs. Working as a consultant for the BBC was really only a hobby job as Miles had retired from his career as a TV producer two years ago, when he reached sixty-five. His wife Bridget still acted, most recently on a TV sitcom about a firm of undertakers. As he switched back to Radio 1 he began to daydream about his early days in TV and radio. He had joined The British Broadcasting Corporation in 1955 aged fifteen. Working at Alexandra Palace in London as a studio boy, he was a messenger and junior assistant to several TV and radio producers and he loved it. In those days his aspiration was to act, just like his hero, Laurence Olivier, or play in a swing band like Benny Goodman's. When the beeb moved production from Ally Pally to Elstree he began to analyse the skills of the directors of the TV shows. Now of course, those early radio and TV performances would be regarded as amateur, but Miles watched and learned. One of the directors of a thriller series about killer plants that ate people, paid particular attention to the young Miles. In those days, whilst luvvies existed throughout the theatre and radio, it was a whispered subject and Miles didn't realise the director Stanley Lumb was grooming him. That was until that day, whilst running a message from the producer of a music hall show to Stanley Lumb. As he stood by his chair he felt a hand creep up his short trousers. Miles was terrified at first, but found he actually liked it and when Stanley asked him to stay behind that evening, he nervously agreed. From then onwards Stanley Lumb began to introduce the sixteen year-old boy into speaking parts on the radio. Very little at first, but gradually he began receiving calls from directors who required a young man in a play. His career as an actor had started. The affair with Stanley lasted for two years until he found another, but in any case Miles had begun to make friends of his own. When the BBC began to make TV programmes from the 'Ally Pally' as they used to call Alexandra Palace, Miles enjoyed a number of parts in several series including *Dixon of Dock Green*, a series about an everyday police officer. Miles played a junior constable and enjoyed the part and later in *The Saint* at Elstree Studios he played a spiv character seen in several episodes.

These flashbacks reminded him of John, another very good friend at the time. Miles' career in TV had continued with parts in plays and programmes such as *Emergency Ward 10*, a hospital series. Miles snapped out of his daydream as the DJ on Radio 1 played a loud indie record, not his cup of tea at all. Deciding he had finished the analysis of the morning DJs on both stations he switched off the radio. He turned on the TV to watch an old *This is Your Life* which featured his favourite actor and producer – him. In 1987 Michael Aspel had caught him out when he was on stage at The Old Vic, a London theatre, and presented him with the famous red book. The programme *This is Your Life* featured a celebrity each week and traced back their career on the stage, in films or on the television. Miles was thrilled, as many old acquaintances recounted his early career and he laughed as clips were shown of his early parts on black and white television. The surprise was his marriage. In 1984 Miles had married Bridget Heany, a Shakespearean actress he had known for ten years. What the research team at *This is Your Life* did not discover was the reason for the marriage as Miles was so obviously gay and Bridget certainly didn't tell them. Bridget Heany was in fact a Romanian actress from Bucharest who, unable to get work, had changed her name in 1974 but unfortunately the immigration office tracked her down and threatened deportation. Bridget's only answer was marriage, but the trouble was she had no male lovers and didn't even like many men. Talking at a dinner one evening, part of a fundraising event for gay rights, Miles found himself offering to marry Bridget — 'purely platonic' he said. So they had married and had lived separate lives, whilst remaining good friends for twenty-three years. Their house was a strange place on occasions, with both of them having live-in lovers. The neighbours found it all very odd but what could you expect from 'theatricals'?

When the thirty minute recording of *This is Your Life* finished Miles went upstairs to lie down. Last year he had noticed some fur-like markings on his tongue. After he left his doctor in Harley Street he was downcast as he had contracted HIV, one of the symptoms being this growth on the tongue. Alerting his partners over the past year had been very difficult, but he felt bound to do so and it also led to the break-up with David who admitted he had AIDS and had not told Miles.

There was a ring at the front doorbell and Miles, looking at his watch, wondered who it was.

"Personal delivery for Mr Easeby," the man said.

"Come in one second," said Miles.

As he accepted the bulky brown envelope he turned but then felt a sharp stabbing pain on the back of his leg. Miles staggered and was about to swear when he dropped to the ground.

Ivan shut the front door, checking his victim's pulse. He was thinking to himself, *Katya was right that these television people are always expecting packages*. He picked up the bogus package, looked around again, then, carefully closing the front door, left.

Bridget came home at 11.30pm with Helen, a young actress she had been infatuated with for some time. Seeing Miles lying on the floor she screamed and it was the younger woman who checked his pulse.

"No pulse I am afraid Bridget – but let's call an ambulance."

The ambulance man declared Miles was dead and moved his body to the hospital. The post mortem showed a massive heart attack, which came as a surprise to Bridget. The dear ol' thing had left her the house and some capital, but his largest investment wasn't returnable – she didn't know why except it was legal.

The Times ran a 'nice' obituary and BBC2 featured a half-hour programme on his career – Miles would have been pleased.

Ivan reported back to Katya. "I think death was even quicker this time, perhaps he had a weak heart" – and another name was crossed off the list.

Constance Spry picked up the CD and smiled to herself. Her record company were once again re-issuing that recording she had first made in 1982, but had changed the title to *Opera Classics of Love*. She didn't mind though, the royalties would be most welcome, but anyone who 'googled' her would find she was seventy-four now and looked a touch different to the face on the CD jacket.

Constance had been a leading soprano for over thirty-five years when she retired in 1992. A wonderful career included performances at the Royal Opera House, Covent Garden, Glyndebourne and the other important opera houses throughout the world. Constance had been made a dame in the honours list of 1993, but she preferred not to use her title.

Joshua, her husband of thirty years, had died last year and she still missed him dreadfully. He had been a fine tenor and they had first met at Covent Garden when they were auditioning for *La Boheme* in 1973. It was love at first sight and a year later they married.

Constance's career had been interrupted by the birth of her two boys, but she had found a superb nanny and was able to resume her blossoming career. If you asked Constance for a highlight, she would find it difficult to answer as there had been so many. Perhaps, the performances for the Queen at the Royal Opera House – Her Majesty had been most gracious – or the occasions singing before crown heads of Europe in Paris and Milan would be the pinnacle of a memorable career. But for Constance, the first time she had sung with Joshua would always be the finest moment.

She loved to live in London and when they began to earn significant money they purchased a mews house in Cheyne Walk, Chelsea. Constance didn't like driving in London so travelled everywhere by taxi, on the bus or using the underground. She used her bus pass, smiling to herself as she was exceedingly rich and could easily afford to pay.

Dmitri, who had been watching her for three days, was intrigued by Constance. *She was such a game old lady*, he thought, but there we are, it was none of his concern. He had decided on a visit to the house, as the people who owned the mews houses opposite were not in residence, so he planned a late night call when he would kill her.

Constance usually retired at 10pm but was curious as to who was ringing her door bell at 10.30pm. Looking through the spy hole, she saw a very old man with grey hair. *Did she know him?* Curiously she opened the door on the chain.

"I am so sorry to trouble you; I am renting number twenty-eight and have locked my keys in the house. I should explain, my wife has gone to the Albert Hall to see *Carmen* in the round and won't be back tonight as she is planning to stay with my niece in Knightsbridge. Could I possibly use your telephone?"

"Don't you have a mobile?" asked Constance.

"By jove, it's Dame Constance Spry isn't it? I have been an admirer since I saw you and your husband Joshua at Covent Garden in *Tosca* in 1981." Dmitri spoke English, perfected in Moscow in 1982, without a trace of an accent. Constance smiled at the memory of the performance that had wowed the critics and the opera world. She even featured a clip on her website. She was warming to this man, what harm could he do at his age?

"Alright, you had better come in and phone your wife."

"I am so grateful," he said as she released the chain on the door. She held the door back as he came in.

"The telephone's on the hall table."

Constance didn't think it was odd the man was carrying a black umbrella, but as he walked alongside her the umbrella seemed to slip and prick her leg. Constance felt very unwell and then collapsed onto the floor.

Dmitri felt her pulse. Incredible stuff the poison they were using, and he kept the tip of the umbrella away from him. Checking he had not left any evidence of a caller, he dangled the leads from the old-fashioned phone onto the floor as though she had fallen whilst about to make a call, then left. He couldn't put the chain back on – still it was a minor clue but it bothered him.

Walking along Chelsea Embankment, he crossed Chelsea Bridge and waited for a bus to Tooting. He didn't have to wait long and sat downstairs at the back as a number of young people boarded – some clearly worse for drink.

Getting off at Tooting Broadway, Dmitri walked to Trevelyan Road, where he had rented a terraced house under a false name. Sighing, he brought up the picture of Constance on his laptop.

"I'm sorry," he said as he picked up his mobile to text Katya.

The media eulogised about Dame Constance Spry. "The best soprano for 30 years" said *The Times* and hundreds of people attended her funeral at St Paul's Cathedral.

Her two sons were shocked by their mother's heart attack. Only last month she had been to see her doctor in Wimpole Street and had been given a clean bill of health, but the post mortem, which was reluctantly agreed by the two men, showed a massive heart attack and that death had been instantaneous, even if it looked as though she had tried to reach the telephone.

Opera mourned Dame Constance and the prime minister mentioned her at question time, with both sides of the house agreeing she was one of this country's special and much-loved singers.

Katya marked another name on the list and looked at who Dmitri was going to eliminate next.

"Lee Morris." The receptionist at the doctor's surgery called out his name and he got up and walked to the small office used as a consulting room. The doctor dressed, as usual, in day clothes, looked up from the papers he had in front of him – *probably a previous patient*, thought Lee as the doctor checked on the screen.

"Ah, Mr Morris," he addressed Lee and looked at him enquiringly.

"I need a repeat prescription doctor."

"I see. Is it something you take regularly?"

"Not exactly," Lee replied. "They prescribed me this at St Antony's." Lee handed the doctor a piece of paper with the word 'Lorazepan' written on it. The doctor tapped into his keyboard and brought up Lee's medical record. He scrolled down.

"That was a long time ago Lee, why do you feel you want this drug?"

"I am feeling symptoms again, doctor."

"What symptoms?"

"I keep thinking someone is following me."

"I see." The doctor continued trawling through Lee's records. "When you gave up work in 2003 you had serious depression and anxiety, do you feel that way now?"

Lee thought for a moment. "No – I have been alright."

"Are you sure you are not just feeling tired?"

"No." Lee began to get agitated; *they never believe you.*

"Well I am reluctant to prescribe Lorazepan. I will give you a short course of Valium." He began to write a prescription. "Now you must come back and see me next week."

Lee took the prescription without another word and left.

As he walked along Tuddenham Road, Lee thought about the last time he had felt depressed. Working for O'Dell Records he had to work long hours and produce the recordings for many of the record company's top stars. He always felt under pressure, smoked cannabis, drank to excess and smoked up to sixty cigarettes a day. He first noticed his hand shaking when he began having disturbed sleep, headaches and felt constantly tired. Week after week he tried to hold it all together, until a new band, Scary People, came to his studio. He disliked this group of ignorant louts immediately and when they began to take the piss, he flipped and struck the lead singer with a microphone stand.

The owners of O'Dell Records had been receiving regular reports of his erratic behaviour during recording sessions, but this couldn't be overlooked and he was retired at age sixty and helped with a pension. He had an income of four thousand pounds per month and so he began drinking even more and one night in the local pub, he began smashing up tables and chairs and was arrested. The police doctor diagnosed mental illness, but still nothing was done. 'Care in the community' was the order of the day. Lee tried to stop the excesses of drink and drugs, but he began to get more and more depressed. Then that fateful day when he attacked a checkout girl in Tesco who was trying to get him to pay for whisky when he had no money. He was arrested and tried for serious assault; he had knocked the young girl unconscious. Fortunately the defence counsel brought in a psychiatrist who diagnosed his chronic depression and he was convicted and sent to St Antony's, a hospital caring for mentally ill people in Norwich. One year later in 2005 he was discharged.

Lee had remained relatively calm since, being weaned off cannabis and alcohol, but remained a determined smoker. Then he spotted this dark-haired man following him. Day after day he saw him. He tried to hide, not get nervous or stressed, but he began shaking again – that was when he decided to go to the doctor.

There he was again, the same man, and coming straight toward him. Lee began to panic, his heart began to palpitate unevenly, and then he felt a prick in his leg and then peace.

Hristo carried on walking down Tuddenham Road until he reached the town centre. He went to the car park where he had left the VW Golf he had stolen and looking at the map, worked out a route for Cambridge, where his next victim lived. Before starting up the engine he reflected on the man. He had definitely spotted him – he must be slipping up and at the end he seemed terrified.

Hristo wondered, not for the first time, what these people had done – still the money was good. He sent a text to Katya confirming the kill.

Martin Ribov parked his Mercedes in the drive and got out, pressed the automatic locking and walked the few yards to his front door. The security light was on – and had been on when he pulled up. *Probably someone walked by the house*, he thought. Martin opened his front door, a solid oak door his ex-wife Miriam had bought, shortly after they had moved into the house in Golders Green, London. He had argued of course – they constantly argued, about wasting money. Fancy spending fifteen hundred pounds on a door. Now she was gone, divorced, but it had cost him fifty percent of his capital and the second home at Sandbanks in Dorset. Luckily he had bought the pension, but those damn lawyers still managed to claim half of the pension was hers. The house, a detached mock-Georgian property over two floors, was his pride and joy. Martin considered he had worked hard to get it and when Miriam told him she was leaving, due to his unreasonable behaviour, he had been determined to keep it. In truth she didn't care for the house. She didn't like the neighbours, the area or his friends. So it hadn't been that difficult : 'quid pro quo' as his solicitor put it. Solicitors – god how he hated them. Spongers taking thousands from you, even dealing with a simple divorce.

Walking into the kitchen he filled the kettle and decided on an instant coffee. His ex-wife had preferred to grind up coffee beans and use their expensive machine, but he couldn't be bothered. Continuing into the lounge, he put the mug of coffee on the table, whoops no mat, and poured himself a stiff Remy. Since she had gone, he drank what he liked and did what he liked. Tonight he contemplated phoning the escort agency and ordering a girl, but no, he felt he would enjoy the pleasures of Tina or Lola another night.

Martin had been a moneylender, concentrating on pawnbroking and occasional personal loans. Before selling out in 2003, he had owned a chain of six pawnbrokers from Paddington to Golders Green. People needed his services and he happily made a margin on the deals that were to be had. Occasionally he did a favour for a gang boss disposing of goods and this kept the hard men off his back. When he reached sixty, he had had enough and sold out to a young man to whom he had been introduced by Sydney Green at the synagogue. He had the asking price and the deal had gone through quickly. It was after that he found

Miriam had cleared her wardrobe and left him. Not as though he cared, he could indulge in his favourite pursuits of racing, women and booze more easily and she had been an argumentative cow for some time. He knew Miriam was living at Sandbanks, a fine house in Dorset, and missed being able to go for the weekend to that lovely part of the world. Perhaps he would buy a property in Marbella; several of his pals had villas. Married for thirty years, Martin had never been faithful. His wife had tolerated his dalliances until one of the girls, a good twenty years younger than her, had called at the front door and announced she was pregnant. Miriam was furious for two reasons, one she was unable to have children and secondly the trollop knew where he lived. Had he brought her to their house? To make matters worse, Martin decided he liked the idea of being a father and gave her, the tart Trudy, a flat in Streatham, London, and a monthly income. He soon got bored with the same girl and hadn't seen his ten-year-old son for several years, even though he carried on keeping them both. Reading *The Times* Martin whistled as he checked various share prices, perhaps he was a little exposed and heavy in equities. Now was the time to re-evaluate his holdings. Earlier, Martin had been to the club in Soho, meeting several of his long-standing associates. 'Friends' was getting carried away, as most of the people he knew were petty criminals, moneylenders or prostitutes. Tipsy after the third double brandy, Martin lurched upstairs, went to his bedroom, undressed and staggered into the en suite bathroom. Managing to pee and then clean his teeth, he went unsteadily back to the bedroom, pulled back the covers and sunk into the bed. Five minutes later he was sound asleep.

Anastasiya opened the front door with the duplicate key. The man, Martin Ribov, had not put on his alarm. It wouldn't have mattered anyway as she was an expert at disabling domestic alarms. The KGB College in Moscow had been very thorough. Anastasiya had lifted Martin's keys from his overcoat pocket in the Pussycat Club in Soho. It had been easy to take an impression and get a key made by one of the many contacts Katya had listed on the laptop computer. Just for tonight, she had dyed her hair blond and worn sexy underwear. She stripped down to her bra, panties and a suspender belt holding up black stockings and climbed the stairs. She could hear him snoring from the front door. Quietly entering his bedroom she walked across to the bedside with the umbrella ready to strike. He rolled over, opened his eyes and looked straight at her. Martin blinked; there was a woman in her underwear standing by his bed. He began to regain his faculties from being comatose due to sleep and alcohol and blinked again.

"Who are you?" he mumbled.

The woman pulled the bedclothes back, as though to get into bed, then suddenly she thrust something toward Martin and stabbed him in the leg. That was the last thing he felt.

Anastasiya laughed as she thought about his face seeing the scantily clad woman next to his bed. *She had eliminated him, but he probably died happy*, she thought. Carefully retracing her steps, she dressed, put on her raincoat and hat; she was already wearing gloves and stepped out of the front door. Tempted to use his Mercedes she thought twice and walked towards Golders Green tube station.

On the tube train she tapped a message to Katya on her mobile confirming the kill. She got out at Kings Cross and changed trains three times before reaching her destination, a bed and breakfast hotel in Earls Court. She had made sure the receptionist knew she was attending an exhibition at Olympia, but she planned to leave first thing in the morning to go to Birmingham where her next target lived.

Miriam, Martin's ex-wife, was shocked when the nice policewoman called at the door of the house in Sandbanks the following day.

"Dead," she kept muttering.

Trudy, his long-time mistress, was astonished to receive a solicitor's letter asking her to attend their offices in Golders Green. Later that week she was told her son Marcus had been left a trust fund of over half a million pounds and she was to receive the interest from the trust until he was twenty-one. The house and Martin's other assets went to three cousins.

Miriam, his ex-wife, didn't attend the funeral.

10TH FEBRUARY 2007 – STRATFORD, ENGLAND

"Laxatives mate, that's what you want to take." Billy was advising his next-door neighbour, Charlie Sprigg, concerning his very delicate problem – he hadn't been to the loo to do a major job for three days and felt bloated. "At your age, mate," Charlie was seventy-four, "you want to keep regular, otherwise everything clogs up."

"Thanks for that Bill," said Charlie, not really listening to the old duffer. Billy, his neighbour in Telford Road, Stratford, was an oracle of knowledge, at least so he thought. In fact, what he hadn't told Billy was he had taken a mild laxative that morning and was beginning to feel he needed to go. Time perhaps to go back to his own house, next door. Billy and Charlie had developed a natural friendship when both became widowers. Billy's wife, Enid, had gone first, bloody cancer. Then Charlie's darling Marilyn had had a stroke and died a year later. The two men had been neighbours in the tiny two-up two-down, terraced houses in Stratford-upon-Avon for twenty-five years. Both had brought up a boy and a girl and both supported Wolverhampton Wanderers Football Club. Billy had been a local government officer; Charlie had owned a successful men's outfitters in Wolverhampton. "I'm nipping back next door Bill and will see you about three'ish to watch the match." The two men always got together Sunday afternoon to watch Sky TV's main match – that's assuming the Wolves weren't at home and playing on a Sunday.

"Okay, mate. See you later. Don't forget I'm cooking today," replied Billy.

Ever since they had lost their dear wives they took turns to cook Sunday lunch, which they enjoyed after the football match on the box.

Charlie had been to the loo, thank goodness, when there was a knock at the front door. Charlie wasn't expecting a visitor, but perhaps it was Bill wanting some mint sauce or something. Opening his front door Charlie was surprised to see a woman standing there – she was wearing a Wolves scarf. Charlie looked at her, did he know her?

"Are you Mr C Sprigg, a season ticket holder at Wolverhampton Wanderers Football Club?"

"Yes," replied a bemused Charlie. The woman smiled, it wasn't a radiant smile and he thought she wasn't attractive.

"Well you have won the prize – may I come in?"

"Prize? What prize?" *What was that accent?* he thought

"Special draw for season ticket holders, free season ticket next year."

Blimey, thought Charlie. *I never win anything.*

"Yes, come in," he said. He closed the door behind her and suddenly felt a sharp pain in the back of his leg. "Ouch!" he said and turned to look at her.

He collapsed immediately and it was in the hall that Billy found him. When he didn't come in to watch the match, at first Billy thought he might be having a bit of trouble with the old bowels, but at half-time he decided to use his door key and see how the old bugger was. That was when he found him in the hall – dead.

Billy was shocked by the sudden death of his old friend. Down the British Legion he was complaining to a group of his cronies.

"I always said if you don't keep regular anything can happen. Look at old Charlie, poor sod."

Anastasiya Stoickkev, travelling as a Dutch national, Agnes Vissar, was pleased with herself: she was getting through her list quite quickly now. That one was quite inventive: using the pretext of delivering a prize, she had killed him in his house and it would look as though he had collapsed in the hall. She boarded the train to Birmingham, still wearing the Wolves scarf, and planned the next hit; a man in a place called Bromsgrove. She would dump the scarf soon, but old gold and black were her favourite colours – she sent a text to Katya.

Frank, was first down to breakfast this morning. Margo would be very surprised he had remembered their fortieth wedding anniversary and intended to surprise her still further, with breakfast in bed. After his heart bypass operation last year, Margo had treated him with kid gloves for several months. But now – things had returned to normal and he was sticking to his diet. He thought about his diet as he prepared a bowl of muesli. *Ruddy bird food*, he thought. *Still, got to keep the weight down and I don't want another scare.* The consultant at the heart hospital had admitted him immediately following his ECG and angiogram which showed he had several blocked arteries.

"Frankly," the consultant had said, "you could have dropped down dead any moment."

What a bedside manner, thought Frank – *certainly scared the shit out of me*.

Frank had left Guildford School of Law in 1962 with a first class law degree. He had joined a London City practice and quickly established a name for himself. Offered a partnership when he was age thirty-one, he was the youngest ever partner in Ogilvie, Dawes and Fisher Solicitors, 57 Fleet Street, London EC4. The firm had many prestigious clients, but it was the young sportsmen and women he mainly dealt with. Contract negotiations with sports clubs started to get serious when the minimum wage for footballers was abolished in the sixties. *It was thanks to people like Jimmy Hill*, he thought. *Those men fought for better wages in order that the stars of United, Chelsea and Arsenal can live like kings today.*

Frank was singing his favourite Abba record, 'Knowing me knowing you', even though he couldn't always remember the words, when he heard the bell. *Must be the postman*, he thought. Answering the door in his dressing gown, he was surprised to see a dark-haired man standing in the porch. *He must have forgotten to lock the outer door*, he thought. "Can I help you?" he asked, looking at the man.

Suddenly the man barged him inside and struck him over the head. The first blow did not knock him out and he was about to cry out when blackness descended.

*

Late that afternoon Margo's sister Miriam and her husband Den called, as arranged, at their detached home in Reigate to collect them. They had arranged to get the train to London to see *Billy Elliot*, the popular West End show. Miriam found the door open and at first thought her sister had left it ajar. Seeing the blood in the hall and then Frank's body, sent her into hysterics. Screaming, she ran back to their Audi. Her husband had to calm her down before she told him what she had found.

Den called the police, then instructing his wife to stay put, he went to the house. "My god, there's blood all over the place," and as he looked at what was left of his brother-in-law's face, he saw why. Frank's face had been battered, you couldn't recognise him. *Christ*, he thought, *what about Margo?*

"Margo," he called out.

The police always said in those TV dramas, don't contaminate the crime scene, Den thought. *But I must find Margo, she could be hurt.* He heard a siren in the distance as he climbed the stairs.

Den found Margo in the main bedroom and promptly threw up on the floor. She was stark naked and had had her throat cut. Den met the police officers as he was coming back down the stairs, white-faced and shocked.

*

CID were called and an investigation was underway. Later on it remained a mystery as to the motive for the two grisly murders. Frank and Margo hadn't an enemy in the world, or so they thought.

Ivan and Katya drove without saying a word. Ivan had killed the last two, but they didn't take turns, it was who was the best one for the job. Sometimes they both killed together, it just depended. Katya's phone buzzed – a text. "Anton's target is dead", Katya said and she got out her laptop and made a note.

"You shouldn't record everything on that thing," said Ivan, but Katya just ignored him.

Michael McGhee gazed at his wife, Trudy, and admired her full breasts and trim figure. *Mind you*, he thought, *I pay enough for that personal trainer and god knows what they get up to in the gymnasium when I am not around.* Trudy was twenty-five years younger than Michael and although she had turned forty, she was a voluptuous woman, 'a head turner' as his brother John put it. Michael and Trudy had married ten years ago, each having had a rather acrimonious divorce. His first wife, Shirley (Shirl to her friends) had discovered his long-standing affair with Trudy, his secretary and PA. Shirley tried to claim half his dosh, but Michael had Charlie Wood have a word with her. Charlie had been Michael's enforcer for thirty years and knew the right buttons to press. Shirley backed down from her claim for fifty million pounds and settled on the house in Hampstead and five million pounds. This still worked out at over ten million pounds – not bad for an Essex girl. Michael smiled to himself.

"Michael." Trudy used that little girl lost technique that always worked.

"What do you want?" Michael replied, knowing his wife was about to tap him for something.

"You know that Charmaine – you know, Paul Carrick's wife?"

"Yeah, I know the one you mean." He thought momentarily about the blond with the tight little arse.

"Well, Paul's bought Charmaine a racehorse."

"What?" said Michael sounding bored and irritated.

"Paul, he's bought Charmaine a racehorse and I want one."

"Oh my gaud, the silly sod. What's he done that for?"

"Charmaine says it's a good tax ruse."

"Tax ruse, my arse, it's extremely expensive to keep horses, ask Jimmy Sutherland, he's got twenty."

"Can I have a racehorse Mickey?" She always purred 'Mickey' when she wanted something.

"How much?"

"Charmaine said Paul paid £50,000 at the sales, for a two-year-old."

"Fifty grand, you must be kidding!" Michael was paying attention now. This was serious dosh.

"Think about it, you will be able to go to Ascot to see your own horse run." Trudy knew how to pull the strings. Michael liked to make out he had class and worked very hard to demonstrate he was no longer the boy from Bermondsey.

"I'll think about it," he muttered. "Let me watch the news at ten now." Michael switched on the massive wall-mounted television in their bedroom and Trudy skipped off to the en suite confident she was going to match that bitch Charmaine who had been boasting all week about her sodding racehorse.

Michael tutted to himself. "Bloody immigrants," he said. "Can't the fuckin' government get a grip?"

"What did you say sweetheart?" said the distant voice of Trudy from the massive en suite bathroom.

"I wasn't talking to you," Michael grunted.

Michael McGhee had made his money in publishing. Well, to be precise he started with a magazine called *Belle* to rival the popular *Reveille*, which featured pictures of bikini-clad girls in 1964. He was twenty-two years old at the time and had inherited ten grand from his grandfather, one of life's successful bookmakers. "Never bet," his granddad had said. "You only pay for the bookmaker's holidays," as he chuckled and jangled the coins in his pocket.

Michael had taken a punt on buying an old run-down print works in Bermondsey. Producing *Belle* had not been easy – getting distribution a lot more difficult. But then, two years later, he had a break. The International News Group made him an offer for the title. He had been distributing through various independent wholesalers and had built up a weekly run of 40,000 copies and this had got to the attention of the giant Newspaper Corporation, who were seeking a men's title to rival the Mirror Group's *Reveille*.

Not one to sit on his laurels, Michael, age twenty-four, bought a new printing press and designed, with the help of Sam Gordon his editor, a monthly glossy men's magazine, called *Encounter*. This magazine went as far as you could go. *Health and Efficiency*, a magazine aimed at naturalists, showed boobs and fannies and it was the only competition. The success of this magazine was virtually instantaneous, so he produced another title , *Blinders*.

Since then he had built a publishing and film empire, based on pornography just within the law. Mrs Mary Whitehouse, an ardent anti-pornographer, had tried to shut him down, but failed. With a mix of sexy photographs and close-to-the-line 'articles' and 'letters' to the editor, Michael's magazines were flying out of the shops. Now he had more or less retired. He had sold the company for seven hundred million pounds last year. Sam, his long time editor, pocketed ten per cent and he trousered over six hundred million pounds. He retained his interest in Sunshine Films, a New York based film company, that made softcore porn DVDs.

Michael listened to the shower and imagined the water running down his wife's ample breasts, such that he didn't hear the creak on the stairs.

Ivan and Katya were expert at house-breaking and knew how to disable most burglar alarms. They had avoided the cameras which swept the grounds around Michael's Surrey retreat, on the fringe of Wentworth Golf Course. On gaining entry through the French window, they had shot the security guard in the kitchen who had been watching one of Michael's erotic videos, but unfortunately for him, not the grounds around the house. Ivan and Katya favoured the silenced Glock pistol, adequate for the task in hand. Each was dressed head to toe in black, including a balaclava covering their heads, both assassins burst into the room. Michael was shot in the head before a single word left his mouth. Listening, they heard the shower and a reasonably in tune version of Abba's 'Money, Money, Money' coming from the en suite bathroom. Katya indicated to Ivan, who went in the bathroom. The tell tale phuts of a silenced pistol told the story. Trudy hadn't even seen the intruder and was shot through the back of the head; a second shot had taken off the side of her face.

At midday the cleaner, Mrs Moody, called. She never came any earlier as they liked to sleep in. Mrs Moody was the McGhees long-standing cleaner; she found the couple and went rushing from the bedroom screaming her head off. Summoning the local 'old Bill' who in turn brought in Surrey's best detectives and finally, Scotland Yard, as they suspected a gangland murder. Michael had paid protection money since he was twenty years of age and had died with his ageing minder, Charlie, slumped over, watching his favourite DVD of Michael's *Girl Assassins*. The Detective Inspector from Scotland Yard's serious crime squad made no sense of the killings and the file was left open as triple unsolved murders.

Katya and Ivan quite liked the car they had stolen from Guildford railway station, but after the triple murder they had driven to Putney, dumped the car in a multi-storey car park and then gone to the underground station. The carriage was empty as Katya got her laptop from the bag she carried.

"I wish you wouldn't use that thing, it leaves a trail," said Ivan.

"I can destroy the data anytime and in any case I have to keep up somehow," Katya replied.

"Who's next?" asked Ivan.

"I am checking. We are doing ours quicker than the others." She looked up before replying," Kensington in London."

The underground train pulled into a station and two people entered the carriage. They sat in silence until Kensington then Katya got off the train. Ivan followed, checking for a tail – you could never be too careful.

2ND APRIL 2007 – CHELSEA, LONDON, ENGLAND

Max Lungrem left his small flat in Chelsea dressed immaculately in a white tuxedo. He hailed a passing taxi and headed toward the Hilton Hotel, Park Lane for this evening's special dinner and presentation. The British Film Institute had tipped him off that he was to receive the prestigious Fellowship of the British Film Institute and he looked forward to once again being in the spotlight. The whole proceeding, that's to say, the awards ceremony, was being shown tomorrow night on television, BBC2, and he could certainly do with the added publicity. Max had been a jobbing actor all his life. He counted himself lucky always in work, as he really could act and enjoyed his stage parts as much as the many films he had been in. He knew he was not a 'top liner', but he was one of those actors people immediately recognised, but couldn't remember their name. His last role as 'M' in the James Bond movie spoof of *Goldfinger* was typical. At sixty-seven he didn't need to work, he had been frugal and had never frittered away his money. In addition, his dear father had left him a tidy sum when he departed this mortal coil. His mother, god bless her, had left his father when he was three years of age and run off, taking him with her, with a Turkish man who had promised her great things. Instead he had dumped her in Istanbul and his father had sent the money for them both to get home. They lived an uneasy life after that. Father was never at home, mother played the field. In the end divorce was inevitable, but Max's father loved his son and continued to meet him and importantly, paid the maintenance.

Max, his real name was Alfred Turnbull, didn't enjoy school much, except English lessons. He found he had a love of poetry and also Shakespeare. When his class put on Macbeth, he auditioned and was selected to play the lead part. Max loved the stage and from the age of twelve kept pestering his father to send him to stage school. Eventually, at age fourteen, he auditioned to join the London School of Music and Arts. He was accepted and so began his lifetime love of the stage.

For over fifty years, Max had appeared in plays throughout the world and acted in films and television. His big 'break' had been the casting of Mr Pickwick in Charles Dickens *Pickwick Papers*, an adaptation of the well known play for a BBC six part television series. He was thirty-two at the time.

Max was a homosexual. He did not flaunt his sexual preference and didn't like the 'queens' who publicaly invited hostility. But when

63

homosexuality was legalised, he came out. Not as though he changed his approach – he didn't. Max was not one to pursue young boys, or visit uncouth public toilets, or Hampstead Heath looking for gay men. If he met a man he liked, he knew immediately if they were gay and if that was the case he courted the man in the old-fashioned way. His long-term lover had been Henry Irvine, a Shakespearian actor. He had died last year of AIDS. Max had been tested as HIV positive but it seemed he would not die of the disease – not yet anyway.

Max adjusted his bow tie; he always carried a small silver mirror in his jacket pocket. The taxi arrived at the Hilton. The approach had been cordoned off for the more prestigious actors and actresses who would be attending the awards. The crowd hardly noticed him walking along the red carpet until one person shouted "Max, can I have your autograph?"

Max looked to his left and saw a dark-haired man standing behind the roped off cordon. He went over. "Can I have your autograph Max? I have always been a fan." Max was intrigued – *what was the man's accent?*

Max looked down at the book and saw it was his book, his autobiography. He had been persuaded by his agent to agree to the autobiography as he had worked with so many famous actors. The book had sold quite well – much to Max's surprise. Max took the pen from the man and noticed his piercing black eyes. He was not a young man, but nevertheless attractive. Max smiled and opened the inside cover to sign, when he saw a note already written in the book boldly. "Meet me later for dinner… please"

Max was somewhat taken aback. Men did approach him, it was common knowledge that he was gay, but this… *well I never*. Max looked at the man. "Please meet me," he said with a foreign accent. Max was intrigued. Max was not impulsive and later would wonder why he had agreed.

"Yes okay, I will be at Simpson's in the Strand tomorrow at 7.30 pm." Max signed the book. "What is your name?"

"Leonid," he replied.

Hmm, thought Max. *Not German then – how intriguing*. The man smiled and his hard eyes softened as he touched Max's hand. Passing back the book, Max smiled and continued down the red carpet.

That night was truly special. No less a man than Sir Richard Attenborough, who had directed him in *Brighton Rock*, extolled the 'wonderful lifetime of service' Max had given to stage and screen. Extracts from three of his more notable films *A Passage to India*, *Henry V* and *Brighton Rock* showed the diversity and acting skills of Max Lungrem. Max had received a CBE in 1995 but this was an honour from his peers at the Film Institute. A lifetime fellowship was conferred upon him. His well rehearsed speech had quotes from several of his films and a very passable James Bond accent – that is the Sean Connery version, brought the house down. The audience were enjoying his acceptance speech and when he closed, he received rapturous applause. Max had brought the house down many times, but he considered this was his finest hour.

There was the usual party afterwards attended by many 'hangers-on' and a few of the award winners, but Max had nowhere else to go, so enjoyed the backslapping and sheep eyes from younger men trying to pick him up. Max had never ever risked tabloid exposure with some 'kiss and tell' merchant and wasn't about to start now – on this of all nights – and hailed a taxi at 11.45pm to return to his Chelsea apartment.

Max had not been able to stop thinking about Leonid all day. *Those dark eyes, what was the accent, Slavic?* It was with some trepidation and dressed in grey slacks and a dark blazer with a cravat, he alighted from the taxi and went to the restaurant at Simpson's. He liked this restaurant on the Strand, they served magnificent roast beef and his favourite bread and butter pudding.

Leonid was waiting for him outside the restaurant. They smiled at each other and shook hands. *Strong hands*, thought Max, *working hands*. Leonid proved excellent company. Max was used to men being regaled by his acting past, the people he knew, the parts he had played, but this man? He seemed so intense, yet touched his hand periodically, enjoying Max's many stories, laughing in all the right places. Still those eyes so dark, so deep and he evaded questions about himself, returning the subject matter to Max and his many acting roles.

It was natural for Max to invite his new friend back to his flat. Not as though he did so expecting to impress him, or perhaps he did. In the taxi the man sat close to Max, casually leaning his hand on Max's leg. Max began to anticipate the sex he knew was about to happen. Reaching his Chelsea flat, in Oakley Street, Max paid off the driver with a handsome tip. Leonid was very complimentary about the décor; the Persian carpets, the expensive drapes and Max went to open a bottle of champagne. He heard the floor creak behind him and half turned as a powerful hand clamped his mouth. He felt the hypodermic in his arm and the flow of what? Max felt remarkably relaxed, and then Leonid half carried, half pulled him to his bedroom. Then undressing him, Max was engulfed in a wave of sublimeness he had never experienced before – it was not cocaine but what was it? The man Max knew as Leonid had undressed him and when he was naked, took another syringe from his jacket pocket and injected Max again in the arm. Max had a moment of euphoria before his heart gave out.

Leonid Kokorov, now posing as a Dutch national, wiped his fingerprints off the syringe, and then he carefully wrapped Max's limp hand around the end to make sure his fingerprints would seem to show he had injected himself. He dropped the syringe near the body and scattered the clothes as though Max had been in a hurry. He thought the police would track back and find the meeting at Simpson's and even possibly the taxi driver, but the CCTV at Simpson's would show a dark haired man, not the blond he really was these days. Leonid sent a text to Katya confirming 'the kill'.

The press were thoroughly unpleasant. Max had never taken hard drugs seriously. He had tried cocaine and cannabis but never over indulged. The police declared a massive heroin overdose was the cause of death and the media had a field day. Max's friends vehemently denied he was a user, but to no avail, the police and the media assumed the worst. Poor Max would have been mortified. A few kind friends attended his funeral but the gossip was all about his 'habit' – didn't he hide it well?

Leonid was already planning his next hit. A woman near Norwich who was living with her daughter in a nice detached house and then onto Marbella for an ex-pat.

"Another hard day at the office" muttered Greg as he looked out of the double-glazed window at the glorious clear blue sky. The sun was already twinkling on the pool and not for the first time, he congratulated himself on selling out in 2003 and moving to Marbella in Spain. He pondered for a moment whether or not he could have got more money for his fifty-branch estate agency chain. But he had been happy enough when the insurance company approached him. Apparently, they had a new managing director who wanted to set up a distribution channel for the insurance company's products through a UK wide chain of estate agents. The deal had not been hard to do, but the two years he had spent in Belgium to avoid the capital gains tax! He frowned as he thought about the non-stop rain. Still, he thought, when he was able to leave Belgium, all of his sale proceeds had been free of the dreaded CGT and he had moved to Spain. He knew that he was paying UK tax, deducted at source, on a number of investments he had arranged prior to leaving dear old blighty, but that was unavoidable. His pension scheme for a start cost him. If he had known then, what he knew now, would he have bothered? Still, hindsight is a wonderful thing.

"Come on Maggie, wakie, wakie." Greg walked into the bedroom with coffee and a plate of toast. Maggie, Greg's partner for the past ten years, was a striking woman and as she sat up, the sheet tumbled from her full breasts.

"Cor blimey Mags, you do tempt a bloke early in the morning." Maggie giggled, knowing full well what she had done.

"Just let me clean my teeth then lover boy and we will see if that Viagra is still working." She could see it was.

Greg had bought a dozen tablets from a bloke he met at the Paradisio Bar in Marbella and much to both of their delight, the pills actually worked. Greg gently slapped her bare bum as she walked by.

Watching the villa was not easy for Dmitri. It was in a gated community and he had chosen to steal a van advertising 'pool services' in Fuengirola. Fortunately the van contained overalls and by speaking English, he had bluffed his way into the complex three times over the last few days. It was obvious to Dmitri that killing this man would not be easy, as he was usually in the company of a big-bosomed, blond-haired woman. The target, Greg Halford, was well tanned, in his late sixties and was shacked up with a woman he thought was at least twenty years younger. He envied him and knew he had to focus on the task at hand. It was getting hotter and there was no air conditioning in this van. Suddenly the blond haired woman came out of the drive, in the cheap Citroen, driving towards the town. Dmitri decided this was the moment. He got out of the van and pressed the intercom on the gate.

"Hello," boomed an English voice.

"Pool cleaner sir," replied Dmitri.

"What's happened to Jimenez?"

"He's not well sir."

The gate started to whine as it swung back.

As he reached the front door, Greg opened it. "Where's your gear then?"

"I need to look at your pool first," replied Dmitri.

"Round the back then old cock."

Dmitri went around the back, as Greg came out of the patio door, carrying a mug and sat on a comfy poolside lounger.

"How long you worked for Pool Services mate?" Greg was a friendly fellow and liked to chat up the home help as he thought you got a better job done.

"Six months," replied Dmitri.

"Do I detect an accent?" Greg looked at him.

"Yes, I came from Slovakia."

"Ah," that stopped Greg in his tracks. He liked the Spanish, but not many other Europeans, *where was Slovakia anyway*?

Lounging back, Greg scanned yesterday's *Daily Mail*, as Dmitri walked around the pool.

"I am just going to get my gear," said Dmitri.

"Alright me old cocker, you do that."

Greg closed his eyes: *just time for a snooze before Maggie gets back and we see if we can break yesterday's record of five times*. Christ he hadn't made love that many times since he was eighteen – he grinned to himself.

Greg glanced at the dark-haired man as he carried in the equipment. Carefully, he put the equipment down. He didn't notice as Dmitri extracted the blade from his bag. He walked behind the lounger and leaning down, cut his victim's throat. Greg gurgled, as blood poured down his chest, but he died very quickly.

Dmitri collected up the pool-cleaning gear and went back to the van. Returning to the villa, he ransacked the bedroom, removing a wad of euros and some jewellery, to make it look as though the murder was motivated by the theft. He left, driving the van toward Marbella.

When Maggie returned to the villa, she was singing her favourite Spice Girls song. Thinking Greg was sunbathing, she went around the back and screamed, as she first saw the blood, then the staring look in his eyes.

The police declared the murder was motivated by the influx of Albanians and Greg's old neighbours stepped up their security. Maggie returned to the UK, having inherited a considerable sum in Greg's will.

Dmitri drove the stolen van to Santander before abandoning the vehicle and boarding the ferry back to Plymouth. He sent a text to Katya, confirming the kill and looked up his next victim on the laptop.

John was having fun. His wife, Jane, was desperately trying to find out where they were going on the long weekend John had arranged. All he would say was that she should pack light clothing as there would be a great deal of walking. John laughed as his wife tried to tease the answer from him.

"How can I plan what to wear?" She implored him to answer. "What about the evenings?" she asked.

"Yes you had better pack some glad rags for the evening darling, but don't overdo it."

"I am not going unless you tell me, John McKenzie."

"Don't spoil the surprise pet, just go with it for now." John had retired six months ago, selling his business to a chain of chemist shops. The time had been right. He had built up the business over the past thirty years with ten shops in Edinburgh, Glasgow and Perth. On the advice of his friend, a financial advisor, he had invested two million pounds of the sale proceeds. Jane and John had spent many an evening discussing whether to pass another one million pounds to their daughter, Clare. John was worried about the fragile state of Clare's marriage. Her husband, Dominic, had already shown he was a womaniser and there seemed no hope for the marriage in the long term. Finally they had agreed to a smaller gift of one hundred thousand pounds and the rest in trust for Clare and her daughters, Melanie and Samantha. They kept the balance of one point five million pounds, mostly in cash and government gilts to provide extra income.

"Please tell me John, enough is enough. I really need to know." Jane continued to coax her husband and knew he would give in soon, he usually did. The day before their trip to mark his retirement, John came clean.

"Okay, I'll tell you. We are going to Venice on the Simplon Orient Express." Jane shrieked, she had always wanted to go on the famous Orient Express to Venice since her sister had bragged about the wonderful trip she had taken two years ago. John had always been working, so they could never easily plan long weekends.

"Shops have to open Saturday, mother," he used to say to Jane. Jane immediately rushed upstairs to change some of the things she had packed. Men, they have no idea what a woman needs to take on a trip! Setting off to Edinburgh Airport by taxi, they had booked to stay overnight in the Dorchester Hotel in Park Lane, London. John had explained that the journey started from Victoria Station, where they boarded the English version of the famous train, for lunch and a leisurely journey to the Channel Tunnel. Then they would disembark the train and board a coach to go through the tunnel. On the French side, they would board a new train, complete with old, but renovated, Pullman carriages and then travel via Paris to Venice. The journey would involve sleeping overnight in couchette-style compartments – *how thrilling*, thought Jane.

The journey was as exciting as they thought it would be. The following day they had boarded the train at Victoria Station for the first stage of their journey. After a sumptuous lunch and copious quantities of wine, they reached Folkestone, disembarked and boarded the coach. A pleasant forty minutes later they were boarding the train on the French side, they could refer to as the 'Orient Express'.

That evening they discovered the joys of this luxurious trip. Dinner in the magnificent dining car, where most guests followed tradition and wore black tie, was superb. Jane wondered where John was putting all the wine and toward the end of a wonderful evening, they staggered back to their couchette. The steward had set up the bunk beds whilst they were at dinner.

"What could be better?" said John, then there was a knock on the door.

"Probably the steward," said Jane.

John answered the door in his floral pyjamas; he had forgotten his dressing gown. A man stood at the door he didn't recognise. It was a steward but not the man they had seen and tipped, earlier.

Speaking in a heavy accent the man said, "Can I just check the couchettes are locked sir?" John glanced behind, *was Jane decent?*

"Yes, come in." John had no time to react as he felt the pain of the bullet and poor Jane barely screamed before Anton Hineva blew her brains out. Anton, an ex-KGB officer, was Russian but travelling as a Dutch national, Bastiaan Meijer.

The company who ran the Orient Express were flabbergasted by the double murder. Never before had anyone been murdered or even robbed on the Orient Express, despite the film suggesting otherwise. The French police said the motive was a robbery gone wrong, pointing to the disappearance of the couple's hand luggage. After their enquiries, the French police announced that the robber must have got off when the train stopped at an unscheduled crossing, but they had been unable to trace the vehicle picking up the robber, or throw any light on the crime. Clare, the surviving daughter, was offered a complimentary trip on the Orient Express to Bath, but she couldn't face it so her husband, Dominic, went with 'a friend'. The Russian, Anton, returned to England on the Calais to Dover ferry and sent Katya a text. He contemplated number nine on his list, a man who lived in a place called Barming, just outside Maidstone, Kent. His notes read: *Widower lives in semi-detached house. Nearest station Barming but advised to use Maidstone Central.*

A photograph was attached and the full address. Anton knew Katya used several of the operatives, he presumed she had a team, to check out each of the targets and take a photograph – to save time. It was these notes he was now reading

Kenny sat, slightly worse for wear, staring at the television. He was daydreaming again and the subject was how six months ago his life had changed. His daydream took him back. It was early November, 2006, just after firework night…

If you called Kenny Mackay a pillock, he would probably agree. He was one of life's chancers. His mother, god rest her soul, had often caught him pinching money out of her purse and he was over forty at the time. Lately Kenny had been drowning his sorrows down The Bull for two reasons, one was the obvious – he enjoyed a pint of bitter – and secondly because of Janice, the barmaid. You wouldn't say Janice was a looker but she certainly knew the art of a barmaid. A low-cut blouse and a sweet smile was all the punter wanted and that's what they got. For some reason Janice seemed to like Kenny. They had known each other since infant school, when Kenny had pulled her pigtails, but with two previous marriages, Janice had been around the block. Janice seemed to think Kenny had something and she knew it wasn't money. Kenny had never married. He had asked women plenty of times, but as his mother had said "What woman in her right mind would take you on?"

He glanced up as another rocket attempted to make some height from the back garden of one of the small terraced houses – *bloody fireworks*, he thought, it was a neighbour's kid's firework party. He checked his tie in the mirror; he was going to meet Janice and left by the front door.

Kenny was a bit boracic, skint, today. He had lost heavily on the horses this afternoon, but was on his way to take Janice to the White Hart in Broad Street, Glasgow, a posh pub. Kenny thought Janice must be about fifty-eight as he was sixty and she had gone to his first school, a primary school in Kilmarnock Street. Lacking the graces or money did not deter Kenny. He really liked her and walking out of his way to the Dundee Road he glanced around and when he felt sure no-one was looking, he untied a new bunch of flowers someone had tied to a lamppost where a poor young lad had died in a motorcycle crash last week. Taking the card attached to the flowers and dropping it, he swiftly walked away. A large bang, and children laughing, reminded him that it was his birthday tomorrow and 5th November, firework night, and he must remember to buy a lotto ticket.

Janice lived in a rented house in Brice Street. The redbrick terraced houses were pre-war and had mostly seen better days. Some people bought the tiny, two up two down, houses and did them up with new windows and a posh front door, but most were in a poor state of repair and when Kenny knocked, several curtains twitched across the road.

Janice had worn her best dress, low cut as usual, and had her coat on before Kenny could make the excuse he had made last time. "I don't feel like a drink tonight darling." They had spent all night in front of the box, with Kenny making feeble attempts to grab her tits. Quickly putting the flowers in water, they were a surprise and looked nice, Janice turned him around and they were out of the front door before he had time to take his coat off. On the way to the White Hart they called in at Mr Patel's, a newsagent on the corner and each bought a lotto ticket for tonight's rollover. "Twelve million quid tonight," Kenny had said. "We've got to have one go." Kenny only had a fiver he had scrounged off Jimmy Clough, his next-door neighbour. Kenny worked on 'the bins' but was due to retire next month. Forty years he had collected Glasgow rubbish and whilst he was now only driving the refuse lorry, he continued to moan about his busy day, getting up at 5am each day to start the round. He didn't mention they usually finished by 11.30 am.

Kenny bought the first drink and then had to admit to Janice he was skint. Janice bought the next three rounds. They left the pub at 10pm, early for Kenny, but Janice wasn't going to spend any more money. *God he can be a useless wanker*, she thought. A few solitary fireworks still lit up the sky with the odd banger going off in the distance.

Kenny sweet talked his way in for a cup of tea and was endeavouring to unclip Janice's zip at the back of her dress, when she said, "Let's check our numbers, we could be millionaires." Turning on the telly, Janice flicked through the teletext to the lottery page. "Today's numbers six, seven, sixteen, twenty-six, thirty-six, forty-six and thirteen is the bonus," she read out loud.

"What did you say?" said Kenny squinting at the screen, he really ought to wear his glasses. Janice repeated the numbers. Kenny went silent, started to shake and felt very ill.

"What is it luv? Are you feeling sick?" asked Janice.

"The numbers – look." He handed her his lottery ticket. Slowly Janice checked the numbers

"Christ – you've won. You got the six." Kenny began to recover.

"You got a Scotch Janice? I need something." Janice kept a half-bottle of Dewars in the sideboard for emergencies and brought out two glasses, pouring a liberal measure.

"To you luv, let's hope not too many punters had the same numbers," said Janice.

In fact, nobody else had selected the numbers and four days later, Kenny was presented with a cheque for thirteen point seven million pounds. The advisors the lottery people had on tow helped Kenny invest some of it, but he insisted on keeping ten million pounds in cash in his bank on deposit.

Kenny didn't marry Janice, but bought a new house on the Edinburgh Road and brought her in as his 'live-in'. Janice was happy to help Kenny spend, spend, spend especially as he had insisted she gave up her job. They went on a cruise around the West Indies for three weeks. Kenny bought a Rolls Royce, which looked ridiculous on the drive of the detached house. He had paid seven hundred and fifty thousand pounds for the house, in the best part of Glasgow, but still the car was out of place. Kenny spent every day at some race track or other, from London to Perth. He spent three million pounds in the first two months and then he found online gambling. Kenny had never paid any attention to the internet, until one of his new breed of so-called mates, a bloke who lived over the road called Colin Cameron, showed him how to gamble online. He lost another three million pounds in a short space of time and in March had less than half of his winnings left. That was when he decided to 'get it all back in one go'. The favourite for the Grand National at Liverpool was a horse he had backed many times. Kenny shortened the odds on 'Line Dancer' when he bet three million pounds to win. Ladbrokes laid off the bet just in case – Kenny stood to win fifteen million pounds if the horse won. 'Line Dancer' fell at Beeches Brook second time round, hampered by a loose horse and leading at the time. Everybody said he would have won easily.

Kenny was now pretty skint. He sold his Rolls Royce, but soon frittered away the eighty grand on useless bets. Janice tried to get him to go for treatment; it was obvious he was addicted. He wouldn't, so she left him, determined not to watch the last of his money make some bookmaker happy.

Later that month, he put the house on the market. The neighbours were secretly pleased to see him go, he was drunk most nights and often sang out loud in the street. He returned to his old street, which hadn't changed. The only person who seemed to care was his old next-door neighbour, Jimmy Clough, who was glad when Kenny bought one of the better looking terraced housed down the road for twenty-five thousand pounds. "At least he can't lose that," he said to Mr Patel in the newsagents.

Kenny was in fact okay. He had his pension from the local authority for forty years on the bins and also those solicitors had 'made' him invest two million pounds in 'things' which gave him a monthly income of just over five thousand pounds and he couldn't cash them in. Janice had come back and together she and Jimmy Clough persuaded him to go to 'gamblers anonymous' and it seemed to be working. Kenny woke from his daydream. *Christ back to reality,* he thought and went to bed.

Six months after his big win, on a dark May night, Kenny's luck ran out. He was knocked down by a car crossing Bridge Street. The police couldn't trace the driver, but the vehicle was found abandoned at Edinburgh Airport long-term car park, a month later.

Kenny left the house and five thousand pounds to his neighbour, Jimmy Clough – all that was left of his lottery win.

Viktorya smiled to herself as she boarded the flight to London Gatwick. It had been an easy hit really. The man was constantly drunk. What a waste though. She had checked up on him and found his lottery win. He had gone through millions of pounds in a few months. *He deserved to die for being so stupid,* she thought and settled down for BA to serve up the modest breakfast on the short flight to London. Glancing at her hit list, she saw her next target was a man in Paignton, Devon. She would have to work out how best to travel, probably by train, she didn't like hire cars, they left a trail. Time for a few minutes' sleep. She reclined the seat and closed her eyes, dreaming of the dachau where she had stayed on the Black Sea in 1988.

Jack Sinclair leaned against the rail watching the jockeys canter the horses around the track. It was 6.30am and his son, Meredith, was overseeing the gallop personally to assess the fitness of Sea Merchant, a three-year-old colt they had entered in the Longstaff Sprint at Goodwood, next month. Jack had been training horses at Strathdown, near Southampton, for thirty years and before him, his father, who owned the yard, had trained many a notable racehorse in the fifties. Meredith had taken over the stables two years ago when Jack's arthritis finally meant he could not ride out himself. Nowadays, Jack had to be content with leaning on the rail watching. Meredith had introduced many fancy ideas, but progress was progress. Jack liked the swimming pool which he recognised helped horses gain, or in some cases regain, their strength and build their muscles.

"Cup of tea Jack?" Monty, one of the oldest stable lads, had wandered over with a mug of hot steaming tea.

"Thanks Monty."

"What do you think then, how's Sea Merchant today?"

"I still think he's not moving smoothly," replied Jack.

"Well, the race is still a month away." Monty had ridden out for Jack in the seventies and they had enjoyed many winners together. "I tell you what, I like the look of that two-year-old chestnut colt, 'Thunder Down', he's going to win races," said Monty.

"Meredith intends to run him in the novices sprint at Lingfield," replied Jack.

The two loved horse racing, it was their life, in their blood. Monty was sixty-five and kept on at the yard as part of the fixtures and fittings. Jack was seventy-one and arthritic due to fifty years of riding and training horses in all weather. They were both shortly to accompany two runners they had to Kempton Races that afternoon. Jack's son, Meredith, was taking Young Ricky, a seven-year-old to race in a handicap race at Lingfield. Young Ricky had already won two races this year and the handicap had pushed him up the weights – he was carrying 9st 11lbs – quite a task for the horse, even on his best form.

Jack was busy making sure the stable lads did the preparation work and most particularly kept the horses quiet. One of this afternoon's runners, Castlebar Lad, an Irish horse, was prone to high spirited shenanigans. The colt was running in this afternoon's Group 4 Handicap against some good seven furlong runners. In Jack's opinion, the horse could step up to one mile or one mile three furlongs and this would be a good test for his speed.

The two horses running at Kempton were loaded in the horse boxes, Castlebar Lad had to travel alone and they set off at 9am to arrive by midday. The other runner that day, 'Scally Wag', was a three-year-old filly, running in the five furlong maiden stakes, a group five race at 4pm. Arriving at the famous Kempton Park racecourse, Jack was reminded of his many winners at this famous track. Both the runners that day were settled and eventually Castlebar Lad was led out to the parade ring. He sweated up a lot and Jack's final words to the jockey, young Pat Smyth, were "He will burst out of the stalls, let him have his head and rely on his stamina to lead from start to finish." Jack's prediction turned out almost right, except Castlebar Lad was caught in the last few strides by Opera Lover who won by a short head. "As I thought," muttered Jack, "needs the extra few furlongs to maximise stamina."

Their next runner was being prepared. The stable were very excited about the prospects. Scally Wag was sired by Moonshine out of Call me a Way, both class horses who had won over forty races between them, including wins in important Group one races. Scally Wag was starting odds-on favourite, which didn't surprise Jack. The filly duly obliged and ran a true race and easily won by a length and a half. *Meredith will be pleased*, thought Jack as the boys loaded up the gear and the horses having been rubbed down, were led into the horse boxes for the return trip to the stables near Southampton.

Jack noticed the dark-haired man coming toward him and vaguely thought it was odd. He wasn't dressed like a stable hand, more like a punter and there was something strange about the umbrella he carried, it wasn't raining. As he walked by, the man seemed to swing the umbrella and Jack felt a sharp contact, "Ouch, you want to look out mate," Jack said. He began to feel woozy and within seconds dropped to the ground. That was where young Billy found him lying face down. Calling for help, the quickest to arrive was a vet, Harry Noble. He shook his head. Harry had known Jack for twenty-five years and was sorry to tell a tearful head lad, Billy, and their jockey, Pat Smyth, that Jack was dead.

The funeral was a grand affair. All the trainers from miles around came and there was a huge floral decoration of a racehorse presented by grateful owners. Meredith could not believe his father had died. The doctor who arrived on the scene had declared death by natural causes, a heart attack, and this was born out at the autopsy. The pathologist had found it odd that Jack's heart had stopped, it seemed free of the usual signs of death by heart failure but he declared death by natural causes.

Egor loved horses and had spent a pleasant day watching the racing and observing his quarry. His passport showed he was a Dutch national called Filip Gerritson, a vet from Amsterdam. The deed was easily accomplished and Egor headed for the exit to board a coach for the railway station. *Another one off the list. That's four this month now,* he thought. *Only two more to complete my list,* as he sent a text to Katya, confirming the kill. Just for a second, he wondered what the old man had done. Still, it was nothing to do with him, just business, and he had a bonus – he had won thirty pounds on the afternoon's racing.

Carl winced as he crouched down to take up his stance to pot the black. As usual, on a Wednesday afternoon at the Highland Club in Oban, he and Hamish Macleod were playing doubles at snooker. The slight pain in his left knee signalled to Carl that either keyhole surgery was necessary on his dickey knee, or he would have to give up the Wednesday match with Hamish and the boys. A crisp ten pound note depended on this shot and the black was situated awkwardly on the green spot with the white up the other end of the table. McKenzie, his doubles partner and his opponent Lofty, Hamish's snooker partner, shifted slightly as they sat on the long green leather divan that had seen better days alongside the snooker table. Carl got up from his position leaning over the table, prolonging everybody's agony as they waited to see if he could pot the black to win the match. He got down again – lined up his shot and hit the white. The agonising wait for fractions of a second as the white ball travelled the length of the table, then a touch on the black moved it toward the pocket and the white travelled off the bottom cushion back up the green baize and settled on the top cushion.

"Christ that was close," said McKenzie to Carl, as Lofty and Hamish surveyed where he had left the white ball.

"You jammy sod," said Lofty, whose shot it was next.

The white ball was leaning on the top cushion. Lofty knew this was going to test his prowess considerably – he hated cushion shots and even though he would never admit it, his eyesight at seventy-four years of age, was not what it was. Lofty knew a miss would give Carl and McKenzie the game. He had to stand up to hit the white and get sufficient force to send it down the table. Lofty wasn't bothered about potting the black – only hitting it. He prodded the white. There was silence, then a shriek.

"Miss, miss, seven away – you lose boys," said Carl. They all knew that they played the rule that a miss on the black when you're all square, and the score was equal, meant the other team won.

Lofty apologised to Hamish as he grudgingly handed over a ten-pound note to Carl.

"Drinks on you," said Hamish determined to get back part of his money.

"Aye, come on lads," said Carl.

They had noticed the stranger sitting at one end of the table, on another of the old and faded leather divans, watching the match, but as the match ended he got up and left.

The Bulgarian, Egor, waited hiding behind the hedge in Carl's garden. He suspected that the old guy, his victim, would be another thirty minutes or so and relaxed as best he could with the umbrella in his hand. Almost as he predicted, about forty minutes later, he heard the footsteps and hoped it was the man, Carl Springer.

Carl was day dreaming as he pondered the match with the boys. Two games to one, he and his doubles partner McKenzie had won and they had lifted ten pounds off that old skinflint Hamish Gordon. Since his retirement, just as the millennium was greeted by his colleagues at the auctioneers where he had been a partner for forty years, he had played snooker with the boys once a week at the Highland Club. His wife had died in 2005 and it was his occasional snooker matches and visits to the club, which kept him from walking into the sea. He missed her terribly, even though his three children and seven grandchildren, made life tolerable; Mary had been the love of his life for so long.

The gate creaked as Carl walked in and it swung back behind him. He probably didn't hear his assailant as he thrust the sharp end of the umbrella into Carl's calf. Death was virtually instantaneous.

Egor looked around; satisfied, he walked to the stolen motor bike he had parked alongside the pub in Albany Street. Before firing up the big BMW, he sent a text to Katya confirming the kill and then headed toward the A85 to turn off on to the A84 to Dunblane, where his next victim lived. Katya was certainly sending him to different parts of the country – he smiled as the wind blew in his face – he was remembering the thirty pounds he won at the races two weeks ago.

One more to go and he would have eliminated the six targets this month.

Ellen Stark felt her mobile phone vibrate in her trouser pocket.

"Hello." The voice on the other end was a man in an agitated state. "Who is this speaking?" said Ellen.

"Oh, I am sorry; it's Daniel Matheson, Julia's husband. Julia is bleeding and I am very concerned."

"Okay Daniel, phone for an ambulance and I will meet you at the outpatients department of St Thomas's Hospital." Ellen scribbled a note for her husband Christopher and picking up her handbag and coat left for the hospital.

As the Audi came out of the drive, the Russian, Hristo, saw the woman was driving. He started up the stolen Nissan Micra and followed discreetly. Hristo had been following the woman for two days and was fairly certain, as she turned down Tooting Broadway, that she was going to the hospital. He knew Mrs Ellen Stark worked as a gynaecologist at St Thomas's Hospital and had practice rooms in Harley Street, London. Following her, one car back, he began to wonder why this seventy-year-old woman was on the list. He had Googled her and she seemed innocuous in the world he usually worked. *What could this elderly woman have done?* Still her death would earn him and that was all that mattered.

Ellen Stark had married late, a widower Christopher Chandler. He was also a doctor, a heart surgeon, specialising in heart conditions specifically arrhythmia – the heart condition whereby a person's heart beats faster or slower than normal. Ellen was a renowned gynaecologist with a successful private practice. Julia Matheson, whose husband had called her, was a private patient of Ellen Stark and had recently had a hysterectomy.

Turning into the hospital's overcrowded car park, Ellen drove to the area reserved for doctors, only to find all the spaces taken.

"Damn," she cursed.

Turning around she drove into the public car parking area. Again, no spaces. Ellen, normally a mild-mannered woman, began a tirade, criticising the hospital administrator, Barry Slater, for the lack of proper parking spaces for staff and doctors. Driving out of the hospital, she toured the streets looking for a space and then, with increasing annoyance, returned to the hospital car park. As she approached the staff parking, a blue Mini Cooper put on reversing lights.

"Oh, thank goodness," she muttered to herself and parked her Audi in the space, nodding thankfully at the Mini driver who she vaguely recognised.

The delay in finding a parking space had resulted in her patient, Julia Matheson, having to go to accident and emergency, as her husband became increasingly concerned about his wife's blood loss. Ellen tracked her down to a cubicle in A & E.

"Have you seen anyone?" she asked, looking at Daniel and Julia.

"No, not yet," muttered a grumpy Daniel.

"Alright, I will wash up and see you here."

Ellen found the junior doctor on duty and introduced herself, explaining her relationship with the occupant of cubicle nine. Accompanied by an auxiliary nurse, all the actual nurses were busy, Ellen returned to her patient's cubicle.

"Daniel would you mind leaving us?"

Daniel muttered, kissed his wife's head and left the cubicle. A short examination revealed that the blood was coming from a tear in the immaculate surgery Ellen had carried out two weeks ago.

"What have you been doing recently Julia?" she asked.

"Sorry, I don't understand," replied her patient.

"Have you been doing any physical exercise?"

Julia thought for a moment. "Well yes, I went cycling yesterday."

Ellen frowned. "Didn't I tell you not to do any lifting or heavy physical exercise for three months?"

"Well yes – but I didn't think – or at least Daniel didn't think cycling was heavy exercise."

"You have torn my stitches," Ellen told her, "and will have to be admitted. I will need to make sure nothing else is amiss." The auxiliary nurse was instructed to arrange a transfer to the gynaecological ward.

Hristo had been waiting, double-parked, near the victim's Audi for a considerable time. He looked at his watch, as he re-tuned the car radio. "Three hours," he spoke to himself, looked at the passenger seat and was comforted by the umbrella that leaned against the seat. Then she appeared. He reversed slightly, seemingly to allow the woman to back out of her space. He got out of the small red Micra, looked around and, satisfied, approached the Audi as she reached her car door. She turned and looked at him – he thrust the umbrella tip in to her thigh.

"Ouch!" she muttered glaring at him. Then dropped to the floor.

Hristo looked around, and then moved her body, to be partially hidden between two parked cars. A car approached. He went back to the Micra and drove off.

Nurse Hempshall was late that morning and saw a red car. Could they be leaving a space? Then she noticed the figure of a woman lying on the tarmac.

After the post mortem revealed a massive heart attack, Christopher Chandler tried to force further investigation. He refused to allow his wife's body to be cremated. For two weeks he held up the anxious relatives, who wondered why Ellen was not being buried or cremated. After a difficult conversation with her sister, Christopher reluctantly agreed to proceed with the funeral, but he ignored her wishes to be cremated and arranged a burial – he just knew they were all missing something.

After he had eliminated the woman Hristo sent a text to Katya and drove to his next target, a man who lived on the south coast of England.

10TH SEPTEMBER 2007 – YORK, ENGLAND

'Arachnophobia, the fear of spiders.' Melanie looked at the poster outside the town hall in York describing a lecture next Wednesday and decided to buy a ticket. The speaker was not known to her, but she knew that the local debating society had some excellent people. Walking down the High Street, she didn't notice Anastasiya tailing her and that wasn't surprising. Anastasiya had been in the KGB for ten years, from 1981 to 1990 and during that time had worked in London, New York and finally in Moscow. Working mostly undercover, Anastasiya was an expert member of an elite squad, set up as an action squad, in an increasing penetrative eighties Russian spy machine. Despite detente and the dismantling of the Berlin Wall, many hard-line KGB remained in powerful positions but not in East Berlin, where she had served briefly. Working with Katya, her job was to turn gullible Western diplomats, by setting up 'honey traps'. Then came the unification of Germany which changed the role of the KGB, but they simply went underground. Anastasiya had been recruited by Katya last year and was delighted to be working with her again. She was curious though – *what had this old lady she was following done to be on the list of persons to be eliminated?* Firstly, she thought her victims might be dissidents being hunted by the present Russian administration. Then, that perhaps they were revenge killings for a past involvement with the British Secret Service. But in truth, none of it made much sense, so she just got on with the task in hand. Now she was going to kill this elderly woman.

Melanie, her intended target, walked to the restaurant on Museum Street where she was meeting her brother Edward for lunch. Her son, who lived at home, had gone on a golfing holiday to Florida and Edward had suggested they have lunch at Georgio's, a small Italian restaurant near his office.

Melanie and Edward were the youngest of a family of eight children. Three of her brothers and one sister were dead. Their eldest brother, Jack, had emigrated to Australia thirty years ago and the surviving sister, Sarah, lived in London. When Melanie and Edward met, they both lived in York not far from the old family home, they enjoyed recounting their frantic and chaotic childhood. Mostly happy times, until their father went to prison. Embezzling money was wrong; her best friend Deidre had told her. Melanie had to leave St Swinton's

School and for a time the family moved to Leeds. Edward was only six years old at the time and didn't understand why they had to leave the terraced house in Easely Street. Two of his brothers had got into a fight at school and Billy had got suspended as he broke a boy's nose. That was it for their poor mother. She sold the house and found a small house to rent in Leeds.

Life goes on and the family had to come to terms with their situation. The children told everybody who cared to ask, that their father was dead and to all intent and purpose he was. Nobody visited him and mother didn't tell him where they had gone. When Alex senior got out of prison he tracked them down. There was a humdinger of a row and the older boys who were twenty-one, twenty, eighteen and seventeen backed up their mother, who had made a new life for herself. 'He' was not welcome and it was made clear he should never darken the doorway again. Six years her father had been 'away', but Melanie still loved him. She was the only member of the family to cry as he walked out of the front door for the last time. A month later, a policeman knocked on the front door.

Was this the family home of Mr Alex Currie? he had asked. Her mother had asked the young constable inside quickly.

"Yes," her mother had replied as Melanie and Billy, the only two children at home at the time, listened at the door.

"I am sorry to tell you this Mrs Currie, but your husband's dead."

Melanie and Billy looked at each other as they heard their mother burst into tears. Later, they discovered their father had drunk a great deal and walked in front of a car – death had been instantaneous. Their mother never recovered from the shock of her husband's death and as her children made their own lives, she slipped into depression. Melanie stayed and saw her mother decline, until one night she came home from the pictures and found her in bed. She called the ambulance, but it was no good, mother had escaped her demons overdosing on the drugs given to her to treat her depression.

When brother and sister met, they had always been close, they didn't talk about mum or dad – it was too painful. They had been the youngest and had never understood why.

Edward greeted his sister with a kiss on the cheek.

"How are you then Ma Mel?" He had always called his older sister Ma Mel as it had been Melanie that cuddled him, made his meals and often took him and collected him from school.

"Very good and what about you Eddie?" Melanie replied.

"Touch of arthritis in the hand, may have to think about stopping writing soon." Edward Currie was a bestselling novelist, with thirty titles under his belt, several of which had been turned into films.

"Oh, I do hope you don't. Why don't you use that dictation machine I gave you for Christmas?"

"You know me sis; I like to read what I write. I'm not in favour of these modern gizmos."

Melanie laughed and they relaxed to choose their lunch from the small but excellent menu.

"Are you keeping your office?" Melanie asked, knowing Edward had been considering writing from home.

"The trouble with writing at home is you get distracted. Anyway my secretary deals with the correspondence. Do you know I am still getting hundreds of letters from all over the world?"

"Can I have the bruschetta to start, followed by the steak, medium to well done?" said Melanie to the hovering waiter. Edward ordered and added a bottle of Pinot Grigio, their favourite white wine.

"Will you come to Tuscany with us this year Mel?" Since her husband died, each year her brothers asked her to holiday with one of them. "I'll think about it," she replied.

The lunch passed quickly, with discussions regarding their respective grandchildren being the principle subjects of discussion. Melanie's daughter, Jane, had three children, all at private school and she relied on her mother for the school fees. This annoyed Edward considerably.

"Why don't they go to the grammar like we did?" he questioned. Melanie had met and married Albert, 'Bertie', when she was twenty-three, after graduating from university. Albert had been a successful solicitor and eventually Mayor of York until his untimely death in 1998. Still, as Edward said, he had looked after the pennies and Melanie was comfortable.

After lunch, brother and sister parted. Melanie was tailed by Anastasiya to Heasons, a large department store in the town centre. Melanie chose two dresses to try on and went to the changing room. As she unzipped her own dress, the curtain to the changing cubicle parted and in stepped a blond-haired woman she did not know.

"Excuse me, this is occupied," said Melanie rather indignantly.

Suddenly the woman lunged and Melanie felt a sharp pain in her leg. Before she could cry out she slumped to the floor.

Must have had a weak heart, thought Anastasiya, as she drew the curtain and left the changing room area. A few minutes later the shop assistant, carrying another dress for Melanie to try on, pulled back the curtain and screamed.

The funeral was attended by all Melanie's surviving family. It was her brother, Edward, who read the eulogy, tears rolling down his cheeks, as he recounted the life and times of his sister 'Ma Mel'.

Anastasiya had left the department store, walking purposely but not quickly and gone to the railway station. As she sat in the first class carriage, the train was heading for London, she sent a text to Katya, confirming the kill, and checked her laptop for the details of the next target – a woman in Luton. She would go all the way to London and then get a train back to Luton – that way she could make sure she hadn't picked up a tail. The old street craft was embedded in her, as she checked her laptop for details of the next target.

Ian Dailly shuffled slowly along the High Street in Reigate. These days he needed a walking stick to help him, but as his wife, Jean, frequently reminded him, at age eighty-seven it wasn't surprising. Ian was on his way to the betting shop to place his afternoon bets. He didn't like online gambling, or using a telephone account, preferring to receive a betting slip which confirmed his bets.

In 1971, he had inherited from his father a mish mash of businesses. Until then, he had refused to 'play the game' and join his father's business. He had joined the army when he left school and after distinguishing himself in Aden in 1967, he was promoted to captain. His CO at the time was Lt Colonel Colin Mitchell, who became a national hero when he led his Argyll and Sutherland Highlanders into the Crater, a district in Aden, retaking the area. Captain Ian Dailly received a Military Cross for bravery as he led fifteen regimental pipers, blaring out 'Scotland the Brave', to reoccupy the Crater. The district of eighty thousand people was retaken with no losses and hardly a shot fired. Later, when Lt Colonel Mitchell was virtually forced to resign, Ian followed suit and initially helped his old CO win the Aberdeenshire West seat in parliament for the Conservatives in the 1970 general election. Then his father died. His mother, a frail eighty-five-year-old, who had lived in the shadow of Alastair Dailly, his father, couldn't run the businesses and relinquished complete control of her affairs to her son, Ian. Ian knew his father had dabbled in numerous businesses, but was surprised to find the company, Dailly Sport Ltd, owned three greyhound stadiums and held majority shares in ten sports stadiums. Realising his father's keen sense of future worth, he recognised the value of the land the stadiums occupied and proceeded to manoeuvre the sale of the grounds. Sometimes this was extremely unpopular – more than one set of football club supporters haranguing him in the press for his uncaring approach. Ian found he really liked greyhound racing and didn't sell the stadiums the business owned. He developed the land previously occupied by a football club or athletics track, as industrial, offices or housing, depending how much each site was worth. He used a complex web of dummy companies and nominee companies to avoid corporation tax, but paid himself a handsome salary and dividends to keep the tax man happy. Jean Dailly, his wife, had brought up their two boys virtually single-handed during his years in the army. At that time, they lived in Edinburgh and both boys were sent to Gordonstoun, the renowned public school in the village of Duffus, Scotland. The education and emphasis on outdoor activities and personal development suited both boys, who went on to Oxford University. Both boys now worked as Directors in Dailly Sport, now a plc. In 1975, Jean and Ian Dailly had moved to Reigate in Surrey to be nearer their business headquarters in London. Moving houses several times they now lived in a substantial 1920's built manor house, near Reigate. Maxwell, the youngest son, had the cottage in the grounds with his wife, Geraldine and grandchildren Lois and Ian, named after his grandfather. All in all, Ian Dailly was a happy man.

The Russian, Ivan, watched the old man walk slowly along the High Street and followed him to the betting shop. *Strange*, he thought, *that this old man, obviously very rich, should drive a Bentley convertible to Reigate and then walk to a betting shop.* Every day he followed the same routine, going on to the Bull's Head in the High Street, for one pint of beer. After which he drove back to his mansion. Ivan had decided to eliminate him in the public car park and waited across the road from the public house. Ian appeared and leaning heavily on his walking stick, headed toward the car park. As he reached his beloved Bentley, he felt a sharp stab at the back of his leg, turned to look behind him and then blackness.

The funeral of Ian Dailly in Edinburgh, at the family grave, was not attended by many of his old army chums, most had passed away, but the regiment arranged a piper and six pall bearers, in dress uniform, to honour a brave soldier. Ian's sons were astounded the 'old man' was dead; it had only been a month or so since the family doctor had said he was as strong as an ox – strange, as the post mortem had concluded death was caused by a massive heart failure.

Ivan left Reigate that day, listening to a play on the radio. He preferred to steal older vehicles, but always chose Mercedes or BMW, for reliability. Ivan had sent the obligatory text to Katya confirming the kill and had checked his laptop for details of his next victim – a woman in Marlow, Buckinghamshire. The portable satnav began chirping out directions. He was going to meet Katya. They were intending to kill the next victim together.

Doris Shinty looked at herself in the hall mirror and talking to herself said, " Not bad for an old girl." Doris had retired last year as a senior partner at GND Chartered Accountants. Today the firm had arranged a presentation at her favourite restaurant, run by two brothers, Robert and David Eyre, in Leonard Street in London's City. Doris had joined the illustrious firm of accountants in 1978 straight from Cambridge University as part of the graduate intake. Steadily, rather than spectacularly, Doris had advanced herself, but it was her affair in 1980 with Walker Steadman, the senior partner, that had changed her life. Walker, who had been her lover for twenty-five years until his death in 2005, had fallen in love. When Doris became pregnant he promised if she had the child, he would keep her place and more importantly for Doris her career path open. They had a little girl, Julia, who was now aged twenty-six years and living in New York. Doris missed her daughter. Her laughter and enthusiasm for life, but she had met an American man who was the love of her life and had followed him to the States, much against Doris's advice. Walker and Doris had never married – he was from an old Catholic family and had five children who he pointed out would hate him. Instead, he kept Doris and paid for Julia to attend the best schools and on to university. They didn't hide their relationship from Julia, but when their daughter was twelve years of age, they had a difficult conversation.

"Why can't I meet my stepbrothers and sisters?" She cried for hours after they explained. How Julia had grown up with such a sunny disposition amazed Doris and when Walker died, it had been heartbreaking to attend the funeral but not make themselves known to the family. Doris knew Walker's wife through office 'do's' and several of the children, as they called into the offices in Fenchurch Street to visit their father. But at his funeral all Doris could do was hold back the tears, as she introduced her daughter Julia. Somehow through a blind trust, Walker had left Julia a handsome sum, making her an independent and wealthy young woman and this was why Doris worried about her daughter's well being. Was this American after Julia or her money?

The limousine taking her to London arrived on time and Doris thought about how she was going to respond to the presentation. The firm had done things well and arranged a Mercedes Limousine to bring Doris from her home in Purley, Surrey, to the City for the luncheon. Arriving at her favourite restaurant, where Walker and she had had many a lunch or dinner before going to her rented flat near Hyde Park, brought back instant memories. A tear formed in her eye which she quickly blinked away – it wouldn't do to show the partners emotion, most of them were so died in the wool, they wouldn't understand what was going on. Elegantly dressed in a delightful dark blue two-piece suit, Doris was greeted at the door by Rodney Steadman, the senior partner and Walker's oldest son.

"You look delightful Doris," he said as he kissed both cheeks. *God,* thought Doris, *Rodney's gushing.*

"Thank you Rodney."

As they entered, polite applause broke out from the partners and senior staff who had been invited to the lunch.

After a superb meal of foie gras, pheasant and fruit cup, washed down by an excellent Chablis and a claret, the speeches began. Rodney eulogised about Doris's achievements in the firm; *was there a knowing look from some of the partners when he referred to her close working relationship with his father, the firm's founder Walker Steadman?* Finally the champagne toast and a presentation of a luxury trip for two on the Orient Express to Venice.

"How wonderful," responded Julia, quoting some amusing stories she had rehearsed.

The lunch ended and Rodney escorted Doris back to the limousine, which was waiting rather precariously on the double yellow lines outside the restaurant. Thanking her host, Doris sank back in her seat, sighed and rested her eyes. Who was she going to go to Venice with? Her daughter probably wouldn't want to go, that left her lifetime friend Margaret – yes she would ask Margaret.

The driver didn't try talking, as he could see his elderly passenger was dropping off to sleep. He didn't notice the BMW motorbike that was following the Mercedes, two cars back.

Viktorya had decided she had done enough groundwork to eliminate the woman Doris Shinty and needed to get on with her list of targets. Deciding to follow the Mercedes on the motorbike she had stolen, she followed the woman back to her house. She had decided she would call at the house and eliminate her.

Doris was awoken by the rather sharp braking,

"Sorry mam, someone's in a hurry," he said as a large motorcycle almost cut them up.

Getting out at her detached house in Purley, Doris handed the driver a twenty pound note.

"Thank you very much mam – my card if we can help again."

Doris went in, noticing again the paint on the front door was beginning to look tired and just as she was about to take herself off to bed for a rest the doorbell rang. Doris looked through the spy hole and saw a blond-haired woman. *What's this?* she thought and opened the door.

"I am terribly sorry to trouble you mam," said Viktorya. "My son has had an epileptic fit and I need to call an ambulance."

"Where is he?" asked a now anxious Doris.

"On the pavement outside your fence," replied Viktorya. Doris went to go out the front door.

"No please let me use your phone." The woman blocked her path.

"Alright it's down the hall." Doris led the way down the hallway and was about to turn, when she felt a sharp prick on the back of her leg. Turning, her eyesight blurred and she collapsed. Doris was as strong as an ox and didn't die quickly, but in the six or seven seconds before her heart gave out, she sent a silent prayer for her daughter.

Viktorya shut the front door and hauled the body into the lounge. Satisfied, she left the house and walked down the road and mounted the old BMW motorcycle she had stolen. Later that day, in a bed and breakfast in Ealing, London, she sent Katya a text confirming her target was dead and checked her next assignment.

Everybody at GND Chartered Accountants was shocked to hear about Doris's sad passing, but only Julia, her daughter, two neighbours and her friend Margaret attended the funeral.

15TH SEPTEMBER, 2007 – WORTHING, ENGLAND

Edmund Cullup was having a pleasant day at the seaside. Sat in his Audi 80, a relic from his long past middle age, when he used the considerable fortune he was amassing to buy and restore cars, he watched a family play with a Frisbee – *daft things*, he thought.

Edmund considered getting out of the car to buy an ice cream cone from 'Mr Whippy', the van he had seen as he parked on the seafront. Worthing in Sussex was a favourite place, his mother's last home before she died. He smiled to himself as he imagined his third wife, Imelda, telling him off as he bought the ice cream 'that inducer of heart attacks' as she described anything edible you actually might like. Dear Imelda, she had divorced him in 2005, finally the frustration of eight years failing to rein in his diet and stop his casual sexual affairs, had beaten her. He missed her more than the others – she had been twenty-eight years younger than him and when he married her, just after his sixtieth birthday, the gossip columns in the *Daily Mail* referred to "that randy rich entrepreneur Ed Cullup marrying again, a woman younger than his step-daughter." Recently, Edmund had sold several of his businesses, the sports shops and the shares in the football club. Contemplating Imelda made him feel randy and he decided to drive up to London to that hotel in Park Lane where the concierge always knew a telephone number to ring. Perhaps he would go up on the Gatwick Express and leave the car at the station for a couple of days, as he didn't fancy driving back to his house in Chichester. *What a pity it was*, he thought, *he had sold the flat in Chelsea*. Still he had got an excellent price and now the market was falling – perhaps he'd buy another. Imelda came into his thoughts again – the bitch tried to renege on the pre-nuptial agreement, but his lawyers had been thorough. It still rankled, though, that he'd had to pay her ten million pounds to keep her mouth shut, as unbeknown to him she had paid a private detective to follow him for over a year and had plenty of ammunition to, in effect, blackmail him. Screwing the wives of prominent people had always been one of Edmund's delights, but he wouldn't want the mud-rakers in the media to find out and splash stories all over the press.

A breeze began to pick up off the sea. He was about to press the electric window button to close the window, when a middle-aged man appeared.

"Can I help you?" enquired Edmund somewhat irritably.

The man did not speak, but much to Edmund's surprise, raised up an umbrella he had been carrying and struck him with the tip in the arm. Despite his advancing years Edmund was a fit man and was about to get out of the car to remonstrate with this stranger, when he felt a seething pain in his chest and blacked out, his head falling through the open window of the car.

Anton looked around, confirmed no one was looking or coming along the seafront and with his gloved hands, manoeuvred the now dead Edmund so that he was leaning back in the driver's seat. Satisfied, the Russian walked along the seafront and got into the old blue Toyota he had stolen in Chichester yesterday. This man, Edmund Cullup, had proved a difficult target. The security at his mansion, outside Chichester, was first class and he was chauffeur-driven on most occasions. Suddenly though, this morning, he had come out of his electric front gates driving an old car. Tailing him, Anton was surprised that he had driven to this shingle beach, a good one-hour drive from his house. Why he had come here he didn't know, but when the opportunity presents itself, you act – KGB manual 1981.

He sent a text to Katya confirming the kill.

Imelda sat ruefully, as the organ began playing something she had vaguely heard before. All three ex-wives attended the funeral. As there were no children, Imelda had confirmed Edmund was firing blanks early in their marriage; his considerable fortune would be divided amongst numerous relatives. They all contemplated how rich they would have been had they persevered with the old bastard. *Still that's life,* thought Imelda, *I had warned him for years about his diet!*

Digby Pratchard-Smyth chatted to his fellow enthusiast, Ernest. The sighting of a rare Black-winged Pratincole had excited all the twitchers for miles around.

"Do you think we've any chance today?" asked Ernest, who, generally speaking, bowed to Digby's experience in these matters.

"Well why not. Morrison," he referred disdainfully to the toad Morrison, a fellow ornithologist who he didn't like, "*claims* to have seen the Pratincole last Wednesday, from this very hide."

Ernest, who did not understand the jealousy between the current president of the Guildford Bird Spotting Society, Morrison Twist and past president Digby Pratchard-Smyth (1990-2001) trained his binoculars on the tree line in front of the lake, fifty yards away.

"Good of Gilbert," who was another twitcher, "to build this hide," said Ernest.

"Why not – he has enjoyed the Society's facilities on more than one occasion." Gilbert was the owner of Dorking Woods, near Guildford, where the rare bird had first been spotted. Digby looked again through the expensive lens of the Pentax camera, refocusing as he saw a bird flying over the lake.

"No, it's not the Pratincole," said Ernest who had noticed Digby suddenly freeze.

Digby Pratchard-Smyth, ex-Guards Officer, 'Daddy was a Brigadier you know', had left the army in 1978 to join his uncle Rupert Fitzwilliam's stockbrokers in the City. After an apprenticeship of two years, when his vampire-like ability to suck out information from the unsuspecting, enabled him to 'learn the business' he began trading. His uncle, initially gave him a small clientele of self made rich people, who he could manage. Digby was a natural. His ability to spot up and coming companies was mirrored by his computer skills. He had realised early on the advantage computer analysis would provide the good stockbroker and had written an effective programme, which highlighted trends. In 1982 the programme, which ran on an early IBM system, gave the firm an advantage they quickly utilised. Building up a clientele had been carefully managed under Uncle Rupert. Then his other uncle, George, the other partner in the practice and Rupert saw their opportunity and promoted their nephew, Digby, to become a junior partner. Thriving on the intelligence Digby's computer programme gave them their clientele, with large sums under management, grew exponentially. In 1991 Uncles George and Rupert gave Digby a full partnership. When Rupert died in 1993, George decided to retire, leaving Digby as senior partner. Digby had constantly upgraded his computer system. The stockbrokers now employed analysts and their own team of programmers. When in 2005, Digby's early warning system began to flag up excessive debt in the banking sector, Fitzwilliam's Stockbrokers began to sell stock, starting with banks worldwide. They saved their clientele from the worst excesses of the meltdown which was to come. Grateful peers and connected persons lobbied the prime minister and Digby was awarded a knighthood in July 2007.

Now Sir Digby Pratchard-Smyth, he was a Freeman of the City of London and widely touted as the next Lord Mayor of London. Since receiving his knighthood, he had activated some of the substantial pension fund he had accumulated and taken a step backward. Mainly to promote his credentials as a future Lord Mayor. Now, here he was in a wood in Dorking, sharing a hide with that wretched fellow Ernest Welling in order to photograph the bird classed as a wader, but which typically hunt their insect prey on the wing. The Black-Winged Pratincole was an unusual visitor to this lake in Surrey. Digby was angling for President of the National Society of Ornithologists and photographs of this rare bird, in an unusual setting, would do his campaign no harm at all.

But it was not to be that day. Had the toad Morrison been mistaken? It was worth a day to try and take the photograph that most likely would elevate him to President of the National Society, but now he would head home. His wife, Lady Anne, was entertaining that evening and he was under strict instructions to be home before six pm. As he approached his favourite car, a Bentley Continental, he thought he heard someone coming up behind him. Just about to turn, expecting Ernest to be there, he felt a sharp prick at the back of his leg…

Hristo had been watching these two Englishmen all day. He had tailed his target, Sir Digby Pritchard-Smyth, from his mansion near Guildford to this private wood. For one minute he had lost him as he entered a wooded area. Then he realised where he was and what he was doing. He was birdwatching from a carefully camouflaged hide. This was too good an opportunity and he intended to kill him in the hide, but then another man joined his victim. Hristo, rather annoyed, settled down and waited for another opportunity. That presented itself six hours later, just as the Russian thought he might have to eliminate both men, his target left the hide heading toward his car – a dark blue Bentley. Completing his task and leaving the body of his victim where he fell, Hristo returned to his car and drove out of the woods heading toward Guildford. Abandoning the stolen Ford Fiesta, he got on the train to London and sent a text to Katya confirming his kill.

Ernest found Sir Digby dead on the floor by the door of his Bentley. The funeral at St Martin's in the Fields, was attended by his surviving uncle George and countless numbers of the grateful clients he had saved from massive losses at the start of the 2007 financial meltdown.

His widow Lady Anne couldn't understand the verdict of the post mortem – heart failure. Digby had been to Harley Street earlier that year and was declared A1 – strange.

Colonel Harriman finished the malt whisky and turned his mind to today's events. He had started Harriman Security when he left the SAS in 2001. He predicted the need for the rich and famous to pay for bodyguards and recruited many of his old colleagues and others he knew from SBS and Special Branch. Men and women who had retired early from the specialist divisions or were invalided out with relatively minor injuries. He recruited them and built Harriman Security based in Park Lane, London.

The telephone rang on the bedside cabinet and he was instantly awake and rolled over to answer.

"Hello."

"Colonel," said a male voice.

"Yes, who is that?"

"It's Sergeant Boyes sir." Despite having retired six years ago, the men who worked for his security firm continued to call him by his old rank and it seemed reasonable that when they referred to themselves, they did also by their old rank.

"Yes sergeant," he replied.

"We have a problem with Dustin, sir."

"What sort of problem?" It was 3am and Colonel Harriman needed his sleep these days.

Now sixty-two years of age, he had left the army five years ago, having served with distinction for over thirty-five years. Colonel John Harriman MC had retired, as far as he was concerned, at the top. He had been commander of a SAS unit based at Hereford and had orchestrated all of the unit's activities, notably in the Middle East and Ireland, and as a young lieutenant at the Balcombe Street siege in London and he had led the assault on the Iranian Embassy to free the hostages. Sergeant Boyes, one of his security men, was talking about a pop star now – Dustin Starr. Whereas the colonel regarded all the young men and women who performed music, ranging from opera to reggae, as pop stars, in fact, Dustin had first worked as an actor in an Australian soap and then come to London having hit record, after hit record. The teenagers loved him.

Sergeant Boyes continued. "I'm outside Alice's nightclub. Starr's inside totally stoned on the cocaine he's been sniffing. I have had to intervene in a fight he was involved in and at the moment he's sitting in the manager's office being sick."

"Well what's new?"

The colonel was used to some of his immature but wealthy clients taking drugs and/or drink and making a fool of themselves.

"The bloke he had the fight with, a young geezer," said Boyes in his colloquial cockney accent.

"Yes, get to the point sergeant, it's three o'clock in the morning," said Colonel Harriman, beginning to get agitated.

"The other geezer's dead, sir."

"Dead," said a surprised Colonel Harriman.

"Yes, the doctor's just been and the fuzz are arriving now."

"Right, Alice's night club you say?"

"Yes, sir."

"Okay contact Mr Toomey, he will meet you at the police station they take him to. Go phone him when you know. Tell the police who you are and tell that idiot not to say one word until Toomey arrives."

Nathan Toomey was Colonel Harriman's 'in house' barrister, who he used when his client was not likely to have a decent brief of their own.

"Please phone me as soon as you are told where they're taking him."

"Yes sir," said Sergeant Boyes, cutting the connection.

Most of the colonel's employees were ex-forces personnel. Many were ex-SAS or ex-SBS, but some were ex-Military Police and Captain Danders was one of those. The colonel dialled out.

"Danders?"

"Yes sir," said Captain Danders immediately recognising the colonel's distinctive voice.

"That punk, Dustin Starr, is about to be arrested at Alice's Night Club."

The colonel explained the story as he knew it and dispatched Danders to the night club to take photographs and collect witness statements before everyone disappeared.

As he settled down to try to sleep, the colonel saw the light flashing on his bedside warning system. His instincts, honed over forty years, made him freeze.

He listened. Getting out of bed he reached inside his bedside drawer for his stun gun and his Browning pistol. Checking it was loaded, old habits die hard, he quickly put on his loafers and moved out of the bedroom listening for the slightest sound. Moving downstairs, he was straining every sinew trying to locate the intruder, he was sure there was one. The man nearly got him, but the colonel, despite his advancing years, was remarkably fit and reacted quicker than the intruder expected as they came face to face. Discharging the stun gun at close range, the man fell like a stone with fifty thousand volts immobilising him. Colonel Harriman looked at the fallen figure dressed head to toe in black, complete with balaclava and quickly went into the library taking out a set of handcuffs from the bureau draw. Swiftly moving back to the prone figure, the colonel handcuffed the intruder by placing his arm under his leg, so that the cuffs were on the wrists but in effect through the man's legs. The man began to regain consciousness as the colonel was phoning on his mobile.

"Hello Mack, I have disabled an intruder in my house, can you bring the van, collect Doheny and take the baggage to the farm?" He leased a disused farm in Norfolk, in which he stored some heavy equipment trucks, armoured cars and armour-plated road vehicles.

Despite being handcuffed, the man began to try and get up and the colonel aimed his stun gun and gave him another burst. He moved toward the man and pulled off the balaclava. *Hmm, black hair and dark-skinned, not an Arab though*, he thought.

The two men he had summoned arrived at his mews house in Chelsea twenty minutes later.

"Evening colonel, you've some rubbish for disposal," said Corporal Mackenzie, known affectionately as 'Mack' by all his mates.

"Hello Doheny," said the colonel to the other man.

"Colonel", he nodded. Doheny was a giant of a man. Six feet, six inches of muscular power, who had been retired early from the SAS at thirty-three, due to a dodgy knee which the layperson would never notice but ended his army career.

"Take him to the farm," said the colonel.

The two men nodded knowing not to discuss their business in his house. Despite the fact the house was regularly swept for bugs, you could never be too sure who was listening with the remote systems available these days.

They put the man into a trunk they had brought in and heaved it into the white van marked 'Benson Office Cleaning Services'. The colonel knew the men would begin working on the intruder tomorrow. Who was he? Why had he broken in? He had discovered a hypodermic the intruder had dropped. What was the compound clearly intended for him? He decided to send the syringe to a laboratory he used for analysis. Meanwhile, the colonel went to the utility room to determine how the man had broken in. The man had deactivated the audible alarm, but had not realised a warning blinked in the colonel's bedroom and a buzzer was briefly activated. "Ah there it is," he looked at the wires in the alarm cupboard noting two of the wires had been cut. *A little careless though*, he thought.

Picking up his mobile phone he called Sergeant Boyes.

"What's happening sergeant?" He said, referring to the earlier message when one of his clients, an Australian soap star, Dustin, had been involved in a fight at Alice's, a nightclub in London.

"He's been taken to West End Central, Mr Toomey is with him." The colonel knew he meant West End Central police station.

"Is he compos mentis?"

"No, off his trolley," replied Sergeant Boyes, referring to Dustin's habit of mixing cocaine with alcohol.

"Alright, stay there, Michael will be with you shortly to help."

Sir Michael Forbes was Harriman Securities' main solicitor. The colonel phoned him and then phoned Dustin Starr's agent and explained his whereabouts and current state. The theatrical agent, John Randle, a rather flamboyant character he did not like, ranted and raved about the 'reason for security'. The colonel simply said, "Mr Randle stop this tantrum, or in precisely three minutes I will withdraw my men and the lawyer." Randle began to realise that perhaps he had gone too far.

"Look, all I am saying is why didn't someone stop him before he got in this aggro?"

"Mr Randle, we are security consultants not babysitters. If your *star*" – he used the word sarcastically – "chooses to pump his nose full of shit and then bravely start a fight, there is nothing we can do about it."

"Alright, sorry I sounded off. Have the press got hold of it yet?"

"That's not my department, Randle, I suggest you get over to West End Central yourself," he said and put the phone down.

The colonel made two more calls, arranging to meet Major Smith and his other Senior Officers at their Park Lane headquarters, first thing in the morning.

THE CHASE

1ST OCTOBER 2007 – LONDON, ENGLAND

The senior management of Harriman Security waited for the colonel to start the meeting. He handed out hastily prepared reports. "Read please, gentlemen."

Colonel Harriman waited a few minutes until the four men, who sat around the table, looked up.

"As you can see, there is not much to go on." He paused. "But I think the hypodermic will contain something pretty nasty, so I have to conclude someone is trying a hit on me."

Major Smith spoke first. "I will call Stewart Danvers and Slim Field to come in immediately and provide around-the-clock extra security for you colonel". The other officers around the table all nodded.

"The thing is," said Captain Norlington, who had been 'retired' early by the army when he nearly killed a group of four yobs who had made the mistake of terrorising his elderly mother in Bermondsey, South London, "anyone who has a grudge will find a way sir, can I suggest you move residence temporarily to my flat?" The colonel remained impassive, but inwardly loved all his men. He had never married due to his army life but he considered all his men as his family. He was six feet two inches tall and at one hundred and eighty pounds considered himself to be fighting fit despite his sixty-two years.

"I don't think so, but thank you," he replied a little indignantly. "Right, Captain Johnson, you go to the farm and supervise the gathering of information – and we don't want him dead, just at the moment." All the officers had killed many times in their career in the army and would happily deal with anyone who threatened their 'family'.

"What we know so far is very sketchy, I'll put out some feelers and see if anyone has heard anything," said Major Smith.

"Enough of this. What's the situation regarding the singer Dustin?" asked the colonel.

Major Smith, who was in charge of logistics and administration, replied, "Our brief, the firm's usual barrister, is at West End Central. Dustin still isn't able to answer any questions, but the police are keeping him there."

"Right, when he regains his faculties, the police will interview him, possibly charge him, and then probably release him on bail – you had better get two more operatives over to the police station to support Sergeant Boyes as there is bound to be a pack of press wolves." Colonel Harriman didn't like the press.

Major Smith referred to their other security and protection clients and one by one they discussed the different jobs. "We have an interview with one of the new Russian oligarchs, an oil billionaire, at Claridges at 11.30am and a request from that industrialist, Daniel Levy, to increase his security."

"I'll go to Claridges," said the colonel.

"Do you think that's wise sir?" said Captain Norlington. Norlington was always looking out for the skipper, not surprisingly, seeing as he saved his life in Iraq in 1991 by flying a rescue mission fifty miles across hostile territory to find his crashed helicopter. The colonel had anticipated Norlington's attempt to walk out, he had been injured but had been the only survivor of the chopper. The colonel found the crash site and was dropped off with an SAS sergeant. They discovered Norlington half a mile from the crash site and he and the other SAS member, Sergeant Finch, carried him for three days before they reached British lines.

"You come with me then Peter." He glanced at Captain Norlington.

The group finished their business and Colonel Harriman ordered a car to take them to the fashionable hotel, Claridges. He was wearing a shoulder holster and packing his favourite handgun, a Browning. Captain Norlington was also armed, but preferred the Glock.

Katya watched the men come out of the Harriman Security HQ. Leonid had told her he was going to hit the next person on his list last night but he had not reported in. The next person was a man called John Harriman and since Leonid had not checked in, Katya had been investigating this target, John Harriman, and she didn't like what she had found. The information she had given to Leonid had included the man's address but little else other than his age and marital status. Perhaps they should have checked him out.

Katya had been observing the man since this morning. She would describe him as six feet one, maybe two, inches tall, one hundred and ninety pounds. On the list she had been sent, his height and weight were shown as five feet eight inches and two hundred and fifty pounds. Yes, he was Mr J Harriman, but the target was a J D Harriman. She had googled his business address and he was referred to simply as Colonel J Harriman. As she sat in the black Mini Cooper, stolen yesterday, her mobile rang.

"Someone's watching you, phone box two hundred yards to your right, I am checking as he is taking photographs."

Monty, one of the Harriman field operatives, had spotted the woman was watching the building and began snapping her with his Pentax camera with the telephoto lens. The colonel didn't appear to be in any danger and his brief had been to see if they were being watched – they were. Monty spoke into his mouthpiece. "Bandit at the kerbside, sat in a black Mini Cooper, definitely watching the building. Female, blond hair, late forties, early fifties". Monty became aware of an old man approaching him with a walking stick. Monty had been an SAS spotter in Belfast and had served in the Lebanon and many other hotspots. As the old man, actually an ex-KGB agent, Ivan Dinov, reached Monty he seemed to slip, Monty moved to avoid him, when he felt the needle in his leg. *Christ,* he thought, *the old guy's…*" and then his heart stopped and he slumped to the floor. The old man picked up the camera quickened his step and walked on, turning the corner into Upper Grosvenor Street. He then spoke into his mobile.

The colonel noticed the woman in the black Mini Cooper start the engine and not too quickly, head off down Park Lane where she had been parked kerbside.

"Monty down, repeat Monty down," said Sergeant Quick, who had moved to his aid. The colonel and Peter Norlington drew their weapons and rushed toward the prone figure. The colonel felt his pulse and nodded to Peter and Sergeant Quick.

"Let's keep this as private as possible. I shall phone Sir Anthony Greenford," who was the head of MI6, "and ask him to perform a clear-up operation and come over, we need a chat," said the colonel.

The MI6 boys were at the scene fifteen minutes later and removed the body of Monty Stanton from the foyer of Harriman security where he had been carried. Poor Monty, he had survived many of the world's hotspots to die in the streets of London, but killed by whom?

Sir Anthony Greenford had known Colonel Harriman for nearly thirty years, ever since some unpleasant terrorists tried to capture him in Northern Ireland in 1978.

Carrying a silver-tipped cane, Sir Anthony was the epitome of a British aristocrat, but actually, his code-name had been Cobra, because he was a deadly adversary. "What's this all about John?" he asked as the colonel indicated for the head of MI6 to sit.

"Tony," the colonel replied, "As yet, I don't know." He then briefed him on the attempt on his life last night, the woman observer, who clearly had an accomplice, who spotted and killed Monty. After the briefing, which might concern internal security, Sir Anthony left with the fingerprints of the man they had captured and taken to the farm. After disabling the man at his flat, Colonel Harriman had put the man's hands on a glass and taken a Polaroid picture.

Monty was a single man, the colonel liked to employ bachelors. Grieving widows were not his scene as he had seen too many in his lifetime, but the men who would attend Monty's funeral were all angry, very angry. Monty's camera had been stolen, and the CCTV footage in Park Lane, didn't show the team how Monty had been killed. Whilst the cameras picked up the black Mini Cooper, the occupant, a woman, could not clearly be seen. The number plate had been checked through a contact at Scotland Yard and was false.

The whole episode was a mystery and Colonel Harriman had asked Sir Anthony to check foreign agents, particularly Bin Laden operatives. The last action John Harriman had performed, before he retired, was to lead a successful raid on the Pakistan border and kill Bin Laden's then second-in-command, Abou Bin Mattmoud. Perhaps this was a simple reprisal, but John Harriman had his doubts.

The man they had captured proved to be stubborn. Sir Anthony had not offered to take over his interrogation, knowing Colonel Harriman's men would be able to work more thoroughly than the frequently handcuffed secret service. Terrorists have rights, the establishment insisted. "Bollocks," thought the fighting men who put their lives on the line and who saw the civilian atrocities at close hand.

Captain Johnson had arrived at the farm in Norfolk by helicopter and was supervising the interrogation of this swarthy dark-haired man. He wasn't proving an easy nut to crack.

"Okay increase the voltage." Leads had been tied to the man's testicles, and he sat tightly bound with leather straps to an old kitchen chair.

"Right." A switch was turned on. The man screamed in agony.

"Come on, tell us your name and all this will stop," said Corporal Mack. Doheny hit him around the face, hard enough for his nose to begin bleeding.

"You will tell us you know," said Captain Johnson.

"Okay again." Mack went to the power supply and threw the switch. Once again the man screamed, his eyes bulging in the sockets, he had endured at least twelve hours of interrogation.

"What's it to be, more of the same, or will you tell us your name?" said Captain Johnson.

The man raised his head with a great effort; he could smell his skin burning and spat into Captain Johnson's face. Doheny stepped forward, smacked him in the month again and they repeated the electric shock treatment.

After the man had lost consciousness, Mack decided on a different tactic. For most men, knowing their manhood was being destroyed was enough, but this guy was a professional – they all knew that they had to use the water.

Undoing the leather straps, they lifted him, still unconscious, and bound him to a plank, length wise, with his head sticking over one end. They hauled the plank up and positioned it on top of a large barrel, almost like a seesaw at a children's park.

"Blindfold him," said Captain Johnson.

As he regained consciousness the man did not struggle, he was conserving energy but as he was tied to a board, he dreaded what he thought was going to happen next. Ever since the conflicts in Iraq and Afghanistan, the CIA had developed a new water torture. All you had to do was turn a person almost upside down and then pour water into their mouth and nose. As the person was blindfolded the effect, after a very short while, simulated drowning. The man was tough, but knew this was likely to break him. Captain Johnson's mobile rang

"Anything?" said the voice on the other end.

"Not yet, but I am hopeful in the next hour or so."

Dohoney began to roll out the hose and then went back to turn on the water. Mack positioned the hose and began to pour the water onto the upside-down face of the man, who spluttered as he fought not to swallow the water. Three times he withstood the intense feeling of drowning, just regaining his breath as they paused. By the fourth time, he had had enough.

"Okay," he spluttered.

Captain Johnson held up his hand. Dohoney picked up the board with the man strapped on it, as though it were matchwood, Mack loosened the straps and Dohoney checked the plastic restraint was still secure around his hands at the back and then dumped the man in a chair.

"Right," said Captain Johnson, "you have one chance to tell us what we want to know. Any attempt to delay or tell us lies will result in a repeat of the water – you understand? Nod if you understand." The man nodded. "What is your name?" asked the Captain. The man paused.

"Leonid."

"And your last name, other name?"

The man mumbled, "Kokorov."

"What is your nationality?"

"Bulgarian."

"You are Leonid Kokorov?" The man nodded. "You tried to kill Colonel Harriman, why?"

"On list," replied the man Kokorov.

"List? What list?" said Captain Johnson.

The Bulgarian, an ex-KGB agent, was beginning to think again and he pondered whether to reply. Just as he paused Captain Johnson said, "Okay, put him back on the board." The man shook uncontrollably.

"No, no I will tell you."

"What list?" repeated the Captain.

"Every month I am given a list of people to kill."

"Every month, how long have you been operating in Britain?"

The man thought. "Nine months," he replied.

"How many people have you killed in this time?"

The dark-haired man paused again. "Vingt," he replied in French.

"That's twenty in English, is that the right number?"

"Yes."

Johnson was taken aback. "Twenty murders, why? What is the reason for these murders?" Again the Bulgarian paused.

"I don't know."

"What do you mean you don't know?" Johnson said, sounding impatient.

"It's true. We have not been told the reason by our handler."

"We! How many agents are there carrying out these murders?"

"I don't know exactly."

"Well how many do you know of?"

"I only know my handler."

"But you think there are more?"

"Yes."

"And they are killing people too?" asked Johnson.

"Yes," the Bulgarian replied. Mack whistled.

"Where do you live?" asked the Captain.

"In London."

"Precise address."

The man paused for a moment. "London, 14 Mellison Road, Tooting."

"Who is your controller?"

This was getting into dangerous ground for the Bulgarian. He knew if he revealed any more information he was as good as dead.

"What protection will I have?" he asked. Dohoney kicked him in the calf.

"About as much as the twenty people you've killed mate."

"Leave it out Doheny," said Captain Johnson. "We can discuss what happens afterwards, when we have thought about what you tell us."

"I want a guarantee," said Kokorov.

"What guarantee? You are hardly in a position to bargain," replied Johnson.

"If I tell you the controller I am a dead man."

"You are a dead man if you don't tell us chum," said Captain Johnson. "Remove his blindfold."

Dohoney roughly pulled off the blindfold. The Bulgarian squinted as the light hit his eyes.

"Tell us what we want to know and we will recommend you are protected," said Johnson. The Bulgarian made up his mind.

"My controller is a man called..." he paused as though he had changed his mind.

"His full name? Nationality?" said Captain Johnson.

"Ivan Dinov – Russian," he replied.

"Where do you meet?"

"We rarely meet, only once every other month, when he gives me list of new names and new mobile phones."

"And then, where do you meet?"

"He telephones on mobile and gives instructions. We never meet same place twice."

"When did you last meet?" The Bulgarian thought for a minute.

"Seven weeks ago."

"Where did you meet?"

"Leicester Square, Odeon cinema."

"So a meeting is due soon?" asked Captain Johnson.

"Yes."

"What are you required to do after you make the hit on the target on the list?"

"I send a text to a number using the mobile given to me."

"What number?"

The Bulgarian paused. "Now it is 07884 717471."

"How many names are usually on the list you are given?"

"Usually three or four names and addresses."

"Each month you are expected to kill four people?"

"Yes."

"I want the names of people you have killed."

"But I can't remember them all," replied Kokorov.

"Try. Start from the most recent."

The Bulgarian began to reel off the names of the targets he had eliminated then he said, "Max Lungren."

Captain Johnson asked him to repeat the name – he did. The three ex-SAS soldiers looked at each other. He reached seventeen names, but was having trouble remembering who he had missed, but certain there were more.

"Okay we will come back to that later," the captain continued. "I want you to put addresses to these names."

They spent the next hour matching names with addresses. "Can I have a drink?" asked Kokorov.

"Mack, give him some water. How do you eliminate the people selected?" asked Captain Johnson.

"I am required to make as many as possible look like suicides."

"With this?" Captain Johnson held up a hypodermic.

They had sent the contents to the MI6 laboratory for analysis and replaced it with water. Johnson moved toward the man and put the tip of the hypodermic needle against his skin. The Bulgarian shivered.

"No, no. Don't do that, I will tell." Captain Johnson moved the needle away from the skin. "It is a cocktail," said the Bulgarian.

"Ah," said Captain Johnson, "and who supplies you?"

"My handler Ivan. He gives me small bottles."

"And how else do you kill people?"

The Bulgarian went through his methods. "A push on a tube station, a drug overdose, a hit-and-run accident and if there are two to kill, a burglary then I knife or shoot them."

Captain Johnson wanted to kill this man like he had never wanted to kill before. A veteran of countless SAS operations, he had killed many times and been responsible for extracting information from terrorists, but never did he have the urge to kill a man like he had now.

Mack could sense how close this Bulgarian was to death – he knew Captain Johnson as a hard ruthless man, who would not blink an eyelid in killing this murderer, but he knew they may not have found out everything they could – What about the other assassins, perhaps the man had more information he could provide?

"Captain." Mack broke the spell. Captain Johnson looked at the shaven-headed man in front of him.

"Mack?"

"Where does he live?"

"Where are you living now?" The Bulgarian looked bewildered.

"But I told you, number 14 Mellison Road, Tooting." Mack had broken the spell and for now had saved the Bulgarian's life.

"Bind him around the chair until I get him picked up," instructed the captain.

Captain Johnson went out to his car parked in a derelict barn and telephoned the colonel.

"I am coming in with surprising results – it's not good. Send a unit to…" he gave the Bulgarian's address. There are others, so far unknown. Alert the lads to watch themselves, these are professionals."

Colonel Harriman had been busy. The photograph and prints of the captured man had also been sent to the CIA and Interpol. The British SIS came up with a result, first naming the man as Leonid Kokorov, a Bulgarian national and ex-KGB.

"What the hell is an ex-KGB operative doing trying to kill me?" he said looking quizzically at Norlington. The colonel's telephone rang.

"Yes?"

"It's me sir, Sergeant Boyes."

"Report."

"That loser Dustin Starr has been charged with manslaughter and bailed to appear at Marylebone Magistrates Court tomorrow."

"Alright, well it's over to Toomey," their expensive barrister, "to deal with the legals. Stay with Dustin, try and keep the press off him."

The colonel, flanked by Captain Norlington and two other ex-SAS men left their Park Lane offices for a meeting with Sir Anthony Greenford, the head of MI6, at his headquarters on the Thames Embankment.

Katya, who was sitting on a bench in the park opposite using high –powered binoculars, picked up her mobile.

"Meet me at the Grosvenor Hotel tea room, Victoria Station, 10am tomorrow," she instructed then terminated the call.

Katya liked the Grosvenor Hotel in London's Victoria Station; it was a good place to rendezvous. Two ways out, one straight onto Victoria Station. She sat in the tea room, shortly before 10am, waiting for Ivan to join her. Earlier, to make certain she didn't have a tail, she had doubled back three times, jumped the tube and also changed bus twice. If she was being followed they were using a large team and were good, very good, but she didn't think anyone was there.

Ivan came in, saw her sitting at one end of the tea room and joined her. Katya was pleased he had cut his dark hair very short, a crew cut they called it over here. They sat close together, as though they were lovers, which of course they were. But today was about business. Ivan, who had been planning the death of the next target, listened.

"Leonid must have been lifted," Katya said, speaking perfect German.

"We know he has not used the usual code to call in and inform you of a success," she said.

"No," he replied. "And from our observation yesterday his target, who is this man Harriman, is very much alive."

"I have also been doing some checking – discreetly, this man Colonel Harriman should never have been targeted."

"What do you mean?" asked Ivan. Katya leaned closer, whispering.

"He's an ex-SAS colonel, impressive field record and now runs a respected security firm."

"Do you think they've killed Leonid?"

"I just don't know, but they wouldn't have got him easily." Katya swept the large tea room with her eyes again, as she had been doing throughout. "I do know that they went to MI6 headquarters very early this morning." All the time Katya was speaking, she was looking around the room, keeping one hand over her lips to avoid lip reading. "I think it's time you had a holiday," Katya said.

"I was thinking much the same," Ivan replied.

"You were Leonid's contact, if he is alive and being interrogated, he might give you up."

"Yes, as you can see I have become Hans Vogel, a German police officer." Katya already knew Ivan's second cover story; she had given him the documents.

"Are you going home?" She meant the flat they shared in Berlin.

"Yes, I will send you a message when I have arrived, look after the children," he referred to the other Russians and the Bulgarians, his ex-colleagues in the KGB.

Briefly they touched hands, Ivan got up and left. Katya paid the bill in cash and left, using the Buckingham Palace Road entrance and boarded the first bus which had pulled up at the bus stop outside. Now Ivan was gone she had to phone Ludvig. He would not be pleased, but at least he could not order a hit on her lover Ivan. Katya knew that's exactly what he would have done, he would have said.

"It's nothing personal, but he's the only link Leonid knows and must be eliminated."

Captain Johnson was ushered into a rather austere room. The headquarters of the Security Services was functional, but that was all he thought. Sitting at the fire was the head of MI6, Sir Anthony Greenford, Colonel Harriman and Captain Norlington. A helicopter had whisked Captain Johnson from the farm in Norfolk, to Battersea helipad in London and a car had been waiting to take him to the Albert Embankment, the headquarters of MI6 near Vauxhall Bridge.

"Sit down Captain," indicated Colonel Harriman. "Report please."

Captain Johnson began to consult a black notebook and without interruption, recounted the information obtained from the Bulgarian at the farm. When he had finished, Sir Anthony summarised.

"So, briefly, we have a group of probably three people. We know they are men and women, who are deadly assassins, killing people on lists provided and by the estimates from what one of their number has said, something like sixty people have been murdered in different parts of the UK, in the past year. We suspect their killers are ex-KGB assassins and probably are Russians and/or Bulgarians operating here under a false identity and passport. We don't know the cell leader or the reason for the 'kills'." Captain Johnson nodded.

"Anything to add John?" he looked at Colonel Harriman .

"Tony, this might be a threat to national security, but I am beginning to doubt it. What agency or agencies should we involve?" The men knew the British often had a problem. There was no equivalent of the American FBI in Britain.

"I think, for the moment, we notify and brief the Special Branch and all chief constables and hopefully John, you will continue to dig up what you can. As I don't think this is an external security problem MI6 cannot become involved."

"We most certainly will. I don't like this, not least because my name was on this list and they've killed one of my men."

"Sir," Captain Norlington, never one to sit by, interrupted, "surely the first thing to do is attempt to apprehend Ivan, the Bulgarian's Russian handler."

"Yes I agree," said Sir Anthony. "I will arrange to circulate his photograph if we have it in central records and his last known description. I am sure he will realise by now, that he may be compromised and will run. We need to have a code red vigilance at all borders and see if we can collar him."

The meeting broke up with Sir Anthony promising to forward details of the Bulgarians last known contacts and a photograph of his handler Ivan Dinov. Outside in the street they were discussing their action plan when Colonel Harriman's mobile rang. It was the action unit sent to the Bulgarian's rented flat at Tooting. "Not much here sir, a Dutch passport, he was posing as Gillis Vardink, a few clothes, food and little else."

"Okay, put a device on the door so we can determine if anyone visits and then return to HQ." The colonel, together with his bodyguards who had been waiting on the embankment, started to walk to hail a taxi.

"You know Peter," he didn't look at Captain Norlington, "this is a very sinister situation. Who and why is someone killing so many people?"

Captain Johnson hailed a cab and the five of them piled in. The two bodyguards had to sit in the drop seats and as they were all big men it was a tight fit in the London black cab.

After meeting Katya, Ivan left through the Grosvenor Hotel front entrance to avoid any CCTV cameras that covered Victoria Station. He walked down the Buckingham Palace Road around the corner to the coach station. Constantly using his fieldcraft, that had kept him safe for twenty-five years, he swept the area behind him. *No*, he thought. *I don't think anyone is following me – mustn't get paranoid.*

He boarded a coach to Brighton; he had decided on this Sussex town in southern England after discussing the times of coaches at the ticket office. Ivan was aiming to leave England from Shoreham Airport, a small private airport some ten miles from Brighton. He had worked out a route. Fly from Shoreham to Paris or alternatively Le Touquet and on to Paris and then catch a train to Berlin, where he would lie low at his flat in the eastern quarter.

The journey to Brighton was swift once the coach had left behind the outskirts of London. After Purley the coach joined the motorway, the M23, which lasted for twenty miles or so, he thought. The coach did not stop until it reached Gatwick Airport, when it picked up some more passengers and a number of people got off.

Ivan hadn't considered using a main airport; if they were looking for him it would be foolish to risk the more vigilant security staff at a major airport.

The countryside on the way from Gatwick to Brighton reminded Ivan of his home in Russia. He was getting too old for all of this – perhaps this would be his last job. Reflecting on the six hundred thousand pounds he had amassed in the Cayman Islands, he decided he would talk seriously to Katya about stopping their line of work soon.

Ivan got off the bus at Brighton Bus Station and asked for directions to the railway station. He hadn't any intention of going by train, but wanted to lay a false trail, just in case. Walking briskly up West Street, he stopped at a taxi rank and asked the first cab driver, "How much to Shoreham Airport?" Satisfied, he got in. The journey only took twenty minutes; he paid the driver and walked into the airport terminal. Ivan knew this would be a small airport as it only flew light aircraft, but he found what he was looking for, 'Flights to France'.

"Nothing going today I am afraid sir," said the elderly man at a counter in the main terminal. "Fog in the channel, no one is flying today."

"Is there a taxi rank?" asked Ivan.

"No, but I can telephone for a taxi," replied the man. Ivan nodded.

"Yes, thank you." There was a delay and he sat for thirty minutes waiting inside the main entrance and pondered what to do now. When the taxi arrived, he told the driver to go to Hove railway station. The man on the desk had provided a timetable showing trains to Southampton and he saw he had to change for Weymouth. Ivan decided to catch the hi-speed ferry from Weymouth, a port on the south coast of England, to St Malo in France, via Guernsey. He knew there would be very little security at Weymouth Harbour or St Malo.

Hove station was quiet at that time of day and he settled on a seat along the platform watching the entrance and the platform on the other side. The wait was annoying, but eventually the train arrived going to Southampton, but stopping at all stations until Portsmouth Harbour. He had purchased some sandwiches at the small canteen at Shoreham Airport and woofed down the cheese and pickle. He liked English cheddar cheese. Feigning sleep, he had lowered the head of his anorak over his face, he pondered on his situation. So far, so good, but the tricky bit was to come – Weymouth. There would be customs officers and possibly police at the port . He hoped the Bulgarian, Leonid, had resisted interrogation, assuming they had him… He changed trains at Southampton, prior to which, the journey had taken some time, as the train stopped at every station and it was getting dark. Since he had left Katya at 10.30am, he had been travelling or rather, often waiting for connections for six hours. Ivan looked at his watch: 5pm; he doubted he would get a ferry today. He would go to the ticket office, buy a ticket for tomorrow and then find a seaman's hotel to stay the night. His German passport would not attract much attention as the hotel would be used by all nationalities.

Arriving at Weymouth railway station, he got off, asked directions for the ferry terminal and walked the short distance. Going into the ticket office he was directed to another building for Condor Ferries.

"No sir, no more crossing today, the last one went at 3pm. Yes, the earliest would be 9am tomorrow", the elderly women replied.

Ivan bought a return ticket, again to throw off anyone who questioned him. He would be visiting Guernsey and then St Malo, returning to England next week. His cover story was simple, he was a German police officer on secondment to Scotland Yard for two months to study English policing. He had a week's holiday and always wanted to see where his father had been stationed during the war – Guernsey.

Picking up his ticket, he thanked the woman on the desk and asked where the local hotels were. He was directed out of the port to an area where, apparently, there were numerous hotels of different classes. She recommended the Premier Lodge. He thanked her and left.

Studying the choice of several hotels, he chose the crumbling Sir Francis Hotel, which clearly had seen better days. Inside was no better, with old furnishings and worn, faded carpets. Ivan approached an elderly man on reception. He didn't even have to leave his passport when he checked in. *What an odd country where security measures are so lax*, he thought.

Ivan barricaded the door of his room with a chair. He had asked for a view of the front street which the night manager had thought a bit strange, but these foreigners, who could say what made them tick. Anyway, it was a quiet night and his cash was most welcome. Ivan slept fully clothed, with his knife handy. It was a shame he had to dump his Glock in a litter bin outside Weymouth station, but you cannot travel passing through border controls these days with a pistol very easily.

The night was dark and he only slept fitfully. The hotel didn't have a dining room; in any case he wouldn't have gone down for breakfast. He had paid cash for the room in advance and slipped out at 7.45am. Walking into McDonald's, he knew from the same establishments all over the world, he would get a reasonable breakfast and hot coffee. The ferry was due to leave at 9am, so he walked across the road to the port entrance. There was a queue of cars lining up to board the cross channel ferry and a separate queue for the hydrofoil to Guernsey operated by Condor Ferries. He knew customs were around, but there was no sign, so he waited until the crewmen indicated that foot passengers could board, showed his ticket and went to the upper deck. There was a breeze blowing light rain, but he wanted to watch who was boarding.

Maurice Toomey had been a customs officer for twenty-five years, working mostly the ports but also several airports. The photograph of the man, purported to be Russian or Bulgarian, but travelling using a Dutch passport, had come in at 3pm yesterday and was in front of him. He studied the CCTV, rewinding the tape. This was a possible. A man, middle-aged, had bought a ticket yesterday and had boarded the fast hydrofoil to St Malo, via Guernsey this morning. There had been no reason to check his passport, but Maurice had a hunch. He picked up the phone to the port police.

"Morning Jack," he said to the desk sergeant.

"What is it Maurice, fretting over Portsmouth beating Man United?"

"Ha ha," Maurice replied, the two were old friends and both shared a love of football.

"Listen mate, you seen that photograph, came in yesterday –'red alert' looking for a white male, fifties. Could be travelling on a German, Russian, Bulgarian or Dutch passport?"

"Yes," replied Jack.

"Well, I have a hunch he's just boarded the Condor hydro."

"You sure?"

"No – but I have blown up the photo on my CCTV screen and there is a strong resemblance."

"Alright Maurice, I'll check it out."

Jack Howard was a career policeman who had transferred to the port police twenty years ago. Not for him walking the beat or sitting in a lay-by waiting for unsuspecting motorists. He loved the sea and to work in such a close proximity, occasionally going out and boarding suspect craft was great. Normally Jack would be accompanied by Pete Lineham, but he had been called to an argument between several motorists in the queue for the ferry to Le Havre.

Jack boarded the St Malo hydrofoil and began to systematically search the boat. He went into the lounge, then the toilets, but there were no locked doors. He had already searched the car deck, so that only left the upper deck.

At first he couldn't see there was anyone up there. Then he saw a figure in a dark anorak, with the hood up, leaning against the front rail. He approached cautiously, there was no point taking risks, if this was the man he wasn't on the red alert list for no reason. He approached from the side, hand on his truncheon.

"Excuse me sir," he got nearer the figure. Suddenly he felt a sharp pain in his chest.

Christ, he thought, *I've been stabbed*. He went to back off and felt another searing pain in his chest, and then all went black.

Ivan looked around; nobody was on the top deck. Hastily he checked the man's pulse, a policeman, he was dead. He grabbed the legs and manhandled the body to a large trunk-like box he had seen against a wall. The large box was locked. He got out his keys and easily picked the padlock. Opening the box he could see it was only half full – ideal. He heaved the body, into the box and covered it with tarpaulin, god this man was heavy, replaced the lock and then examined his clothing. There was blood on his anorak. He decided against throwing it overboard. Fortunately, he had purchased the reversible one, so he simply turned the hood around and pulled the sleeves inside out.

The ships siren let up a long signal. The hydrofoil was about to leave. *Would anyone notice the policeman had not got off?* he thought.

The powerful boat reversed engines and began to move away from the dock. *Clearly they hadn't missed him yet,* he thought. *Time for a look around or at least get a coffee.* He went downstairs to the toilet to check his appearance.

The journey to Guernsey was uneventful and then the loud speaker spluttered and a man announced that as there was going to be a delay of one hour before the onward journey to St Malo, he decided to get off and take a walk.

When Jack didn't call back, Maurice thought he had, as usual, got sidetracked. But when Pete Lineham phoned and asked if he had seen Jack, he began to get concerned. Pete alerted control and a full scale search of the port was ordered. The captain of the hydrofoil received a call from Inspector Charles Nurdin, of the mainland police, who he knew well. Had they seen Jack Howard?

The captain said that he would make enquiries. It was one of the deck hands who remembered Jack coming aboard just before they departed, but no one could verify he had left. The crew began a discreet search of the boat.

"No captain," said crewman Harris, "nothing's turned up, I don't know where he's got to, perhaps he got off and we didn't notice."

Special Branch received the call from Inspector Nurdin just after 12.30pm. The sergeant knew Jack Howard; he had worked with him before on several occasions.

"I don't believe Jack has just disappeared. Send a message to Guernsey police to search that hydrofoil from stem to stern."

Guernsey doesn't have a large constabulary but ten officers were sent to the harbour at St Peter Port.

Ivan, who had disembarked, watched the police arriving from the quayside and knew it was only a matter of time before they found the body. Looking around the harbour he spotted a small motor cruiser with a man climbing aboard. Ivan approached. "Excuse me," he said in his best accented English. The man looked up from the deck.

"Yes, can I help you?" Ivan looked at the boat which he saw was a Princess and had a powerful twin 480 hp Volvo 74P diesel engine, just what he needed. Ivan showed his forged police badge.

"Hans Vogel, German police officer, Interpol. We are visiting boats in the harbour to warn owners about a criminal gang that are stealing boats and using them to run drugs to England."

Ivan had thought that this man, a gullible Englishman, would invite him onboard but he didn't.

"Thanks, warning noted," said the tall fair-haired man. Ivan's senses told him not to pursue this approach, but conscious of his need to get out of St Peter Port harbour, he persevered.

"Can I come aboard?"

Commander John Cunningham had started his career in the navy by joining the marines. After two years, he transferred into the special boat service, the Royal Navy's equivalent of the SAS. He had served in Iraq and along the coastal waters around the Persian Gulf and had joined the SAS on several ops in Northern Ireland. He didn't believe this man's story, but the only way to find out what he really wanted was to invite him onboard. Cathy, his wife, was shopping in town, so he didn't have to worry about her being on board.

"Okay," he replied. The man, who John guessed was about fifty maybe fifty-five years old, nimbly walked along the short gangplank and hopped over the rail. John moved toward him. "As I was saying, a group of criminals, mostly Albanians, are operating in the Channel Islands." Suddenly the man lunged with an open switchblade in his hand. John sidestepped and caught the man's arm in a lock forcing him to drop the knife. The man used his free arm and struck John on the side of the head. John's hold loosened as he felt a sharp punch into his side; he returned that punch with a blow to the man's head.

Ivan recognised this was no islander playing with his toy boat and decided to retreat. He jumped onto the rail and across the gap to the boardwalk. Running, he was making a hasty retreat, when his legs were tackled and he went down. Reaching out his hand, he touched a metal rod; he grasped it and lashed out. *This man was strong*, he thought, but he connected with the improvised cosh and the man's hold slackened. Ivan kicked out and caught him full in the face, feeling the hold on his legs loosen; he hit the man again with the metal bar and cut his face, blood pouring from the wound. Ivan heard a shout, got up and ran off down the boardwalk. John was annoyed with himself, he should have had him, but instead he was cut and bleeding heavily, blinding him in one eye. The bastard had run off again, but this time John didn't pursue him. Another man had shouted and reached John, who was dazed but trying to get up.

"You okay mate?"

"Have you got a mobile?"

"Yes," replied the man.

"Call the police; tell them to come to the marina sharpish."

Ivan slowed his pace – never run, you draw attention to yourself. As he reached the place where he had left his holdall, he picked up the bag and went into the public toilet, time to change identity.

3RD OCTOBER 2007 – GUERNSEY, CHANNEL ISLANDS

The police car screeched to a halt at the entrance to the marina and three policemen rushed down the harbour steps leading to where the injured man lay. An ambulance, siren blazing, stopped next to the police car.

John Cunningham was surrounded by people trying to help stem the flow of blood from a nasty head wound, when the police arrived.

"Stand back please," said a uniformed man apparently in charge.

Inspector Griffin was not used to crime, at this level, on his patch. Firstly, the body of a mainland police officer had been discovered on the hydrofoil from Weymouth, now a fight, which could be connected. Kneeling by the prostrate man the Inspector said, "What happened? I'm Inspector Griffin, Guernsey police?"

John Cunningham reached into his back pocket and showed his ID. "Ah, Commander Cunningham," the Inspector's tone changed. John began to describe his attacker.

"A man, about five foot ten to five foot eleven, short dark hair, aged about fifty to fifty-five years, boarded my boat, the *Princess 45* over there, and attacked me with a knife, probably a flick knife. We fought and he ran off. I pursued him and brought him down, but he had some sort of metal bar and hit me twice. Unfortunately, the blood from the wound poured down into my eye, so I couldn't see where he went."

"Did anyone else here see this man?" asked the inspector looking around. A small rugged, slightly balding man stepped forward.

"I saw a man hitting this man and went to his aid. As I shouted, the guy looked at me, got up and ran off – that way," he pointed toward the marina steps.

"Thank you sir, please wait here, we will want to interview you further."

The inspector spoke to another officer, who using his mobile, radioed a message to their headquarters. The Guernsey police force was now stretched to their limit and the head of police, a superintendent, would have to ask for help from nearby Jersey and the mainland.

The ambulance men arrived and examined John's head wound.

"It's not too bad sir, needs stitches though. We will take you to the hospital." They helped John on to a stretcher, which he told them was totally unnecessary, as he used someone's mobile to phone his wife Cathy who was shopping in St Peter Port.

Ivan came out of the public toilet, walked down to the office and brought a ticket to Sark Island. Sark is the smallest of the four main Channel Islands. "There are no cars, but lots of places to walk and a number of hotels," the ticket office clerk told him. Ivan had changed his identity to a Latvian, Eduard Eglitis, from Riga. His cover story had changed slightly, as he was now an older retired man, who was following the footsteps of his brother who had been a prisoner of war in Guernsey during the Second World War. Ivan had used his grey wig and make-up to age his appearance and now resembled his own father who really was eighty-five years old!

A policeman rushed by him, taking no notice of the elderly man and Ivan boarded the boat to Sark.

SAME DAY – LONDON, ENGLAND

Colonel Harriman sat at the head of the long table, addressing his officers. Even though they were a private security company, each of the men retained their rank and status, as far as the colonel was concerned. "Major?" He looked up at his trusted adjutant.

"The last sighting of the man, Ivan Dinov, was a CCTV camera in the Buckingham Palace Road yesterday at 10.30am. However, there is a report coming in from our friends at Special Branch, that there has been an incident in St Peter Port, Guernsey on the hydrofoil out of Weymouth."

The colonel interrupted. "Who have we got down at Portsmouth these days?" he asked. Major Smith had expected the colonel would want an immediate follow-up and had already rung 'Sparky', the affectionate name for Corporal David Cheeseman, ex-SAS, a communications specialist.

"I have sent Sparky across to Guernsey, by speedboat, to see if there is a link to our man," replied Major Smith.

"Good," replied the colonel, never one to overindulge praise on his officers – it was their job after all.

The major continued, "Special Branch and our boys are working on the list the Bulgarian, Leonid Kokorov, gave us of his victims. There doesn't seem to be any connection." He looked at the report in front of him.

"Out of the sixteen victims and there are apparently several more, he can't recollect precise details, thirteen are men, three women. All over sixty and ten are over seventy years old. No links in occupation, service record or religion." They had at first wondered if the murders were politically motivated – but no. "His victims are mainly in the southeast of England. Several are double murders, involving a husband and wife," Captain Harrington raised his head slightly.

"Captain," said Colonel Harriman. "Have the police produced a list of deaths reported this year, concentrating on men and women over age sixty?"

"Yes," replied Major Smith. "It doesn't help us much, as there were over three hundred thousand deaths of men and women over age sixty."

"Let's narrow that list down to how many deaths of over-sixties were suspicious or mysterious accidents," said Captain Harrington. The colonel nodded but knew that would take some time. The Bulgarian had told them that all the assassins were also using a poison which was being analysed.

"That actor," asked Captain Johnson referring to Max Lungren who they had previously occasionally worked for, "did we manage to get any CCTV on his murder?" The major looked at another file and extracted three photographs.

"Yes, this is a photograph taken at Simpson's, but the man is well disguised and is probably the Bulgarian we are holding." He passed the A4 photographs to Captain Johnson.

Max Lungren, an actor of some repute, was one of their clients who had been murdered. They had traced his last evening to a dinner he had at the restaurant Simpson's, just off the Strand. The police had found a taxi driver who remembered taking two men to Lungren's flat in Chelsea. The waiter at Simpson's had given a good description and done a 'fotofit' of the man. The police had attempted, without success, to match the description of photographs and the 'fotofit' drawing to known criminals, the colonel suspected they had the man who murdered Lungren in custody even though the police had closed the file as death by a drug overdose.

The colonel's telephone rang. He picked it up. "Thank you Tony." He put the receiver back on the cradle. The colonel liked the old-fashioned telephones with a dial, not the push-button modern version. "A known accomplice of the man Ivan Dinov we are hunting, a woman, ex-KGB called Katya Gatchevske, was photographed by CCTV and computer matched, coming out of the Grosvenor Hotel. The camera on the corner of Buckingham Palace Road picked her up and one of Tony Greenford's MI6 boys curious to a possible FSB involvement spotted her after running the tapes after Ivan was seen in the vicinity," said the colonel.

"So that's another one," said the major, "possibly the women seen in the black mini outside our office."

The meeting broke up at midday with Captain Harrington and the colonel leaving to meet Sir Anthony, the head of MI6, to compare notes and unofficially co-ordinate the manhunt for Ivan and now Katya.

"If all these assassins have murdered roughly the same number of people and there are at least three killers, they have possibly murdered up to sixty people – we must find the link," said the colonel.

"It's extraordinary," said Harrington. "What on earth could it be about?"

Sir Anthony, the head of MI6, was also puzzled. Why would ex-KGB officers be murdering British citizens with no apparent link? There obviously must be one, but what was it? He had concluded that this was not about national security or their overseas operations and after discussing the murders with the home secretary, they had decided to involve Scotland Yard. The chief constable and Chief Superintendent Stern, a senior detective had been asked to attend a meeting with Sir Anthony's old friend, Colonel Harriman. This whole investigation started when one of the ex-KGB assassins had tried to kill the colonel. This was their first mistake as his security firm were staffed with some of the best ex-SAS officers and men who had been in the Secret Intelligence Service. Chief Superintendent Stern listened to the report from Sir Anthony and Colonel John Harriman, whom he had met previously.

"Questions?" asked Sir Anthony.

"If the three assassins have been identified as ex-KGB, isn't this a job for Special Branch?" asked the chief superintendent, never one to take on something he didn't like the look of.

Looking at the chief constable, Sir Anthony replied, "Special Branch will be involved, but the prime minister and home secretary require a police investigation to commence. There should be the fullest co-operation with Colonel Harriman and I am to be kept in the loop."

"What about MI5?" asked the chief constable.

"Yes, they will be briefed," replied Sir Anthony who was not keen on the internal security force.

The meeting had broken up, with a less than happy chief superintendent. He considered that potentially his team, stretched as they were already, would have to drop quite a few other enquiries to concentrate on these murders, which he still thought must be political – and he wasn't going to be the fall guy, that was for sure.

3RD OCTOBER 2007 – KENT, ENGLAND

Ernest Sadler OBE was looking at his scorecard somewhat apprehensively. Ernest had been a professional golfer. Not a very successful pro golfer, but he had usually earned enough from the European Tour to keep him from having to earn his living doing a 'proper job', as his father used to put it.

Since he had joined the Seniors Tour, he had earned more money from after dinner speaking than prize money from the tour. Mind you, he had won the Channel Islands Senior Tour match last year, by one stroke, from Gary Mark. Some of his old pals on the European Tour had not played senior golf, preferring to pack it in gracefully. Ernest had nothing better to do. No wife or family to live out his twilight years gracefully with. That was a regret, but still you can't be playing the field and expect happy families. He had married a beautiful nurse called Susan, in 1975. Susan was ten years younger and damned attractive. But the tour, oh the tour. It took you all over Europe and into temptation. Susan found out and that was that. He hadn't resented losing half his assets or even the flat in London; after all it was his own fault. Almost despite himself, and since the divorce, he salted money away. It was his dad who really disciplined him to save. Being the son of a Welsh miner made it difficult to fritter money away, you simply felt too guilty about sacrifice and stupidity. When he did have a top ten finish in a golf tournament, his dad always said, "Right now Ernest," he never called him Ernie like everybody else did, "half of it into a pension plan now, you know your career is likely to be short." *Dad was right of course and in those days a divorcing wife didn't get half the pension pot, not like today*, he thought ruefully. *I wonder how time has treated Susan, by god, she was a cracker*, he thought. Why he was thinking of his ex-wife now, he did not know. They had divorced over twenty years ago and he knew she had remarried. To some doctor, he had heard. Still she deserved a good man; she was the nicest person he had ever met. What is it about, when you have a poor round of golf, makes you melancholy? He had played Sandwich Golf Course so badly and this was the last UK Seniors Tour match this year. It was almost as though it was the first time he had seen the course. Instead of that, it was the scene of his greatest triumph – second in the British Open 1984, god if he hadn't missed that putt on the sixteenth green. *Look at that card today,* he thought, eighty-three, a score of eleven over par. *Blimey I had better give up soon or I'll be a laughing stock even on the Seniors Tour.*

For once Ernest declined a swift G & T in the bar and decided to head for home. Loading up his aging Volvo estate, he got into the driver's side, when a woman tapped on the window. Never one to ignore a lady, Ernie pressed the button and the window lowered effortlessly. She was smiling, *not bad either, about fifty,* he thought. He liked blonds.

"Would you autograph my programme Ernie?" Was that a foreign accent? Ernie took the pen and programme, turned the pages to his photograph and was about to sign across his picture, when he felt a stab in the arm. It was the last round of golf he would play and it had not been a very auspicious end to his playing career.

They found Ernest slumped over the wheel of his Volvo. "Real sad, had a heart attack," said Jack Dalby, another senior golfer on the tour.

"He was sixty-nine you know," said Andy Forman, who had beaten him by one stroke in the British Open in 1984.

A few of his old rivals came to the funeral. Susan, his ex-wife, also came and found herself crying, she had never stopped loving him, her first and last love.

Katya had picked up the programme and the pen – no point leaving them — and had driven back up to London. She had dumped the stolen black Mini and now had a Ford Fiesta. Three more to go and she could go to Berlin. *I wonder if Ivan's made it,* she thought. First she had to go back to London and see Ludvig – something she was not looking forward to.

Ivan, now travelling as Eduard Eglitis, a Latvian national, was walking around Sark enjoying the island and its environment. He particularly liked the lack of people. He was told that in October the weather could be inclement. *How quaint the English put things*, he thought. The rain had in fact put off many possible visitors to Sark, but Ivan loved it. The lack of police, was an added bonus. He had been here a day now and was considering when to leave. The hotel, where he was staying, was pleasant enough and there were only two other guests. He took breakfast very early before the other guests appeared and had dinner early, that way he avoided questions and having to make small talk. The hotel staff, what there were of them, regarded him as a bit eccentric.

Deciding to leave in two days time, he smiled to himself as he contemplated retiring to the West Indies. Katya might take some persuading: he knew she had been enjoying being Ludvig's number two again. But still, they had over a million pounds sterling between them and could live very well in Barbados with that amount. Perhaps they would stay there or perhaps visit the other islands, an enjoyable thought. Katya, ever being the cautious one, wanted to retire to South America, Colombia or Argentina. "Difficult to be extradited from there," she had said. But on balance, he preferred English-speaking places.

Slowly he circumnavigated the island, going down on to several fine sandy beaches. He met precisely no one, exactly how he liked it as he contemplated the journey to Berlin.

Katya began to dial. She was dreading this conversation, as she knew Ludvig's temper from old. He was a cunning and ruthless man and no doubt she was risking her own life by not running.

"It's me, we need to meet."

"British Museum, Egyptian Art, two-thirty today." The line went dead.

Katya picked up the bottle of hair dye, looked at herself in the mirror as a blond and then opened the packet of Excellence hair dye. When she had finished dying her hair black, she toned her eyebrows with a dark eyebrow pencil – her appearance was now completely changed. Clicking the underneath of her laptop, the hidden section sprang out and she extracted the German passport and credit card. Katya had changed all Russian operatives from Dutch nationals to Germans and left the Bulgarians with their alternative papers and now had decided she would become Anna Krall, from Leipzig, an English teacher by profession. Examining the passport, the photograph she had arranged to be taken in Sweden of her as a dark-haired German, date of birth 18th May 1962, looked back at her. *That will do*, she thought and checked over the hotel room in Earls Court. Satisfied she had left nothing incriminating, she packed her holdall and left by the fire escape. Katya had paid her bill in cash that morning so the hotel had no reason to investigate this guest or alert the authorities, but she did not want anyone to see the dark-haired woman leave.

Outside the hotel, Katya went around the front and walked briskly, but not too fast, toward the tube station. Buying a single ticket, she boarded a tube for the Metropolitan Line and got off at Holborn. Walking from Holborn Station, she suddenly broke into a run and crossed the traffic lights running up Southampton Row, before cutting into a mini supermarket. Watching out of the window, Katya saw no sign of being followed and after buying a London A-Z street map, came out of the shop, turned left after half a mile, into Russell Square. Katya was deliberately going around in a circle and turned left again into Bedford Place. Crossing over she was obscured behind a van and waited; nobody following. Walking down Bedford Place, Katya turned right into Russell Street and into the British Museum forecourt.

Checking again she wasn't being followed, Katya stood just inside the main entrance pretending to read the guide to the museum. Having had several meetings here before, Katya already knew the layout. A few minutes later she went to the section showing Egyptian artefacts and art and stood looking at a mummified figure in a glass box. The glass was a useful mirror and she saw Ludvig just before he appeared beside her.

"Shall we have coffee?" said Ludvig.

He led the way to the tea room. Katya sat down as he ordered two coffees at the self service cafeteria. Sitting opposite her, he sipped his black coffee as they both scanned the nearly empty room.

"Report please," he said in German. Katya reported, also in German, most of the events of the past twenty-four hours in a matter-of-fact way. Ludvig listened without interruption.

"So where is Ivan now?"

"He has gone."

"Gone where?"

"I don't know, he used the mobile to tell me he thought his cover might be blown so he was leaving."

"Katya, this is most unsatisfactory, if Ivan gets caught as well, that leads to you and also to me."

Katya was watching Ludvig closely, if he was going to kill her he would be using the hypodermic and he was not carrying an umbrella. She kept her hands perfectly still on the table but was ready to kick away any second.

"You have changed identities to a German?" he asked.

"Yes." Ludvig sat thinking for a moment.

"This is what we will do. You take the latest list; divide it up amongst Anton, Anastasiya and Hristo and the remaining Bulgarians. I take it the Russians have all returned to England as Germans?" he asked. "And the Bulgarians? You have issued new passports?"

"Yes," replied Katya.

"Instruct them to carry out the assassinations from the new list, add Leonid's number of targets to the others. You will kill the six named on your list and the three on your previous list, and then leave the country. As soon as the others have completed their tasks, tell them to leave as well. I will meet you in Berlin at the usual place in thirty days."

Katya noticed that a small, dark-haired man had entered the cafeteria. He somehow didn't seem right for a visitor to the museum. Fearing the worst, she got up to leave, Ludvig caught her arm.

"And Katya, don't ever give me away. If the British don't kill you, I will." He had that dangerous look on his face that she had seen before.

Ludvig released her arm and she turned away. Katya was right about the dark-haired man, he was Ludvig's link-up man, an ex-CIA operative, Franklyn Lime, and he came and sat down.

"Did you see that woman?" Ludvig said.

"Yes."

"You will have to kill her in Berlin." The American nodded.

Ludvig got up, leaving the American quickly finishing his coffee, and left the museum heading down toward Holborn tube station. Franklyn Lime, an alias for Max Schneider, a German, tailed him, but couldn't detect any other parties. Max's parents had changed their name when they emigrated to the USA after the Second World War and he had been recruited by the CIA after he graduated from Yale. He spoke perfect German and passable French, hence the attraction. He was posted to Germany during the Cold War and 'turned' by Ludvig. Max had been caught in a 'honey trap'. Thinking he was dating a Swedish girl, but she turned out to be a 'he'. Compromising photographs were shown to him, but still he had initially resisted. But the money proved to be the key – the Russians offered him more money than he dreamed possible – he became a double agent and Ludvig, then head of the KGB in Berlin, ran him. Having remained undiscovered, he had retired from the CIA five years ago, and now worked semi-exclusively for Ludvig, who used him to kill.

MURDERS CONTINUE…

5TH OCTOBER 2007 – LONDON, ENGLAND

Jack Solomon was not a religious man, but today his granddaughter, Clare, was getting married at St Peters Church, Streatham in London. *Strange*, he thought, *the connection*. He had been born in Streatham; actually Tooting in St James Hospital, but all his young life had been spent in Valley Road, Streatham. Jack remembered his school life, firstly Sunnyhill Primary School, then Aristotle School, Brixton. *Brixton was a different place then to what it is now*, he thought. You daren't mention it, but when he went to Aristotle School in the sixties, there were no black children in the school. *Now there are probably no white faces*, he thought – *how things change. Mostly for the better*, he reflected

If his wife Sylvia, had been alive today, she would have loved seeing their daughter Susan's delight as their granddaughter, Clare, got married. It seemed that these days couples didn't get married. He couldn't think why not, after all many of the couples living together sacrificed legal rights and for what? Freedom to move on? Lack of commitment? But it seemed to him that people really wanted both those things. *They wanted love and security, so why not marry*, he thought.

He reflected on when he had proposed to Sylvia. They were at the Locarno, Streatham, a large dance hall, long closed down. He had had a few lagers, got down on one knee and proposed. All his mates thought he was a daft idiot, but Sylvia loved it and accepted. They had been married thirty years, until just when they were able to enjoy retirement, she had told him that she had cancer. Sylvia, his beloved wife, only lived another eight months. But today was his granddaughter Clare's day, she was marrying a nice young man, Gary, whom he had met several times and liked.

Jack had retired two years ago, after forty years building his successful motor dealers in Guildford and Woking, Surrey. But he was lonely and missed Sylvia terribly. His two children, Susan and Peter, were always inviting him to their houses, but he didn't like to overstay his welcome and went back to his empty house in Godalming, Surrey, not far from the first garage he owned.

Success had not come easy for Jack, but when he got the Datsun car franchise he quickly expanded and made a packet. Datsuns were a popular car to buy in the eighties and nineties and when he sold out the business, his had been the largest franchise in the South of England.

The organist began to play Mendelssohn's Wedding March and he looked around to see his granddaughter; she looked lovely in her white dress. A tear came into his eye. Clare, she looked just like his Sylvia and he wiped the tear away. A hand held his; it was his son's wife Linda, a lovely girl whom he was very fond of. "She looks wonderful Dad," said Linda. Jack nodded, fighting back more tears. It wouldn't do, at sixty-eight years of age, to be crying at his granddaughter's wedding.

The ceremony was familiar and after the formalities they assembled outside for photographs. Jack wandered around the side of the church for a cigarette. He had never managed to give them up, even after Sylvia had died.

A woman approached, carrying an umbrella. *Strange*, thought Jack, *it doesn't look like rain*. He felt a sharp prick in his leg. Jack had gone to join Sylvia.

They tried not to let Jack's heart attack spoil the wedding, but Clare was sobbing uncontrollably when they broke the news.

"Can't understand it," said his son Peter. "He only had a check up last week."

The post mortem confirmed a heart failure, but a diligent police inspector thought it was an unexpected death and forwarded the file to Scotland Yard, as requested.

Katya sat on the top deck of the 109 bus she had boarded at Streatham Hill and looking around saw nobody near her. She got out her laptop – another to note down and claim the bounty for – that was how she looked at it. Every one she killed earned her a tidy sum and meant it would be sooner, rather than later, when Ivan and she could retire. Now who was next…

5TH OCTOBER 2007 – LONDON, ENGLAND

Colonel Harriman was not a patient man at the best of times. He liked to act decisively – get things done. These murders were frustrating him and still they were no further forward. The Russian, Ivan Dinov, known to the CIA, Interpol and MI6 as a dangerous ex-KGB agent, who had been spotted in London and then linked to the death of a Port Authority policeman in Guernsey, continued to elude the searchers. Corporal Cheeseman had been sent to Guernsey to assist the local constabulary and the newly appointed police crime co-ordinator, Chief Superintendent Stern, had sent a team of detectives. Cheeseman had telephoned yesterday with a good description of the man who had rather foolishly, tried to steel Commander John Cunningham's powerful motor boat in Guernsey harbour. Colonel Harriman hadn't met John Cunningham, but he had heard good things about the SBS man, from Admiral Reach, an old friend. It was a break the man Dinov attacking John Cunningham; they knew he was on the island, but where? Chief Superintendent Stern had indicated that after one more day they would assume Dinov had got off the island, but Colonel Harriman was not so sure.

Walking through into the board room in his London office, he sat at the head of the table. The men seated around the table stopped talking and waited for him to speak.

"Gentlemen, we are flailing in the water. Where is Dinov? What do you think Captain Harrington?"

Captain Harrington, ex-SAS, was a very astute man and had done some computer simulations on Dinov's possible escape route.

"I think he is still in the vicinity sir. There were no other ferries out of St Peter Port that day and the harbour master reports that there were few other craft leaving the harbour. The police stopped the hydrofoil to St Malo for three hours and virtually tore it apart in case he had gone back on board. "There have been no further reports of boats missing. I think he is holed up there."

"So do I," said the colonel. "We will send two more men with you Harrington to help with the hunt."

"We are getting very thin on the ground sir," said Major Smith, the colonel's second-in-command. "With our men protecting dignitaries and pop stars and hunting for this man, we can't take on any more work at the moment." Colonel Harriman nodded.

"Prioritise, major, prioritise. What other news?" he asked.

"I have a report from MI6 on the poison the attackers have been using," said Major Smith. He passed around an A4 sheet.

"Well I'll be damned, they've refined the ricin poison," said Colonel Harriman as he read aloud the footnote. "The ricin poison used in assassinations has been refined with the venom from a sea creature called the sea wasp," he continued. "The sea wasp is a jellyfish (*Chironex fleckeri*) with one of the most deadly poisons known to man. In the opinion of the National Scientific laboratories, anyone injected with this poison would suffer heart failure and die within ten seconds, or sooner, if they had a heart condition or were old."

"Charming," said Captain Johnson.

"As you know," said the major, "we have also confirmed the identity of the woman outside HQ two days ago."

"Go on," said the colonel.

"Her name is Katya Gatchevske, let's call her Katya." They all laughed. "She is also ex-KGB, served with the man Ivan Dinov, rumoured to be working in Iraq and also with the Taliban in Afghanistan," he continued. "The CIA, Interpol and MI6 are preparing a report on her, we should have it by tomorrow. Meanwhile, I suggest we publish her last known photograph and see if someone has seen her." The major looked around the table.

"A dangerous game," said Captain Johnson. "If she is staying with someone she might kill them if she realised they've recognised her."

"Yes, but we don't have much time, Dinov is gone, she is probably our only link in the chain," said Captain Harrington.

"I agree," said the colonel. "Let's get a photograph in all the nationals and London papers. Say she has escaped from prison and should not be approached as she's a dangerous terrorist."

The meeting broke up at 11.30am with Captain Harrington arranging for the company helicopter to take him and two others to Guernsey to continue the search for Ivan Dinov.

Livingstone Handley booked into the Kings Hotel on the seafront at Paignton. Before his wife, Cecily, had died they had travelled, usually in July, to Torquay or Paignton, to enjoy fourteen days 'by the sea', as his dear wife had put it. This year he was going later, to avoid the crowds of happy people. Livingstone had been a professional footballer, spending twenty years playing at various levels, including when he was aged twenty-two, playing three seasons for Leyton Orient in the old Third Division. Unfortunately an achilles injury, when he was thirty-two, meant he had to retire from the professional game. But Livingstone had listened to his mentor, Brian Phillips, the ex-manager of the O's, who had told him to take his FA coaching badges. Livingstone passed and after an early apprenticeship as assistant manager in a non-league team, he applied for a job managing Fourth Division Hartlepool and much to his surprise, got it. After three successful years, when he took Hartlepool up a division, he moved on to manage Burnley, but when he failed to gain promotion to the old First Division, he was sacked in 1987. Livingstone Handley had always been adventurous and when Brian Phillips recommended him to a team in Los Angeles, he went over to America to coach the LA Galaxy team. It was early days in American soccer, as they called it, but Livingstone and his wife Cecily enjoyed the all year round climate and made lots of friends. When he reached sixty, they returned to the UK, somewhat reluctantly, but there was no prospect of work in the States and Livingstone wanted, much to Cecily's annoyance, to continue coaching or managing a team.

Cecily had been frugal with their money over the years, sadly they had no children and she had squirreled away a tidy sum. Investing cautiously, they were set up to enjoy a long and happy retirement. Fate can be a double-edged sword. And so it was when a car, driven by a joy rider with three of his mates egging him on, crashed into Cecily's Austin Metro as she drove slowly across the lights in High Street, Hartlepool. She was taken to hospital with a painful whiplash injury. The doctor in A&E was a very sharp cookie and having spotted Cecily's irregular heartbeat, suggested further tests. Immediate surgery was proposed, but the prognosis was not good. Cecily had severely blocked arteries. Who would have thought that one minute you would be looking forward to retirement, spending time together gardening, walking and going to football and the next facing a heart surgeon who was telling you that your wife had not survived the operation. It had been too late. Livingstone spent a lonely spring in Hartlepool, his old mates were great, but he missed his Cecily more than he could explain. He cheered Man United and sometimes went to Newcastle or Sunderland, as a special treat with his pal Mickey Flynn, another ex-professional player from the old days.

Making up his mind to go to Torbay had been easy. He liked to walk and this time stayed in the King's Hotel, Paignton, a sea-front hotel, so that he could walk along the promenade. It was beginning to get dark, so he decided to walk to the end of the pier, do a lap, and then go back to the hotel for dinner. Livingstone heard footsteps behind him, the old strikers' instinct I suppose, he half turned and then felt a terrible pain at the back of his head – then nothing.

The Bulgarian Dmitri, had followed Livingstone to the end of the pier and seeing his chance coshed him and chucked him over the rail.

They found Livingstone's body washed up the next day – the hotel had not noticed he was missing, but he had his room key in his pocket, so the police were able to find out who he was, "Good footballer in his day," said Nigel Smith, the editor of the *Hartlepool Gazette*, as they wrote Livingston's obituary.

"I just wish they had caught the mugger. Fancy chucking him in the sea, the bastard," replied Maurice, the sports editor. Still they did him proud with a super piece and they wore black arm bands at the Hartlepool match on Saturday. Detective Sergeant Mortimer of the Torbay police decided to send the file on his death to Scotland Yard – it was a suspicious death. You just didn't get muggers murdering people on Paignton pier.

Dmitri sent a text to Katya and took out his list to see who was next.

The Honourable Peregrine Harrington-Smyth was enjoying himself. He had been invited by the Lloyd's Shooting Club to a shoot in Piddinghoe, East Sussex. Lloyd's of London, the premier insurance underwriters, the place where major and some very minor insurance risks were placed everyday, was where Peregrine had worked, for over thirty years, prior to his retirement. During that happy period, he had been the underwriter for the Wilcox Syndicate number 1071, writing aviation risks. Peregrine's father was Lord Harrington-Smyth of Dorchester who was now ninety-two years old. His mother, Lady Jane, had sadly died ten years ago. *But the old bugger lives on*, he thought to himself. Peregrine had been president of the Lloyd's Shooting Club for over ten years and enjoyed a day's shooting. He always considered pheasants to be rather stupid birds – they barely flew and then only a few feet off the ground. Duck, on the other hand, were a fast and high-flying opportunity to demonstrate what a good shot you were.

Today was a duck shoot, and it was an opportunity to meet Tubby Lincoln again and the other club members. Peregrine had retired from his syndicate at Lloyd's in 2002 and now, five years later, he enjoyed regaling old times with fellow underwriters, some also retired.

Life had been kind, except he had never married. An unkind rival at Lloyd's was once heard to say, "Who on earth would want to marry that pompous, self righteous prig? Anyway I've heard he's gay." Peregrine did not exhibit his sexuality in public, but truthfully he was not a sexual man. He preferred a glass of good malt at the Reform Club in London, or a night at Covent Garden watching ballet, to chasing women or boys and he had, at times, a penchant for both.

The beaters began to whistle and noisily frightened the ducks into breaking cover and taking off. Some fluttered into the air and a barrage of shotguns opened fire.

That was when Tubby moved along the line of shooters to gossip with Peregrine about the new Underwriter on Aviation Syndicate 12. *Where was the old boy?* he thought.

Suddenly he saw a leg sticking out and going closer, realised Peregrine was on the ground. He saw immediately he had been shot in the back and much to the initial annoyance of some of the members, brought proceedings to a halt.

A doctor was summoned but it was too late for Peregrine, he was pronounced dead at the scene.

The funny thing was the police couldn't work out how Peregrine had been accidentally shot. The shooters were in a line and nobody seemed to be out of order. A verdict of accidental shooting, by person, or persons unknown, was brought in by the Coroners Court. Nobody had noticed the blond-haired man, with his collar up, slip away from the shoot.

Sitting in his hotel bedroom in Sark, Ivan read the obituary in *The Times* and smiled, another nice sum earned, Hristo had completed that hit, an excellent job.

Katya noted on her laptop Hristo's kill, rubbed her eyes and wondered if she should call Ivan, he should be in Berlin by now.

KATYA GATCHEVSKE

7TH OCTOBER 2007 – SARK, CHANNEL ISLANDS

"I'm sorry to trouble you Mrs Smedley," said Ivan to the portly woman who owned the Dixcart Bay Hotel, Sark.

"Hello, Mr Eglitis, can I help?"

"Yes please." Ivan exaggerated his accent and continued. "My father is ill in France and I need to go quickly." He paused to let the information sink in. "I do not wish to delay and wondered if you know of a fisherman who could take me to St Malo?"

"St Malo," Mrs Smedley repeated the name of the town in France. "Well, old Drussell would probably take you in his fishing boat for a couple of pounds."

"Where do I find him?" asked Ivan who was known by Mrs Smedley as Eduard Eglitis, a Latvian national from Rigor.

"I'll telephone him and ask him to call, when I mention there may be some money in it, I am sure he will come," she replied.

"I do hate to press you, but it is urgent," said Ivan.

"Alright, my dear, I'll do it now."

As it happened, Francoise Drussell had had a bad morning. He was out checking his lobster pots, as he hadn't caught many fish that morning, when his mobile rang. A man wanted to get to St Malo in a hurry, cash involved, that was all he needed to know.

Three hours later, Ivan jumped from the small fishing boat onto the harbourside at St Malo. There were no customs, police or anyone else, come to that. The harbour was very sleepy at one-thirty in the afternoon. Ivan had thought about eliminating the old man, but decided it would attract too much attention. No one would link him with Sark or the old fisherman. In any case he was now an old man – a Latvian.

Conventionally for a change, Ivan hired a car from Hertz, using Eduard Eglitis's credit card, and planned his route to Germany. He intended to abandon the car at Strasbourg and board a train to Berlin. He knew eventually the police would trace the hire car back to St Malo, but he would be long gone and would have changed his identity again.

As he drove through the French countryside, always keeping clear of the motorways, he wondered how Katya was. Ivan had loved Katya for twenty-five years and now, as he approached his fifty-fifth birthday, he wondered if he should have had children but it would have meant adopting. Still, what could you do in their profession, he laughed to himself.

Dumping the Fiat car in a multi-storey car park in Strasbourg, Ivan walked into the first public toilet. There, he changed identities from the old man Eduard, a Latvian, to his favourite identity, Anders Andersson. He removed the grey wig and wiped clean the grey eyebrows, returning to his natural brown colouring. He was now Anders Andersson, a teacher from Stockholm on a visit to Berlin checking on venues for a possible school trip. The common currency in most of Europe had been a blessing. No constant changing of money, life was simpler than in the old days of the KGB. He hummed a German tune alone in the carriage of the inter city express train to Berlin. He would meet Katya in a few days and they would get out – the old life forgotten.

Katya felt her mobile buzzing in her pocket. Examining the dial she clicked on 'missed call', hoping it would be Ivan – *Damn*, she thought. *It was Ludvig*. She returned his call.

"Be at the statue in the park, opposite Royal Albert Hall, at 5pm." The phone went dead.

Typical Ludvig. No conversation just instructions. Katya was on a bus, a 159, taking her to Streatham Hill, where she had rented one of her three flats in London. What did he want? He knew the current list had not been completed, there simply hadn't been time. Getting off at Streatham Hill railway station, she walked up Leigham Court Road toward the block of flats, deep in thought.

*

Ludvig had decided to eliminate Katya and then run. This whole thing would start getting out of hand soon. Time to take what he had and depart these shores. Katya and Ivan were the only links to him. If he eliminated Katya, Ivan would come after him and he would kill him too. The plus was that the team would continue with their lists, as they wouldn't know Katya was no more. Money would keep pouring in for the next month, as more victims died.

Ludvig had told the ex-CIA man, Franklyn Lime, to be in position early as he knew Katya would arrive at least thirty minutes before the rendezvous time to check it out. Katya hadn't met Franklyn, so he should be able to get close enough to kill her with a silenced pistol. The statue in Kensington Gardens had been cleaned recently and looked spectacular. Franklyn briefly wondered who it was, still he couldn't spend time looking at it now. The ex-CIA agent gazed around – no sign of Katya. A horse rider in the distance and an old lady pulling a suitcase were the only people in sight. As the old lady reached where he was standing, she moved off the path toward him. What did she want? It was to be his last thought before Katya shot him in the head. Katya knew he was dead before he hit the ground, and began to walk away, pulling her suitcase down the path. A horse rider approached, but couldn't have seen anything. As the rider and Katya came side by side a male voice said, "I knew you would get him."

Katya began to dive sideways and pull her pistol out, but the silenced barrel made speed difficult. In fact, she had no time, as Ludvig fired twice, reined in the horse and fired a third into her head. "Sorry," he whispered, "it's business and you're a link to me."

He rode off back to the stables where he had hired the horse, changed clothes and made his way to the edge of Kensington Gardens, crossed the road and walked down Exhibition Road to South Kensington underground station. He boarded the tube train to Victoria Station and coming in through the Buckingham Palace Road side entrance to the mainline station, he looked at the screen and saw that the non-stop Gatwick Express was due to leave in five minutes. The journey to Gatwick Airport was uneventful and thirty minutes later he was buying a ticket to Prague, paying in cash, at the EasyJet sales desk. He went upstairs to the shops and sat, facing the shopping mall, in Starbucks reading a newspaper. Two policemen passed by with machine pistols strapped across their chests, but neither even glanced his way. He walked to the departure area and passed through security forty-five minutes before the departure time, showing his Swiss passport which wasn't scrutinised. All the man on the desk looked at was his EasyJet boarding pass. The man took his photograph, but what the hell; he had died his hair stone grey to match the passport and looking every bit his apparent age of sixty-five years.

Ludvig wasn't nervous, he couldn't see how they could have been looking for him, only Katya and Ivan knew his involvement. Katya was dead and he doubted Ivan had been caught; he was too wiley an old fox.

The plane touched down three hours later at Prague International Airport; Ludvig went to the left luggage lockers, removed the small case inside and went to the gents' toilet. He came out having changed his clothes and identity to a German, Gunter Weiss, the name of an actual teacher in Dresden. Using one of his disposable mobile phones he phoned Morgan Fryer, the man who had hired him. "Meet me at number three, seventeen days' time," Ludvig knew that Morgan would be right now making arrangements to look up the code number and find it was for Vienna and he dumped the mobile in a wastepaper basket and went to check train times to Vienna.

It was late on Wednesday afternoon. Colonel Harriman had received a call from the policeman in charge of the murder investigation. The chief inspector, an able man, detailed the progress, or rather lack of it, concerning the investigation of a list which had reached forty-five unrelated deaths. There seemed to be no connection between the deceased persons. The police list detailed single men, married men and couples. Some of the murdered people had previously, prior to retirement, been professional. Four accountants, two solicitors, a barrister, ten had been self employed business people, the rest a mixture of ordinary persons with ordinary jobs and lives. Except there were two actors, a racehorse trainer and an ex-professional footballer. There seemed to be no common denominator. The police had cross-checked all forty-five dead people including religion, service in the armed forces, membership of political parties, relatives, they had even checked if they could all be paedophiles, such was the extent of the investigations. But it all revealed very little. The only common factor seemed to be they were all over age sixty. Not all had retired, the racehorse trainer, and accountant and several of the self employed still worked.

The police had exhumed twelve bodies from the list the Bulgarian had provided for Colonel Harriman and tests had confirmed the existence of minute particles of the poison, ricin 'chironex fleckeri', the deadly cocktail perfected to kill within ten seconds. Interpol could find no links with any other murders in Europe. Nor did the combined offices of the Security Services, MI5, MI6, CIA, FBI, Interpol or Scotland Yard, have a clue who made the lethal poison. Nobody had used it before, or so they thought. Lacking intelligence, the Secret Service had turned to tracing Ivan Dinov and Katya Gatchevske.

A manila folder, on Katya and Ivan, had been presented to the colonel by an old friend in the CIA. These two Russians had a long history together. She was known in the eighties to have been the station head for the KGB in East Berlin. Ivan had been her colleague, firstly in Germany and then later in Afghanistan. At the end of the Cold War, they both worked for the Russian Government, before, it seemed, old enemies surfaced and they had to run. The CIA next picked them up in Iraq, working for Saddam Hussein, training his intelligence forces. Then they were 'loaned' to the Taliban in Afghanistan and based in Kabul, it seemed for several years. They disappeared off the radar between 2004 and 2006 and as they were not considered 'players', the CIA did not look for them. Interpol reported a sighting in Madrid of Ivan, prior to a series of explosions orchestrated by the Basque Separatist movement. But no further sightings of Katya. Colonel Harriman had requested CIA and British Intelligence investigate who Katya and Ivan reported to firstly, in the KGB, and then later on their various jobs. To date no intelligence had been received.

*

Ivan Dinov had eluded capture in the UK and then in the Channel Islands. A computer simulation suggested he was most likely to steal a boat and sail to France or Spain, as he was an accomplished sailor. The police in Guernsey reported that no boats were missing.

In the police inspector's office in London's Scotland Yard, the sergeant read his report. "Ivan is well away by now," he told the inspector.

"We have today published the last known photograph of Katya," said the inspector. "Let's hope this brings a lead." The phone rang. "Right, I'll be there in fifteen minutes, are you sure it's her?" He cut off the caller and as instructed, phoned Colonel Harriman.

"Two bodies have been found in Kensington Gardens, near the statue of Prince Albert, they think the woman might be Katya," said the policemen.

"Can I meet you there?" asked the Colonel.

"Yes, by all means."

Katya had disguised herself well, thought Colonel Harriman as he looked at the body of the old woman. No wonder she was such a good field agent – but a dead one now. He knew this meant her superior was eliminating the link up the line. There was no identity on the other dead body, a man, so it would take some time to see if he was known. The colonel suspected that Katya had killed one of her opponents and by the sound of the initial report from the crime scene pathologist Katya had been shot three times, the last a head shot. *Making sure*, he thought.

There was nothing further to gain so the colonel returned to his Park Lane office.

Colonel Harriman had been asked to attend a briefing at Scotland Yard, but was running slightly late. Ushered upstairs to the third floor, he entered a large room where fifteen or so men and women sat around a table and he recognised Chief Superintendent Stern at the head of the table addressing the assembled group.

"Apologies ladies and gentlemen; slight internal problem," said Colonel Harriman, glancing around as he took a spare seat at the end of the table. The chief superintendent nodded and continued talking.

"I was summarising our position. We now realise there are at least three people, one a woman, who are killing British citizens. The assassins, we shall call them that, are, it seems, ex-KGB and at least two are probably Russian. The man that has been apprehended," he looked directly at Colonel Harriman, "is a Bulgarian, Leonid Kokorov, who has been living here as a Dutch citizen, Gillis Vardink. I think that's how you pronounce that name." One of the male officers laughed, but stopped quickly when the chief superintendent glared at him. "If I may continue? The leader of this group, we think is a Russian we know as Ivan Dinov, also ex-KGB. He had previously come to the attention of the security services in Berlin, Iraq, Afghanistan and North Africa and most recently is linked to a terrorist attack by Basque separatists in Madrid. We understand that he works with another Russian, a female, Katya Gatchevske," again the chief superintendent struggled with the pronunciation, "who we believe has been identified as killed in Kensington Gardens, near the statue of Prince Albert, late yesterday afternoon." He paused. "The man Ivan Dinov was tracked to Weymouth, where he boarded a hydrofoil to Guernsey. We suspect he was heading for France, the boat's final destination. We believe a port police officer approached him on board the boat and was murdered. A man we believe to be Dinov tried to steal a motor cruiser from St Peter Port harbour after the hydrofoil had docked, but unfortunately for him he chose to try to steal a boat belonging to a serving SBS officer, who fought him off. He would appear to be on the run in or around Guernsey, but there have been no sightings for five days, inspector." He looked at Inspector Haynes who got to his feet.

"The laboratory has confirmed the victims are often stabbed with the tip of an umbrella, or injected by hypodermic with a deadly cocktail of poisons of ricin, mixed with a poison from a jellyfish. The effect of being injected is death within ten seconds. At the moment we think this is the probable list of forty-four victims." The inspector went through the list, drawing to the attention of the assembled group, the details on the white board behind the chief superintendant. "If you turn to page six of the file in front of you," the entire group opened their manila file, "you will see the work that Special Branch and our unit here have carried out, cross-checking the background of all the known victims and other probable notables. Besides occasional odd coincidences, there is little to go on and we cannot, at this moment, establish a motive for these murders." He sat down. Chief Superintendent Stern stood up.

"Colonel Harriman is known to some of you. He is a private security consultant who was attacked by one of the apparent assassins, a Bulgarian, who later gave us what information about the assassins that we have – colonel anything you would like to add?" said the chief superintendent, rather reluctantly.

"Yes." Colonel Harriman did not stand. "It seems to me that the probability is that there has, in fact, been something around one hundred and seventy-six murders and probably at least one hundred and forty-four." There was a gasp around the room. The colonel continued. "Consider that one man was given lists of people he was required to murder and we know of at least two other assassins and there is probably a group leader. Simple maths." He looked around at the faces, some of which seemed to understand, others looked blank. "Gentlemen, they have been killing people for nine months at the rate of four to six each per month." He stopped to let the statement sink in. "This is most likely the worst linked murder case any of us have ever heard of, or investigated, but with so many murders must come similarities, we just haven't found them yet; furthermore," he continued as the chief superintendent was about to stand, "unknown assassins may still be continuing to murder people." The colonel stopped talking as conversation erupted around the table.

"Thank you colonel for your analysis," said the chief superintendent, rather grudgingly. He glared around the table waiting for silence. "Special Branch has a red alert for Bulgarian, Dutch or Russian nationals and details of known ex-KGB officers who served around the same time as Ivan Dinov, have been circulated."

Clearly, thought Colonel Harriman, *all the Bulgarians and probably the Russians are here on false passports*, so he didn't hold out much hope for Immigration Officers or local police catching a Bulgarian or a Russian.

"In conclusion," said Chief Superintendent Stern, "we must continue to break down the past history of the murdered persons and ascertain the link. We are also collecting all deaths of men and women over age sixty-five and checking to see if there are any further victims." He glanced towards Colonel Harriman. The chief superintendent didn't like the involvement of the colonel in this affair, but the powers that be, had insisted.

That was clearly the end of the meeting, until a young woman spoke. "Excuse me sir." The chief superintendent looked at DC de Courcy, a woman officer he didn't know very well.

"Yes?"

"It occurs to me that this man Dinov has eluded us in the Channel Islands and is probably right now in mainland France. Shouldn't we be asking the French, German and Spanish police and Interpol, to keep a particular look out for him and trace all hire or stolen cars in the vicinity of the French coast around St Malo, his likely point of entry?" The male officers around the table looked at de Courcy aghast.

"Thank you," the chief superintendent said grudgingly. He thought for a second. "De Courcy, I am sure Inspector Haynes has listened closely to your suggestions."

The meeting broke up with a rather red-faced de Courcy being ribbed by several of her colleagues. Colonel Harriman, on the other hand, approached her and said, "You are quite right young lady. He has almost certainly gone and I agree the likely place is France. I will speak to some people to follow up your suggestions."

Within the hour, Chief Superintendent Stern was receiving a summons to the chief constable's office.

"I know how difficult this case is proving John," said the chief constable, "but Colonel Harriman has put a specific request to certain people and additional resources are being allocated to the investigation. Deputy Chief Constable McGuire is taking over the investigation and adding a Chief Inspector Hadden to the team."

"But sir," said Stern

"Sorry John no buts, that's how it is and you are off the case."

Secretly Chief Superintendent Stern was delighted.

*

Detective Chief Inspector Hadden listened to the briefing from Inspector Haynes. One of the old school, the DCI had two years left until he was going to retire, having served thirty-five years in the Met.

"Well this is a right flipping mess inspector. Are you working in teams?"

"No sir, just on specific areas," replied the inspector.

"Right, organise your squad into three teams. Team A, to concentrate on trying to find a link with these murders. Team B, to follow matey-boy into France, make a nuisance of yourself with the Frog police. Team C, to examine any other possible suspicious deaths. The young de Courcy is to be a liaison with Colonel Harriman and is to be kept in the loop by all three teams.

"Got it?"

"Yes sir."

"Right, off you go then lad, let's get cracking." The DCI sat back in his chair. "Thank God I will soon have my retirement papers seeing as this case could be the end of me," he muttered to himself.

At the same time as the chief inspector was organising the investigation, the home secretary and the head of the MI5, Sir Aubrey Granville-Davis, were meeting the prime minister in Downing Street.

"Harriman believes there are upwards of one hundred victims," exclaimed the prime minister. "If he's right then this could create a panic we have never seen before, not to mention damage relationships with Russia and Bulgaria."

"I suggest, prime minister," said the home secretary, "that there is a complete news blackout with immediate effect. I have instructed the chief constable to place his most senior detective in charge and step up the investigation"

"Sir Granville-Davis," the prime minister turned toward the head of the MI5.

"We now believe, prime minister, as does MI6, that these murders are not linked to any threat to national security, other than the obvious falling out with Russia," he continued. "The fact that they are using a new and difficult to manufacture poison, we have called 'Formula B'," he handed over a sheet of paper, "means they have either a very sophisticated laboratory somewhere, or they are being helped, possibly by the CIA or the remnants of the KGB."

"Doesn't that infer a Russian involvement?" asked the prime minister, ignoring the introduction of the CIA into the equation.

"No – not necessarily. You see there are still many ex-KGB who Putin has elevated back into his country's security services and they are selling their, shall we call them 'services'?"

"Talk about the west being capitalist. I think the Russians are just as bad these days," said the home secretary.

"Then there are the French and the Chinese," said Sir Granville-Davis.

"They could be involved?" said the PM incredulously.

"I don't think so, but they certainly could manufacture quantities of the poison," replied Granville-Davis.

"Have you left the Bulgarian they caught with Harriman's mob?" asked the prime minister.

"Yes, because we didn't want to have him in police custody – it removes certain options", replied the home secretary.

"Well, look," said the PM, "I am beginning to smell a huge problem. We must keep the lid on all this. If the media discover a hundred murdered people, there will be hell to pay." The prime minister closed the folder in front of him signalling the meeting was over. As the other two men got up to leave he said "Oh, Aubrey, a quick word."

The head of the security services came back to the table and sat down. "I don't want any misunderstandings. I don't want this story leaking to the press. If there are a hundred or more murders my instinct is to cover it up. Make sure that the Bulgarian cannot be put on trial and if they catch anyone, and at the moment they don't seem to be doing a very good job, I don't want public trials. Do you get my drift?"

"Yes prime minister," replied the shrewd head of security.

"Right I'll wish you a good day then Aubrey." The home secretary was waiting outside and was buzzed back into the Cabinet Office. "Charles, this situation, I intend to call a snap election in the spring. I know it's six months away, but we do not need grisly details of murders by Russians and toxic poisons all over the papers." The home secretary nodded. "Pass the word down to the chief constable that information on this case is to be on a need to know basis only and stress the investigation is top secret. Get all the police to sign the Official Secrets Act."

"What about Colonel Harriman?" asked the home secretary. The prime minister thought for a moment.

"Yes, I see what you mean, arrange to meet him and stress the importance of utmost secrecy – and Charles, take him out of the loop. No further information to be given to him." The home secretary nodded and got up to leave. "Just one final thing Charles, ask the dirty squad to try and get something on Harriman in case we need it and stop feeding him intel."

Colonel Harriman studied a sheath of papers. The Russian billionaire, Leonid Agronov, had requested security during his trip to London next June to attend racing at Ascot. Contemplating the problems this would pose, he decided on an eight man team with a reserve team of two. The rich Russians carried a lot of baggage, he thought, and it was always with some reluctance that he agreed to a security contract. Even if the Russian was a close friend of the Russian president there was always a risk from an old enemy and it was easy to get into Britain by using false passports and identities. Contemplating the security risk, he thought four men should be with the Russian at all times and four men placed around his entourage. The two reserves would shadow the vehicle convoy, park up at Ascot and standby to assist, if required.

Turning to more immediate matters he thought about the teenage pop sensation, 'Julia'. *Top of the Pops she may be*, he thought, *but what a whacko she was.* Two ex-police officers, Susie Chalmers and Rod Lime, were Julia's minders and both hated it. Julia was a model, a singer and a compulsive publicity seeker, who snorted cocaine and drank to excess. *What a role model*, thought Colonel Harriman as he read the latest report from Susie, one of his senior female minders.

Turning to the murders – 'Case X', as he had marked the file— he considered the current situation. The death of Katya confirmed that the overall commander of the operation was not Ivan Dinov. The Secret Service report on both Ivan and Katya had been specific – they were lovers. It seemed unlikely Ivan would kill Katya, but the commander of the OP would, especially after the Bulgarian was captured. So the commander of the OP had probably decided to run, as they knew Katya's lover Ivan Dinov had. The latest report, one day old, from the deputy chief constable was not encouraging. Still no connection between the murders had been discovered.

He picked up a green folder. Ah yes. The pop star Dustin. The man he had struck, who had died of a brain haemorrhage, was a known villain. Convictions for GBH and an attempted murder which their barrister thought would influence the Crown Prosecution Service

Putting down the folder, Colonel Harriman used his old-fashioned intercom to talk to his number two, Major Smith.

"Yes colonel," he replied.

"Smithy, any news from Captain Johnson tracking Ivan Dinov in France?"

"No sir. I am afraid he lost the trail in St Malo. He's pretty certain he stole a car and there are two hire cars unaccounted for that he is asking the French Police to trace."

"Alright, give him one more day, and then pull him off. We are getting stretched and there is no point leaving him to chase shadows."

Colonel Harriman picked up the file and went to his wall safe. He suddenly felt his sixty-two years and decide to go to his flat and rest. Since the attempt to kill him, he had been sleeping 'light'.

DEATH IS A CERTAINTY

10TH OCTOBER 2007 – CHELMSFORD, ENGLAND

When in doubt, say nothing – that had been John Wadkin's formula during his entire business life and he saw no need to change now he had retired. Flo, his wife, wanted him to buy a small house in France. "Somewhere around the Loire Valley" was being discussed at odd moments when the subject came up again. Flo, John knew, had more than earned her right to suggest buying a French dream home, but the trouble was John realised, at their age, sixty-eight and sixty-four, owning a second property might be more of a burden than an enjoyment. Still, she enjoyed planning and was even closing in on the area around Saumur, on the Loire, that she really 'liked'. Saumur was a lovely French town smack bang on the River Loire. The town had a superb chateau and lots to commend the area. But John was reticent and was stalling his enthusiastic wife.

"Let's go down to the area next month John," said Flo.

"If you want dear," replied John, he could visit those wineries he liked and restock his wine cellar.

"Do you think we should go online and look for estate agents in the area?"

Ah, back to buying in France again, thought John.

"Why not dear, do you want me to take a look?" John was the more proficient internet exponent.

"Can you do the search for me and then I will look at the agents." They pulled up in Tesco's car park. "I'll get a trolley dear," said John as Flo strode towards the entrance.

"Alright, but you go and sit in the coffee bar – and John, no doughnut," Flo said very sternly.

John passed the trolley to Flo and headed toward the coffee bar – a self-service place which was already overflowing with husbands and harassed mothers.

John moved swiftly along the counter, ordered a coffee, steadfastly but reluctantly moved past the doughnuts, paid at the till and selected a seat next to the window. Flo would be at least a half an hour doing the weekly shop, so he got up and picked up a newspaper from a table where someone had left it.

My God, he thought, *another knife crime. London is really becoming a dangerous place to live. Living in Chelmsford, as they did, was sometimes not much better*, he thought. Ever since he had retired from Forsyth & Sons, Gentlemen's Tailors, Flo and John had set up a routine. Monday they did the garden, Tuesday cleaning the house – not as though that took long these days, Wednesday into town to meet their friends, Stephanie and Barry. They often went to the cinema; it was reduced price for pensioners on Wednesdays. Thursday they played bridge and Friday they did the weekly shop. The weekend was spent pottering about and occasionally John played a round of golf with their son, Marcus.

This whole business of buying a property in France had started when John inherited a considerable sum from his late mother's estate. John's mother had lived to ninety-two – bless her. John, being an only child, had inherited over half a million pounds. They had some inheritance tax to pay, but still it was a tidy sum. Up until then they had lived very well on the pensions John had set up. Finishing his coffee, John went to get up when a swarthy-looking dark-haired man sat down opposite him.

"Ouch," said John as he felt a sharp prick in his leg.

Flo was going down the frozen food aisle when she noticed that there seemed to be something going on in the café. A crowd had gathered. John always called it the coffee bar – she smiled to herself.

"Someone's collapsed in the café," a checkout girl said. Flo's heart seemed to miss a beat – no, surely not John. She left her three-quarters filled trolley and rushed to the café. Looking around she couldn't see him – and then –

"Oh God, no, it can't be." John lay on the floor; a man was massaging his chest. "That's my husband," she said.

A woman took her arm and sat her down, she phoned her son Marcus. Shortly after, an ambulance arrived. John was declared dead. Marcus arrived just as they were wheeling John to the ambulance. Flo sobbed uncontrollably, "He's dead Marcus, dead. I don't understand it," she said in a state of shock. As he held his mother, Marcus knew what she meant; only last week his father had a 'well man' medical at the BUPA hospital and had been passed A1.

The funeral took place at St Peter's Church. They weren't great church-goers but John would have wanted that.

The Bulgarian, Dmitri, who had stabbed his latest victim in the leg in the supermarket café, didn't wait around for the church service; he caught a train to Norwich, where his next victim lived. He sent a text message to Katya.

Flo never did buy that house in France and, like Marcus, was astounded that the verdict of the post mortem was heart failure.

'Mr Pickle', they used to call him. Sydney Featherstone had set up 'Featherstone's Pickles' in 1969 in a warehouse just outside Wolverhampton. Working on a recipe handed down by his mother, he put in all the cash he had and began bottling pickled onions. Not for him, plain vinegar. There was a secret ingredient – peppercorns. The pickle factory started off slowly, but once Marks & Spencer's placed a large order, there was no stopping them. Next, they developed piccalilli – also with a special mustard which made 'Featherstone's Piccalilli' the most sought after in the Midlands. For twenty years Sydney had built a pickle empire, resisting overtures from Colmans the mustard people and Crosse & Blackwells to buy him out. But then a strange thing happened – at the age of fifty-one, he fell in love.

Sydney had devoted all his time and energy to the pickle factory. He didn't go dancing or drinking down the pub and he didn't meet women. The ladies who worked for him at the factory regarded him as a bit of a catch, but none of them attracted him. Then one day he was walking the love of his life, a Cairn terrier called Delilah, when another dog approached. Tail wagging; the newcomer was a cute little Westie.

"Well who are you with?" asked Sydney as the two dogs introduced themselves.

"Oh, thank goodness, you have her. Thank you so much." Sydney looked up and was smitten. There, standing by him, was a beautiful woman in her forties, with an Audrey Hepburn, his favourite actress, haircut and wonderful brown eyes.

After that initial meeting they walked their dogs together every day. The woman, Joan, was a widow with the same love of animals shared by Sydney and when she found out he was the owner of the famous 'Featherstone's Pickles', she brought him a recipe of a Branston type of pickle which her mother had passed down the family. Well – that was it. A beautiful woman who loved dogs and made astonishing pickle. They married exactly a year after they met and together had continued to expand Featherstone's Pickles, building up an extensive export market. Ex-pats loved their pickles and profits soared, and demand meant they had to move to bigger and bigger factories. When Sydney reached sixty-five, they finally accepted an offer from the giant Rickett & Colman company and sold out for a very considerable sum of money.

They did the usual things – went on a cruise, toured the world, always travelling first class and then settled for breeding terriers in Shrewsbury, Shropshire.

Viktorya had been watching Sydney for several days – not that Sydney knew it. The dogs would be a nuisance; still it meant she could kill him on that green he walked. She watched and waited another day as the man Sydney Featherstone, number four on her list, was often accompanied by a dark-haired woman, he presumed the target's wife. Today he was alone. Timing her approach she shot Sydney dead – one shot between the eyes with a silenced Glock pistol, supplied by Katya. The dogs barked as their master dropped down dead and it would be five minutes before another dog walker curiously approached the four Westies, all whimpering around at the prone figure of a man lying in the grass.

Joan was devastated. They had no children and now she was alone again. What a wonderful man he had been. Hundreds turned up at the funeral, it seemed all the ex-employees had fond memories of 'Mr Pickles'.

After sending a text to Katya reporting her latest kill, Viktorya drove away from the outskirts of Shrewsbury toward the address she had for number five on her list, humming as the radio played a Viennese waltz.

Detective Inspector David Morris sighed. From what he had discovered this man, Sydney Featherstone, had no enemies, so why was he shot dead? No clues, no witnesses, except an elderly dog-walker who 'thought' she saw a dark-haired woman on the green about 3.30 pm.

Yes, he thought, *this was an unexpected death* and sent the file, as requested to Scotland Yard – it seemed they were collating unexpected deaths he didn't know why.

12TH OCTOBER 2007 – LONDON, ENGLAND

Veronica Jane Ash was born in Warrington, England in May 1945. The daughter of Ellen Ash, whose husband, Carl Ash, left for America in 1947 and hadn't been seen or heard of since. Veronica, or 'V' as she was known, was a bright girl, but struggled to concentrate on academic studies, preferring to drawl over film stars and the new celebrities who were pop stars and models. It was no surprise to her mother when, at age fifteen she announced she was leaving school and going to Aunt Lizzie's in London. V's aunt ran a model agency, off the Edgware Road in London and was moderately successful at placing girls with the new up and coming glossy magazines and with publications such as Reveille and Tit Bits where girls posed in swimwear. V's aunt had contacts. Aunt Lizzie had always said she had 'high cheekbones and a beautiful face', which was apparently the prerequisite for a career in modelling. At first Aunt Lizzie found her new responsibility a nuisance and was seriously tempted to send Veronica back to her mother. But then, at a dinner party she regularly held for editors of magazines and newspapers, the influential newspaper baron Lord Rothermere commented how lovely the girl was and that he would be happy to arrange a photographic shoot featuring her soon. *The dirty old man*, thought Lizzie. *I know what he wants, but still the girl does have something.*

Slowly at first, V was introduced to modelling, not smutty stuff, children's clothes, domestic goods that sort of thing. Then the Rank Film Company asked Lizzie for young women to appear in a film they were making with a new singer called Rocky Meehan. V went for a screen test at Ealing Studios in London and was selected to play one of the screaming girls who followed Rocky, early groupies so to speak. V was seventeen years old and fancied a career in films and as young as she was she knew how to get it. She didn't bother with the lead in the film, Rocky, but set her cap at the producer and director, Sam Blenheim. Always one for the ladies, Sam didn't need a formal invitation. The affair kick-started V's acting career – she appeared in three more 'pop' films after that and began to get regular television work. When Sam divorced his wife, he married V, even though she was twenty-five years younger than him. His two children, who were nearly the same age as V, hated her. The marriage lasted three years before V met and fell in love with an American actor, James Gordon.

They were working together on an Agatha Christie murder film, for once not directed by Sam. V became infatuated with the brash young American and ran off to America with him when they finished filming. Sam divorced V in 1969. Fortunately for her, he had played around himself during their brief marriage and his penchant for young women had got him into hot water with a sixteen-year-old girl when he was producing a musical at Pinewood Studios. The girl terminated the unwanted child, but V found out and threatened to expose his sordid activities to the press if he didn't co-operate with a fast divorce settlement. He did. The affair with James Gordon didn't last long, but V liked Hollywood and stayed on. V had a knack for meeting influential men who inevitably fell in love with her and she was cast by the director in one of Elvis Presley's films as the love interest. This film was followed by several more, usually she played a beautiful woman hotly pursued by the leading man and that's exactly what she was. At age thirty she married again. Another man much older than her – this time one of the co-owners of the Los Angeles based Lexus Studio, a huge American film company. For a while V behaved, but then she fell for Stewart Ince, an up and coming actor she met when working on a series for American television about a cattle farm. Hank Lenihan wasn't a man to tolerate his pretty wife messing about with young actors and promptly got her removed from the TV series and then initiated divorce proceedings. V didn't do very well out of that settlement and decided to return to England.

The glamorous and somewhat notorious V, enjoyed the new era which was opening up in England. New studios opened at Pinewood where she was cast as a Bond Girl in Diamonds Are Forever. Chat show hosts loved her – she knew all the gossip and teased her way on the Michael Parkinson show and Russell Harty interviewed her twice.

As she got older, V's film parts began to dry up, but then she was offered a series of light porn movies in Los Angeles. It was on the set of one of these movies that she met husband number three, Jack Rivaldi, a lawyer. Jack worked for the mob, who were funding the film V was making. Criminals mixed easily in the film world; they liked being seen with the celebrities. Jack adored V and showered her with gifts, bought her a house in Beverley Hills and showed her off to his connected pals. They were married for twenty-one years before a heart attack killed probably the only man V had truly loved. Returning to England she settled down doing the odd TV interview and wrote her autobiography.

Actually it was a young man called Stephen Druce who wrote the book, but V provided the titbits. The book was a best seller.

Now in her sixties, V looked at herself in the mirror. *Not bad for an old girl,* she thought and completed her make-up. Malcolm Milner, an old friend from her days at Pinewood Studios, was taking her out to dinner. Now sixty-two years old, she hadn't done any work for quite some time but the public, her public, still remembered her. Malcolm arrived promptly at 7.30pm and they set off in a cab for 'Kudos', the fashionable restaurant in Knightsbridge. She didn't notice and neither did Malcolm, the dark-haired man on a motorbike, who had waited until their taxi arrived and then followed. Anton had recognised her name on his list straight away. He remembered how attractive she had been, but a job was a job. After the couple had eaten, Anton followed them back to her flat, just off Park Lane. The man went in and he waited. An hour later the man left. Anton picked the lock on the entrance door, a simple Yale lock, and went up to the first floor. He had been to her flat before. Using a plastic card, he easily opened the front door and cut the door chain. Slowly working his way along the hallway he heard singing. *Not bad,* he thought and inched closer – she was in the bathroom. V had her back to the door as he crept toward her. Sensing someone was there, she went to turn, but found her head in a vice-like grip. She dropped her cleansing cream and tried to scream – nothing came out – then blackness.

Her body was found by her cleaner on the floor of the bathroom two days later. The police established the cause of death as asphyxiation, she had been strangled. "A very strong person using their bare hands" the report said.

The film world and the public came out in their droves to V's last performance – her funeral in Warrington. The police made no headway solving the murder and there appeared to be no motive. The papers were passed to a newly formed squad at Scotland Yard, investigating murders.

Anton watched a rerun of one of her old films in his hotel that night. *Shame really,* he thought. *I wouldn't have minded screwing her* but they said not to and Anton always did what Katya told him. Only one left on his list – was funny he hadn't heard from Katya for sometime but he sent her a text confirming the hit as instructed.

12TH OCTOBER 2007 – LONDON, ENGLAND

Colonel Harriman took the call from his old friend and listened. "Alright, I'll meet you at the usual place at two-thirty," he replied.

There was a knock on his door. He had been at his Park Lane office all day discussing his business operations. "Come in," he answered a second knock on the door.

The young policewoman, de Courcy, came in. "Excuse me for interrupting colonel, but I have just been instructed to return to Scotland Yard."

"That's alright dear," he smiled at the young woman. He had been very impressed at the efficiency and common sense of this young police officer and had already made a decision to endeavour to recruit her when this murderous affair was over. "You go ahead Maureen," he called her by her first name. Reluctantly the petite, dark-haired woman left the colonel's office. She had developed an enormous admiration for his attention to detail and army discipline, which was not always apparent in the police force.

Maxwell Harding, who had fought so bravely in the first desert war with Iraq, coughed at the colonel's door. Max, as they all knew him, was excused many of the formalities as he hobbled into the room. Max had lost both legs when a kerbside bomb went off on the road to Basra. The unarmoured jeep he had been in, had been thrown across the road. Max considered he was lucky; the other three members of his SAS unit had been killed.

"Yes Max?"

"Sorry to interrupt colonel, thought you would want to know straight away." Colonel Harriman looked up from the file on his desk and Max continued. "George Doheny is on the mobile; four men identifying themselves as Special Branch have turned up at the farm and want to take the Bulgarian into custody." The colonel picked up his mobile and selected a number.

"Hello, chief constable, I understand four members of Special Branch have just turned up at the farm where we are holding the Bulgarian, is this legitimate?"

"Yes John, I am sorry you haven't had a call," replied the chief constable.

"Okay, we will pass him into their custody."

"Are you on your landline or mobile John?" asked the chief constable. "Mobile."

"Fine, thanks very much for the call." The policeman put the phone down.

"Okay, Max, tell them to let them have him." Max left the office to relay the colonel's instructions. Meanwhile the colonel buzzed his number two, Major Smith.

"Smithy, can you come in?" Major Smith, a thick-set man in his early sixties, knocked and entered the colonel's office.

"John?"

"Sit down Smithy." He paused. "We seem to be being cut out of the loop on these murders." The colonel explained to his friend that suddenly their prisoner had been taken without prior warning, the young policewoman had been instructed to return to Scotland Yard and his good friend, Sir Anthony Greenford, the head of MI6, had asked for a meeting later that day. "It's obvious they are distancing us," said the colonel.

"What do you think – cover-up?" replied Smithy.

"I wouldn't be surprised", the colonel replied. "When Doheny and Mack," who were the two men who had been guarding the Bulgarian prisoner, "return make sure you put the film in the strongroom." Colonel Harriman's men had filmed and recorded the intelligence gathering and not told anyone. "I'll see you later," said the colonel. He had arranged to meet Sir Anthony Greenford for a late lunch at the Officers Club in Pall Mall.

Ivan sat by the window in the Café Rouge, a small nondescript café in Central Square near Zurich railway station and the old town. As he sipped his coffee, he reflected on Katya. Ivan had travelled to Germany from France and after waiting five days in Berlin at the flat they shared in the Franz Strasse, he knew he had to move on to their second rendezvous point. Amazingly efficient, Katya always calculated all eventualities and had agreed with him that if she didn't meet him in Berlin then he should move to Zurich. *Such efficiency*, he thought. *Yet where was she?* He knew her last few targets would take up at least a week, but she had sent him a text telling him she wasn't intending to finish her degree as it was getting warm in town. He knew this meant she was going to run. That was five days ago. Ivan and Katya had worked together in the KGB for twenty-five years before the old Soviet Union broke up. She had been his section head, but more than that, they were lovers. When they fled from their beloved Russia, a year after the wall came down in Berlin, old enemies had surfaced under President Gorbachev. They had gone to the Middle East and peddled their unique skills in Afghanistan, Iraq and afterwards Saudi Arabia. In Saudi they had met a group who were very militant, later to be called Al Qaeda. They asked them to train operatives in Afghanistan and Libya. Still sipping his coffee, Ivan reflected on the change of events. Gorbachev was replaced by Yeltsin and once again the power struggle in Moscow changed. An earlier head of the KGB and his number two, a man called Ludvig Korotski, returned to prominence in Russia. Through channels, they put a toe in the water and found out that they would be welcomed back to Russia. It was ironic really, that a rather liberal president and mostly unbeknown to him, was allowing many of the old guard to return and take up powerful positions. Katya and Ivan joined a rather sinister group later called the Russian mafia but their stay in the homeland didn't last long. They were killers really, assassins who would kill to instructions. Ivan reflected on the growing lawlessness in his home country. Powerful men were running things now and he doubted whether Katya or he would ever be able to walk the streets of Moscow again – too many enemies.

Finishing his coffee, Ivan scanned the square, and then went to the back of the cafe, apparently going to the toilet, but in fact he slipped out of the back door.

Walking purposefully, he returned to his hotel, taking a roundabout route. Certain he had not been followed; he lay back on the single bed in his hotel room. He got up to look out at the street; as usual he had selected a room at the front of the hotel. Nothing. Making up his mind, he looked at the timetable on the small bedside table and began packing his overnight case.

As he packed, he contemplated changing his appearance and nationality again. Deciding it was unnecessary and that he would travel under his Swedish passport, he checked the hidden, lead-lined, compartment in his small suitcase where he had placed a false French passport, in the name of Claude M Chassued, a forged driving licence and credit cards. The metal compartment had been developed by the Russian KGB when x-ray machines were introduced at airports to enable operatives to travel without risking false papers being discovered.

He left the hotel as quietly as he had arrived and walked to Zurich railway station. He had decided to enter Britain by the Eurostar from Paris, a favourite route. There were barely any checks and you sat in comfort as the train sped from Paris to London's St Pancras Station. If you felt uncomfortable for any reason, you could get off at Ashford, in the Kent countryside, and travel the final journey to London by stolen car or on the ordinary rail link. He decided to get off at Ashford anyway, why risk the cameras at St Pancras Station?

The journey from Zurich to Paris was uneventful, except a rather large woman kept trying to engage him in conversation, which he resisted with curt nods. Ivan, ever careful, changed his mind; he had used the Eurostar before and decided to fly to Stockholm from Paris and onward perhaps to Gatwick or Dublin. As usual he bought a return ticket even though he would not be returning, at least not soon. He would wait a week at the third rendezvous in Stockholm and then, if Katya did not come, go looking for her.

16TH OCTOBER 2007 – LOCH LOMOND, SCOTLAND

Stewart McCall was striding purposefully down the seventeenth fairway at Loch Lomond golf course. He had hit a good drive, but it had gone right, so he cut away from his playing partner towards a small copse of trees, hoping that his ball was sitting up in front of the trees. Just as he was approaching the trees he saw another golfer pulling a trolley and heading in his direction. They were going to meet at the trees. Curiously, Stewart wondered how this man had hit such a wayward shot to be just off the fairway he was playing. He must have been playing the first hole and hooked his shot rather badly. The man seemed to be standing in the vicinity where Stewart thought his ball had landed. "If you see a Dunlop number four it's mine," he said casually, looking at the man.

Strangely, the man didn't say a word, just pointed. *Funny fellow*, thought Stewart, but he had, it seemed, found his ball. Stewart walked over to where the man was standing and pointing. He parked his trolley and removed a number six iron from his golf bag and went to look at the lie. "Where did you see the ball old man?" he asked, as he couldn't see his ball amongst the light rough. The man moved towards him and curiously was carrying an umbrella. Stewart felt a sharp prick in his leg, looked at the man, went to raise his club to strike him but instead crashed to the ground.

Hristo looked around, the other player was walking down the fairway one hundred yards away looking for his golf ball, so he dragged the body of the man, Stewart McCall, into the copse of trees, swiftly went and pulled his victim's trolley and left it sideways on the floor of the copse. Walking slowly away, pulling his own trolley, he went directly to the clubhouse, abandoned the trolley near where he had found it and went to his car. He had stolen a blue Ford Fiesta yesterday from Edinburgh and followed Stewart McCall from his house in the suburbs to Loch Lomond golf course. The umbrella had injected a lethal dose of the poison in his victim's leg – it had been easy, another five thousand pounds earned. He drove to Glasgow, where he dumped the car, sent a text and then caught a bus to the railway station. He had to go to Carlisle next to kill a woman called Muriel Lanson.

17TH OCTOBER 2007 – HAMPSHIRE, ENGLAND

It was beautiful day in October in the Hampshire countryside, with clear blue skies and a surprising temperature of seventeen degrees centigrade. Anastasiya had changed her identity to Agnes Vissar, a Dutch national, and moved, renting a flat in Southampton, southern England. The latest list of her targets included three people who lived near Southampton. Strangely her last text, ten days ago, to her controller, Katya, had not been acknowledged. Usually a report of a confirmed kill was met with a text reply of the letter 'A'. Not this time.

Since then, she had killed an elderly man in Dorchester three days ago, using the poison and was now researching eliminating a woman, who lived in Bridport, not far from Southampton. She estimated a drive of perhaps one hour and a half, driving her stolen car carefully and obeying all traffic rules. Training with the KGB in the early eighties she had almost missed the 'fun times' as Katya put it. Leaving Moscow University, Anastasiya had been recruited at age twenty-one and principally used as a deadly 'honey trap'. The head of Moscow Station told her the industrialist Egar Svertin and the politburo member Ivan Gratsky were traitors and deserved elimination; these had been her first two victims. Her long legs, blond hair and angelic face made her an ideal assassin. Men were flattered by her attention and unlike most women, Anastasiya had no scruples. Her KGB instructors considered her one of their finest recruits – pity the Cold War was over.

Anastasiya was driving on the M27 towards Bournemouth, intending to spend two days observing Mrs Marilyn Walker, who lived in Bridport, Dorset. Driving in the centre lane, she watched her speed, didn't exceed the national speed limit, even though she knew the BMW 3 series could easily reach speeds of over one hundred and twenty mph. Constantly checking her mirrors, Anastasiya spotted a rather old car coming up fast on the outside lane of the motorway. *The British*, she thought, *mostly obeyed the rules, but when driving, many people regularly exceeded the speed limits, even though there were CCTV cameras all over the place.* A car passed on her outside. Suddenly there was a loud bang, the car veered and struck the front of her vehicle. Anastasiya fought to control her car, but the blow to her front offside had sent her across the lane and into the path of a large lorry. The lorry driver braked hard, but he was doing fifty-five mph and couldn't avoid hitting the BMW and propelling it with metal screeching and sparks flying down the carriageway. Suddenly the BMW flipped over whilst continuing to be pushed down the inside lane. Several other cars were caught in the crash. By the time the emergency services had arrived Anastasiya was dead.

The police were quickly on the scene, closing the motorway for three hours, as they arranged for the broken heaps, which used to be cars, to be removed and the dead and injured to be taken away by ambulance. Sergeant Hawkes had called in the number plate of the BMW immediately, as the woman, who was dead at the scene from massive head injuries, didn't have any identification. Discovering the car had been stolen, he reported his findings to his Inspector; a small brown holdall with binoculars, spare underwear, slacks, blouse and strangely a flick-knife. In addition, an umbrella was removed from what had been the back seat. The inspector, a bright young career copper, had reported the findings to his local Special Branch officer, who in turn, after examining the umbrella, called the chief inspector at Scotland Yard who had issued a bulletin detailing suspicious deaths and listing of all things, umbrellas as notifiable up the line. Then all hell let loose. A helicopter came down from London, all the woman's possessions were taken and the body removed. A list of names had been found in a secret compartment in the holdall, along with a Dutch passport and a vial of liquid.

Chief Inspector Hadden considered the accident as a stroke of luck. A wheel had come off an old Jaguar on the M27, causing a multi-vehicle pile up. This woman, he doubted her real name was Agnes Vissar or that she was Dutch, was clearly one of the assassins. Why else would she be carrying the deadly poison and the means to inject the victim – the black adapted umbrella? The woman's face had been badly smashed up, but he was hoping her fingerprints would tell him who she really was. Maybe their luck was changing, as they also had the names of three people who were, it seemed to him, very lucky, as they were clearly future intended victims.

A day later the CIA identified the ex-KGB operative, Anastasiya Stoickkev, from fingerprints obtained when a KGB head of station defected in 1985 – he had trained her, one of the deadliest female assassins the KGB ever used.

17TH OCTOBER 2007 — PAIGNTON, ENGLAND

George Drinkwater was a creature of great habit. Every day he walked his dog, a red setter called Ruby, to the beach at Broadsands. Broadsands, as the name suggested, was a pleasant beach near Paignton in Devon. Favoured by the locals, Broadsands was not so well known by the 'Grockels' – the local name for the tourists who invaded Devon each year in the early spring and through the summer. At this time of year, with a stiff breeze blowing in off the sea, he was usually alone, but today, as he threw the ball for Ruby to fetch, he noticed a figure walking towards him. The man didn't have a dog and it was unusual for George to meet someone at eight in the morning on the beach, particularly this time of year, so he watched as the man approached.

"Not so good today," he smiled as he spoke to the stranger. Ruby came running over and then strangely growled. "Here Ruby, come here," George said, surprised Ruby was growling. The man was now within touching distance and that's when George noticed the umbrella. "Christ, what did you do…?" George's voice trailed off as he fell on the beach and died. The dog was barking and dancing around his master totally confused.

Egor, walked away, went to the car park, sent a text and reversed out of the parking bay. There were no other cars in the car park and as he drove back towards the Brixham Road, he pondered on his next victim, who lived in Newcastle in the north of England.

It was an hour later when a couple who were out dog-walking spotted George. Ruby hadn't moved from his side, crying as she knew her master was dead. George's neighbours were shocked. Since his wife had died two years ago, George kept very fit dog-walking and playing bowls. It was incredible he died on the beach at Broadsands and poor old Ruby, at twelve years old nobody wanted a red setter, in any case she barked all the time now.

Chief Inspector Haddon was not a happy man. Yesterday he had presented an updated report on the murders the hit squad had been investigating. The chief constable had almost reprimanded him for continuing an operation he had been ordered to investigate ten days ago. But surely it was his duty to report further likely murders showing that the killers, he knew for certain there were more than one, were still active? And what about the work done by that girl de Courcy? She had now established a link between a probable one hundred and forty-one murders, which had eluded his squad, Special Branch and the Secret Service? If it turned out to be the missing link, it would cause incredible reactions, here in the UK and in the USA. Surely it was his duty? He had not attempted to take the credit for the remarkable detective work the young DC had put in – *She is going to be something else,* he thought. *Still, why should I care that the chief constable was not pleased. Funny though – he almost seemed angry. That's what you get promoting young blokes as top brass. Seasoned coppers, that's who should receive important promotions,* he thought.

The chief inspector was pondering his lack of advancement; everyone knew he was a brilliant detective, as he crossed the road. He didn't even see the vehicle, as it hit him square on and he was dead before he hit the ground, his weak heart had finally given up.

News of the death of Chief Inspector Haddon reached Detective Constable de Courcy as she reported for duty the following day. Tears filled her eyes, as she heard about the hit and run. Then she started to think. *Coincidence or something more sinister? Who to ask?* She went to the ladies washroom and made a call on her mobile.

COVER-UP

19TH OCTOBER 2007 – LONDON, ENGLAND

The prime minister sat in the cabinet office waiting for the home secretary. He looked at his watch. Charles Henderson was usually very punctual, what was delaying him today? Frederick Haverley-Court, his principal personal secretary, knocked and entered.

"The chief constable and Sir Granville-Davis are waiting and a message from Charles Henderson: delayed in the house. He will ring shortly."

Damn the man, thought the prime minister. He knew the home secretary was a shrewd politician who coveted his job. He had edged him out by ten votes at the last leadership election, but he had then been forced to invite him to join his cabinet, due to his popularity in the party. He didn't trust him and the subject they were discussing that morning was political dynamite. "Alright Frederick. Let's get on with it. Show the chief constable and Sir Granville-Davis in." The two men entered the cabinet room.

"Good morning gentlemen, please sit down." Both men acknowledged the prime minister and sat opposite him. The chief constable who had instigated this meeting got out four manila folders, marked 'Top Secret'.

"The home secretary has been delayed", the prime minister paused, "but we will commence the meeting without him."

Sir Aubrey Granville-Davis, the head of MI5, glanced at the chief constable; both men were experienced enough to sense that politicians were playing their usual games.

"Right chief constable, you asked for this meeting, over to you," said the prime minister.

The chief constable, Sir David Burch, had been a serving police officer for twenty-eight years. He had been one of the earliest graduates, from Manchester University, to be fast-tracked through a graduate training programme and he was the youngest ever inspector in the history of Manchester police at twenty-four years old. It helped that his father and grandfather had both been chief constables, but his rise through the ranks had been meteoric. Some malicious colleagues claimed the lodge, he was an active Freemason, had also influenced his amazing career advancement. Chief inspector by age twenty-eight, a superintendent by age thirty-two and the chief super three years later. He had to wait three more years before he became an assistant chief constable. Then as far as he was concerned, the breakthrough. He jumped deputy chief constable to be appointed chief constable of Manchester Constabulary before his fortieth birthday. Lord Justice Tregorney, his godfather, said at the exclusive dinner party held in his honour,

"We have witnessed the extraordinary rise of David. His grandfather, Sir Phillip, would be very proud." David Burch, the subject of the toast whose father had recently retired from the Devon-Exmouth Constabulary, beamed proudly and later was to hear his father add, "he has a great chance to become the youngest Metropolitan Police Commissioner in the history of the force." And so he was – appointed three years ago just after his forty-fourth birthday. The unsuccessful candidates for the London Metropolitan Police Commissioner's job, regarded as the ultimate top copper, resented his rise through the ranks, his name was often spoken jealously, but nevertheless enviously, by chief constables and assistant chief constables and his colleagues.

Sir David Burch, waited until after the other two men had read their folder then said, "As you know, prime minister, we have scaled down operation 'Phoenix'" – he had personally thought of that name— "but something's come up, which is important." Sir David handed out a further A4 sheet to the prime minister and Sir Granville-Davis, and continued, "The investigating officer, Chief Inspector Hadden, was ordered to terminate the investigations, but against direct orders, he carried on. Two days ago he came to see me with evidence that suggested a conspiracy by one of the world's most important businesses." Both the other men were reading the A4 sheet.

"My god," muttered the prime minister, "he has established proof of this?"

"Well, as you will see, the evidence is very conclusive without the chief inspector having interviewed the CEO of the company or any of the directors." The prime minister's political brain was turning as he finished reading. This could be a disaster. Relationships between the USA, Russian and the UK strained. A public outcry and worse, a probable downturn in confidence in the financial institutions would be the likely result. Perhaps a run on the stock market? His political instincts began to take over.

"Who knows about this?" He referred to the sheet and folder. The chief constable who had anticipated the question passed a copy of a further A4 unmarked white cartridge sheet to both men reporting the death of the chief inspector. The prime minister frowned.

"This Detective Constable de Courcy, tell me about her," asked the prime minister ignoring the report of the man's death in a hit and run. Once again the chief constable's antenna was working and he passed another two page report to both men.

"Hmm," said Sir Granville-Davis. The prime minister's eyes also fell on the reason for the head of the Secret Service's gasp.

This girl, woman, thought the prime minister, *is the great granddaughter of Countess de Courcy, one of the wealthiest families in the world.* The family owned the de Courcy Bank as well as countless businesses throughout the world. Also, their families were head of the Swiss bank of the same name – de Courcy. "What on earth is this woman doing in the police?" asked the prime minister.

"I was curious myself," replied the chief constable and discreetly made enquires. "Apparently, she is one of those people who feel they should start without any of life's advantages – from the bottom, no favours, and no influence."

"But why the police?" asked Sir Granville-Davis. The chief constable had talked to Superintendent Sylvia Franklin, the most senior of his female officers and asked the very same question.

"Her great grandmother served in the Secret Service during the First and Second World Wars – it seems she thought the police might be as exciting."

"Who was her great grandmother?" asked the prime minister, fearing the worst.

"Prime minister, she was a de Courcy." David Burch, who already knew the answer, watched as the prime minister's face coloured – the de Courcy dynasty could not be trifled with and they donated millions to party funds.

"Has she signed the Official Secrets Act?"

"Yes," replied the chief constable.

"Good," the prime minister replied. "Sir Granville-Davis, anything to add?" The head of MI5 had kept relatively quiet whilst the chief constable presented his report and said, "We have intel that the man we are seeking, Ivan Dinov, is in Sweden under an assumed name. He is a direct link to the main co-ordinator of this affair. Discreetly examining the deaths of people over age sixty since we ceased investigations, leads me to believe another twenty-five people have been murdered since then."

"So the assassins," the prime minister couldn't think of a better word to describe the people killing his countrymen and women, "are still operating?"

"I believe they are, but we still don't know how many, but the deaths are in two areas of southern and southeast England." Both men waited for the prime minister to absorb the information they had provided and for instructions. They had been told to cease the investigation – it was to be buried – never happened, but what now? Nobody asked after poor Chef Inspector Hadden who had been killed in a hit and run.

*

The home secretary, the Honourable Charles Henderson, sipped his coffee in the members' tea room at the House of Commons. Sir David Burch, the chief constable, had briefed him yesterday evening at the City of Westminster lodge meeting. They were close friends, despite the age difference. Charles Henderson was, at fifty-seven, in line for being grand master of the most important Masonic lodge in Britain. If, and only if, he became prime minister, would he resign from the Masonic movement, but he didn't consider it necessary when he had been invited to join the cabinet. After all, Prince Michael and dozens of titled people were members of the lodge – why should he resign? The prime minister hadn't wanted him in the cabinet at all. Charles had lost the leadership election, but when the votes were counted, it was clear the party was split. The prime minister had no choice but to offer him a cabinet post. However, they shared a mutual distrust for each other and this affair could bring one, or both of them down. *Best leave it to him to make a decision*, he thought. He might, after all, hang himself, but he couldn't help wondering who had killed the policeman the chief constable briefed him about called Hadden— *Hit and run my arse*, he thought.

The two men left the Cabinet Office, each reflecting on their careers. Sir Granville-Davis had two more years before his well-earned retirement. Sir David Burch had planned to enter politics in two or three years time.

What the prime minister proposed, no instructed, was basically immoral and probably illegal, but they both were trapped in different ways. One, Sir Granville-Davis yearned for his house on the River Dart, just outside Dartmouth in Devon. The other to enter politics and become the prime minister himself.

The prime minister suspected that Charles Henderson deliberately didn't appear until midday, over an hour after the earlier meeting had ended. He knew he had to brief him, but realised Charles was distancing himself. It was a high risk game the prime minister was playing.

"Well, what are you proposing?" asked Charles Henderson, the home secretary, emphasising for the tape recorder in his pocket, on the word 'you'.

"Nothing – it's best to do nothing." It was easy for the prime minister to lie.

*

Colonel Harriman sat studying the two sheets of paper which had arrived in a typed envelope thirty minutes ago. His doorman said a middle-aged man had handed him the envelope. The description of the man was vague, as was the CCTV, as he was wearing a raincoat with a large trilby hat which covered most of his face.

There was a knock. "Come in," said the colonel. Major Smith walked into the sparse office. The colonel didn't believe in unnecessary clutter, hence there was a single desk in the room, a hat stand and two chairs. "Read this Smithy." Major Smith picked up the two A4 sheets of plain white paper.

"Do you know how the info arrived?" he asked.

"Yes, a middle-aged man brought it by hand thirty minutes ago," replied Colonel Harriman.

"Terry," who was their receptionist, "couldn't give a description?"

"No," he replied .

"If the information is sound, what next?" asked Major Smith.

"For the first time in my life Smithy, I am considering betraying my country."

The prime minister and the home secretary sat opposite each other at the broad office table, reading the latest report on the nationwide murders and particularly the death of one of the assassins, a Russian woman. Both had spent the last twenty-four hours pondering what to do about 'the problem'. The home secretary, the Honourable Charles Henderson, looked up.

"Yes prime minister?"

"It is time to bury this matter in more ways than one. Instruct Aubrey Granville-Davis to close the whole investigation down – he will know what to do."

"Are you sure prime minister?" The home secretary, the natural successor for the leadership should the prime minister be ousted, would really have liked witnesses to his personal reluctance to close down the operation to apprehend the murderers, but still he had all the conversations on tape.

John Wyndham had been prime minister for five years, winning a majority of one hundred and fifty seats for Labour in 2003 and was politically astute. He was also well aware Charles Henderson, his home secretary, coveted his job. "The situation, as I have discussed it," he didn't mention who he had 'discussed it' with, "is now that the people heading up this murder squad or squads have either been killed themselves, by the ultimate leader, or have fled the country."

"But what about the latest woman, now directly connected as an ex-KGB assassin – the one in the car crash near Bournemouth?"

"That's precisely my point. We have one in custody, two, maybe three are dead and one or two have fled. How many more can there be?"

"Harriman thinks it likely there are more," said the home secretary.

"Harriman, Harriman how I wish he wasn't involved in all this." The home secretary, who was a slow reader, finished his last page. "Shall I instruct the chief constable myself?" asked Charles Henderson. The prime minister thought for a moment.

"Yes, but make sure the whole investigation is closed down. Nobody is to discuss the decision with Harriman — and Charles," he paused. "All documents to be shredded, except the signed copies of the Official Secrets Act that all the investigators have signed."

Charles Henderson left the meeting with the prime minister an unhappy man. He knew that if the investigation surfaced at a later date, he was a sitting duck. All his political senses told him to cover his back. He wrote a handwritten note to Sir Granville-Davis and the chief constable, careful to keep a photocopy of each.

On the express instructions of the PM, close down operation 'Phoenix' immediately. PM also instructed to destroy all paperwork, except the signed Official Secret Act statements by officers and others. Do NOT tell Harriman.

IVAN DINOV

20TH OCTOBER 2007 – LONDON, ENGLAND

Ivan sat back, as the British Airways jet from Stockholm to London Gatwick began accelerating down the runway. Manfred Ottoman, a German he had employed before when he had worked for the KGB in Berlin, was sitting behind him, three rows back in an aisle seat. He was taking a calculated risk – nobody would expect him to return to the UK, but he had to find out what had happened to Katya. Not admitting to himself that she was captured by the British, or worse dead, his normal passive manner had become agitated. If she was in captivity he would get her out. He wouldn't think about her being dead.

As the British Airways A380 jet landed on the southerly runway at Gatwick, Captain Andrew Browne thanked everybody for flying BA and hoped to see them all soon. *Funny,* thought Ivan, *how things change. Once, not many years ago, you rarely heard from the captain. Nowadays they were all PR experts* – he smiled to himself. Ivan had decided not to use his Swedish passport, relying on one of his older aliases, Cornelius Bakke, a Dutch flower grower from Amsterdam. Ivan spoke fluent Dutch, Swedish, French and German and as he approached passport control, he took on the personality of the expert fruit and flower grower, visiting the UK on business. Mainly to visit various garden centres. The customs officer, an elderly woman with a grim determined look on her face, asked him the expected questions and he passed through. Ivan didn't bother to look for Manfred, who was covering his back, as he had already told him to meet him outside the new Marks & Spencer shop in the South Terminal. Ivan liked M&S, as the British called the store; he went inside and purchased a sandwich and a bottle of water. Manfred arrived without acknowledgement outside M&S; went inside and also bought a snack. Both men headed toward the train station and paid cash for a return ticket to Clapham Junction. Ivan had a safe house in Putney and was intending to catch a bus from Clapham. Manfred would watch for anyone tracking him. The train and bus journey to Wadham Road in London, near Putney underground station was uneventful. Strolling purposefully down the road, Ivan stopped at number 75, looked around and entered the terraced house and ten minutes later he was joined by Manfred.

The skill with counter-surveillance, was to expect the unexpected, so Ivan left the house by the back door and entered an alley at the bottom of the garden. Coming round in a loop, he entered the street one hundred metres down the road using the alley between the houses, which were built in the mid 1930s. Carefully, he surveyed all the cars in the vicinity of the safe house. One man sat in a Volkswagen Golf talking on a mobile phone. Just as Ivan began to think of moving on, a woman came out of number 25 and got into the car. The man started the engine and whilst having a seemingly heated conversation with the woman, drove off. Ivan looked around carefully, nothing else concerned him and he retraced his steps back to the rear garden of number 75.

Inside, Manfred was oiling a Walther PPK, which had been hidden under the floorboards for ten years. Setting up safe houses and safe deposit boxes containing money and false documents, had been part of Ivan and Katya's brief in the late eighties and early nineties. Although the KGB had officially been disbanded, the up and coming Putin had resurrected many of the old comradeships, with instructions to build a spy infrastructure in London, New York, Berlin and Paris. Ivan had not been part of Putin's favoured ex-KGB officers, but he knew someone who was. That man had died after revealing much useful information, including the whereabouts of a safe house in London, that even Putin did not know – 75 Wadham Road, Putney. Using one of his several disposable mobiles, Ivan punched in the number of Colonel Harriman's private phone. After two rings the phone was answered.

"Harriman."

"Colonel – you are looking for me and I wish to meet you. Meet me at the Bella Napa coffee bar opposite South Western Magistrates Court, Lavender Hill at 10am tomorrow. Come alone; if I see anyone else I will never call you again." The line went dead.

21ST OCTOBER 2007 – LONDON, ENGLAND

The morning started well, with a light breeze and intermittant, hazy sunshine; Colonel Harriman entered the coffee bar, which was really a snack bar, and sat down near the back of the empty premises. A man, Greek or Italian, the colonel had never studied languages, asked him what he would like. Ordering a coffee he sat, controlling his heartbeat. Outside, dressed as British Telecom employees, were Captain Johnson and Sergeant Quick. In a car fifty yards away was Captain Norlington and Slim Field. Colonel Harriman could feel the small pistol in the ankle holder. The Turkish or Greek man brought his coffee. A door behind the colonel opened and an elderly man hobbled out of the toilet. He walked slowly, purposefully, and then sat next to the colonel.

"The tip of the stick you feel against your leg is loaded with the poison I am sure you have identified by now. Any alarming movement by you, or anyone else, will result in your death, nod if you understand." The colonel nodded. "You know me as Ivan Dinov. I want to know what has happened to Katya Gatchevske. Just tell me quickly and to the point." The man spoke perfect English with no trace of an accent. The colonel pondered for one second. *Could he reach his pistol? He thought not. Could he throw over the table and evade the apparent hypodermic needle at the tip of the man's walking stick? A very high risk, so playing along was his only hope.*

"Tell me now and don't lie. I am getting nervous."

Colonel Harriman doubted this man ever got nervous but said, "She is dead." The man slumped in the chair, but instantly recovered.

"When? Where?" he said.

"Fourteen days ago, near the statue of Prince Albert, opposite the Albert Hall – she was shot three times at close range."

"How do I know you are not lying and don't have her?" The colonel thought for a moment.

"The person Katya Gatchevske was, in fact, previously a man. The post mortem revealed that he had undergone a sex change operation, probably in Amsterdam, thirty-plus years ago." Ivan's hand, holding the walking stick, moved.

"Careful please. I have told you what you came to find out," said the colonel.

"Who killed her?"

"Not me or the British police or Security Service."

"What was the gun?"

"The bullets taken from her head were fired from a semi-automatic pistol."

"A Russian gun?"

"Yes." The colonel felt the need to move his leg. "May I adjust my seating position?"

"No." The old man remained silent for a few seconds. "The leader of the squad that you are seeking, who has orchestrated the deaths, is a man called Ludvig Korotski. He will be trying to find me, to eliminate me as well, as I am the only remaining link to him, other than the American."

"The American?"

"Ah, that interests you I see. Well here is what we will do. I will give you a complete dossier of the operation, including the American. In return, I want an amnesty and Ludvig killed."

"I'm not sure," the colonel went to speak.

"Colonel. I know you, don't tell me you are not sure or as you British say 'all bets are off' or is it the Americans?" He laughed at his own joke. "Kill Ludvig, take photographs." Ivan took an envelope from his pocket. "Here are his aliases, usual dead drops, safe houses and deposit boxes, and a photograph."

"I realise you have been monitoring our conversation. The British Telecom van outside and the black BMW down Stormont Street, are your men. Do not take any action for three minutes, or the vehicles will ignite. I will call you tomorrow at 5pm for an update." At that, the elderly man rammed the end of his walking stick into the colonel's leg. Colonel Harriman cried out and slumped over the table. The old man muttered to the Greek owner about his friend feeling sick and left through the back entrance.

Captain Johnson, who had been listening to the colonel's conversation, waited for two minutes. No one had spoken a word since he had heard the clump. The captain thought for a few seconds then spoke the pre-arranged signal, 'Cascade' and Sergeant Quick and he approached the café

Captain Norlington, who had been waiting in the BMW, left the vehicle and approached the café from Sugden Road, suddenly there was a mild bang and thick black smoke poured from under his car. Slim Field opened the door and got out as smoke filled the interior. Using his walkie talkie, Captain Norlington called Captain Johnson. "Smoke bomb this end, under the car."

"And here as well," replied Sergeant Quick, as the BT van was engulfed in black smoke. Captain Johnson had drawn his Walther pistol and entered the café. Sweeping the room, he saw a grey-haired man looking at the colonel.

"Sir, sir, are you okay?" he said shaking Colonel Harriman. Taking one look, Captain Johnson phoned for an ambulance and called to Norlington.

"H is down; I have called for an ambulance." Just then Captain Norlington came into the cafe through the back door.

"No sign of our quarry," he said. Captain Johnson was feeling for H's pulse. "His pulse is strong."

The private ambulance they had summoned arrived from Chelsea Hospital. The colonel was stretchered off, not having regained consciousness.

Somehow Norlington sensed that the Russian Dinov had not permanently harmed the colonel, just as he had only set off smoke bombs to distract whilst he left the scene. Calling the major at the security firm's HQ, he arranged for their private physician, Dr Emsley, to go to Chelsea Hospital, whilst the other members of the team dispersed.

*

Colonel Harriman opened his eyes and tried to sit up. "Now stay put colonel – just for a few minutes," said Doctor Emsley. Not used to taking instructions, the colonel struggled to get up. "Come on old man, rest for a while," said Doctor Emsley, doubting this stubborn man would listen.

"I cannot afford the luxury doctor, now please help me up." The colonel checked he wasn't in any danger before leaving the hospital and supported by Captain Johnson, got in the waiting Lexus. The engine was started and they headed toward the colonel's house in Chelsea.

At his house, settled in his favourite armchair, the colonel relived his meeting with Dinov. The briefing only took ten minutes as Colonel Harriman filled in the blanks and they all agreed a course of action. Major Smith was to control the operation searching for Major-General Ludvig Korotski, ex-KGB head of Moscow station also known as a Dutchman, Arse deGroop or a German, Gunter Weiss.

Colonel Harriman, called in all favours. People, who they had not contacted in years, received a call if they were deemed useful in the search for the man they thought headed up the operation to murder British citizens. Twenty-four hours passed without any positive news, and then a French Secret Service officer, whose life had been saved by Paul Macroix, an ex-paratrooper who worked for the colonel in Paris, received a phone call. "Meet me at the foot of the Eiffel Tower at 4pm." Paul met the man he knew as Jacque, who handed over a single sheet of paper. A man called Gunter Weiss had entered France by car from Germany, four days ago. The border crossing at Strasbourg was being trialled for a sophisticated fingerprint, photograph and voice recognition system which was being pioneered by the French, for a Swiss manufacturer. All passports were scrutinised, fingerprints surreptitiously taken and where possible, the motorist's voice recorded. All three were then entered into a computer and checked for known criminal activity. The fingerprints of the man who had just crossed into France were identified as belonging to a Gunter Weiss, in connection with the murder of an American diplomat in Berlin three years ago. The murderer was suspected to be a German national, so it fitted. The man was also wanted in Lyon for passing a substantial quantity of counterfeit euro notes in 2006. His fingerprints, having been identified were passed to Interpol, who linked this man with the person the British were looking for. He was also a man on the CIA tracker list if he surfaced; they wanted to know, and whether he had crossed the border into France. The man had been tracked by French detectives to a hotel in Avignon using his alias, Gunter Weiss. The French had a sophisticated system whereby all foreign nationals had their details sent overnight to a logging station in Paris. When Gunter Weiss had booked in, he had been identified.

SET-UP

Colonel Harriman wanted to lead the snatch himself but realised that the after-effects of the drug used by Ivan Dinov were not entirely out of his system. Captain Johnson would command and co-ordinate the capture of the man who had ordered the Bulgarian to break into the colonel's house and who was likely to be the leader of the group who had murdered British citizens. The colonel's personal mobile rang. "Harriman." His facial expression didn't change as he responded to the call. "Come now, to my HQ. Don't report your movements to a superior and don't delay." He terminated the call.

Using the intercom, he summoned his management, in effect all ex-officers from the armed forces or secret service and several other members of his security firm, to the board room. He then phoned Terry on reception to warn him of the imminent arrival of a guest, to be shown up straight away. This time he didn't phone his old friend, Sir Anthony Greenford, the head of MI6, who had been present at most of his previous meetings.

*

The group assembled at 10.30am at the London HQ of Harriman Security. It consisted of three ex-SAS officers, an ex-Special Boat Services commander, the colonel's adjutant, Major Smith and a retired Special Branch superintendent – the elite management of Harriman Security and two sergeants, both also ex-SAS. The colonel summarised the situation, starting with the murders, the extent of the hit squad, the death of one of the ring-leaders, probably killed by the organiser and the meeting of another of the assassins, one of the main organisers at the café near Putney. The man, ex-KGB as most of the murderers seemed to be, wanted the firm to find a man called Ludvig Korotski. It was likely the man Dinov wanted to eliminate Korotski as he seemed to be the person who murdered the woman Katya. "We have been promised full details of the operation from this man Dinov if we give him Korotski."

"It seems to me that the man who drugged me," said the colonel, "is clearly aware of his vulnerability and has reversed the situation, promising to deliver full organisational details, in return for the apparent head of the operation, the man he has now identified as Ludvig Korotski. We now know that Korotski is at the Hotel Orangerie in Avignon using a German cover, registered as Gunter Weiss. He probably has a minder. We do not know who the other man is." There was a knock on the boardroom door.

"Come in." Colonel Harriman got up from his chair as Terry showed in Detective Constable de Courcy. "Ah, my dear come in, we are just discussing the operation and your input would be invaluable."

"I am sorry colonel, but I have signed the Official Secrets Act and feel I cannot discuss the case."

"Understandably so – wouldn't ask you to. So let's just bring my officers up to date," he continued. "Gentlemen, I have invited the detective constable here because I believe she is in great danger." Colonel Harriman outlined the death four days ago of Chief Inspector Hadden, significantly, he said, after he had delivered a revised report to the chief constable on these murders. "That report is known to us, and points, thanks to some brilliant detective work," the young woman blushed, "to a conspiracy of global proportions, involving a company in the USA," he continued. "I have asked the detective constable here as my personal guest, as I fear she may be perceived as knowing too much."

"But colonel, surely no one would harm me?" the young woman said.

"My dear, you have discovered a great deal. In some quarters it might seem expedient to bury the truth and only two police officers knew it and one is now conveniently dead."

"Who is your immediate superior female officer?" asked Major Smith.

"Inspector Jane Green," she said.

"Ring her on this mobile," he handed her a phone, "and tell her you are sick and won't be in today, stomach problems – if you know what I mean?"

The detective constable blushed again. When she had made the call Colonel Harriman suggested she wait for him outside the boardroom and buzzed Terry to organise coffee. She looked as though she could use a drink.

The men then continued to discuss the extraction in France of the organiser, Korotski, travelling as a German national called Weiss. They decided a team of eight would carry out the extraction, taking Korotski to a small airport outside Avignon. From there, he would be brought to Colchester airport in Essex and then to the farm the firm owned for a debriefing. The other man, Ivan Dinov, would then be lured to the farm and also captured. At that point they would have both key players. Captain Johnson was to lead the extraction in France. The colonel knew Captain Johnson was extremely volatile and ruthless and he stressed that he didn't mind what happened to the minder accompanying the organiser, but, he stressed, the man himself must be brought back alive. The meeting broke up an hour later, during which time they discussed a number of scenarios as to what to do once the information they already suspected was confirmed and names could be added to this criminal affair. Colonel Harriman followed his officers from the boardroom and sat down alongside Detective Constable de Courcy. "Now young lady, it is important you disappear for a while. Is there somewhere you can go?" The young woman thought for a moment.

"My grandmother has a house in Brighton, I can go there."

"Good, one of my female operatives will accompany you – by car, I suggest, to avoid CCTV cameras at the railway stations. Come back into my office." He led the way to his sparsely decorated office and using the internal phone summoned Amanda Hodge, one of his operatives. "Amanda, this is Detective Constable de Courcy. I want you to accompany her to her grandmother's house in Brighton. Use a hire car from Hertz up the road." Amanda nodded, knowing better than to ask questions. "Oh, and get a weapon from the armoury. Detective, go with Amanda, you can trust her implicitly." He didn't add she was a crack shot and also ex-SAS.

23RD OCTOBER 2007 – AVIGNON, FRANCE

"Major-General."

"I have told you not to call me by my old rank," said Ludvig.

"Yes sir."

"Now what is it?"

"We have been here several days now and I don't like the security of the place, shouldn't we move on?"

"I am waiting for someone, we will both stay until I say so." Ludvig was travelling as Gunter Weiss, an alias he suspected was known and he was deliberately staying out in the open. He had also spotted what he thought was probably French police who had been watching the hotel for the past twenty-four hours.

*

Captain Johnson walked slowly toward the Hotel Orangerie in Avignon. The building had four storeys, with balconies on the front bedrooms and an alleyway alongside which went around the back. He already knew the layout by researching the image on Google Earth and from a report given to him last night by Corporal Danvers. The corporal had been in the Engineering Corps before becoming a paratrooper and drew for Captain Johnson the building exits and a suggested approach. The best way to exit the premises was through the kitchens and out the rear door which led to an alley. They could park a van, fairly unobtrusively, as though it was a delivery. Corporal Danvers, on the pretext of looking for the toilet, had gone into the kitchen, acting the Englishman abroad and smiling all the time. He mapped out in his mind the geography of the place and whether the dumb waiter, the service lift connected to each floor, went to the basement or kitchen. Unfortunately it was to the basement, where the corporal discovered the hotel laundry and the destination of the service lift from each floor. Presented with the internal and external plan of the hotel, Captain Johnson had decided to attack boldly and exit out of the back door from the kitchen area of the hotel as French paramedics. The logistics member of the team of eight had hired a white van and they decided to dress as a medical team with a doctor and in the uniform of French paramedics under raincoats. Four of the team would ascend the stairs and the rest use the lift to the first floor. Their target was a room on the first floor which faced the front of the building, and one man was positioned outside to make sure their quarry didn't escape over the balcony. On investigation, one of the adjacent rooms, number fourteen, was occupied, but as luck would have it, one of the team had checked in, requested and been given room eighteen on the other side. Taking his case upstairs he entered room eighteen. Rodney Birtles, Rod to his mates, laid out the small armoury they had brought from England on the bed. Two of the them would be using Stasi sub-machine guns and the rest silenced Walther PPK pistols. The stun grenades would hopefully disable the occupants of room sixteen and no shooting would be necessary. Captain Johnson didn't underestimate this man; he was the ex-station head of the KGB in Moscow, a master of disguise who was both ruthless and cunning. The Russian also had a bodyguard, reported to be a tough-looking man about six feet tall with dark hair. The French police, who were rather conspicuous to Captain Johnson, were called off. Captain Johnson finished his final 'walk-by', dropped the paper in a public waste bin, which was the signal to commence the operation and entered the hotel lobby. Murchinson, an ex-corporal who had been thrown out of the SAS for excessive force when arresting two members of the IRA in Belfast in 1985 (one died the other was seriously wounded) followed Captain Johnson into the lobby. He collected Birtles' room key; who was booked in, under an assumed name of course, and was joined in the lift by Johnson and Norlington. They went to the second floor, and then came down the fire escape to the first floor. Captain Johnson, Norlington and Murchinson now joined by Birtles, walked slowly along the passageway on the first floor and slipped into room eighteen. Laid out on the bed were weapons. Johnson handed Murchinson and Norlington silenced pistols, held up four fingers, which indicated the connecting door was to be blown in four seconds. The muffled explosion blew out the door lock. Murchinson kicked in the door and Captain Johnson threw in the two stun grenades. Two explosions and in went Murchinson, followed by Johnson. Birtles and Captain Norlington watched the front hallway. Captain Johnson appeared at the door. "Only one dead bloke in here – it's his minder by the look of it, though there's not much left of his face."

"Okay, let's abort, everybody out," shouted Captain Johnson. The team left by the fire stairs, went out through the kitchen and all got in the Peugeot van parked in the alley. The driver, Mickey Osborne, didn't ask why there was no Russian. The man at the front of the building, Corporal Danvers, walked slowly towards his Citroen to follow the van, making sure they were not being tailed. As he went to get in the car, he felt a sharp prick in his leg and then blackness descended.

The eighth member of the team, an ex-RAF pilot, who had been more used to flying RAF Tornadoes than the firms ten-seater Falcon 2000 Executive Jet, went through his preparations. His mobile rang. "We are aborting Tony, be with you in forty minutes." Captain Johnson began to be concerned when Corporal Danvers didn't report in. "Can anyone see Danvers behind us in the Citroen?"

"No sir," replied Murchinson, the nearest to the back window looking out for the yellow car.

"Christ, what a mess, where the hell is he?" said Captain Johnson.

*

Egor Constini, the second of Ludvig's minders, a Bulgarian, ex-KGB muscle, available for a few thousand dollars, heaved the thick rope which had been placed halfway along a large branch. Corporal Danvers was being pulled up in the air by his legs, so that he dangled upside down and as he began to regain consciousness he struggled. He swung his legs and received a kick in the head for his trouble, someone muttered in a language he didn't recognise.

Danvers tasted blood in his mouth, but decided he might need the saliva in his mouth so didn't attempt to spit it out. The bottom half of a man appeared in front of him. The man kneeled down so that Danvers saw his face. It was the face of a very old man, white hair with a white moustache, but the eyes, a deep penetrating blue, were clear. "Ah, awake I see. So I will answer your questions first and then you will answer mine," he didn't wait for an answer. "I evaded the pathetic attempt to capture me by walking straight past two of your men on the stairs. I had already been warned of their approach and that you were the only man left to watch the front. Now I want some information from you." Danvers glanced past the man and could see he was in the middle of a thick forest. The other man stepped into his eye-line, walked behind him and for what seemed to Danvers an eternity beat him with a thick tree branch across his legs and did the same around the front. His testicles and head were then the main targets. Danvers knew, from his SAS training, that he could withstand a certain amount of beating – but this. His face felt wet, he suspected it was covered in blood. The bastard had broken his nose. His testicles and backside hurt like hell.

"Look, all this will stop and I will give you a drink if you tell me your name," he heard the older man say. Danvers knew that this technique, the surrender of a small amount of information, would eventually lead to him telling them everything they wanted to know, so he remained silent.

"I am getting, how do you say, pretty pissed off with you and up until now I have been kind. You have one more minute, and then we will start again." Danvers swung slightly, hanging upside down from the bough of a tree and in a semi-conscious state he considered his options. If he told them anything, it would likely lead to a torrent of information. He tested his legs again – still tied securely as he hung like a sack of potatoes. His head faced downwards, about a foot from the ground.

"You are a stupid man – now you will learn real pain. Okay Constini."

The other man began to heap twigs and small branches and then having satisfied the leader, an instruction was passed and he lit the fire. Danvers felt his body being moved upwards slightly, then let go. Christ he was swinging head first across the fire. The first pass of his body above the fire felt warm to his head and scalp. On the return swing he smelt his hair burning and agonising pain. He heard another instruction, in the unknown language and felt himself being lowered onto the fire. The pain was incredible – he heard himself screaming and he smelt his flesh burning. Again he felt himself moving, this time he was raised up. The old man kneeled down. "Come now, surely you have had enough of our improvised, is that the right word, little game. What is your name?"

"Danvers," he sobbed. "Please pour some water over my head." He could feel and smell his flesh burning and the pain, the terrible pain.

"In good time," replied the man. "Now, tell me, was this kidnap an attempt by Colonel Harriman, the CIA or the British Secret Service?"

"Harriman," he barely managed to reply, the pain was so intense he nearly passed out.

"Has Harriman found the Russian, Ivan Dinov?"

"Don't know," replied Danvers.

"Now don't be silly" – he nodded and the Bulgarian lowered the helpless Danvers toward the now robust fire.

"Don't know, swear don't know," Danvers screamed as flames engulfed his head, burning what was left of his flesh.

Mercifully he felt himself beginning to faint from the agonising pain. Then water, cold water, but the pain, he couldn't stand the pain. "Okay, you don't know. What do you know? Are they any nearer solving the reason for the deaths?" Again Danvers replied he didn't know. Danvers was basically a foot soldier, Ludvig decided, but at least they had found out Harriman was the one after him –perhaps this colonel needed a little lesson.

"What shall we do with this?" the Bulgarian asked, kicking Danvers' disfigured head.

"Blow his brains out from the rear, so as his face cannot be recognised, then burn all his fingerprints to prevent his identity being easily established." The other man took his pistol from his jacket and shot from behind. For Danvers, death was a merciful release.

The two men made no attempt to bury the body. Anyone finding him hanging upside down from the tree would report to the local police who would have great difficulty identifying the man and might decide it was a gangland or drugs-related murder.

Checking around they had left no clue as to their identity Ludvig made a decision. They drove off in the Citroen and abandoned it at Avignon railway station. Ludvig was going to travel to Vienna to meet the American, Fryer. Ludvig had a safe house in London that he was positive was unknown and completely cold. He would plan his next steps there, maybe to kill this Colonel Harriman, who was becoming a nuisance, but he did need to find Ivan.

SOME YOU WIN...

23RD OCTOBER 2007 – LONDON, ENGLAND

The Secret Intelligence Service in the UK had been significantly boosted during the Cold War and also later when the Berlin Wall came down and the need to protect the mainland from the IRA and lately Muslim fundamentalists became essential. However, despite their resources, finding this girl was proving difficult, until one of their informants rang at 6pm yesterday. "The woman detective is in Brighton chaperoned by a woman – one of Harriman's." The head of the SIS used his red desk phone.

"Beresford – get in here."

The door opened and a dark-haired man in his thirties, clean-shaven, but with a scar on his forehead entered. "The girl's here." He handed him a note. "Private contract – both women to be killed. Tell the contractors to make it look like a bungled burglary."

Beresford left without saying a word, a trick his previous superior had told him – never talk about something illegal, it could be recorded and used against you later. *Such a shame*, thought Beresford, *I rather liked her,* as he made a call.

Amanda Hodge had worked for Harriman Security for two years. She had been recruited when she left the SAS; Amanda had joined the army in 1998 and passed the arduous training for the SAS in 2003. Thinking about those days was frustrating. Trained by the SAS to a peak physical condition, an expert shot, fluent in French and a Cambridge graduate of Arab studies, she expected frontline postings in Afghanistan or Iraq. But no, she was always left as liaison or worse, as a decoy. Frustrated, she confronted her CO, who told her in no uncertain terms, that he was not having the daughter of General David Hodge killed in action during his watch. Far from helping her career, her father's reputation and position as Joint Chief of Staff hampered her every step.

Finally, having had a request for covert activity once again declined, she resigned from the squad – in anger and frustration it must be said.

Her father, finding out the news of his daughter's resignation, telephoned his old pal Colonel Harriman and virtually sold his daughter to him. Well that was how the two men described it over a couple of large malt whiskies at the Officers Club in Pall Mall. For his part, Colonel Harriman was delighted to employ the young woman. An expert in Arab affairs, who spoke Urdu and French, was extremely useful.

Now Amanda found herself baby-sitting. Alright, the detective constable was great company and a friendship had already formed, but still she longed for the real action. The two women had an easy journey to Hove, and settled into the house owned by the policewoman's grandmother. Resisting the temptation to open a bottle of Chardonnay that was in the fridge, they had sat talking about their respective aspirations and careers to date. Amanda was very pro-Harriman Security, having already been 'in action' protecting a Russian from an attempt to kill him in London.

Lurking outside number 36, The Avenue, Hove, the two Albanians planned their entrance. Georgio had already climbed the rear garden fence late last night and checked the back entrance. A back door, protected by the look of it, by a four or five-lever dead-lock, the French windows looked more promising. The brothers Georgio and Marcus were hired thugs. Part of an infamous Albanian gang operating in south-west London, they had no panache and were enforcers in the protection arm of the business. Their boss, a ruthless gangster, who arrived in England using a false passport when Greece joined the EU, had already been paid handsomely for the two deaths and tipped off about a police informer in his ranks. Given two thousand pounds, each of his men expected an easy kill when they learned the targets were two women living alone. England – the land of milk and money, they thought. Georgio, was a dark skinned, swarthy man with a ponytail and a gold earring. The taller Marcus, was broad shouldered and as strong as an ox, but he lacked Georgio's cunning or brains.

They had planned their entrance, laughing as they contemplated a little 'afters'. Marcus would kick in the French windows and they would kill the women, maybe after a little fun. From the photograph they had seen, at least one looked attractive. At 2am Marcus duly broke the lock on the French window and they entered the house on the ground floor.

Amanda heard a noise and came to life instantly, listened and then, only pausing to pick up her Walther and a clip, pulled on her panties and quickly moved next door. The young policewoman had not been asleep and the sound of the French window being forced was enough to get her out of bed. Picking up the stun gun and pepper spray, she was about to go and warn Amanda, when her door opened. Instinctively, she moved behind the door to zap the intruder with the stun gun. Just in time she realised it was Amanda.

"Did you hear that?" she whispered.

Amanda nodded and pointed to her lips. She led DC de Courcy to the bed and indicated that she lie on the top, loosening her pyjama top, to reveal her pert breasts. A creak on the landing, told Amanda the intruder was close. She moved to a clear firing position across the room, behind a high-backed chair.

Marcus edged the door open and slowly, gun raised, entered the bedroom. He had already tried another door which had been locked, this one though was open. The curtains were half drawn and moonlight streamed into the room. He saw a young woman lying asleep on the bed. *By all the gods, she has a fine pair of tits. I think I'll play with this one first,* he thought.

Georgio had gone to the other rooms on this landing. The first room he entered had a large double bed, but no sign of any occupant. The next bedroom had a single bed. The sheets had been pulled back. He felt the bed – still warm. *Where was she?*

Marcus moved slowly forward, silently for a big man. He pulled a cosh from his pocket – stun her first, it would make what was to follow easier. He moved to the side of the bed. The woman was on her back breathing with easy breaths. Suddenly he lurched toward her, a shot rang out. Marcus felt the entry wound, half turned, before dropping dead across the bed.

Georgio was halfway along the hallway when he heard the shot. *Why had that fool fired, this was to be fun – then the kill,* he thought. Entering the bedroom he saw what looked at first glance like Marcus lying on top of a struggling woman. Speaking in their traditional tongue, he told his brother to stop, they must find the other woman, when a female voice said, "Lower your gun and put your hands on your head."

Georgio turned slowly, *where was she?* He squinted in the low light. *Ah, behind the chair.* "Come now just a little fun," he said. "No harm done."

Amanda stood holding her pistol in the trained stance, her body slightly sideways on, but Georgio couldn't help seeing that her bare breasts were revealed through her nightdress and a smile broke on his face.

"Come now, you would not shoot an unarmed man." Slowly his hand moved to the second pistol tucked in his waistband.

"Put your hands on your head," said Amanda urgently. Georgio moved with great speed, diving sideways, as he pulled his Beretta from his waistband. Two shots rang out. The detective constable, still on the bed, finally pushed the dead man off her.

"Amanda."

"It's okay, both men are down. Turn on the light." Amanda moved painfully toward the man on the floor and kicked him with her foot. Satisfied, she moved toward the man on the bed. Perfect head shot. He was dead. Feeling weak she slumped and dropped the pistol onto the bed.

"Amanda you're hit."

"Yes, it's my side." Blood was gushing out of the wound. The young policewoman rushed over and picking a top from her drawer she pushed it against the wound.

"Can you hold it here whilst I phone the colonel?"

Picking up her mobile, she dialled Colonel Harriman. After explaining what had happened, he told her to take Amanda to A & E at Brighton Hospital. Leave the two bodies; he would take care of things.

Colonel Harriman rang off. *Those bastards, right that's it, I have got to get the wolves called off.* He used his mobile and phoned Major Smith. "Get Sergeant Quick and drive to the A & E at Brighton Hospital. Amanda's hit. Go and cover and bring both out if you can, to my flat." He made another call after consulting his computer system.

"Ah yes," he said. "Can I speak to Chief Constable McGleish please?"

A women's voice had answered ."Can I ask whose calling?"

"Tell him it's John Harriman." There was a pause for a few seconds as the call was re-routed.

"John you old devil, how are you, do you realise the time?" John Harriman and Alex McGleish, the Chief Constable of Sussex, were old friends from Oxford University, both had been in the successful team that won the Varsity rugby match in their final year.

"I am good, thank you, Alex, and you and Sheila, how are you both?"

"Very well indeed, John. Did I write and tell you my son Angus remarried?" The tone of the conversation changed slightly, as both men remembered Angus's first wife, Susan, the daughter of another university friend. Susan had died of cancer three years ago, leaving Angus with two children aged fourteen and twelve years.

"Yes you did. I sent him a note."

"Thank you John, he would have appreciated it. Now I am always delighted to hear from you but I sense this is not a social call."

"As always, your instincts are correct Alex. Let me fill you in as best I can – is your line secure?"

"No, so don't tell me the story – just how I can help."

"Okay. One of my people has been wounded, gunshot, protecting a young woman, a policewoman as it happens. They have just gone to Brighton Hospital. Two men broke into their house in Hove and attempted to murder them. Can you arrange for one of your best men to interview the women, they will fill in the gaps. You will need to get your forensic people to 36, The Avenue, Hove, where there are two dead men." Alex whistled.

"God's teeth, John, what's this all about?"

"Can't tell you over the phone. I am sending two of my men down to help protect the women, one of them, Major Smith, will have a note for you."

"That's good enough for me, John. It will be done and I hope to see you under more convivial circumstances soon."

"I am already lining my stomach." Both men laughed.

"Take care John."

"You too Alex." The connection was cut.

Colonel Harriman used his mobile to phone his number two, Major Smith. "Smithy, can you take a letter to Alex McGleish en route to the hospital?"

Colonel Harriman was not a man to sit idly by whilst thugs were hired to murder women, and dialled another number. "Is that the prime minister's secretary?" He had been given the out-of-hour's telephone number in case of emergency. A sleepy voice answered.

"Yes."

"Colonel Harriman speaking. I would like an urgent meeting with the prime minister, about a matter we are involved in."

"I'm sorry sir, the prime minister's diary is full for at least two weeks."

"I am quite certain that when you inform the prime minister that I have called and that a certain matter is about to hit the press, he will see me immediately."

"I will phone you back," said the prime minister's personal secretary. Five minutes later Colonel Harriman's mobile rang,

"The prime minister will see you at four pm this afternoon."

*

Ivan Dinov sat in a deck chair on Paignton seafront, watching the holiday makers. Happy people, argumentative people, children crying, young men courting – *the whole of life's treasures were here*, he thought. *And my poor Katya. How she had longed to sit on a beach at our dacha on the Black Sea.* Lately she accepted that Barbados or St Kitts was the likely destination, but that bastard had killed her. Thirty years she had worked for him. They had been together for twenty-five years. Tears didn't enter his eyes, but he longed, no yearned, for revenge. This evening he would call that Colonel Harriman on a disposable mobile phone. *I wonder if he is closing in on the bastard*, he thought and then he began to study a young man who was practising handstands on the beach.

The chapel at Newcastle Crematorium was full to overflowing. William 'Willy' Morris had been a popular man in Newcastle, not least because he liked to flash his money around. During the eighties, he had built up a chain of betting shops throughout the north-east. Flirting with the criminal fraternity, it was rumoured he bankrolled numerous armed robberies. He lived life on the edge. Inspector Wells, who had been in charge of a serious crime unit in Newcastle, had been after Willy for twenty years and sat at the back of the chapel of rest. Of course, the criminal fraternity recognised the policeman, just as he made a mental note of who attended the funeral.

Willy had inherited an 'on course' betting business from his dad in 1981. Up until then he had happily supported his dad's business, by attending race meetings and setting up their stand on his own for the best part of two years as his dad's heart condition got worse. When 'Big Joe' Morris died, Willy decided that whilst a good 'on course' bookmaker certainly made money if he learned to lay off the tricky bets the big dosh was made by the betting shops. Willy opened his first shop in a suburb of Newcastle in 1983 and found he liked being in the dry, as opposed to getting soaking wet at race courses. More to the point, he made money and then opened another shop, then another. During the next twenty years he expanded and built a mini empire of thirty betting shops throughout the north-east of England.

Early on, he had met and nurtured a big hitter, Frankie Wiseman. It also helped that Willy married Frankie's sister, Kate. Frankie Wiseman was a thug and controlled much of the criminal activities in the north-east. Time and time again Frankie had fought off attempts by the Manchester mob and a Glasgow team to take over and he did so by fear and ruthlessness. Willy and Frankie were quite a team. Willy laundered all Frankie's illegal cash through the betting shops and provided cash when needed. Frankie was finally sent down in 1995 for armed robbery. Willy was charged with possession of stolen property, but the jury couldn't agree a verdict. With Willy still outside, Frankie maintained his hold on the north-east until he was paroled in 2004, having served half of an eighteen-year stretch.

Willy had not contemplated retirement, but when one of the big chains of betting offices made him an offer, he decided to sell out.

Frankie wasn't best pleased, but accepted that Willy needed to back off, having discovered that, as his 'ol man' before him, he had a dickey heart. Kate, Willy's long-suffering wife, watched as Willy slowly deteriorated and passed away.

Supported by her brother Frankie and his wife Judy, Kate sobbed uncontrollably. She had loved her husband, who had been a good man, or so she thought. Frankie knew otherwise of course, but why tell her now.

The dark-haired man, whom Inspector Wells had observed entering the chapel of rest, was not known to him. To Egor Dunayavskaya, a Bulgarian who had already eliminated twenty-nine people, it was good news, as last week he had two people to kill – after this only one – another woman. After the brief service Egor followed the mourners to the garden of remembrance and saw his chance. The woman, Kate Morris, stayed in the archway reading the cards on the flowers and wreaths. Kate looked up to see a dark-haired man she didn't recognise, carrying an umbrella. *Strange,* she thought fleetingly, *it doesn't look like rain,* and then glancing at the card on a beautiful bouquet of lilies, she felt a prick in her leg.

Frankie found his sister collapsed across the mass of flowers. The doctor was called and declared her dead. Later, an autopsy revealed a heart attack as the cause of death. As his sister and brother-in-law had no children, Frankie inherited a two million-pound estate, but cursed his 'stupid' brother-in-law for listening to that prick of an accountant, Julian Davis, and buying some crap investments for half of the money he had got from the sale of the betting shops.

Egor got the train to Sunderland, where he would connect to Manchester, and sent a text to Katya. Funny she had not been in touch with a new list of instructions.

Marcus parked his Mercedes 140 perfectly, making certain that he was squarely between the parking bays. Last year he had seen a middle-aged woman scrape the car next to her as she attempted to get out of the parking space at Waitrose – and she had just driven off. *Standards these days*, thought Marcus as he reflected that years ago, most people would have left a note of their name and address, admitting liability.

Marcus Hall, aged seventy-five, prided himself on his independence. He visited Waitrose every Monday, the best day to shop, as far as he was concerned. Somehow the produce always seemed better, fresher and the sell-by dates were longer. On Tuesday he went to a bridge drive in the local village hall, on Wednesday he met Alfred Sams and they went for a walk along the seafront and sometimes up onto the cliff top. Thursday was washing and cleaning and he often took a trip to see his daughter Melanie in Hastings. Friday he went to Rotary – the club met at the local Conservative Club in Seaford and the weekend was spent pottering around Lindfield Cemetery to lay fresh flowers on his wife Maude's grave. Marcus had been a widower for two years and still desperately missed his 'Old Duck'. Hence his routine – he found he coped better.

Carefully walking with his trolley up and down the rows in the supermarket, Marcus picked up and examined the items that interested him. *It must be his accountant's training,* he thought – attention to detail and all that. Finishing his week's shopping, he bumped into 'Bunny' Warren, an old friend from Rotary.

"Fancy a coffee?" said Marcus. Both men were retired professionals. Bunny had been partner in Fish and Warren Solicitors and Marcus a partner in Woodscott & Brewer Accountants. "See the chancellor has sold our gold off at a rock-bottom price."

"Why on earth politicians are allowed to deal in real things is beyond me," replied Bunny. The two men ordered their coffees and one of Waitrose's cakes 'made in our in-store bakery', it said.

"How is Cecilia?" asked Marcus, referring to Bunny's invalid wife.

"Oh, so-so," replied Bunny.

The two men chatted about the economy, interest rates and investment returns before parting company as Bunny stopped to buy a lottery ticket. Marcus didn't bother, considering it a waste of money, having calculated the odds against winning were too great, years ago.

As he loaded his bags into the boot, Marcus didn't see the blond-haired man walk up to him, but suddenly felt a sharp stabbing pain in his leg. He turned, but then collapsed; the trolley ran across the parking space next to his car and collided with a large 4x4 being parked by a woman. She was about to get angrily out of her car, when she saw the man on the floor. Quickly she reached him, turned him over into the recovery position and felt for a pulse – nothing. Later she explained to the policeman, that she had felt sure there had been a tall man in a raincoat, but he was nowhere to be seen afterwards.

The police autopsy showed death from heart failure, but Inspector Faulds sent the file to the unit at Scotland Yard. After all, two people had been certain a male five feet ten inches to six feet, wearing a raincoat, had approached the deceased person and the inspector had a feeling all was not as it appeared.

Dmitri had travelled from Seaford Railway Station to Brighton, then doubling back, caught a bus to Newhaven, where he boarded a ferry for Dieppe. He had sent a text to Katya without reply and had completed his list of targets. The only thing to do was return to Russia and await further instructions, and planning his route, he intended to travel by rail to Germany and then on to Moscow. *It was curious,* he thought, *no communication from Katya.*

24TH OCTOBER 2007 – VIENNA, AUSTRIA

Ludvig walked apparently aimlessly along Taborstrasse in Vienna toward the internet café. Since his arrival by train from Avignon via Paris, he had spent a day relaxing. He had even picked up a prostitute yesterday and indulged his grotesque sexual habits, leaving the girl unconscious in a seedy back-street hotel. He had, of course, disguised his appearance and had now changed identity from the middle-aged German schoolteacher, Gunter Weiss, to a shy man from Dresden, Ulrich Wilger, a retired shopkeeper. Humming quietly, Ludvig was pleased with himself. He calculated he had amassed over six million pounds in his Cayman Island bank account but he proposed to pull the plug on the whole operation. That might involve killing the man who gave him the job in the first place – Morgan Fryer. He didn't know for certain why Fryer wanted these people dead and he couldn't care less. Each month a million pounds was deposited into his bank for administering the operation and he had received a 'bonus' of a further half a million pounds due to the success of his operation. Ludvig gave Katya, who regretfully he had had to eliminate, an extra £500,000 to co-ordinate the op in London, but that had been money well spent as the whole operation had gone like a dream. Ludvig had sent Morgan Fryer a message to be at the rendezvous point in Vienna today at 4pm. Fryer would have travelled overnight from New York to London and then on to Vienna. Ludvig had contacted another old colleague, an East German, Dieter Belman. Now he had eliminated Katya and Ivan Dinov was on the run, Ludvig needed another pair of eyes to watch his back. *Old habits die hard,* he thought, but Dieter needed the money and accepted the familiar role as cover agent without any persuasion.

Approaching the Hotel Neuwaldegg on Neuwaldeggerstrasse, Ludvig checked his watch – 3.55pm. Fryer would be inside in the foyer. Dieter would be watching his back. Ludvig felt his mobile vibrate, he answered: "Ja." Dieter's Russian was not good so Ludvig answered in German. Listening he clicked the phone off. Dieter confirmed that Fryer was in the foyer and that he had spotted at least one and probably two likely minders, a man and a woman. The man, dark-skinned, black hair and blue suit was sitting facing the swivel door of the hotel. The woman, a brunette in a dark blue suit and white blouse, was in the seat three away from Fryer. *Why do Americans always wear blue suits?* pondered Ludvig.

Ludvig entered the hotel walking slowly through the foyer toward the lifts. Fryer got up and followed, so did the man and the woman. Ludvig went into the coffee bar on the ground floor and chose a seat facing the doorway. Fryer came into the room, saw him and came and sat at his table.

"May I join you?" Fryer asked in Russian. Ludvig nodded, scanning the room for Fryer's shadows. The woman had come in first, sitting facing Ludvig's table, but across the café some twenty feet away. Ludvig didn't see the man. Dieter, his own man, sat on a swivel chair at the counter watching Ludvig and the woman, whilst apparently reading a copy of *Der Spiegel*. Glancing at the woman, *not bad looking,* thought Dieter, *but where was the man?*

"You requested a meet," said Fryer. Ludvig continued looking around as he spoke.

"The operation in Britain has been suspended. Three of my people are ill, so I have decided to leave things for a while."

"I see." Fryer had his back to the door but knew Sharon was close and the Cuban Sanchez had just entered the coffee bar. "Is this a permanent cessation of business?" asked Fryer.

"I think so. It is hot in Britain now," replied Ludvig.

"Do you expect to go back?" asked Fryer.

"Not at the moment but anything is possible," replied Ludvig.

"Okay, good job. I'll be in touch." Fryer got up, but as he went to leave, Ludvig handed him an envelope.

"Read it in your car," he said. Fryer walked toward the coffee bar door. Ludvig scratched his nose – that meant let him go, but watch his minders.

As Fryer reached the pavement, a black Peugeot 406 pulled up and he got in to head back to the airport. The Cuban, Sanchez joined him in the back seat. "Well that was simple enough. I don't think he intended to hit you," he spoke in a lazy Spanish-American drawl.

"Don't underestimate him; he is one of the deadliest killers you will only ever meet once. I shall be glad to get out of this place." He opened the envelope and examined the contents – a single sheet of paper. Typed on the pale blue paper was a paragraph:

A solicitor in London has been instructed to send a dossier on my firm's activities to the Chief Constable at Scotland Yard, if I don't text him every week. You don't know the day of the week or the firm but rest assured any move on me will be your downfall. Incidentally they also have a recording of every conversation.

So that's it, thought Fryer, *he has insurance in place, no wonder he was so confident about withdrawing from the contract.* Taking out his mobile he spoke urgently, making two calls. "Leave him. Yes you will still be paid," he replied to the voice on the other end. The two snipers Fryer had carefully placed opposite the hotel, one in the front bedroom, the other on the roof of an apartment block, would not be eliminating Ludvig today.

Ludvig had watched as the dark-skinned man followed Fryer out of the café. The woman got up, glanced at Ludvig and left just as her mobile rang. *Just calling off the troops,* thought Ludvig, imagining Fryer reading his note. Ludvig's own mobile rang. A Russian voice said, "You were right, I have spotted a marksman on the roof of the apartment opposite, but he is folding up his rifle and he seems to be leaving." Ludvig terminated the call without reply and then sent a text to his shadow Dieter.

"I'm leaving laundry exit, tell Gregory." How many people the American had placed around the hotel Ludvig did not know, but his insurance policy was in place and he doubted Fryer would risk a double-cross. *Maybe I should contemplate killing him, hmm,* thought Ludvig as he left.

The Citroen pulled up at the rear of the hotel, Ludvig got in. "Take me to the station," Ludvig instructed Dieter. "We are going to London to find Ivan, you tail me as usual."

Vienna station was busy. Dieter hurried, keeping pace with Ludvig, some thirty feet behind him. Ludvig had given him a ticket in the car – one way to London, via Paris. *Strange to be going back to London,* thought Dieter, *but you don't question Ludvig.*

The colonel took a cab to Downing Street, accompanied by Captain Norlington. Arriving, they were let through the security checkpoint and walked to number ten. The door opened as they arrived.

"Colonel Harriman?"

"Yes, and you are?"

"Frederick Haverley-Court, the PM's private secretary. He is expecting you, this way please."

The man dressed in a lightweight blue suit led them upstairs and they knocked and entered the cabinet room where so many decisions were taken.

The prime minister was sitting reading in the centre of the huge table, he looked up and came around the table to shake hands.

"I am sorry colonel, but your colleague has not been screened and has not signed the Official Secrets Act, so he will accompany Frederick downstairs for afternoon tea."

Captain Norlington looked at the colonel, who nodded. As Norlington left, Sir Aubrey Granville-Davis entered. "You two know each other," the prime minister said.

"Yes," replied Sir Aubrey. Colonel Harriman nodded, he knew the head of MI5 alright. The prime minister returned to his seat in the middle of the table.

"Now colonel, or may I call you John? What's happened, your message indicated the matter was urgent!"

"Yes," responded Colonel Harriman. "Yesterday, evidence came my way that there had been at least fifteen further murders." Silence… He continued. "Then it was reported to me that a few days ago the chief inspector, who had led the investigation, had been killed in a…" he paused, looking at Sir Aubrey, "hit and run accident. Now there has been an attempt to murder Detective Constable de Courcy, who had been taking a rest with one of my colleagues."

"Oh dear. I am sorry to hear that. Is the girl alright?" asked the PM.

"Yes," Colonel Harriman looked directly at Sir Aubrey, "the hit failed and both the men who tried to kill the women are dead." There was a slight shift in position by the head of the Security Service. The colonel continued. "The reason for my call is that I believe the whole story is about to break on the internet, with details of many of the murders, and the story is linking the death of the chief inspector. The prime minister looked at his head of security.

"Do we know of this?"

"No prime minister."

"Who is your source?" asked the PM.

"I am sorry, but I am sure you understand I cannot break a confidence."

"So when is this story likely to break?" asked the PM.

"Well… I am keeping the lid on it, but if there were any more deaths, say for example the young DC de Courcy, then the story would almost certainly be on the internet news channels and then all hell would break loose."

The prime minister sat for a second, wrote something on the pad in front of him and then looked up. "I think we understand the situation. Thank you for coming to see me." At that Colonel Harriman stood, they all shook hands and he left.

*

The prime minister hadn't taken long to realise Harriman was threatening him. At first he churned inside. *How dare he come in here and threaten me, the prime minister.* Then he considered the options. Like all politicians he compromised. "Call off the dogs Aubrey," he told the head of the Secret Service, "for now."

25TH OCTOBER 2007 – PAIGNTON, ENGLAND

Ivan had sat long enough on a deckchair at Paignton on England's Devon coast. *By now,* he thought, *the Harriman Security people would have made an attempt to capture Korotski and he was certain they would fail.* He knew very few organisations were proficient at truly covert operations. Yes, Harriman was expert at SAS-type operations – seek and destroy – but not covert watch and then lift operations. Korotski would spot Harriman's men and run. Katya had been a skilful operative and she always suspected that Major General Korotski would eliminate her if things turned nasty. So, she had prepared a list of his likely safe houses. One of which she told Ivan he considered completely clean, completely without risk. He was wrong because Katya knew exactly where it was and Ivan was going there now to kill the bastard. Ivan used his disposable mobile to phone Harriman and was told 'there was no news'. He suspected he was lying and dumped the mobile.

*

The Albanian, Jak Bardhi, had arrived in London in early 2007 using a fake Italian passport. He had heard that the Romanians were cornering the lucrative prostitution and drugs markets and wanted to see the opportunity for himself. As soon as Romania was invited to join the EU, he organised twenty of his best men giving them all Italian passports and returned to London. In the space of one week, he had eliminated the two Romanians running a central London prostitution racket and taken over their territory. He met the other influential parties, the Turks, the Chinese, the blacks and several London gangsters and did a deal. He was not a greedy man; he only wanted a slice of the action – namely central and southwest London. An uneasy truce was established. During the war in Serbia, when he had been supplying guns to both sides, he met an Englishman called Maxwell. This Englishman he had known immediately was a spy. He tried a honey-trap using a gorgeous Kosovan woman but the man had outwitted him and turned the tables. So much so he had to get out of Serbia rather fast, as the Serbs didn't seem to like him supplying guns to their enemies. When he launched his campaign to oust the Romanians, the man he knew as Maxwell paid him a visit. He told him in no uncertain terms, that his remaining in England, was very much dependent on his co-operation. Now and again they would ask him to do a little job for them. Usually it was eliminating people. Three times in the past year he had 'co-operated'. Now two of his best men had not reported in. Georgio was a stickler for keeping him informed so he knew something was wrong. His mobile rang.

"Meet me at 11am Café Nero, Clapham Junction station forecourt." He didn't like it but you didn't disobey Maxwell. He had tried to stop the bastard blackmailing him early on and had 'lost' two men who were deported in double quick time back to Albania. So he was sitting in the window overlooking the ticket office when he saw him come in and purchase a coffee. Joining him at his table Maxwell spoke quietly.

"So, you employ idiots?"

"What do you mean?" replied the Albanian.

"Both your men are dead; they failed to deal with the targets." The Albanian had suspected that Georgio and Marcus had failed, or they would have contacted him by now.

"So do you want me to try again?" he asked.

"No," replied Maxwell.

"I have lost two of my best men; they are worth more than the payment."

"Tough."

At that Maxwell got up and left. *One day*, thought the Albanian, as a nerve on his face ticked, *I will kill that man – perhaps soon.*

LUDVIG

25TH OCTOBER 2007 – LONDON, ENGLAND

Colonel Harriman sat up in bed drinking his favourite drink, a decaffeinated cappuccino coffee. The new coffee machines made terrific coffee, almost better than Marco's in the King's Road, Chelsea. As he contemplated the murders, he couldn't get it out of his head – they were actually closing down the investigation. No conclusion, still no closer to motive for probably over one hundred and eighty murders of British citizens, even though that young DC de Courcy had come up with a theory. *Typical of the shits of course*, he thought. *Who cares for the poor sods paying taxes keeping them in their elevated positions; well I do!*

Turning on the television in his bedroom, the BBC news was reporting a horrific crash near Bournemouth. He listened for ten minutes, went to the bathroom, the old bladder wasn't what it used to be, and after reading for a few more minutes, retired for the night. The colonel never took sleeping pills, he liked to be alert at all times, but tonight, as he lay unable to get off to sleep, he searched his mind for any clues they had missed. *Of course*, he thought to himself, *whatever the reason, the killer came for me, it is shared with one hundred and eighty other poor dead souls.* Getting up from the bed, he sat at the bureau in his room, and taking out a note pad began to jot.

Background, Job, Forces, Enemies, Nationality, Service Men/Women, Age, Education, Hobbies, Clubs, Associations, Lifestyle, Sex, Wealth, Residence and so on, he wrote. *There must be something else here but what? Is it what the young DC thinks it is?* Leaving the desk he returned to bed, turned off the light and settled down. He often found writing down his thoughts helped him settle and sleep.

That same day, Ludvig Korotski had boarded the Eurostar at Paris. His favourite method of entering the UK was through the tunnel and getting off at Ashford International Station. There were few formalities;

in any case his documents were perfect. Ludvig had travelled by train from Vienna to Paris, where he had stayed for one day – now was the time to go to London. The journey was completely uneventful. The German, Dieter, still tailed him watching for a suspicion of any contact, but there was none. *The English are funny,* he thought. *So clever in many ways, yet leave their borders open. Mother Russia is not so stupid, President Putin has re-established excellent border control, as i know to my peril. Such a pity not being able to return home. Still once I have eliminated Dinov and Colonel Harriman,* he thought, *I will travel to South America for a holiday.*

Ludvig decided to get off the Eurostar at Ashford International where he presented a forged Swedish passport using his favourite Swedish alias, Sven Andersson; he had changed identity again. After Ludvig passed through passport control, a signal was sent to an office on London's South Bank.

"A man who we think is Ludvig Korotski is in the country. Came in via Ashford using the alias Sven Andersson – a Swede."

The German, Dieter, was getting bored with this assignment. Back in England again, and as usual he trailed the major with not the slightest sign of any surveillance. *The man is paranoid,* he thought. *Nobody could possibly realise we have returned, he changes identity so much even I cannot remember who he is now.*

They drove in the stolen Fiesta, in silence, toward London and their destination, a house in Epsom, Surrey, aiming to arrive about midday.

Later that day, posing as television aerial installation men, they recced the house. Ludvig laughed to himself as he thought how they had stolen the TV repair van. They had just dumped the Fiesta and were walking down Sevenoaks High Street when a man pulled up in a white van, got out and ran into a shop. Ludvig nodded to Dieter, they both got in the van and drove off. *How foolish to leave your keys, but how easy,* he chuckled to himself. The ladder on the top of the van had proved really useful as they checked out the house in Epsom. White overalls, found in the back of the van, added to their disguise, enabling them to disable the alarm and wander around the house.

Deciding to enter that evening by the French windows, they watched from the third stolen car, a silver Audi (they had dumped the van earlier) as their quarry drove onto the hardstanding alongside his house. They expected he would be surprised that his alarm did not go off when he entered, but like most people would think he had either not activated it properly when he left that morning, or assume there was a fault and call the alarm company tomorrow. They waited, watching a downstairs hall light come on, it was 8.30pm and they settled down patiently, as they waited for darkness in the house.

The two shadowy figures, both dressed in black with balaclavas over their heads, approached the front of the house. It was a small semi-detached house in a close and at 2am the street was quiet, except for the occasional dog barking. *Animals sensed things,* thought Ludvig. Ludvig and Dieter had travelled to Ashford, Kent on the Eurostar from Paris. Ludvig liked to get off at Ashford and steal a car around the terminal. People went away for days or weeks leaving their car in the multi-storey car park. Ludvig had never heard of this suburban area, Epsom, but had decided to go for the number two in the Harriman organisation, rather than risk the top man. After all the Bulgarian was no fool and he had captured him.

At 2am, satisfied that the occupant had gone to bed and that no activity was obvious in the area, Ludvig and Dieter broke into the house through the French windows. The old-fashioned French windows were easy for the ex-KGB operatives and in minutes they were in the through lounge. Using a pencil torch, a thin light helped them avoid the furniture. Slowly they went upstairs, both were armed. As they suspected after they had recced the house earlier, their target was sleeping in the larger, middle bedroom. They could hear his snoring from the top of the stairs. Suddenly the snoring stopped and both men halted, listening, waiting. Silence and darkness. Ludvig indicated Dieter to go ahead and they crept along the landing silently. The door to the bedroom was open, Dieter entered. A figure lunged at Dieter, who crumpled and fell to the floor. Ludvig, who had deliberately hung back, waited. A man in pyjamas turned on the light, immediately seeing Ludvig. He turned.

"Stop or I will kill you," said Ludvig. The man stopped. "Hands on head – now," Ludvig barked. "Go lie on the bed face downward, keep hands on your head."

As the major slowly edged toward the bed, he was calculating his chances of turning the tables. One was down, but the other had him cold. If they had come to kill him, then he would already be dead, so perhaps the best course of action was to wait and see what they wanted. He could hear the other man slapping the unconscious man's face until he moaned and the second intruder, who he had hit over the head with a vase, began to recover. "You are good, but not that good, so don't even think of doing something stupid," said Ludvig sensing the man lying on the bed was thinking about reacting.

"Du Hurensohn (you son of a bitch)." Dieter sat up cursing. Dieter found his gun, picked it up and got up.

"Nein," said Ludvig sternly, as Dieter went to shoot the figure face-down on the bed. "One move out of place and my companion will kill you, major," Ludvig referred to Major Smith's rank for the first time.

"What do you want?" Major Smith knew that there was a reason for the intruder stopping the other man from killing him.

"You are the second in command of the Harriman Security, yes?" Ludvig said already knowing the answer. Major Smith nodded, hands still on his head.

"I have a request for the colonel, but first my friend is going to tie you up. You have already given him a giant headache," Ludvig laughed.

"Hands down," Dieter said. Major Smith was roughly bound expertly and very tightly.

"Now listen major," said Ludvig. "Your colonel is wondering what is going on, why all the deaths, what is the connection, yes?" Ludvig prodded the major's leg with his pistol.

"If you say so," replied Major Smith.

"I will give him all the information he needs and evidence against the originators, but he must do something for me first."

"And that is?" replied the major.

"You are hunting for Ivan Dinov. I want him too," said the masked man.

"And?" questioned the major.

"You have the resources to find him quicker than me." Ludvig took a folded sheet of paper from his back pocket. "Here is a list of all his aliases and an up-to-date photograph. When you find him, telephone the number on the bottom of the paper and when I know where he is, I will email you with the information your colonel requires."

"That's it?" Said major Smith. "We give you Ivan Dinov; you give us the complete story and the people behind it?"

"Yes, but," Ludvig paused, "when you find Ivan Dinov you must back off. If I see any of your men or other agents, I will not send the information you require – is that clear?" Ludvig prodded Major Smith.

"Yes, it's clear, but why should we trust you?"

"You have no choice." At that Ludvig fired the stun gun he had found in the bedside cabinet earlier and Major Smith collapsed after receiving 15,000 volts in his back.

It took Major Smith two hours, after he woke up from the effects of the stun gun, to free himself and phone Colonel Harriman. Thirty minutes later Captain Johnson and the colonel arrived. The major repeated the message and after examining the sheet of paper left by the intruders, Colonel Harriman decided to call a meeting tomorrow at the Park Lane headquarters of Harriman Security. As they talked Doheny arrived, Colonel Harriman had asked him to ride shot gun at the major's house for the rest of the night.

Promptly at 10am Colonel Harriman entered the boardroom. Already present were his senior officers and Sir Anthony Greenford, the head of MI6. Sir Anthony and Colonel Harriman were old friends and the colonel had decided to include him in their discussion. "Let me start by saying that it is quite clear that the people leading the investigation into the murder of countless British citizens, have decided to cut us out of the loop – major… " Colonel Harriman looked toward his second in command to bring the assembled group up to speed with the attack on his person last night.

They all sat quietly as Major Smith recounted his capture. Captain Johnson felt his anger surge as the major elaborated on his ordeal and finally the stun gun which knocked him out. Captain Johnson was a first class officer, but was inclined to be headstrong, especially when a man who had saved his life in Beirut was threatened. "Can we find these men sir?" Captain Johnson said angrily.

"I don't think we can, captain," replied the major. Colonel Harriman looked up, "We have an opportunity to find out who's behind these murders and I believe we have a duty to pursue this opportunity. But it will, in my view, take us in conflict with the government. I have invited Sir Anthony here, not in an official capacity, but as a stakeholder (Sir Anthony had 5% of the shares in his wife's name) in Harriman Security Ltd." He held up his hand. "Sir Anthony has a conflict of interest and I will ask him to comment, if he is able, but he will not be present when we discuss whether we go after this man Ivan Dinov – Sir Anthony."

Sir Anthony Greenford was a career spy. He had first come to the attention of the secret service at Cambridge in the late sixties. A bright student, he excelled academically in languages and at sport, notably rowing and rugby. A Cambridge blue at both sports, he was recruited to join the Foreign Office on leaving university in 1970. His father, the noted diplomat Sir Roger Greenford, was the British Ambassador in Moscow during the very difficult days of the late sixties and early seventies. Anthony Greenford was intrigued by the apparent activities of the KGB and the Embassy's own officers and spent every vacation when he was at university in Moscow. When an obvious honey-trap, a beautiful blond Russian girl, tried to pick up Anthony at a Swedish

Embassy party, he confessed to his father that he would like to join the Secret Service. His father counselled him against this; hence he joined the Foreign Office. But the intrigue and the excitement of a life in the Secret Service continued to attract Anthony, such that when the permanent secretary of the Paris Embassy asked him if he would be interested in talking to Pilkington-Smyth, the then head of MI5, he readily agreed. That was the start of his career in the world of espionage and counter espionage. Promotions came readily and he distinguished himself in the field in Ireland and with counter terrorism in the UK. Sir Anthony was persuaded to switch departments in 1981 and work for MI6 and now headed up that department. Sir Anthony met Colonel Harriman in Belfast in 1978. Lieutenant John Harriman was working undercover for the SAS; Anthony Greenford was at the British Embassy in Dublin. The Irish and British governments were tracking a particularly dangerous wing of the IRA. This splinter group had been responsible for bombs in several Northern Ireland towns and a mainland bomb in London. Anthony Greenford nurtured an informant who fed him information – good stuff. Then one day his informant told him that the leader of the splinter group, Sean O'Connor, was going to cross the border at Crossmaglen. A detachment of the SAS and an army unit were sent to apprehend him. Anthony, always in the thick of things, had positioned himself illegally south of the border at the crossing point, waiting for developments. Suddenly, his passenger door was wrenched open, he tried to pull out his pistol but was confronted by two armed men, one of them struck him in the mouth. They got him out of the car and were pushing him toward a Land Rover hidden amongst some trees, when a voice said, "I'd leave him where you found him boys."

Both men turned, raising the pistols in their hands – two shots rang out. The man next to Anthony cried out and fell to the ground, the other Anthony couldn't see. Anthony turned to find a man dressed in camouflage fatigues holding a pistol.

"Come on," he said, "before his friends arrive." Before he left the man took out a camera and photographed both men and dabbed their prints on a small vacuum flask. "We will use your car to cross the border – you drive." Later Anthony had to move heaven and earth to find out the name of the man who saved him, but it took six months before he was able to meet John Harriman, a lieutenant in the SAS. They had been firm friends ever since.

Colonel Harriman had been speaking for a few minutes, as Sir Anthony daydreamed about the day he had met the man in front of him. "Sir Anthony," said Colonel Harriman. "You have no objection if we only ask you to comment if we are missing something of national importance." Sir Anthony nodded.

Colonel Harriman picked up a white A4 sheet. "I received this note this morning, anonymously." He began to read out loud. "At least fifteen more victims have been identified; here are some of the details; a widow, Mrs Diane Home, age seventy-five, lived in Salisbury, Wiltshire. Struck whilst in church, apparently died of a heart attack. Post-mortem revealed the deadly concoction of poisons injected into her leg. She was a retired fashion editor.

"A couple, Mr and Mrs James Trundle, male aged seventy-nine, female seventy-four, both murdered in Bournemouth, shot at close range probably a Glock hand gun. He was a retired accountant, she a housewife.

"Smedley Woolcott, age seventy, retired sports agent fell on the train line at Andover Station. A witness swore a man had pushed him on to the line, but no CCTV or other witnesses.

"Sir Marcus Hall OBE, aged seventy-six, retired solicitor. A witness in Bridport, Hampshire said she thought a man had struck 'the elderly gentleman' with an umbrella. Post-mortem revealed death was heart failure caused by the poison ricin and the cocktail mix."

Colonel Harriman paused to let the report sink in, "Gentlemen it's simple, there are at least two assassins still killing people. The deaths on this list are in southern England usually Hampshire or Wiltshire, or in the north, or Scotland. One man could not be responsible, as these deaths are much too far apart for the killer to have travelled from one end of the country to the other in the time."

Major Smith passed around a file. "Major Smith has prepared a report detailing what we know of Ivan Dinov, the man we have been chasing for the past week. To summarise, he is aged early to mid sixties, medium height, frequently has dark hair. He is a brilliant linguist, speaking English, French, German and obviously his native Russian. Completely ruthless, he is an ex-KGB section head in East Berlin and the CIA have reported him working in Iran, Afghanistan, Libya, Saudi Arabia and Pakistan. He has been linked to atrocities in Spain, Egypt, Afghanistan and Iraq. He always worked with a woman, Katya Gatchevske, now deceased. He is freelance and in fact would not be welcomed in Moscow as he was an opponent of President Putin in the eighties. He is the master of disguise – a ruthless killer who we think partly orchestrated this operation."

"Sir," Captain Norlington spoke for the first time. "Do we have any idea who else he might be working with?"

"Major Smith," said Colonel Harriman.

"The CIA have, in their own words, 'struck out on this one'," replied the major.

"Then we have to catch Ivan Dinov," said Captain Norlington.

"Or if the leader is the man Ivan Dinov told us about who paid the major a visit, he is also a clever and dangerous man," added the colonel, "and he wants Dinov, presumably to eliminate him. In short they are trying to kill each other and each is supplying us with the information we need."

MURDERS CONTINUE

26TH OCTOBER 2007 – LONDON, ENGLAND

Ivan was impressed. The Virgin train to London's Paddington station had been on time and had been very comfortable. He then travelled by underground train to Victoria Station, using counter surveillance techniques, twice by 'hopping off' and 'hopping on'. Usually he had Katya or another watching his back, but he had let the Bulgarian who had been covering him return to Sofia. For what he had to do, had to be 'one to one'. Changing buses twice, Ivan reached his final stop and got off the number 159 bus at Clapham Common.

Twenty-four years ago Ludvig Korotski, Ivan's old boss running the KGB activities outside Russia, had set up a series of safe houses in London and the South of England. All but one had been properly declared in KGB records. It had been Katya's job, as Ludvig's number two, to purchase the properties through nominees and dummy companies, but she had accidentally come across one property in London that Ludvig had purchased using state funds that he had not recorded or accounted for. Katya had told Ivan as they had pondered informing the minister, but decided to keep the information to themselves, perhaps a useful card to hold in the future. Ivan was certain that Ludvig would use the house as his London base for several reasons. Firstly, there was the obvious: he thought nobody knew of its existence. Secondly, he probably had a stash of documents and weapons hidden on the premises.

Ivan walked by the address on the Clapham Common Southside. It was a large Victorian house in need of some TLC. The Venetian blinds on the lower windows were all closed; there was no sign of life. "Good, he's not here yet," muttered Ivan to himself. Walking the length of the road, Ivan discovered an alley. Looking around he checked for the umpteenth time – no sign of any surveillance – and went down the alley.

The Controller's operatives had all been assigned their positions and to avoid confusion each had a code number.

Mickie, number six, pulled up in the milk float. "I think I have him, gone around the back shall I follow?"

"No leave him, number two." The call sign for Sheila Marsh, who was sitting watching from the window at number 18 Southside. "Number two, go hang out some washing."

"Number three, a man is approaching down the alley, it could be our man. All units stand by."

Ivan walked quickly along the alley, pausing briefly at the back of what he thought was number 16 Southside. He was about to climb the close-boarded fence when he heard a door close from the house next door. Dropping back down, Ivan peered through a gap in the fence and saw a woman carrying a washing basket. He stayed very still. She finished hanging out some shirts and underwear, both men's and women's. *Hmm*, he thought, *mixed family unit next door*. She went back indoors.

"Number two here, no sign of him around the back."

"Number three here, he's here alright he has just climbed the fence." The man who was number three was Dave Edmunds, who was at the rear of number 18 looking from the top bedroom.

"Right if he breaks in or lets himself in, we go and get him – stand by."

"Captain are your men ready?" said control.

"Ready," he confirmed

The Controller referred to the SAS squad who had arrived minutes ago and when the suspect disappeared around the back, they had alighted from their vehicles. Eight crack SAS soldiers, heavily armed, waited instructions.

"Number five here, the man is trying to break in," the man reporting was dressed as a tramp and had come down the alley from the other direction.

"Soon as he is inside we take him. Numbers two, three, four and five go in the back. Captain take your squad in the front and people, I would like him alive," said control.

Ivan used his skeleton key and turned the lock. He knew he would have about twenty seconds to disable the alarm, but in any case he had rightly judged that nobody would bother, even if it did go off. Inside was the tell-tale sound of an audible alarm warning. He walked speedily through the kitchen, the control box was likely to be in the hall. He saw a cupboard and looked inside. Yes, he looked at the system, produced wire cutters, snipped two wires and then applied his connector. The alarm immediately stopped. The small palmtop computer he had attached to the alarm system, informed the system all was okay, by searching for the most punched in sequence and repeating it.

Just as Ivan was about to explore the house, all hell broke loose, the front door was opened and three black clad men in army fatigues faced him in the hall. Ivan was about to run back the way he had come, when two men came from the kitchen, both pointing pistols at him and a hooded soldier who had followed him down the hall shouted "Hands on your head – do not move," menacingly pointing his machine pistol as he walked towards him. *Christ,* thought Ivan, *after all these years I missed something.* He raised his hands.

"Captain here, we have him coming out the front."

"Excellent, number one, please organise the repair of the house immediately."

Flanked by two SAS men, a handcuffed Ivan was bundled into the back of an innocent looking white Ford Transit van which left immediately, followed by the SAS squad vans and number five in a VW Golf.

"Number five here, convoy heading to Saxon Court."

"Number two, three and four resume surveillance – one more fish to catch."

*

Sir Anthony sat in his office at the MI6 headquarters overlooking the River Thames. The intel from the CIA had been good. They had 'turned' an agent who had been working directly for the head of the KGB over twenty years ago who had given them two safe houses in London. For two decades the CIA had kept the information to themselves until the British had asked for links to Katya Gatchevske. The CIA headquarters in Langley, Virginia kept records dating back nearly one hundred years and a trace on Katya revealed she had been KGB. The interesting thing had been her partnership with Ivan Dinov and significantly they both worked in the 1980s for Ludvig Korotski. It was Ludvig's number two who had set up the two 'safe' houses in London and Sir Anthony had followed a hunch and staked out both and the one at 16 Southside, came up trumps.

Colonel Harriman replaced the telephone. He still had a business to run and his resources were painfully thin. The Russian oligarch Danil Alexseer, one of the three Russian billionaires whom he provided security for, was demanding more operatives to join the two already at his disposal. The colonel shuffled his operatives using his online system. Two of his usual employees were unavailable and he pondered for a few seconds the loss of Corporal Danvers, who was almost certainly dead. All his people knew they were in a high risk occupation, but nevertheless…

His thoughts turned to the young policewoman, Detective Constable de Courcy. Amanda Hodge had told him she was a very courageous young woman acting as decoy with only a stun gun and pepper spray to protect herself with. Amanda was still in Brighton hospital, she had lost a great deal of blood, but the wound, a bullet had creased her side, would heal quickly. The colonel pondered on recruiting more operatives, but they were and had to be, so choosy. He would make the young DC an offer once this was all over, subject to talking to her grandmother. He smiled to himself as he thought about that family – the de Courcys. The young policewoman had checked in at the Grand Hotel in Brighton, insisting she would not leave until Amanda was able to journey back to London.

"Colonel Harriman," he answered his mobile.

"Ah John, you might care to know, one of the two gifts mother wanted has been purchased. We are waiting for the other," the phone went dead.

He wondered which one they had apprehended. Anyway either way the chances were that the remaining Russian would be after him, or at least make contact using his landline. He called his number two, Major Smith.

"Smithy, come to my office will you?"

Major Smith was one of a rare breed of former SAS men who had been captured by the IRA and had lived to tell the tale. During an operation in Armagh, informally known later as 'Bloody Sunday', the Parachute Regiment became engaged in one of the worst engagements of the conflict. Lieutenant Smith, as he then was, found a useful vantage point as a spotter looking for an IRA sniper firing from a block of flats.

The two SAS men were on the balcony of a four-storey building sending info to the Paras on the positions of possible snipers, Unfortunately for them, the occupants of the flat they had been spotting from returned, having been themselves involved in the early skirmishes with the army. The shock of finding two dishevelled men on their balcony was brief as all of the three men pulled pistols. Both the lieutenant and a corporal were taken to an IRA safe house and interrogated for two days. Both Smithy and the corporal gave up small snippets of intel, nothing serious but sufficient to stop the beatings. The corporal was unfortunate; he had admitted a lower rank and the hard man of the Provisional IRA wanted to kill someone. Lieutenant Smith, complete with serious injuries, was exchanged for a dissident held in the Mays Prison in Belfast, Michael O'Shaunessy. He had been caught earlier that month attempting to plant a bomb in Belfast city centre. It had taken considerable persuasion by the colonel of the SAS in Hereford, to convince his superiors to arrange a swap. Admittedly they thought they were getting two for one, but the body of the corporal was never returned.

Smithy had blamed himself for the capture and it was only after the SAS commander gave him a dressing down for not recognising the truth that he was just unlucky, that he began to deal with the guilt and returned to active duty. Smithy swore to get revenge and nearly a year later shot dead all the callous men who murdered the corporal. A tip-off to the RUC, the Ulster police force, had led to information as to the whereabouts of the men who by now were on the most wanted list. The SAS mounted a snatch operation to lift the men led by Captain Smith. Smithy caught them cold in a farm house in County Armagh. They resisted and he shot two of them the other threw down his gun. His superiors were not amused he had killed two possible sources of information and he remained a captain for three more years serving in Ireland and Iraq.

Colonel Harriman had recruited the retired Major Smith as soon as he decided to set up his security firm. He had worked with him many times and knew he was a dependable and first-class officer. The men had a mutual respect .

"You wanted to see me John."

"Yes Smithy. I am getting concerned – look at this printout." He passed the major a breakdown of their personnel and their assignments.

"I see what you mean, the loss of Corporal Danvers and now Amanda has left us thin on the ground."

"I think we are going to have to return to the field ourselves Smithy unless we can find two or three new recruits. Have you got any pipeline candidates?"

"As a matter of fact there is a captain about to retire from the regiment. He's forty-five and been pen-pushing for over a year now."

"Good record?" asked the colonel.

"Yes, first class – wounded in Afghanistan rescuing a unit of Paras trapped by Taliban forces a year ago."

"Has the injury healed?"

"Yes, but we would have to respect he has had muscle grafts to his right leg and limps slightly."

"Still, another pair of hands. Why don't you approach him soon? Meanwhile, I am reluctantly pulling off one of the boys looking after the detective constable, de Courcy," he grunted, "who is staying at great expense at the Grand Hotel in Brighton." It was unlikely they would attempt another try at the young detective constable, but the colonel believed in the exception rather than the rule and a slight concern did not go away so he had left DC de Courcy with one bodyguard.

27TH OCTOBER 2007 – CARLISLE, ENGLAND

Muriel glanced at herself in the mirror – satisfied, she picked up her umbrella and her handbag, shut the front door and left for London. She was catching the 8.10am to Kings Cross, to meet two old friends. Muriel Lanson had been the editor of Life magazine, the biggest selling women's magazine of the eighties and nineties. Before she had retired in 2001, after an uninterrupted reign as editor of more than twenty years, she was renowned. Some of her staff were scared of her – she could be belligerent and very angry when an article failed to meet her high expectations. But that was why the magazine outsold its peers every month for twenty years. Two hundred and forty-six issues – Muriel could remember the front page of many of them. The 'exclusives' with Princess Diana, Madonna, Gorbachev, Donald Trump, Tony Blair, Prince Andrew – it simply went on and on, her list of coups. She was, in fact, Dame Muriel Lanson, but she never used the title, she still felt a little bit of a fraud, after all she was 'only' the editor, she hadn't written the pieces. Admittedly it was usually following one of her famous dinner parties that she secured an interview with the rich and famous. Failures – yes she regretted, that despite all her persuasive powers, she was a beautiful and formidable woman, she could not persuade Prince Philip to feature. Too many skeletons, she suspected. The train was on time and Muriel settled down in the first class compartment.

Hristo had followed his next target, a woman, Muriel Lanson to the railway station and watched as she bought a ticket. She purchased a magazine and boarded the London train. He hadn't bought a first class ticket and was forced to sit two carriages away. Still the train was crowded, he doubted he would get the chance to kill her on the train, but he had to be careful not to lose her in London. The train got even more crowded as they stopped at York. Luckily for Hristo he had decided to buy a ticket to the train's destination, but he would have got off if necessary.

Muriel had dozed some of the journey, but spent most of the time writing. She was writing a book about a young woman's rise to fame and fortune in the film industry. The book was a little more erotic than Muriel had intended, but when she began to chart the life of this woman her own fantasies and sex life seemed to transfer to her heroine.

She blushed as she read her latest pages – god, if only she had had that much fun!

Pulling into Kings Cross, only five minutes late, Muriel let the crowds get off the train before disembarking with her overnight case. A porter offered to carry it, but she politely declined – *she was after all sixty-two not eighty-two,* she thought. Suddenly, she felt a sharp prick in her calf, she felt unwell virtually immediately, went to sit down, then blacked out.

Hristo had skilfully jabbed the woman Muriel with the top of the umbrella. It had been good of her to wait until everyone had got off the train. At first he thought the porter was going to interfere with his plan, but when she shook her head, he followed her down the platform toward the ticket barrier, then looking around, stabbed her in the back of the leg. Strolling through the ticket barrier he inserted his ticket, and then heard a commotion behind him, but he didn't look back and walked slowly toward the exit marked 'underground'. Hristo had already decided to change his appearance and got the tube to Hammersmith, where he booked in at the seedy Orchard Hotel. Katya supplied him with 'safe' overnight stops, usually run-down hotels in quiet areas, but before he checked in, he visited a gents toilet and changed his overcoat to a zip jerkin and put a trilby hat on to hide his blond hair.

Later Muriel's funeral made all of the national papers due to the list of dignitaries who attended. Members of the Royal family, film stars, television presenters and most of Fleet Street's good and the great turned out. Muriel's sister Kate heard great things about her sister. The funny thing was Kate knew her sister had been for a full medical only a few weeks ago and the coroner's verdict of 'heart failure' seemed somehow wrong. Still what did she know, she was only a doctor.

Earlier Hristo had one more name on his list, a man in Sunderland, and realised that he would have to get a train back up to the north of England. He sent a text to Katya adding 'running out of friends to visit, please send more', he liked killing people.

27TH OCTOBER 2007 – DARTMOUTH, ENGLAND

Sarah and David Wilson lived in an old terraced house, five minutes from the ferry at Dartmouth. When David had retired as chairman of the Principality merchant bank in London, Sarah and he had spent two months deciding where to live. Their house in Ascot was very grand, but seemed empty these days, as all three of their children had long gone. Two daughters had married and both now divorced, the other child, John, was an actor and although linked with countless women, usually actresses much younger than himself, he never looked like 'settling down' as Sarah put it. They could go to the south of France, to their lovely property just outside St Agulf. But no, David said it was too hot in July and August and anyway both the girls virtually lived in their four-bedroom villa and when in close proximity to both his daughters he wanted to shout at them to find a decent man, not the rubbish they usually brought home. They decided to stay in England, but it was by chance they discovered the 'escape' as Sarah called their charming cottage. David always liked the south-west area and when shortly after he retired, they decided to take a well earned holiday, Sarah suggested Dartmouth and they rented a house overlooking the River Dart. On one of their excursions into Dartmouth, they spotted the 'For Sale' sign on a beautiful white timber clad cottage near the town centre. They obtained the keys, the property was empty, a probate sale, and they promptly fell in love. The cottage wasn't as sumptuous as their Ascot house but that was part of the attraction. It was perfect. A hideaway, only two bedrooms so children and grandchildren would not be able to stay. They called the cottage 'Wilson's Last Stand', it was their joke. They didn't consider that they were being selfish, it was just that after a hectic life and the last few years clearing up both daughters' messy divorces, they wanted time on their own. The life was idyllic just the two of them, with occasional visits from friends and Sarah's sister Emily and her husband George. They often frequented the super restaurants in Dartmouth or Brixham and they sailed a small thirty-eight-foot yacht around the coast and sometimes spent time on the Isle of Wight or the Channel Islands. The first year of retirement had whistled by. Both their daughters had two children and they were their main outgoings – school fees. All four grandchildren boarded, two at Winchester and two at Roedean, a girl's school near Brighton. David had set up a trust fund, so it wasn't that painful and both daughters had done well from acrimonious divorces. Life was good.

That was until that fateful day when, returning from a rather splendid dinner at a pub in Totnes, they discovered a break-in at their cottage. Perhaps, if David had not gone into the cottage, Sarah would not have felt she should follow him. Both were shot at close range. The police later said that forensics had shown that a Glock pistol was used from about five feet away; both were shot twice, once in the chest followed up by a head shot. The chief inspector from Devon and Cornwall Constabulary sent the papers to the special unit at Scotland Yard who were requesting details of unusual deaths and murders, because it didn't make sense. Why had a man and his wife, who it seemed had no enemies in the world, been murdered in this professional way? The chief inspector thought it looked like a hit but a thorough investigation had not uncovered a single clue as to the killer or a motive.

The Bulgarian, Egor Dunayavskaya, now masquerading as a Dutchman, Filip Gerritsan, had decided to shoot both the man and the woman as there was no other choice. He couldn't see how he could kill them both with the poison and it seemed simple just to shoot them.

He sent a text to Katya and began planning to leave England, as he had finished his latest list. He would go to the rendezvous in Paris; perhaps he would get news there.

CAPTURE

27TH OCTOBER 2007 – LONDON, ENGLAND

"Elderly woman approaching." Number two picked up the message from number three and trained binoculars on the woman. The woman walked past the gate of 16 Southside slowly.

"There is a dark-haired man on the other side of the road – could be covering the woman," reported number three.

"I see him," reported number six, who was on the face of it delivering milk to the houses in the street.

In the command centre, a black van one street away, the operational head made a decision. "Scramble the backup – code red."

The sergeant in charge of the SAS unit waiting at Clapham Police Station signalled to his unit, a cranking up motion, and all eight men sped out of the door. The police inside the building were glad to see the back of them monopolising their canteen. Two unmarked black Transit vans with smoked glass windows headed towards Clapham Southside.

"The woman has gone down the alley," reported number six. "The man is approximately fifty yards behind her."

"If the man turns down the alley, take him out number six."

"Acknowledged," he replied.

"The woman is at the back gate," reported number three.

"Sergeant, how close?" asked control to the SAS unit en route.

"ETA one minute," replied the sergeant.

"Same procedure as before sergeant, except you have a key to get in," said control.

"Affirmative," he replied

"The woman is walking up the back path of number 16," said number three.

"All operatives listen, two, three, four, seven and eight go in the back way thirty seconds from now," ordered control.

"Number six reporting, the man has been taken down in the alley. He was carrying a pistol."

The elderly woman used a key to gain entrance to the back of 16 Southside. Had she noticed, a close inspection might have revealed some slight wood chipping around the lock, otherwise all seemed as it should be. The alarm was triggered, so she moved toward the cupboard under the stairs. She punched in the code, not noticing the repair to the system, when the front door burst open and a number of hooded men rushed in. The woman fired her pistol, the first man fell, others came behind him. The woman ran back the way she had come and faced four men, one of which fired a tazer. The woman fell, unconscious.

"The house is secure," reported in the SAS sergeant. "Ambulance required – man down."

"Number two here. We have the woman, tough old bird, tried to shoot us before we tazered her."

"Take her to the usual place and also the man in the alley," instructed control.

The woman was handcuffed, blindfolded, gagged and bundled into one of the Transit vans with number two and number three. The man who was shadowing her was literally heaved into the back of the other Transit, shortly before a third and fourth transit appeared. Three SAS soldiers also got in the van with the man, the rest of the squad and the sergeant, left for Chelsea helipad, via a hospital in Chelsea, where they were taking the wounded man.

"Number five, clean up. Sergeant, I expect you will pass on our congratulations to your men," said control.

"Yes I will," the sergeant replied.

"Good job sergeant – I hope your man is not badly wounded."

"Thank you sir," he replied.

"Numbers four, seven and eight follow on behind the Transits and take over security at Saxon Court when the SAS leave."

"Affirmative," they all replied in turn stating their number.

Members of the Secret Service took over from the SAS once the small convoy reached Saxon Court.

Visible from the road going north from Brighton toward London was a large imposing country mansion set in grounds at least five hundred yards from the motorway. There was no immediate slip road, the only approach was from an earlier slip road on the motorway if you were travelling south to Brighton and then through country lanes. Arriving at their destination the SAS soldiers and the MI6 operatives bundled out the man and were slightly gentler with the woman, although extremely careful, she had after all seriously wounded a SAS trooper.

Both the prisoners were put in separate soundproof cells. The imposing early Victorian house had been converted into a training school with secure accommodation and was used when the security services wished to interrogate a person outside of Special Branch involvement. Normally interrogation was by skilled Secret Service personnel, but not in some instances, especially if it was deemed excess force might be necessary, then they used 'specialists'. There were no twenty-four hour holding rules at Saxon Court. Prisoners were not given a phone call. In fact no one knew they were there and the prisoners certainly had no idea where Saxon Court was or who held them.

After several hours, the first of their prisoners, who they already suspected was Ivan Dinov, was brought by number two and number three manacled, blindfolded and gagged, to the interrogation room. His blindfold and gag were removed as he was strapped to a chair. Ivan blinked and looked around. *Professionals*, he thought, *this might prove difficult.* A man pinned his arm as a needle was inserted and an injection, he suspected the so-called truth drug sodium pentothal, was flooding into his veins. His clothes were cut away, leaving him naked.

"What is your name?" a voice asked. Suddenly Ivan in his subdued state felt an enormous surge of electricity up his right arm and he jumped immediately. "What is your name?" the voice asked again. Once again a surge of electricity swept into his body – this time through his leg. "What is your name?" again the voice. Ivan felt like he was having a 'heart to heart' talk with a friend.

"Ivan Dinov," he said – they would know who he was anyway. *Save strength,* he thought, as he tried to control his mind from being taken over by the drug.

"Why did you go to number 16, Southside, Clapham Common?" No response. The operator sent the current through both arms and both legs simultaneously. Ivan screamed. "Answer the questions. Why did you go to number 16, Southside, Clapham Common?"

"To kill Korotski," Ivan replied.

"Why did you want to kill this man Korotski?" the voice asked. Again silence. The voltage was increased. Ivan's body racked in pain as his muscles spasmed, sweat poured down his face. "Answer! Why do you want to kill Korotski?"

"He killed Katya," mumbled Ivan.

"Louder!" the voice instructed.

"He killed Katya Gatchevske," said Ivan. Ivan was soaked with perspiration and he knew he had to give some information to stop the interrogation.

"What were you and Katya doing in this country?" asked the voice. No answer. A charge of electricity racked his body and Ivan screamed a piercing scream and nearly bit his tongue off. Blood was running out of his mouth, and then a charge of electricity was applied to his testicles. He screamed in pain.

"Alright, alright, but I want to do a deal," he barely whispered.

"Deal, you think you are in a position to do deals?" Another electric charge swept through Ivan's body, again his muscles spasmed and his body only stayed in the chair as he was strapped in. During KGB training the more extreme training officers had subjected some of the trainees to torture, which included electricity – but nothing Ivan had faced before had prepared him for this. "What were you and Katya doing in this country?" the voice asked again.

Ivan paused and another bolt of electricity passed through his genitals and his body – he screamed again.

"Eliminating targets," he said so quietly they couldn't hear him.

"Repeat louder."

"We were eliminating targets," Ivan replied, anxious to delay more torture. Ivan racked his brains; *keep thinking*, he thought to himself. *What knowledge did he have to prevent all this?* There was a pause.

"How many targets?"

"Tens, twenty, fifty or more, I lost count. Katya knew," replied Ivan.

"Why did Katya know?" the voice said.

"She was Korotski's second in command; all the arrangements were through her."

"How did Korotski decide the targets?"

Ivan thought for a second. "I only know that usually Katya sent each operative a list of six targets, which included a profile, some information and usually a photograph," replied Ivan.

"How many field operatives were there?" the voice continued. Ivan paused, but he saw out of the corner of his eye a man's hand turn to the 'on' switch.

"No, no, I am thinking," he said. "Eight," he replied.

"Confirm louder. How many operatives?"

"Eight," he repeated.

"Give me all their names, then later you will write them down." Ivan began to list firstly the Russians: Anton Hineva, Anastasiya Stoickkov, Hristo Penev, then the Bulgarians: Viktorya Abamova, Dmitri Baich, Egor Dunayavskaya, Ivan Gelperin and Leonid Kokorov. With the Bulgarians, he took longer because he didn't personally know them all.

"Are those their real names?" the voice said.

"Yes, as far as I am aware," Ivan replied.

"When did you commence this operation?" the interrogator asked.

"Over one year ago," Ivan replied.

"Give him a drink of water, he is being very co-operative," the voice said. Ivan gulped down the water and the man poured some over his testicles.

"Now Ivan, answer this next question truthfully, or you are going to die when the switch is turned on." Ivan suddenly realised they had soaked his genitles, would the electricity and water kill him? He doubted it but to take a chance… The muscles in his leg twitched involuntarily.

"Who did Korotski receive his instructions from?" the interrogator asked. Ivan thought for a moment and they gave him a few seconds.

"Come now Ivan, we know the answer, you are not telling us what we don't already know." The voice sounded softer, sincere. Ivan, who for once felt out of control, was considering the truth of that last statement. Did they know, or not? Did he hold the key to getting out of here alive, or not?

"Now Ivan, answer the question or die," said the voice.

Ivan decided, "Korotski met an American, we thought ex-CIA, in Sweden and Berlin. He was the contact between us and whoever wanted these people killed."

"Not enough, we know that already, who gave the contract?" Ivan began to sweat and for once in his life, felt trapped.

"Answer!" shouted the voice.

Ivan began talking again. "Once, after a meeting with Korotski, Katya followed the ex-CIA man to New York. He went to a building in Manhattan."

"What building?"

"It was a building with many storeys, as the Americans say, a skyscraper." Ivan was beginning to formulate an idea.

"What business operated from the building?" the voice asked less angrily, knowing they must have obtained more information.

"Katya wrote down the businesses. She could not go after the CIA man, there was security, but he went to the first floor." There was a pause; Ivan knew his inquisitor was receiving instructions.

"You will write down the name of the businesses," the voice said.

"I cannot remember them all – but Katya has them on her laptop computer and lots of other information she collected," Ivan replied. There was another pause and once again Ivan knew the man was receiving instructions.

"Where is that laptop now?" The voice was softer, conciliatory. Ivan paused for a second as though making up his mind.

"A safe deposit box at Paddington railway station in London," Ivan replied.

"Where is the key and what is the number?" asked the interrogator.

"The number is twenty-seven, the mechanism is number coded. She would have used her old KGB number 462764." Ivan knew Katya's old KGB number off by heart as his was one digit higher.

"Take him back to the cell," the interrogator said. When Ivan had left, instructions were relayed.

"Number two, go to Paddington, and collect whatever is in the box. Number seven and number eight organise the doctor to check his tongue, but keep him manacled, hands and ankles and be careful, he is very dangerous." They left Ivan in his cell pondering on his future, blindfolded and manacled.

*

Colonel Harriman picked up his mobile.

"Hello."

"John, we now have both. Will talk soon."

*

Ludvig Korotski was not uncomfortable in his cell. He didn't like being blindfolded or manacled, but so far they had left him to think. It was probably the British Security Service that had him and he knew lots of things they would like to know.

The German who had been shadowing Ludvig, captured at the house in Clapham, quickly gave up what little information he had. His name was Dieter Belman and he was also ex-KGB. He had not been part of the original team built by Katya and Ivan Dinov. Korotski had approached him in Berlin to act as his bodyguard and for extra surveillance; he had only been working for him for three weeks.

They decided he knew very little and proposed to eliminate him. He had no CIA or Interpol record and had only served in the KGB from 1989 to 1991 and only then, on home soil, but nevertheless, they didn't want to let him go or put him on a public trial.

27TH OCTOBER 2007 – SAXON COURT, ENGLAND

Number two had returned with Katya's lap top computer, via the London headquarters of MI6 on the south bank of the River Thames. There, the computer was left to be analysed, a report to be given to the director by 9am tomorrow morning. The computer technician, a boffin who preferred machines to people, complained, but immediately began to examine the Dell laptop. It had not been difficult to crack Katya's code and he quickly ascertained that there were ten killers, including Ivan and Katya, but not including Ludvig Korotski. Ludvig supplied the names of the victims and some background to Katya who arranged meetings with the field operatives at the same time supplying disposable mobiles, the deadly poison, false papers and details of the victims, often extensive. Sometimes a spouse was listed.

Number two took the false passports, cash and credit cards to number one, together with a sheet of paper with ten companies in Manhattan and the names listed of ten killers. Fifteen minutes later, an urgent red coded message was sent to a diplomat at the British Embassy in New York, really a senior MI6 agent, to go to the address of an office block in Manhattan and send a report back on the businesses in the building and any possible connection to the UK.

A red alert was issued to mainland police, British security services, Interpol and the CIA to trace and apprehend Anton Hineva, alias a Dutchman, Bastian Meijer, Hristo Penev, alias Albert Smit, the Bulgarians Dmitri Baich, alias Daniel de Groot, Egor Dunayavskaya, alias Filip Gerritsan and a woman, Viktorya Abamova, alias Liv Brusser. Another man, Ivan Gelperin's, name had been deleted by Katya, they didn't know why, so added him to the list of wanted suspects.

*

At the SIS location in Surrey, the service doctor visited Ivan Dinov and looked at his tongue. He had bitten into it during interrogation, but it did not require sewing up – it would heal, the doctor said, but eating would be uncomfortable. "So what?" said number four.

Ivan Dinov sat blindfolded and manacled. He was thirsty, but refrained from requesting water; KGB training had said 'in captivity only ask for the most important things as it may be the only thing you get'.

He used the time to think. He would have to give them more and contemplated what might save his life. Fortunately, Katya had insisted they document all of the contacts they had made worldwide before and since leaving the KGB in somewhat of a hurry in 1988. After their hasty flight from Russia, they had worked for Al Qaeda, the Taliban, the Iraq government and the Iranians and had met some of the key members of Bin Laden's inner circle. They also knew several 'sleepers'. Agents who had been planted into the USA over twenty years ago by the KGB and importantly, a ring of agents who lived and worked in the USA, but were really Muslim fanatics. In Britain there were three sleepers, also all Muslim fanatics they had helped to train and equip with false identities. But the most significant of the intel he could trade Ivan knew was the code-name of the mole in the British Security Service. MI5 had a high ranking officer who was a Muslim sympathiser and had fed important information for the attacks to take place on the London Underground. Ivan knew that this man had also given up a British MI6 undercover agent in Tehran two years ago, who had been tortured and shot. Ivan knew that because he had helped with the torture but he wouldn't tell them that. He reflected how Katya and he had remained at liberty and felt confident he had enough intel to negotiate. The effect of the drug they gave him was wearing off.

*

Number one read the report. He had been in the office since yesterday reading the transcript of the 'interviews' with Dinov and the Bulgarian and having meetings with number two and the psychiatrist he used to determine the mental state of the prisoners. The result of the meetings had been a general conclusion that Ivan was giving up intel only very little at a time. They thought Ivan was confident he had something they wanted. They decided that the Bulgarian knew very little. The other prisoner, a woman, had been manacled and left.

"No breakfast or liquids for either, make 'the woman' stand up manacled and blindfolded for three hours. Then take her to the 'shower room'," a colloquialism for the wet room where high-powered hoses and freezing cold water were used to weaken the resolve of stubborn people. "Take off the woman's clothing and the wig, leave 'her' naked." Number one had known Ludvig Korotski was disguised as soon as he heard they had apprehended a woman.

Number two, accompanied by number four and number five, hauled Ludvig to his feet. "Now you will stand. Any attempt to sit and you will be beaten. We know you speak perfect English so don't bother replying." Ludvig was still disguised as a woman. He had changed into his favourite, the grey-haired elderly woman, at a service station toilet outside Ashford and he was still dressed in the wig and clothes as Ingrid Bergan, a Swedish national. After an hour, he tried to lean against the wall of the padded cell and the door opened and he received a sharp reminder across his legs. *At least,* he thought, *the bastards had to stay vigilant,* but he knew he would tire as they had kept him awake all night with loud music and frequent visits to the cell.

*

The colonel's mobile rang.

"Hello."

"John, the matter is getting interesting, let's meet."

"Okay, Aquarium Southside – say 2pm."

"Good choice, we are dealing with some right sharks."

Ivan Dinov had been left alone and not been interviewed again he thought for at least four or five hours. He didn't know precisely how long he had been locked in the room, but since the torture he had been fed twice and he had slept on the mattress on the floor, albeit fitfully. Ivan was wondering why they had not resumed his interrogation when the cell door opened. Two men he had not seen before came in.

"Come on, get up." They yanked him up from the floor and frogmarched him out still manacled. This time they went much further than before. *Where were they taking him?* He began to feel apprehensive. One of the men knocked on the door.

"Come," a voice said from inside. One of the men yanked off his blindfold.

Ivan was surprised to be entering a rather pleasant room and blinked at the first daylight he had seen for some time.

"Ah, Ivan, come and join me."

A rather distinguished-looking man, greying at the temples, was sitting at a desk at one end of the room. Ivan was dumped on a chair, still manacled, the chain clunked as it hit the floor. Ivan looked at the man sitting behind the desk, blinking as the autumn sun shone through the windows.

"Tea?"

Ivan accepted a mug of tea from one of the men who had half-dragged him to this room. The tea was not hot; not taking any chances, thought Ivan, of him throwing scalding tea over one of the guards – very professional, must be MI5. The man behind the desk began to speak.

"Now Ivan, you must know you are in a very perilous situation. Some of the people I work with would like you to disappear – permanently." He stopped talking, allowing the statement to sink in. "Me," he paused, "I believe you have a great deal you can tell us and it's my job to find out what you know. Now tell me about Ludvig Korotski."

Ivan saw no point in withholding information about Ludvig and gave a full account of the Russian's past history, coming right up to date with his approach to Katya to manage an operation in the UK.

"Good, we have recovered Katya's laptop and examined the hard drive." The man behind the desk was reading a sheet of paper. "Your friend Katya was very meticulous." He carried on reading and turned the page. "Hmm, you realise that I could have you shot now. You have helped murder one hundred and ninety-two British citizens. You will not be tried in a court of law and sentenced to life imprisonment. The public in Britain will not hear of your despicable acts. You only have one chance to save your life. What do you know might interest us that will save you Ivan?"

Ivan studied the man. *Yes, that's what I would do, kill the perpetrators of the murders, no public trial – he's not bluffing.* "Well?" the man said.

"You have a mole in the Secret Intelligence Service. I know his face, but not his name. But first, what is in it for me?" The man put down the piece of paper he had been holding.

"Ivan, you are not in a position to bargain. You either tell me what I want to know or you will die this morning and be taken for cremation. Nobody will miss you or mourn for you, a callous and ruthless murderer."

"Alright, but I must know who I am talking to and I want a new identity and to be flown to a place of my choice. Finally I want the privilege of killing Ludvig Korotski."

"My name is Sir Anthony Greenford; I am the head of MI6." Ivan knew the name but not the face, the head of MI6 had been virtually a recluse for over twenty years – but how did he know the man sitting in front of him was really Sir Anthony Greenford and the head of MI6?

"I need more, I want to see your passport and the home secretary, what's his name, Charles Henderson?"

"Come now Ivan, you ask too much. I can show you my passport, but how does that prove who I am and as to meeting Henderson that's out of the question." Ivan thought for a moment.

"What about if I knew of another mole, this time in the White House administration?"

"We might be interested – and your conditions remain?" replied Sir Anthony.

"Yes, I want to have the assurance of Henderson, the home secretary, that I will be released and flown where I choose."

"You realise that we will not release you until we prove conclusively the intel you provide?"

"Of course," replied Ivan.

"Very well, I will see what I can do." Sir Anthony nodded and Ivan was picked up from both sides and taken toward the door. Sir Anthony selected a number on the red phone, but before he dialled he asked another question.

"Oh, by the way, why was the name Ivan Gelperin deleted from Katya's computer?" asked Sir Anthony.

"He changed his mind and was eliminated," replied Ivan.

"Ah, I see." Sir Anthony nodded and Ivan was blindfolded and taken back to his cell.

*

Ludvig was concerned. *Why hadn't they started their interrogation?* They couldn't be checking anything he had told them – because he hadn't given them anything – yet. Still manacled to the wall, at least he now had a bed. He didn't realise Ivan was in the cell two doors down.

*

Chares Henderson was about to go to the House of Commons when his personal assistant, a charming young woman, Penny Hardcastle, with whom he had been flirting for three months, knocked at the door.

"Telephone call on the red phone."

"I'll take it in here. Charles Henderson." He recognised Sir Anthony Greenford's voice.

28TH OCTOBER 2007 – LONDON, ENGLAND

Frederick Haverley-Court had been the prime minister's personal secretary since the general election of 1989. *Today was going to be particularly difficult for the PM*, he thought, as he looked at the on-screen diary. A meeting this morning with the French foreign minister still pushing for a further change in the EU constitution, a meeting early this afternoon with the chancellor to discuss the worsening economic situation, prime minister's questions in the house at midday which would be awkward today as the opposition leader intended to raise the PM's commitment to hold a referendum on the new EU treaty. Now a call from the head of MI5, Sir Aubrey Granville-Davis, urgently requesting a meeting. Reluctantly he had scheduled in the head of the Secret Intelligence Service for 10am, a quick thirty-minute meeting before the French arrived.

Sir Aubrey was shown into the cabinet room and sat waiting, a briefcase by his leg. In hustled a clearly agitated prime minister and that pompous twit Frederick Haverley-Court. The head of MI5 pulled out a red file which was the signal for the prime minister to excuse his private secretary.

"Tell me Aubrey," the PM said, rather agitated. "I have a very busy schedule today."

"You might be interested to know, prime minister, that MI6 have apprehended both the co-ordinator and we think one of the senior protagonists, in the nasty affair we have been discussing." The prime minister looked up.

"Well, what's the problem, that's good news isn't it?"

"Well," he paused, "that rather depends."

"Oh, get on with it man, depends on what?"

"Really, as homeland security is involved, these two men should be interrogated by MI5. However the head of MI6, Sir Anthony Greenford, won't pass them over, claiming that there is significant intelligence to be gathered on foreign agents, included Bin Laden and other Muslim terrorist activities abroad including cells and other intel."

"Well is he right?"

"Sir it's homeland security I am concerned about and these two men should be turned over to MI5 immediately."

"Very well I will talk to the home secretary. Now I am sorry but I have the French foreign minister outside – I must get on."

At that Sir Aubrey Granville-Davis left more confidently than when he had arrived. The prime minister called Frederick, his personal secretary.

"Ask the home secretary to call by this morning, before question time and wheel in the French and Laurence," who was the foreign secretary.

*

The home secretary, Charles Henderson, had a political nose like a giant antenna. He sniffed the air as he considered the memo on his desk. *The PM wishes to see you before question time.* Since receiving the message he had examined the questions the prime minister faced at midday in the house and decided that none were connected with his department – although there was the question of ratifying a new EU treaty without a referendum. The party had promised, at the last election, a referendum if there were to be changes to the EU treaty and its power base. But the prime minister and a significant number of cabinet members were opposed to giving the public their say. Charles knew he had sat on the fence. Now what could 'he' want?

Promptly, at 11.25am, the home secretary arrived at number ten Downing Street and was, as usual, shown into the waiting area outside the cabinet room. Five minutes later, the PM, who had a tactic of keeping you waiting, sent the loathsome Frederick, his secretary, a man the home secretary would sidetrack as soon as he was PM, to show him into the cabinet room.

The PM sat in the centre of the large desk surrounded by papers. "Ah, Charles, please sit." He carried on examining a sheet. "Sorry, just reminding myself of the running order for questions in the House. Do you realise the Liberals are intending to push for a vote on this referendum nonsense?"

"Yes, I heard prime minister."

"Well I am having none of it. Now, what did I ask you to call for?" He pretended to rack his brains. "Ah, yes. Aubrey Granville-Davis tells me MI6 have taken two principals in this murder affair – you remember we closed the file last week, or was it the week before?"

"The week before last, prime minister."

"Well Aubrey is not happy. MI6 are conducting an interrogation and he feels it's all linked to homeland security and his department should be in complete charge. I have decided, all things being equal, he is right. Can you talk to Sir Anthony Greenford and tell him to hand these men over?"

"I will talk to him today, prime minister."

"Good, well must away to the House." He referred to the House of Commons. No mention of sharing a car – *God, the arrogance of the man*, thought the home secretary.

*

The home secretary used the secure line in the PM's outer office to contact Sir Anthony Greenford, the head of MI6.

"Meet me at the House of Commons tearoom at 4.45pm." It wasn't a request as Sir Anthony acknowledged.

The home secretary called for his black Rover, he had asked for a newer vehicle but the PM said they must keep supporting the British motor industry, *twit*, thought the home secretary. Arriving at the House of Commons he met Lord Brotherton, a crony from the House of Lords.

"Angus, are you going to the dinner at Lady Rothermere's this evening?" He always called Charles Henderson by his second Christian name, following their time at Eton together.

"Yes I am old boy," replied Charles Henderson.

"Good, I have a hunch we may have to think about recruiting support soon." He winked at his old Etonian friend, who had put his head down the toilet during his days at Eton College many times.

"Look forward to it," replied Charles.

The home secretary entered the debating chamber as the PM took his seat on the front row behind the dispatch box. Forcing the foreign secretary to move up, he squashed into the benches, he smiled, no leered, at those sitting on the opposition benches and nodded to his opposite number.

The debate was a lively one. You had to admire the skill of the PM as he evaded the important issues and skirmished with the leader of the opposition and the other party leaders. Mind you, everybody knew that one of the party leaders was having a drink or two and most of the time they waited to see if he slurred his words or fell over. He did not and commenced a very energetic attack on the PM and his catalogue of broken promises to the British people.

It was all to no avail, the PM refused to agree a proper debate and flannelled sufficiently for his own side to avoid a vote on the issue. The questions moved on and a back-bench opposition MP caught the Speaker's eye. "Right Honourable member for Chertsey," the speaker announced. Rodney Weddon MP stood up.

"It has come to my attention that this government has blocked an investigation into countless murders that have been taking place throughout the British Isles during the past eighteen months." The House suddenly went silent, murders, murders, what was the Right Honourable Member for Chertsey talking about? "Will the prime minister deny he has personally stopped this investigation?"

For once the House of Commons had gone silent. The Speaker saw a number of MPs stand waving their order papers and recognised 'the member from Stepney'. The Labour MP Marcus Trethwick stood up.

"Mr Speaker, if and I say if, there are matters to investigate, surely it should be left to the appropriate authorities, not debated in this house?"

"Prime minister," the Speaker recognised the PM who stood to speak.

"The Honourable Member for Stepney is quite right, I have no knowledge of what the Honourable Member from Chertsey is talking about, but the house is not a debating chamber for so called crimes." He sat down.

At that, more than two dozen MPs stood up, trying to attract the Speaker's attention, but sensing the government were in trouble, the Speaker ignored them and moved on.

"The prime minister," the Speaker said.

The PM expertly moved the subject on to yesterday's questions in the House when he said he would report back... and so the most famous parliamentary chamber in the world moved on. At the end of the prime minister's questions, he bustled out of the chamber, instructing his personal private secretary to locate the home secretary and ask him to come to his rooms in the House.

The home secretary had slipped away during the later stages of prime minister's question time to the member's tea room in the House of Commons. He had earlier telephoned Sir Anthony Greenford and arranged for the head of MI6 to meet him where they could sit quietly on the balcony overlooking a busy River Thames. Various colleagues had approached him about the opposition MP's question on murders 'throughout the country' but he had skilfully dodged all questions pushing the onus back toward the prime minister. He had considered himself very clever to pass the snippet to the opposition MP, Rodney Weddon who was an old pal from Oxford University days and now the seed was planted. It couldn't have gone better, the PM had lied to the House... triumph poured through his body as Sir Anthony Greenford sat down.

"Ah, Sir Anthony, how kind of you to meet me," said the home secretary somewhat condescendingly.

"Home secretary," replied Sir Anthony.

"Sir Anthony, the PM has asked me to enquire whether it is true that your department has apprehended two of the men suspected as connected with these gruesome murders we were investigating?" he emphasised 'were'.

"Home secretary, a team of MI6 operatives have indeed captured a number of men who we are talking to at the moment. We don't yet know if they are the men responsible for the crimes, but we have established a link to 'overseas matters' of utmost importance to the security of the realm."

"Overseas matters." Charles Henderson cleared his throat by taking a sip of tea and continued. "These overseas matters, would you say they take priority over homeland security?" he said, planting the thought firmly.

"Most certainly, minister, in fact there is, I must stress, only a suggestion at this stage, that one of the men knows the identity of a mole high up in MI5."

The home secretary put the piece of walnut cake he was about to tuck into down and looked at Sir Anthony for the first rime. "Mole in MI5," he muttered and then thinking for a few minutes he said, "Look, the PM has instructed me to tell you to pass these men to MI5 for them to investigate these matters, but what you have told me changes everything – you carry on, but report your findings directly to me."

"Yes, minister. I will get on then."

At that Sir Anthony Greenford got up from the table, nodded to the PM's private secretary as he scurried into the tea room and left.

Returning to the south bank of the River Thames, Sir Anthony pondered the meeting he had with the home secretary. He knew the man was a devious politician and suspected that the question the opposition MP had asked in the House of Commons today had been set up by him. How else would the MP know about the murders? So it was probable that the home secretary was angling for the story to break and the PM would be forced to consider his position and possibly resign. He had, after all, lied to the House. It was also interesting that the Head of MI5 had found out that his department were interrogating the two probable co-ordinators of the murders. He now had to consider that he had a mole in his department reporting to MI5. Deciding to drive down to Saxon Court to oversee the interrogation himself he called for his driver.

*

Ludvig Korotski had been kept manacled, blindfolded and on his feet for twelve hours and was reaching the point where he would drop down and no amount of beating would get him up. He heard the cell door open again. What did they want? He was standing, no beating was necessary. The two men grabbed him and frogmarched him out of the cell into another room. His clothes were cut away and the woman's wig he had used to great effect was pulled off. He stood naked, still manacled and blindfolded, as suddenly freezing cold water hit him from a powerful hose. Knocked off his feet he fell to the floor.

"Get up you bastard." One of the men came over and kicked him. Slowly Ludvig got to his feet; still manacled, the chains had now rubbed raw the skin around his ankles.

Again a jet of freezing water hit his body. This time he stayed on his feet. For twenty minutes he was subjected to what he knew was an attempt to weaken any resolve he might have left. What his British captors didn't know though was that in 1978 he had endured two hours of such treatment in KGB headquarters in Moscow. *Do they think Russians are soft?* he thought.

With his hands and legs manacled Ludvig wasn't in any position to resist, but nevertheless was dragged unceremoniously back to his cell and dumped onto the floor. Stark naked, his teeth began to chatter as he shivered uncontrollably. The spy-hole blinked as someone looked in. Cursing himself, he reflected on his capture. He had been stupid to assume no one knew of the Clapham address. Slowly he got his body under control. His KGB trainer had said, "Concentrate the mind Korotski and you can overcome most things."

It didn't seem very long before they came for him again. This time he was frogmarched to a room. He noticed the padded walls and how dimly lit it was. Then he saw the wooden plank fixed in the middle, just like a children's seesaw. But Ludvig knew this was no children's playground toy. Still manacled, he was lifted and fixed with leather belts, with his back flat onto the wooden plank. Ludvig's head, slightly protruding, was at one end of the plank of wood. He knew what was next. The two men who had brought him to the room moved out of his sight and another man pulled a large object under his head – he didn't immediately recognise what it was. Then out of the corner of his eye he saw a black hose being unrolled next to him. The plank was swung down and his head was in a large metal container, he was blindfolded.

"Okay, let's start," a man's voice said. He couldn't see that another man dressed in a wet suit approached with a hose. Suddenly a torrent of water poured down his face into his mouth and nose. Ludvig tried to switch positions, but his head was firmly fixed and he couldn't move. He began to choke – the water stopped. He felt the plank was being lifted up.

"I want to know your name," the same man's voice. Silence, Ludvig didn't reply.

The plank was moved again and his head was in the metal bath, *yes that's what it was an old-fashioned metal bath*, he thought. He sensed that the man with the hose approached. The water was turned on and again Ludvig tried to hold his breath, but water was running up his nose, he began to choke. He couldn't stop the feeling he was drowning, he choked and spluttered. The water stopped.

"We can do this for as long as you like, now what is your name?" Ludvig knew he could not take much more. The feeling of drowning, as water poured down his face into his nose and mouth, the lack of oxygen, but he wasn't going to give in – yet.

"Again," said the voice. Twice more Ludvig endured the deadly torture until he knew he could take no more. "You can stop all this you know. What is your name?" the voice asked.

Ludvig spluttered. "Korotski, Ludvig Korotski."

"Ah, I am glad you are helping yourself," the voice said. The two men who had brought him to the room undid the leather straps, picked him up and carried him down the room. He was placed in a chair and his blindfold removed. A powerful light was turned on and trained straight into his face, Ludvig could not see his inquisitor. "We know a lot about you Ludvig. Why are you organising the killing of British citizens?"

Ludvig thought for a minute – *how much to tell them, when should he play his trump card?* "I don't know," Ludvig replied.

"Oh dear, we are going to have to start all over again," the voice said. Two men roughly picked up Ludvig.

"No, no I will tell you."

"Don't waste our time Ludvig, you have one more chance."

"I was approached last year by a man I knew from the old days."

"His name?" the voice said.

"An American, his name is Morgan Fryer."

"How do you know this man Fryer?" the voice asked.

"He was CIA, at Berlin Station in the early eighties," replied Ludvig.

"You had done business with this man before?"

"Yes," replied Ludvig.

"What did he ask you to do?"

Ludvig paused for a second. "He asked me if I was interested in setting up a unit in the UK, to eliminate people," replied Ludvig

"Eliminate people – you mean kill people?"

"Yes," replied Ludvig

"Did he say why these people were targets?"

"No."

"You did not ask?"

"No."

"How much were you paid?"

"Six million pounds," he lied, he had received much more.

"Six million pounds is a great deal of money, how many people had you to arrange to be killed to earn this sum of money?"

"I was to receive a list of names each month. I didn't ask how many, money was paid each time the people on the list were eliminated."

"Good, Ludvig, would you like a drink of tea?" Ludvig nodded, thinking to himself, *classic as I am co-operating, now comes a reward.*

A cup was brought to his mouth; Ludvig drank the hot sweet tea. "Now Ludvig, tell me exactly when you started on the first list?"

Ludvig lost track of time but he answered all the questions, until the key question was asked. "Ludvig, who is actually behind this affair?"

Ludvig had expected that his inquisitor would want to know the answer to this question, but was in a quandary. *If he gave them everything, what had he got to bargain with?* Ludvig realised that he had some information from the old days, including some 'hot' stuff, but would this be enough to save his life? "I had Fryer followed by one of my most trusted members of my surveillance team to New York. I knew he worked for a security company." Ludvig cleared his throat.

"Do you want water?" asked the voice.

Ludvig nodded, it bought him more time to decide what to tell them. Ludvig drank out of the cup which had been put to his mouth by one of the men who had tortured him.

"Now Ludvig you were saying you had this man Morgan Fryer followed to New York, who followed him?"

"Katya and Ivan."

"Their full names please."

"Katya Gatchevske and Ivan Dinov."

"Ah, yes," the voice replied. Silence in the room. "Why did you choose those two to follow Fryer?"

"They were the best."

"I see."

"Now tell me, what did they find out?" Ludvig knew he was trapped. If he didn't tell them they would resume the water torture and he knew he couldn't endure much more of that.

"Well?" the voice barked now.

"Okay, they followed Fryer and documented where he went, who he talked to. I have full details on my laptop."

"Where is your laptop?"

"I have a post office box in east London."

"Address?"

"The post office is in Dalston Lane, London, number sixty-five."

"Key operated?"

"Yes."

"Where is the key?"

"I don't have it."

"Don't stall now Ludvig, we will get very angry."

"I am telling the truth, the key is in my flat in Stockholm on a bunch (he lied). I don't need to go to the post office each time I am in the country."

"What is the number of the box?"

"Nineteen," replied Ludvig – he knew they would break into the post office and remove the contents.

"Ludvig, I am curious… " The voice trailed off. Ludvig waited for the next question. "Why did you kill Katya Gatchevske?"

"Kill her?" He sounded incredulous. "I did not kill her."

"Come now Ludvig, we know you shot her in that park in London." Silence, Ludvig didn't reply. "Ludvig we don't intend to use what you are telling us as evidence in a murder trial – why did you kill her?" Ludvig thought about his answer.

"I didn't, the man Ivan Dinov killed her," he replied.

"Ludvig – are you saying a man we know was out of the country killed his girlfriend?"

"Yes, I believe he did."

"If you tell me crap, Ludvig, you will be put back on the board. "Take him back to the cell, he can think about his answer for a short while."

Ludvig was picked up by his arms and manhandled back to the padded cell. The door slammed behind him as he sat naked on the stone floor, still manacled hand and foot.

NEW YORK

4TH NOVEMBER 2007 – NEW YORK

Sir Anthony Greenford gazed out of the window as the British Airways Boeing 777 banked on the approach to New York's Newark airport. Sir Anthony preferred Newark; it always seemed less intense than JFK, in any case the flight number, BA 0721, was the first flight out of Heathrow that morning. Travelling first class, he was embarking from the plane before his two agents, Wilkinson and Frimley, were even approaching the exit door. *How ridiculous*, he thought, *that I am not authorised to agree executive travel for agents*. Waiting, having been ushered through the American immigration control by an official, his two agents, who were in truth his security, appeared. All three men had overnight bags and were greeted by Mike Adcock the 'special' attaché at the British Embassy and led to a black British Embassy Ford Galaxy car. Looking out through the darkened windows, Sir Anthony grimaced – he didn't like New York. Washington was tolerable, but New York – urg!

A meeting had been scheduled at the Embassy for 2pm, their time, with Michael Rosling, acting director of the CIA and Janet Street, the US secretary of state. Sir Anthony was alone, as both of his visitors were shown into the sumptuous room at the British Embassy and were introduced. He knew Michael, but not Janet Street, a rather striking dusky woman, whose reputation for tough action was known worldwide. His guests sat down and were offered coffee.

"Thank you for coming at such short notice." Sir Anthony had only requested the meeting yesterday. Unzipping a leather document case and removing three files marked 'Strictly Confidential, Eyes Only', he passed a file to each of them.

"If you don't mind a little light reading before we talk."

Both Mike Rosling and Janet Street were excellent at speed reading, but both looked taken aback on reaching the bottom of page one. Sir

Anthony had set up the briefing by firstly detailing the operation against UK citizens, then the means, the organisation, but it was the number of people killed he knew had startled both of them. When they turned the page their faces changed – Jesus Christ, ex-CIA people involved – they read on. It seemed that the British had broken the conspiracy and now knew why these horrific murders had taken place. Also, a bonus appeared to be the Intel being extracted from two Russians, who were both ex-KGB. Janet Street muttered to herself again. Sir Anthony knew she had reached that part of the report detailing the person or persons responsible for the deaths. *Nearly finished*, he thought. Janet's eyebrows rose for the third time as she said, "Christ not another."

Michael finished reading and they both looked up.

"Forgive me that I have been unable to give you any advance intel on this matter. The British government felt it wise to keep the whole thing under wraps."

"Understandably so," replied Janet Street, crossing her legs.

"As you can see, we now know who has activated this terrible sequence of murders and Her Majesty's government are seeking justice. Yes, justice. But in what form — that's what I am here to discuss."

Michael Rosling was a career member of the CIA. He had risen through the ranks, after an outstanding career as a field officer and was now near his pinnacle. He had no intention of losing what he had gained and sat waiting to be invited to comment.

"What do you see as the options, Sir Anthony?" asked Janet Street. Sir Anthony paused.

"Well…" He outlined the two options. One was a very public trial. The Americans responsible would be extradited back to the UK to stand trial for one hundred and ninety-seven murders of UK citizens. The other… the Americans would deal with the matter internally themselves, with summary justice for the protagonists and compensation for the victims paid by the giant corporation who employed two of the men responsible.

"How would the compensation for the victims be paid without alerting the media?" queried Janet Street.

"We imagine that a mistake has occurred with previous payments to the victims and in the light of this a full repayment of original capital would be made."

"I see," said Janet. "When do you want an answer, Sir Anthony?" she asked.

"Today," he replied.

Janet nodded, closed the file and then said, "The mole in the White House when would we find out who that is?"

"Immediately we agree a course of action," replied Sir Anthony.

"Thank you Sir Anthony, I will be in touch later today." Janet got up, shook hands and was followed out of the room by Michael Rosling, who hadn't said a word. In any case he knew better, the conversation was almost certainly being recorded, the Brits were quite cute like that.

Sir Anthony had a pleasant lunch at the Embassy with 'Badger' Warren, Sir Edgar Warren to anyone else. Badger and he had shared a room at Oxford in their first year and both were ardent potholers, joining the University Potholing Club. Badger had saved Sir Anthony once in the Mendip Caves, when he got stuck going through a narrow tunnel. With the water level rising, he dug his friend out by chipping away at the rock, until he was able to pull Anthony through. They had shared a friendship ever since and each was godparent to the other's son.

"I imagine it's another of your delicate little matters, Anthony?" said Badger.

"Yes 'fraid so old boy. Can't even tell you."

"Will you be around for dinner with Sweet Pea tonight?" Badger referred to his wife – Eunice.

"I certainly hope so," Sir Anthony replied.

Both men enjoyed their lunch, reminiscing and talking about old friends. Badger noticed that Anthony declined all offers of wine, even the first-class Embassy claret; it must be a serious matter.

*

The home secretary pressed the red button and took the call. "Sir Anthony… " The call was from the Head of MI6 in New York on the Embassy secure line.

"Home secretary, I have to report that the Americans have decided to tidy matters up their end."

"And compensation?" he asked.

"Yes, the corporation will be forced to pay back all the capital originally invested, to each of the victims' estates."

"Good and what of the other matter?" Sir Anthony knew he referred to the mole in the White House.

"They are in our debt."

"Excellent, good work Sir Anthony. We will talk again Thursday."

Joseph Garcia sat at his desk deleting details of the computer program he had titled 'Pots of Gold'. Not as though he had recorded much after Morgan Fryer told him that the Russian guy, Korotski, had stopped the operation. He had always known there was a risk someone would put two and two together and make four, but he had examined his involvement and decided there was no link to him. Since he had left the CIA in 1998, he had done very well for himself. Head of security for the London and American Insurance Corporation, a six-figure salary and huge bonuses. He had had a brainwave in 2006 and, reflecting on the start of the affair, he thought he hadn't really been serious. But Randolph Wilson Jnr., the chief operating officer, had refined his idea and activated it. Now was the time to get out – he had enough money, Wilson had paid him a bonus of two million dollars last year. It was late; nobody else was around as he entered the lift in the L and A building on the 42nd floor. A man he had not seen before was standing outside the lift door on the ground floor.

"Can I help you?" Garcia said, looking across and wondering why nobody was on the security desk. Suddenly he was looking down the barrel of a silenced pistol and another man appeared.

"We want to talk to you." The other man approached and he felt a sharp pain in his neck, he felt himself falling, then blackness descended.

Randolph Wilson Jnr was the grandson of one of the illustrious founders of the American Insurance Corporation. His grandfather had started a life assurance business in 1922, just before the Great Depression. The Social Security Act of 1935 set up a programme to ensure income for the elderly and Randolph Wilson Senior decided to set up an insurance corporation. In 1984, the company bought a British company, the London and Counties Life Assurance Company plc, to form one of the largest insurance companies in the world, operating in twenty-five countries – the London and American Insurance Corporation.

Randolph Jnr. had inherited the family shares when his father died in 1992, aged eighty years, and had set about 'modernising' as he called it. Unfortunately, all the frugal senior managers that had worked hard to make sure the corporation made exceptional profits since the mid 1960s had all steadily retired. Randolph's new appointments were often misguided and the giant corporation made a loss on its worldwide operation for the first time ever in 2005. The board were not best pleased and Randolph, who only held eleven percent of the stock, now found himself under pressure. When in 2006, his chief operating officer in the UK, Glen Rydor, had told him that the UK's figures were not looking good, he was not in the best of moods. Then the head of security, Joseph Garcia, the cousin of a senator from Ohio, came to him and jokingly reported a far-fetched idea he had. It was unconventional, but it just wouldn't go out of his head. Randolph did some sums. It was possible to make in year one over four hundred million pounds nearly eight hundred million dollars if the plan was put into place. It was never discussed at board level; he simply gave Garcia the nod and left him to it. In 2007 the plan had instantly resulted in the ailing UK arm of the insurance corporation turning around a deficit, to a profit of two hundred and ten million pounds, a staggering four hundred million dollars. Randolph had given Garcia a bonus.

Randolph enjoyed a sumptuous lifestyle. He had a M2 sixty-foot catamaran permanently tied up at Dennis Conner's North Cove yacht marina, on the Hudson River in lower Manhattan. He was a member of the exclusive Trump National Golf Club, Bedminster, New Jersey and had a superb apartment overlooking the west side of Central Park. His wife, Elizabeth, was the only daughter of the Ronaldsons from

Boston. Jackson Ronaldson, her father, owned a chain of hotels including the prestigious 'Eagles Nest', which dominated the skyline in Las Vegas, and his daughter had also inherited from her grandfather a considerable sum. Randolph was very rich and enjoyed the opulence and lifestyle, but being summoned to a meeting with Janet Street, the secretary of state, was not his idea of a good start to the day. What did she want? He didn't like her, as even though he had contributed a substantial sum to the Republican cause, he still hadn't been invited to dinner with the president. His earlier dealing with Janet Street involved a congressional hearing when she was a senior fellow of the American Economics Institute. They were arguing that American insurance companies should reduce their premiums to enable the lower paid to take out medical insurance. Randolph, as chairman of the National Association of Insurers, had sat through a difficult hearing when she, as a special advisor, criticised the insurance industry. He didn't like her and catching the early train to Washington was a nuisance.

The US State Department had a modern building, but it wasn't that often meetings were scheduled there. Usually, Randolph knew, Janet Street, who enjoyed the prestige and trappings of her position, would use her office at the White House.

Randolph got out of the limousine and went to the reception. Passing through security machines he was shown to an office on the sixth floor, where he sat alone, pondering the reason for the meeting. Randolph fidgeted as he sat on the leather chair opposite an empty matching chair.

The door opened and in swept Janet Street, followed by two men he didn't know. She seemed icy, barely acknowledging his presence. She opened a red file, moved several pages, and then looked up at him.

"I have called you here to account for the appalling crimes you have instigated in the British Isles." Randolph flushed, *what did she mean?* "You, and it seems you alone, are responsible for the instructions to your 'head of security'," she looked down at her file, "a certain Joseph Garcia. Is this so?"

"I don't think so," stammered Randolph.

She continued unabated. "You authorised this man, Garcia, to embark on a truly terrible plan to murder British citizens and to date over one hundred and ninety people have been murdered as a result of your action."

Randolph, white as a sheet, remained silent.

"Do you acknowledge this terrible operation was agreed by you?"

Randolph sat, his right leg shaking, perspiration running down his face, but his business brain was still working. He muttered, "I don't know what you're talking about."

Janet Street nodded and one of the men produced a recording device and pressed a button. Randolph heard Garcia's and his own voice in a conversation. *Oh God*, he thought, *Garcia recorded everything*.

"Do you deny that's your voice?"

Randolph put his head in his hands.

"I thought not, now this is what you are going to do." Randolph listened as the secretary of state outlined how his corporation were going to arrange for the British company to write, regretting an error when the insurance plans were set up and refunding the original investment in full, plus interest, to the estates of all the deceased persons.

"But..." he started to talk but nothing came out.

"There are no buts, you will do as I instruct you, or you will be extradited to the UK to face murder charges, and... " She paused before getting up. "You are most fortunate you didn't murder any of our citizens." Janet Street, still looking very angry, headed toward the door.

Randolph was accompanied by the two men back to his apartment in New York, where they collected his passport and the keys to his boat. He had been informed that he would report back to Silus Markell, an under secretary of state, to confirm the letters and cheques had been sent. He was told, in no uncertain terms, that he would be immediately extradited to the UK if he failed to meet this deadline.

Glen Rydor the chief operating officer of the British subsidiary of the London and American, was summoned to New York. He had known of the terrible plan, having been briefed by Randolph late in 2006. At first he had been shocked and refused, but then that bastard Garcia had shown him the photographs. Glen Watson Rydor, married with two children both at university, was not the pillar of propriety he made out. Pictures of him, with young boys, would be given to the press and loaded on various internet websites. He fell into line and gave Garcia a list of the largest investments. Afterwards he ignored the staggering change in mortality rates noted by his London actuary. He knew 'they' were somehow responsible, but when his ailing London-based insurance company turned around a potential loss, into an excellent profit, he happily pocketed the large bonus that came his way.

The meeting, with a pale Randolph accompanied by two men who were not introduced, was short and to the point. He was to personally write to one hundred and ninety seven executors of estates and refund the deceased insured person's original capital investment, plus interest. The cost of five hundred and seventy one million pounds was to be funded from British reserves and by a transfer of four hundred million pounds from the New York office. Randolph still didn't know how he was going to explain that to the board of London and American, Glen Rydor was told that he would be sacked for incompetence shortly after the cheques had been sent out, with no severance pay.

He went back to London with no choice and a list. He arranged for the letters and personally signed all the cheques. He left the London and American British headquarters building in Leadenhall Street, London, went home and was found at 6pm, when his wife came home: he had hanged himself in the garage.

Randolph received the news of Glen Rydor's demise without emotion. He couldn't contact Garcia who had been missing for several days. The chairman of the London and American was demanding a special board meeting to discuss, as he put it, 'the serious outpouring of finances from New York to London'. Randolph simply tendered his resignation, leaving a letter on his desk and headed for his house outside Boston.

Later the news channel, CBC, reported that he was walking in the garden, it seemed, when he disturbed an intruder and was knifed to death, no motive was apparent as there was money and credit cards in his pocket and his expensive Rolex watch had not been stolen.

The board of directors of London and American held an emergency meeting. A finance director was appointed to investigate why the London and New York offices had cleared over six hundred and eighty million dollars of cheques in the past few days and apparently London had paid out another three hundred and fifty million dollars. Once the shareholders and the markets found out there would be a run on the company's shares and each of the directors would lose millions of dollars as their personal shareholdings fell. The board members were fuming and knew Randolph, who had authorised these payments, was dead – some sort of mix-up. The British division of London and American had repaid millions.

TIDYING UP

9TH NOVEMBER 2007 – LONDON, ENGLAND

Colonel Harriman, took the call from Captain Johnson.

"The code is green" was all he said and the phone call terminated.

Sir Anthony's arrival was announced and John Harriman got up to await his old friend. "Good to see you, Anthony."

"And you John," replied the head of MI6.

After the formalities of morning tea, brought in on a silver tray, the two men sat chatting.

"Thank god it's over," said Colonel Harriman.

"Yes, and financial restitution made, albeit to the estates of the deceased persons."

"I still don't quite understand why those people were murdered," said the colonel.

"Let me explain. All the murdered persons were linked: they had each purchased a life annuity with the London and American Insurance Corporation. Most of the annuities were purchased by single persons with no guaranteed term or the guarantee had passed. Sometimes joint life annuities had been purchased. So if the person or persons who had bought the annuity died the annuity simply ceased – the insurance company pocketing the balance of capital they had been expecting to pay."

"Sorry Anthony, I still don't follow."

"An annuity provides a regular income paid, usually monthly, by an insurance Company after the policyholder has given over a capital sum called the purchase price. The amount called the annuity is paid until the policyholder or both policyholders die. The annuity might have a guarantee to pay, often for five years, but after this period it will go on until the death of a single annuitant or both if a joint annuity. It's a good way of providing a guaranteed income," said Sir Anthony.

"Ah, I see now," replied the colonel. "Presumably the earlier the person who bought the annuity dies the more money the insurance company makes," he added. "But why was a husband and his wife murdered?"

"Because they had a joint annuity. If both were killed, the annuity payment would cease and once again the insurance company would be able to pocket the balance of capital originally invested, called the purchase price."

"But how could all that be worth paying the Russians and their hit team?"

"Oh, it's big business John. Each of the people murdered had invested large sums, between a half a million pounds and in one case, thirty million pounds. Multiply the amounts pocketed by the insurance company in not having to continue the annuities and you have hundreds of millions – believe me it was huge."

"That young Detective Constable de Courcy was on to it – or nearly on to it before they closed down the investigation," said the colonel.

"Yes and so was the chief inspector who died," replied Sir Anthony.

"What are we going to do about his murder?" The colonel put his cup down.

"It irks me to say it, but we have no proof so it is difficult to arrest the man responsible."

"What do you mean?" asked Colonel Harriman.

"Sometimes, John, there are things I can't tell even you, but rest assured justice will prevail."

"If you say so."

"By the way, it's interesting how the chief operating officer of the British end of the London and American Insurance Company and the CEO of the group have both died," said Sir Anthony.

"Yes," replied the colonel.

"Coincidence, I suppose." Sir Anthony held out his hand.

"I am glad I am never on the wrong side of you John."

"Don't be silly old friend." The two men shook hands and parted.

John Harriman sat at the table. *Justice* he thought, *had it been done? What about the two Russians and their team of killers, some of whom had not been caught?* John knew if he had his way, the team leaders, those two Russians would be sharing an unmarked grave by now.

Ludvig Korotski didn't know where they were taking him. After what he calculated was about ten days (he had made a mark on the floor each time darkness came) they had given him some clothes and ordered him to dress. He had been manacled and then driven blindfolded. When his blindfold had been removed, he found he was at a small airfield, but he remained manacled. Four men accompanied him... two of them he knew from his captivity and interrogation, two he did not. Ludvig judged the flight time of the unmarked Lear executive jet at around nine hours, so he thought he could be in the USA or perhaps Mexico, or somewhere in Asia. His leg manacles had been removed on the aircraft, so he was able to walk down the aircraft steps, even though he was now handcuffed to his escort.

"Where are we?" Ludvig asked. He struggled to walk handcuffed down the stairs leading to the tarmac.

The man next to him ignored his question as he was escorted across the tarmac to a waiting car. Ludvig sat between two guards, he had seen the two other men who had been on the flight get into a second car. As they left the airport he saw a sign – Bridgetown – they were in Barbados! Ludvig liked Barbados, but would have preferred a South American country – more chance he could disappear when finally they left him alone. He had every reason to believe he was being released as he had drip-fed important information promising more when he was given his freedom.

As they drove up the west of the island, an area Ludvig was familiar with, they approached a fairly new build, consisting of various apartments close to a marina. The man handcuffed to him said, "right, up the stairs" and they entered an apartment on the first floor. The other man produced a key, released the handcuff from his guard and then, much to his surprise, he was handcuffed to the arm of a large armchair. His two guards, the men who had collected him from the house in England, left the room. Another man he had not seen before entered He was in his forties, greying at the temples, tough-looking. He took out a pistol from his pocket. Ludvig began to sweat – surely not, he had done all they asked. The man screwed on a silencer, then walked over to the chair and proceeded to wrap a strap around his upper body, tightening it so he couldn't move.

"But why? I have given you everything, done all you asked – why kill me now I have much more to tell you?"

The man didn't answer, walked behind him and yanked his head back. As he felt the cold, sharp edge of the knife, Ludvig knew there was no more to say… and died.

The man went to the door, signalled another man to come in, who glanced at the slumped body of Ludvig and nodded. Carefully, not to cover themselves in his blood, they undid the strap binding him to the chair, unlocked the handcuffs and carried the body into the bedroom, dumping it on the bed facing away from the door.

Wiping up the drops of blood with a cloth covered in bleach they checked for any sign they had been there, satisfied they left. One of the men sent a text – 'the code is green'.

Ivan Dinov looked out over the aqua blue waters of the Caribbean and pondered his future. *Would they leave him as promised in Barbados, or was there a twist in the tale?* Up until now his bargain had been a flight by executive jet to Barbados, where he had a flat at St James, on the western side of the island, in return for names and contact details. Two weeks of intensive interrogation. He had given up one of his aces early on – the name of the British spy, high up in the Secret Intelligence Service. He knew the man well, as he had recruited him in Moscow in 1981. It hadn't been difficult, the man had a penchant for young girls, Ivan simply obliged. Today they would have called him a paedophile. He had provided the incriminating photographs, always impossible to deny, and a recording, which had been found by his interrogators after they visited a safe deposit box in Berlin. Ivan had realised that his life remained on a knife edge and gave up numerous Basque terrorists, Al Qaeda and Taliban contacts, mostly in Iran and Saudi Arabia, but two in Europe, who he knew were responsible for the Madrid bombing in 2004. But then, just as he thought he had done enough, it still seemed as though he was going to be killed, he used his final ace in the hole. He gave up the American. He had held out for a few days, but his life versus old loyalties – no contest. The American had been a special achievement of Katya's in the early days of the Russian liberal leaders. Katya was a transsexual and it was that which hooked the American. He simply couldn't get enough of her and when she proposed a lifetime of enjoyment, he readily agreed. Since then, for over twenty-five years, his darling Katya had visited the American, now apparently a happily married man, and reminded him of his true sexual urges. The man was given titbits of intel, which helped his career and he advanced up the ladder of the CIA. He became director of the CIA in 1999 and Katya and Ivan had enjoyed seven years of important information fed to them in bit-sized chunks, which they sold on. In return they gave him several of the most unimportant Taliban militants, several members of Al Qaeda and the second-in-command of the Osama Bin Laden group. That last coup got the American promotion. Still, Ivan had to give him up and that intel was what it seemed had saved his life.

Landing at Bridgetown, the executive jet taxied far away from the terminal. The steps were lowered and he and four men got into a waiting car. Ivan was dropped outside the steps leading to his apartment and the car sped away. Ivan was beginning to think they were going to keep their word, but nevertheless cautiously entered his apartment. Ivan and Katya had bought the apartment in 2003, before the property explosion on Barbados at the fashionable marina, in the favoured St James area. Remembering their purchase together of the furniture he, just for a second, thought of Katya, and then his thoughts turned to now. He went into the kitchen, yes there was coffee and he put the electric kettle on. Picking up his holdall, he went to the bedroom. His instincts took over immediately. A body lay on the bed covered in blood – he looked closer. Christ it was that bastard Ludvig Korotski, someone had cut his throat. *Time to get out of here*, he thought. He pushed aside a chest of drawers and found the loose plank in the floor, which he removed. Feeling into the hole, something snapped and caught his fingers. As he withdrew his hand, he saw he had activated a rat trap. *What game was this?*

Hearing a creak, Ivan spun around. Two men faced him, both holding pistols. "What's this, we had a deal," Ivan said.

One of the men deliberately aimed his pistol and shot Ivan in the kneecap. Ivan screamed in pain as he fell to the floor. The other calmly walked up to him and shot him in the other kneecap. Ivan was in excruciating pain, *who were these men?* As the other man moved towards him, Ivan pleaded.

"I know something else, something about a British politician."

The two men, who hadn't spoken, looked at each other then both turned their guns down on Ivan and fired. Ivan was shot in the chest twice, and one of the men then leaned over and shot him in the head. The other man went to the gas stove and opened the door, turning the gas tap on. They sprinkled petrol all around the two bodies and moved them close to the stove. His colleague lit the candle on the adjacent table and they left. They had checked nobody was at home downstairs, or the flats next door, but remained close by until the explosion and resultant fire just in case. The flat was soon engulfed in flames, time to leave.

One of the two, a tall burly man, used his mobile from the car taking them back to Bridgetown airport. "The code is green," he texted and cut the connection.

Far away in Washington, an interceptor had picked up the message brought to him by a FBI computer analyst in Langley, Virginia. Later on, the new head of the CIA would study the two messages and consider the deaths of the two insurance directors and the burnt bodies found in Barbados, identified as two Russians wanted by the CIA and start to wonder, *did the Brits knock them off?* He still had the ex-head of the CIA, that rat Morgan Fryer and the insurance company's security man, Garcia, and all were scheduled for elimination.

John Harriman was contemplating refusing a new job. He didn't like turning down business but his resources were stretched. He had forty-four field personnel and four staff who manned the headquarters office in Park Lane. Unless his number two, 'Smithy', and he returned to working in the field he had no spare operatives. As he pondered the problem his secure line rang.

"John."

"It's Toomey, colonel." John Harriman had already recognised the deep baritone voice of the barrister they always used for legal matters.

"Go ahead," he replied.

"Dustin Starr has been charged with possession of a class 'A' drug but the CPS have dropped a manslaughter or grievous bodily harm charge," the barrister said.

"Well that's the best we could expect." The colonel referred to the death of a man at Alice's nightclub when his client, the pop star Dustin Starr, had punched a man who fell backwards, cracking his head on a table, and died of a brain haemorrhage.

"The man who died had been drinking excessively and had already assaulted a young woman who was sitting with Dustin. Apparently he swung a punch at Dustin hitting him on the shoulder. The witnesses all stated Dustin was just defending himself," replied the barrister.

"What is he likely to get?" asked the colonel.

"Oh, a fine or maybe community service, it's his first offence."

"Have you informed his agent?"

"Yes, he is not exactly ecstatic."

"That's not our problem. Thanks Nathan," and he rang off.

Harriman Security provided bodyguards for a number of celebrities and pop stars. John Harriman rarely approved of their behaviour and his operatives often found themselves dealing with minor public affray problems. The instructions were quite clear: do not interfere unless the client is being threatened verbally or physically. His operative, Sergeant Boyes, had acted as best he could and hadn't had the chance to intercept the man who died.

*

For Colonel Harriman and the team at Harriman Security, life went on. But they never forgot their old colleagues, both murdered during the investigation, and as they all stood silently in their local pub, The Grapes, just off Park Lane, the colonel called for a toast.

"To Corporal Danvers and Monty Stanton. May they rest in peace – the code is green."

The prime minister had gone to Chequers in an attempt to get away from the baying media. Ever since the article had appeared in the German magazine, *der Speigel*, suggesting there had been an unprecedented cover up of mass murders in the UK, the media had been after him.

Reflecting on events of the past six months, he wondered if he should have had the home secretary deal with everything to do with the affair. Now he was firmly in the driving seat. But what did they really have? Speculation, no proof. The Sunday papers arrived and he rapidly scanned the front pages. Nothing – good. Inside *The Times* on page three, was an article, written by that bastard, Sam Vine, referring to the article in the German magazine and a question in the House, by that Tory Rodney Wealden. Still they had nothing except speculation; he would hold his nerve and not answer questions.

Monday was usually a quiet day in the House of Commons. Most of the MPs were either in their constituencies or doing other work, but today a stream of weary-looking MPs and the cock-a-hoop opposition, joined bemused Liberals and others in a packed chamber for prime minister's question time. The prime minister took his seat to a crescendo of noise, mostly from the opposition benches. The Speaker, the Hon Harold Mackie, called for order.

"The prime minister." For ten minutes he spoke of unimportant matters until he had finished his notes.

A flurry of hands went up.

"The Honourable Rodney Wealden."

Rodney Wealden, Tory MP for Chertsey in Surrey, stood up. A hush descended on the house.

"The House has been grossly misled and lied to by the prime minister." The noise was drowning out the Speaker's voice.

"Order! Order!" he shouted.

The prime minister sank back in his chair as Rodney Wealden described how over one hundred and ninety UK citizens had been murdered over the past eighteen months, by a group of assassins seemingly brought together for the purpose of increasing the profits of the London and American Insurance Corporation. He even had a tape. As the opposition MP called for the resignation of the prime minister many of the members in the House roared their approval and his own party remained silent.

An experienced politician, who had manipulated and manoeuvred all through his political life, he knew he was finished, he rose.

"The prime minister," roared the Speaker. The House fell silent.

"The Right Honourable Member for Chertsey may be substantially correct." Uproar in the house.

"Order! Order!" shouted the Speaker as the prime minister remained on his feet.

"I do not propose to discuss the circumstances or the reaction by Her Majesty's government, to an unprecedented situation here and now." Again there was uproar as dozens of MPs stood up waving their order papers.

"Order! Order!" roared the Speaker as the prime minister remained at the despatch box.

"Instead we shall appoint a cross-party committee to examine the facts of the matter and report back to the House," he said rather unconvincingly.

"Resign! Resign!" echoed around the chamber.

"Order! Order!" The Speaker was having trouble, the house was in turmoil.

The prime minister, white as a sheet sat down. *Was it his imagination or did he feel faint?* As he slumped forward, his head struck the base of the wooden rostrum in front of him, pandemonium broke out. Several doctors from all sides of the House attended him, but it was no good – he was dead.

A week later, at Westminster Abbey, the prime ministers eulogy was given by Lord Blackwater, the leader of House of Lords referring to 'a fine man, great orator, who had done much for this country'. An autopsy was carried out but no suspicious chemicals were discovered, even though he had a new security guard that fateful day who had moved an umbrella in the back of his limousine on the way to the House of Commons, accidentally pricking the PM's leg. After the post mortem, the verdict was 'a heart attack', but Charles Henderson, the home secretary, couldn't help wondering if he had been killed – if so why? What he didn't know was that the cocktail of lethal drugs using a ricin base had been changed to delay death by approximately sixty minutes, and it was now virtually unidentifiable.

The extraordinary thing was the home secretary did not get elected by the party to lead them in the leadership contest prior to the general election. He was beaten by the charming Sarah Waterside. No baggage, they said, from the murderous affair that the all-party select committee which had been set up to investigate what they had called 'the worst example of commercial greed they had ever seen'. Needless to say the select committee did not see the evidence held by the security services, confirming that the government knew very early on about the deaths, nor was the death of an investigating policeman linked or the attempt to murder another police officer.

The head of the Joint Intelligence Committee led the tributes to Sir Aubrey Granville-Davis who had been the head of MI5. He had died of a heart attack following the intelligence Ivan Dinov had supplied which had been confirmed after his interrogation. Few people knew he had been the mole planted by the Russians thirty years ago into the MI5.

The London and American Insurance Company's shares collapsed. Part of the giant insurance company was sold off. All of the directors found themselves unemployed.

*

Colonel Harriman closed his eyes, only to sit bolt upright as he heard a knock on his office door.

"The final report on the London and American affair," said Major Smith.

"Thanks Smithy."

As he read the file, a copy secretly passed to him by Sir Anthony of the select committee findings, the colonel began to feel very tired. So many had been killed before they had helped stop the murders. Still, justice had partly been done, even if the Americans wouldn't confirm that the treacherous ex-CIA man, Morgan Fryer, or the man who planned the whole sorry exercise, Garcia, was dead. Walking across to his shredder, he carefully inserted a number of files. Wouldn't do for anyone to read of his role in the affair – *time for a break*, he thought, *leave Smithy to run the show for a week or so.*

As he read the final file he reflected on the list of Russians and Bulgarians who had killed so many people, a small red cross denoted that all but two were dead, the woman Viktorya Abamova, a Bulgarian, eluded them, as did the Russian Hristo Penev – still they would show up sooner or later and with most of the security forces in the world looking for them, including the Russians, it shouldn't be long.

Colonel Harriman closed his eyes – perhaps he was getting too old for all this. Then he remembered he had an interview with the young woman de Courcy and got out his electric shaver to tidy himself up – appearance was important – *death was a certainty*, he thought.

Previously Ted York published...

ROSIE

Born in 1878 to an East End London docker's family, Rosie finds herself a mysterious benefactor, who pays for both her and her sister to be privately educated. While undoubtedly talented in the school room, Rosie longs to take to the stage at the Britannia Theatre in Shoreditch, London. As a beautiful, intelligent and talented actress she is popular with the Britannia theatre crowd and, thanks again to her benefactor, is offered a part at the Theatre Royal Drury Lane. In 1900, Rosie accompanies the cast of "Much Ado About Nothing" to Paris. The excitement of the world fair, the Exposition Universelle, and the summer Olympics are surpassed when Rosie meets Frederick, the son of a rich Swiss Merchant Banker. A whirlwind courtship leads to a grand wedding in Westminster Abbey.

As her life changes from actress to society lady, she mixes with Lords and Ladies, Princes and Kings. Flirting with the early feminist movement, Rosie's life unfolds with relentless excitement as she works for the early forerunner of the British Secret Service.

Rosie is a woman of the twentieth century. A charming and likeable heroine, she will appeal to readers looking for a heart-warming rags to riches saga.